DELTA ZONE—

With an explosive spray of sand, something big and metallic raised itself from the shallow depression—a killing machine, a warrior robot, a behemoth from Hell. A segmented, flexible tail curled up its back, and mounted at the end of it was a giant laser, a laser which was even now targeting in on them. . . .

DEATH HUNT
ON A
DYING PLANET
GARY ALAN RUSE

A SIGNET BOOK

NEW AMERICAN LIBRARY

SIGNET TRADEMARK REG. U.S. PAT. OFF. AND FOREIGN COUNTRIES
REGISTERED TRADEMARK—MARCA REGISTRADA
HECHO EN CHICAGO, U.S.A.

SIGNET, SIGNET CLASSIC, MENTOR, ONYX, PLUME, MERIDIAN
and NAL BOOKS are published by NAL PENGUIN INC.,
1633 Broadway, New York, New York 10019

First Printing, October, 1988

1 2 3 4 5 6 7 8 9

PRINTED IN THE UNITED STATES OF AMERICA

*For Virginia Mae Ruse
and Layton N. Ruse,
my parents . . .*

*and for all my friends
in the South Florida
Science Fiction Society*

*and for new friends Jonathan
and Charlotte Pendragon.*

With special thanks to everyone who gave editorial input to this project, in its various stages of development from start to finish. Your help is deeply appreciated.

G.A.R.
Miami, Florida 1988

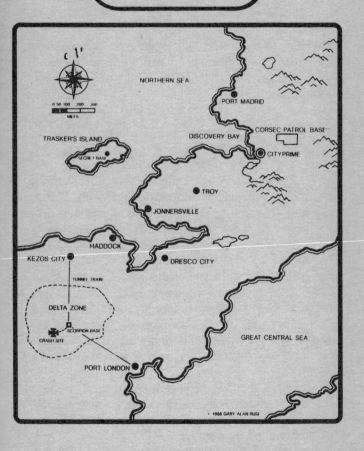

1:

GIFT OF GLORY

IN THE FRIGID BLACKNESS of space, an ancient starship orbited Coreworld. A dead ship, abandoned and silent, a relic of a past nearly forgotten, with mysterious symbols of old Earth fading on its hull. The enormous vessel was almost a mile in length, its outer shell of pressurized compartments forming a long, thick tube surrounding the inner core of power generators, life-support equipment, and structural framework.

The starship's shuttle bays were all empty, its human cargo long ago disembarked and transported to the planet's surface below. A single word, sun-bleached almost to the point of disappearing altogether, was painted in characters twenty feet high and surrounded by an oval made up of the flags of many nations. Nations that were now but dimly remembered legends. That word was *Glory*, and it was the vessel's name.

It had been a space derelict for centuries, nothing more than a glimmering speck of light visible in the nighttime sky of Coreworld. But now, suddenly, intruders disturbed its slumber.

Roddi moved through one of the ship's darkened corridors, as quickly and quietly as his mechanical legs would permit, searching for the answer to a mystery. A robot roughly the size and shape of a man, Roddi was grateful that *Glory* was still spinning about its central axis, creating enough gravity to make walking easy. And although he did not need air himself, his sensors told him that the ship's seals had held and kept an atmosphere.

A small light in the center of his chest cast its wide beam ahead, illuminating his path. The eerie corridor he traversed was flanked on both sides by row upon row of suspended-animation cabinets, four deep and three high, with space between the vertical tiers for access. He knew that there were over three thousand such devices in *Glory*. And although the empty cabinet had once sustained life during a lengthy space-flight, they now looked unpleasantly like coffins. He had seen enough of those on Coreworld, where the radiation-cleansed corpses of plague victims had been buried in hastily excavated crypts.

Roddi did not like thinking about human death. The beings that created him should be powerful, all-knowing, and wise. Not fragile, not mortal. The truth often saddened him as much as it puzzled him.

Abruptly, sounds came from behind him, somewhere in a distant corridor. It reminded Roddi of the urgency of his mission, and that his own existence was not very secure at the moment.

He broke into a rhythmic, mechanical jog, relying on the thick insulation on the soles of his feet to deaden their metallic ring against the flooring. The beam from his chest light bounced in an irritating way, but not enough to interfere with his vision.

At the end of the corridor he stopped to check his handheld scanner, a piece of University gear. Its tiny indicator lights blinked and its screen glowed with a computer-generated map of *Glory*'s interior. The strange signal which had brought him here was still being received, but the arrow that was supposed to indicate the signal's source within the ship had disappeared from the screen. How could he know which way to go in this impossible, darkened maze of a vessel if the device did not tell him?

"Work, you stupid little twit of a machine!" Roddi said impatiently, tapping its case with a metal finger. "Or we'll both get our circuits blasted to molten sludge."

Seemingly in response, the arrow indicator flashed on and began to blink rapidly, pointing the way.

Roddi studied it a second, then looked up and chose the cross corridor he must take. He hurried off in the direction indicated by the device, and hoped it was not malfunctioning.

The glowing map showed a compartment within the ship, accessible from this corridor. Within minutes, he was there. The door was closed, and it was labeled with a sign reading "Laboratory C."

Roddi tried to open it. It was a sliding door, powered by servos within the wall. It would not yield, and probably could not, without electricity to run the servos. There was no time to experiment, and he doubted he could break it down.

Opening an accessory compartment in his torso, he extracted a small laser pistol. It was fully charged.

"Half power should do," he muttered to himself as he set the controls.

He quickly aimed and triggered the weapon. A ruby beam, needle-thin and barely visible, touched the door and began to etch a burning line across its surface. It seemed to take forever. He looked back down the corridor for some sign of the ones he knew were searching for him, then quickly redirected his chest-light beam, lest they see it. They would find him soon enough, without his help.

Abruptly, the door broke free and fell inward with a dull thump. Roddi gave a brief jerk of surprise, then silently cursed himself for not paying attention. With his laser still in hand, he stepped through the opening, careful not to touch the glowing edges.

His chest light slowly revealed the compartment, and it was indeed a laboratory, judging from the counters and equipment cabinets. But the place had been stripped of its equipment, either by the original colonists or by later visitors. The empty shells of built-in gear cratered the walls, and cut cables dangled everywhere. Roddi had heard humans speak of buildings and caves that were haunted by the ghosts of people who had once lived there. He found himself wondering if electronic circuits sometimes left behind their own kind of residue . . . phantom signals, ghosts. Or did intelligent, psychogenetic robots like himself? Perhaps. And if any place had ghosts within its walls, surely this ship did.

Roddi checked his scanner. The glowing arrow still pointed to the far wall of the compartment, but he could see nothing there to account for the signal. What worried him even more was that although he was so close, the signal seemed to be growing weaker.

"There has to be something!" Roddi approached the wall, and on an impulse, extended his open hand to it. The sensor circuits in his palm picked up a trace of power. Encouraged, he searched further.

In a moment he located a circuit buried within the wall, a circuit that was still alive with power, though not very much. It was a locking mechanism, not terribly complicated, and took no more than a moment to activate with simple coded signals. Hardly a challenge at all. He might have found it boring if not for the danger that drew steadily closer.

There was a moment's hesitation, then in response to his signals a section of the wall creaked, unsealed itself, and slowly grated open. It revealed a hidden compartment, lying just beyond the first.

This was a strange twist, even for humans, thought Roddi. Cautiously, not certain what to expect, he entered the second compartment.

He did not need his chest light to see here. The room was illuminated by emergency lights, red-hued and faint, but still bright enough to reveal details. This place was also a laboratory, but its equipment was still intact and, incredibly, still functioning. The answer lay at one end of the room, where shielded nuclear power cells stood, their cables connected to a grid of equipment and computers, all with multiple backup devices. The frequent flickering of the lights suggested that the power cells were finally exhausted and beginning to fail. That would explain the steadily weakening signal.

But it did not explain the new mystery Roddi found here. The clutter of equipment framed an object that stood in the center of the compartment. The long, transparent case resembled the suspended-animation cabinets he had seen throughout the ship, but was clearly unlike them in design. It was unlike them in another important respect, as well. The others were empty. This one was not.

Lying motionless within the case was the body of a young woman, perhaps in her late twenties or early thirties, slender and what humans might term attractive. She wore an old-fashioned lab smock over close-fitting slacks. Her sleeves were rolled up past the elbows, and attached to both arms were boxy devices with fluid tubes and electrical cables leading out of them. Similar devices were strapped to her bare ankles.

Even more astonishing, the equipment dials and readouts indicated that she was alive. The oddball, patchwork system seemed to be attempting to revive her, though it was quickly running out of power.

Roddi was beginning to feel his processing capabilities overloading. There was so much to consider—the danger from without, this bizarre discovery, his desire to fulfill his mission for the University, his sudden concern for this human. What to do? He was automatically storing visual and auditory records of everything around him, but he was also attempting to understand the equipment so that he could assist. It seemed impossible. He lacked advanced medical programming, and the equipment, though archaic, seemed very complex.

Suddenly, he saw the young woman stir. She was coming out of a sleep that must have lasted, if his calculations were correct, seven centuries. For that was how long ago *Glory* had left the world known as Earth.

Mechanisms within the cabinet whirred to life, releasing latches and seals, shutting off valves. The lid of the case opened a crack, started to rise, faltered, tried again. The lights faded with the effort.

Acting quickly, Roddi grasped the edge of the lid and strained upward. The lights brightened again as the drain on the power lessened.

The girl was already moving by the time Roddi had the lid fully open. She rose to a sitting position, her eyes still closed, her hands held to her temples as if cradling a headache. Stirred by her movements, a cloud of pinkish vapor rolled out of the case and quickly dissipated.

Roddi's head rotated briefly toward the doorway as footsteps, and something worse than footsteps, began to echo more loudly from an adjacent corridor.

Half to himself, half to the young woman, he said, "Oh, do please hurry."

Straightening suddenly at the sound of his voice, she pried her eyes open and looked around. Her confused gaze took in the flickering glare of the emergency lights, the failing equipment, and the metallic figure looming over her. Her pretty face took on a troubled look.

"What . . . what's wrong—?"

"Much," said Roddi. "Let me help you out of there."

He quickly unstrapped the devices at her ankles and arms, disconnecting their intravenous connections, electrodes, and monitoring circuits. The equipment was different from the cryogenic systems of the other suspended-animation cabinets, and Roddi was surprised by the lack of those systems' characteristic chill.

"You're not cold," he said.

"Well, you are," the girl replied, recoiling from his touch, and studying him more critically now. "And just who, or what, in bloody blue blazes are you?"

"I am called Roddi," he said with an irritated tone, "and I am a psybot, and if you knew what was heading this way you would not be wasting our time with silly questions."

"Questions aren't silly if you don't know the answers," she said defensively, then frowned toward the doorway. "What's headed this way?"

Roddi helped her from the case and began pulling her toward the door. "Can we talk about this as we move?"

"I'm trying," she said as she lurched forward on legs

that did not want to bend. "But take it easy—I'm still a little stiff."

"Exercise is good for that."

They made their way through the outer laboratory and reached the doorway. The young woman paused, leaning unsteadily against the wall and running a hand through blond hair that reached almost to her shoulders. "Marinda . . ." she said softly. "I'm Marinda Donelson."

"Pleased to meet you," said Roddi. "And I'm glad your mind is functioning. But if you're still weak from your reawakening, I shall carry you."

Her posture straightened abruptly. "You will not! I can get around on my own, thank you."

She pushed weakly past him and stepped out into the corridor, turning left and marching along with more pride than precision. Roddi hurried around her and gently wheeled her about to the other direction.

"Let's go this way, please," he said. "You'll meet a nicer class of people."

As he attempted to hurry her along down the corridor, Marinda said, "What is it you're so afraid of? And why is the ship dark? And what on earth is a psybot?"

"Psychogenetic robot," Roddi said absently, glancing behind him as they moved. "The rest I'll have to explain when there's more time."

They were nearly at the end of the corridor when Marinda stopped in her tracks, transfixed by what she glimpsed through a viewport in an outer bulkhead. Moving beneath them with the ship's rotation was the glowing sphere of Coreworld, its oddly shaped continents and cloud structures clearly visible.

"Oh my God," said Marinda, staring in awe at the sight. "We did it. We actually did it. We reached the

16

other star system after all. And Fenton's experiment worked. I'm living proof of it."

"Let's keep it that way," said Roddi, giving her a tug to get her moving again. Then his head rotated quickly as a shout came from behind them. "Oh, glitch. That's what I was afraid of."

There was enough urgency in his tone to tear Marinda's attention away from the viewport. Looking down the corridor, she saw what he saw. Appearing around a corner were six or more large, hulking, shadowy figures. At least two of them had shapes that were decidedly not human. All carried lights that tore through the darkness with a chilling glare, bathing Roddi and Marinda in their combined glow, and stealing what safety the darkness offered.

Roddi jerked Marinda half off her feet as he pulled her toward a cross corridor that might give cover. A ray beam seared down the corridor, through the spot where they had stood, scorching the bulkhead beyond.

"Halt!" one of the shadowy figures called out after them. Then again: "Halt!"

Roddi decided running was wiser.

2:
DESCENT INTO DANGER

"WHO ARE THOSE PEOPLE?" Marinda asked breathlessly as she ran alongside her psybot companion. She found it easier to keep up now that fear-induced adrenaline was flowing through her veins.

"CorSec Guards," said Roddi. "Short for Corporation Security Guards. A nasty bunch. And, I might add, not all of them are people."

They fled down the cross corridor, which curved up and away with the shape of the hull. They quickly turned left down the next main corridor, doubling back in the direction of the docking ports that seemed so far away. And always behind them, the clanging and clattering sounds of pursuit.

This corridor was much the same as the others Roddi had taken to reach the laboratory. And it too was lined on both sides by a seemingly endless row of suspended-animation cabinets. Roddi's chest light sent reflections dancing across their transparent domed lids as he and Marinda ran down the aisle between them.

The fear which gripped her could not keep Marinda from looking into each cabinet she passed. Looking, and noticing, and growing puzzled.

"Empty," she said. "All of them empty. Where's everyone gone?"

"Transported by shuttle down to Coreworld—that

planet you were looking at," explained Roddi. "Why weren't you taken down with them?"

She looked at him wonderingly. "You're asking me?"

"Sorry. I thought if you knew what you were doing in that hidden lab . . ."

"I do," she said, drawing a quick breath. "Long story."

Suddenly, lights in the ceiling above sprang into flickering life, the abrupt change after darkness startling them. The light was weak and milky, fluctuating from moment to moment. An ancient light tube above them flared and exploded as power surged through it. It rained tiny fragments around them, making Marinda duck.

The lights seemed to be coming on throughout this section of *Glory*, and Roddi glanced back as the sounds behind them grew louder. The direction of his gaze drew Marinda's attention like a magnet, and just as she looked, the CorSec Guards rounded the corner and came into view. She thought that being able to see in full light would be a help. It took only a glimpse to change that opinion.

"Two humans," said Roddi, doing a quick tally, "possibly cyborgs. The rest are armored fighter robots. Many weapons."

It took but a moment to say that—only a moment for Marinda to see with chilling clarity just what was stalking them. The two men were dangerous-looking enough, without a shred of humanity showing in their brutish faces. The robots were even worse—black hulking things with armor-plated flat surfaces and thick stalks of legs that ended in flattened pods instead of feet. There were four pivoting, articulated arms on each robot, two arms with weapons sockets instead of hands. The heads were low turrets, faceless and expressionless, with multiple eye lenses shielded behind heavy sheets of viewplex.

Roddi and Marinda ducked low as an impressive array of weapons were aimed in their direction. Ray beams flashed overhead, sending sputtering chunks of debris flying from suspended-animation cabinets right above them. Each beam made a shrill, screaming hiss of sound as it hit.

They ducked behind a row of the lowest cabinets, working their way through to the very edge of the corridor. If they could just get around another corner and avoid giving their pursuers a straight line of fire, they might elude them long enough to get away. Roddi briefly glanced at the small hand laser he carried, and wished he had brought something more powerful with him. Not that it would do much good against so many CorSec Guards.

Roddi saw an opening in the corridor wall just ahead. It should be just the passageway they needed. He quickly extracted the scanner unit from his accessory compartment and studied the ship's diagram on the glowing screen. But the unit was still malfunctioning. Their position on the map was not indicated, and the details seemed incomplete. He stowed the device angrily. They would just have to chance it. He motioned for Marinda to follow him and stayed low as he led her to the opening.

The CorSec Guards were gaining on them, closing the gap. The humans were hunting for them through the rows of coffinlike cabinets, while the robots avoided the restricting narrowness of that path and continued to follow down the corridor's center aisle, their turret heads constantly scanning for a target.

Roddi and Marinda reached the opening at last and ducked around the corner, ready to break into a run.

But as they straightened up for the sprint they were forced to come to a shuddering halt. This was not a cross corridor at all. It was merely an equipment alcove, not much deeper than it was wide. A dead end. Perhaps literally, thought Roddi.

They whirled on their heels, hoping there was still time to slip out and head down the main corridor. But time had run out. Most of the guards were already within view, and within range. They could not take a step without drawing fire.

Marinda sighed deeply. "I don't suppose this could just be a bad dream."

"I don't have dreams," said Roddi. "But I share your wish. Now get behind me."

"What?"

"Just do it."

She complied. "This is very gallant and brave of you, but I don't see—"

"I want you to line yourself up with me," he interrupted. "Your arms with my arms, your legs with my legs, so none of you is exposed to them. Understand?"

She nodded and did as he asked, resisting the temptation to peek around at the danger that now faced them.

"Surrender!" shouted one of the human guards ahead of them in the center of the corridor. "This is your last chance!"

Roddi meekly dropped his laser pistol and kept his arms still. "I offer no fight," he announced loudly. So loudly his voice rang and echoed through the corridor.

Softly, he said to Marinda, "I have activated a built-in forcefield projector. It will shield us both, for a time. And my body shell is painted a color that resists the particular beam weapon they're fond of. Until they burn their way through me, you'll be safe."

22

"Roddi," she said, tears unavoidably welling up in her eyes, "you don't even know me. Why—?"

"Sssh," he quieted her. "I could be wrong. They may not kill us. Though knowing their masters as I do, death might be preferable."

The CorSec Guards began to advance, their arsenal of weapons leveled at the psybot and the young woman. A step closer. Two steps. Halfway through a third.

Then abruptly, in the next instant, one of the robots approaching them jerked forward as if struck from behind, exploding in a blinding glare of energy that sent fragments in all directions. Almost simultaneously, a second flash of light and a thundering sound came as a second robot was destroyed in midstep. One of the humans twisted in agony as a blue beam scorched through his back and out his chest, lighting up his body from within.

Chunks of metal debris flew at Roddi and Marinda, twisting and burning through the air, with sharp jagged edges ready to bring maiming death. They stopped just short of them, deflected by Roddi's forcefield.

The remaining human and robots were scrambling to get clear of the destruction, seeking what cover they could find on either side of the alcove, interested only in their own survival. Marinda and Roddi could wait. More ray fire chased them, encouraging their flight.

"About time," Roddi said.

Marinda sensed he was not talking to her, and peered around his head to see who the words were for. She was right.

A man stood on the other side of the corridor, directly behind where the CorSec Guards had been before scattering. Marinda gasped at the sight of him.

The stranger was tall and lean, his posture rock-hard and straight. A hooded cape covered most of his close-cropped hair, but was folded back from his shoulders to free his arms for fighting. A large beam pistol was in his right hand, and his left hand, which looked oddly metallic, was closed in a tight fist. That fist, and the rest of his left arm up to the elbow, was ringed by a cluster of tubes, two of which still had traces of smoke issuing from them. His face was a grim mask, his mouth tight-lipped and brooding. Without speaking, he motioned for them to run toward him.

Roddi deactivated his forcefield and darted forward. "Let's go!"

Marinda followed his lead, shaken, her heart pounding. She no longer felt the groggy sluggishness that had followed her reawakening.

They raced into the corridor as the man directed, and as they passed him, he snapped, "Head for the ship!"

Roddi angled around him and took off down the corridor's center aisle, with Marinda close behind him. The man in the cloak stayed rooted to the spot for a moment, thrusting out his left arm toward the CorSec Guards, who had taken up positions behind the banks of suspended-animation cabinets. Triggering his launcher gauntlet, he fired three more armor-piercing missiles with quick precision, then with his right hand laid down a barrage of withering particle beams from his protoblaster. He made no attempt to hit specific targets; he merely discouraged immediate pursuit. The results looked like the grand finale of an old-fashioned fireworks display.

Then he turned and fled down the corridor after Roddi and Marinda, as explosions erupted and reverberated behind him. His cape billowed out, and he ran with an odd loping gait that was almost, but not quite, a limp.

As they ran, the ship's restored lighting began to flicker and fade. The corridor was soon sputtering in and out of darkness, making their flight all the more hazardous. A cross corridor yielded access to the main corridor Roddi had originally followed, and they turned first one corner, then another. Running, running, always running.

Roddi continued his steady, rhythmic jog, but Marinda was beginning to flail a bit as she ran. She was in good shape normally, but this was all just too much, too soon, after awakening from suspension. Abruptly, she stumbled, falling to the corridor deck.

She was on her hands and knees, the wind knocked from her, unable to rise or even call out. Roddi continued away from her, unaware of her fall.

Suddenly a strong arm wrapped around her waist and lifted her in one movement. The man in the hooded cape had not even broken stride, and was now carrying her along as he ran.

The ship's lights fluttered one last time, then quit altogether, plunging them into darkness. Only Roddi's chest light illuminated their way.

The psybot observed, "The reserve power generators you switched on must have given out."

"Least of our worries," came the reply.

Long minutes elapsed before they reached the entry chamber that connected to the airlocks and docking port. The ship that had brought them to *Glory* lay just outside, its power grid patched into the docking mechanisms and airlocks. It offered at least some measure of safety and hope of escape.

Roddi plunged into the entry chamber first, heading for the second airlock gate in the row along the outer bulkhead.

"Control lights are still on," said Roddi, "so the power is still—"

His words stopped abruptly as a weapon flashed within the long chamber. Roddi spun a quarter turn as he took a hit in the shoulder.

"Vandal!" he shouted, as much a warning to his friend as an outcry from the injury.

Vandal needed no further warning. He had spotted the attacker as Roddi was hit. A CorSec Guard, apparently left behind to cover the airlocks, crouched at one side of the chamber, ray pistol in hand. He was turning to aim at Vandal, whose gun arm was burdened by the girl's weight.

Marinda looked up sharply, feeling impossibly awkward with Vandal's arm about her midsection, her legs dangling and her hands clawing for support. She saw the CorSec Guard's weapon flash directly at them and jerked her eyes closed, expecting to die in the next instant.

Vandal had no time to release Marinda and free his gun arm. There was not even time to attempt a missile launch. He pivoted, throwing up his left arm in a desparate attempt to block the path of the ray. He succeeded, and the ray struck Vandal's missile gauntlet dead center. Marinda screamed as a shower of sparks and metal particles sprayed from the gauntlet.

The ray struck an empty launch tube, and the damage sent a missile flying from the loaded tube next to it. The missile whizzed toward the ceiling of the chamber and detonated against power conduits.

The explosion distracted the CorSec man momentarily, making him hesitate. Vandal swung his launcher around and triggered it. A missile shot out.

It missed the man. The ray damage had wrecked the targeting circuits, and the missile went past the guard, not detonating. Vandal's launcher gauntlet began to smoke and sputter, in imminent danger of exploding.

The CorSec man ducked and rolled from the spot where the missile had hit, and if he was surprised that it had not gone off, he wasted no time thinking about it. Starting to rise from a crouch, he aimed at Vandal once more.

Vandal did not waste any time either. Their lives were on the thin edge. He pointed the gauntlet directly at the man and opened his fist, fingers fully extended. He flinched as circuits fired and the gauntlet was propelled from his arm.

It flew straight for the CorSec Guard, with Vandal's metallic left hand still at the front end of the launcher, and slammed into the man, high on his chest, knocking him back against the bulkhead. As it struck, the open fingers of the hand clamped upon his throat.

Terror-struck, the guard dropped his weapon, his eyes rolling down to stare at the disembodied hand. As he tried to break the grip of the clutching fingers, more sparks and smoke began to pour from the damaged gauntlet. He began to run haphazardly, clawing at the launcher with all his panicky strength.

Wordlessly, Vandal hurried toward the airlock booth. Roddi was already opening the door, and quickly sealed it behind them once all three were inside.

Vandal set the girl down on her feet and steadied her, holstered his protoblaster, then looked to Roddi. "How bad?"

"Could be worse," said the psybot, glancing down at the scorched spot on his left shoulder. "Cosmetic damage to the shell, and some loss of control in my arm, but nothing we can't repair."

Marinda gazed in confusion and mild horror at the end of Vandal's left arm, where the hand was missing.

There was no blood. At the end of the arm, where the wrist should have been, was a flattened surface bearing a socket and power connecters. She wondered if the rest of the arm was artificial, too, or if it was only from the elbow down. She did not voice the question, but saw in a glance that the man called Vandal had read it in her eyes. She looked away.

The airlock was ready. Roddi released the latches and raised the floor hatch.

He clambered down the ladder in the side of the tubular docking port, leading the way. Vandal helped Marinda down, then entered the tube and pulled the hatch closed after him.

Below, Roddi reached their ship's entry hatch and activated the unlocking mechanism. He stood back while the hatch opened, then went through into the ship itself. He helped Marinda in, watched as Vandal entered, then closed the hatch, locking it securely.

"Sit over there," Vandal told Marinda, pointing with his good hand at a padded seat behind those of the pilot and copilot. It was a small ship, a bit cramped, and not at all new-looking.

Marinda took her seat as instructed, and watched as Vandal swiftly opened an equipment panel in the bulkhead, removed a plastic-covered object, and tore open the wrapper with his teeth. A new artificial hand was inside, and Vandal carefully snapped it into place at the end of his arm. He took a moment to flex the fingers, making sure they worked, then swung into his seat behind the controls. Roddi took his seat alongside.

"Break us free," snapped Vandal.

Roddi reached for a control door labeled "Docking Disengage," raised it, and pressed the button. Latches could be heard releasing overhead, and there was a sudden lurch as the ship broke free of its port.

Marinda looked out one of the side windows. She could see a second ship, larger and bearing an emblem with the words "CorSec Patrol," attached to a nearby docking port. It took no effort to guess that it had brought the guards who had pursued them through the corridors of *Glory*.

As Vandal maneuvered away from the great starship with thruster jets, the semblance of gravity they had felt while attached to the spinning vessel faded to zero. He laid in a course for Avalon, the third moon of Logres and their destination.

"Thanks, Vandal," Roddi said abruptly. "For saving us back there. Twice. Though I don't know how you wiped out those battle robs with single shots."

"I've fought that type of unit before," Vandal said grimly. "They have a weak spot. A direct hit over their power cell, and the released energy does most of the damage. They should discontinue that model."

"Let's not tell them," Roddi observed. He studied Vandal silently for a long moment, aware that his friend's seeming calm after combat hid feelings better left undisturbed. Finally, he said, "Shall I beam a message to the University?"

"No. Let's get out of the area first."

Vandal fired up the engines, ready for the long flight back to Avalon. But escape was not to be that easy.

An explosion rocked their ship as they drew away from *Glory*, startling everyone. Roddi saw the cause of it first, pointing with alarm.

"I see it." Vandal worked the controls of his vessel, bringing it around.

As the ship swung farther, Marinda could see another CorSec ship approaching them from the planet below. The ion cannon at its nose was still glowing from the shot that had struck them.

Vandal had already switched on weapons power and was watching the targeting grid superimposed on the forward window. When the glowing red grid covered the nose of the approaching craft, he hit the trigger.

The jolt as he fired shook their ship almost as badly as the initial hit had. Their interior lights dimmed as the medium-sized grazer weapon fired a burst of gamma rays at the CorSec patrol vessel.

His aim was on target. The ion cannon and much of the nose of the CorSec ship vaporized. Disabled, the ship ceased hostile action and began to limp toward the orbiting starship and its comrade vessel.

"Well," said Roddi, "that puts them out of it."

"Us, too." Vandal was fighting with the controls now, and flight indicators were spinning madly, showing damage readings. "We took a good shot. Our engines may fail . . . life-support systems are on the edge."

Roddi looked at him questioningly. "Avalon . . .?"

"Never make it. Best we can hope for is a landing down there."

"Down there?" Marinda said, staring at the planet looming large below them. She knew nothing of it yet, but if that was where the CorSec Guards came from, it boded ill for their chances there. She looked to Vandal, but saw nothing in his grim countenance to reassure her.

The ship's nose dropped steadily and they began their uncertain descent. Down . . . to Coreworld.

5:

REPORT AND ASSIGNMENT

RAZER STUDIED HERSELF IN the mirrored wall of the luxurious private apartment, and was pleased by what she saw. It was not an act of vanity, or even of pride. It was merely a look of appraisal. A self-imposed inspection as routine as the regular maintenance she performed on all the hundred or so weapons she owned and used with such deadly skill.

"I'll be with you in a moment, darling," said a man's resonant voice from the next room.

Without looking away from her reflected image, Razer replied, "Take your time. Waiting only enhances the pleasure."

Though she was in her mid-thirties, there was nothing about her face or figure to suggest she was past her twenties. Razer was tall and athletic, but not lanky. Her body was perfectly formed and proportioned, so unless she was standing next to someone it was impossible to gauge her height. Her voluptuous curves owed as much to expert conditioning as to hereditary beauty.

The lushness of those curves was amply revealed by the sheer lounging suit she wore. The jacket was short, ending high above her waist, with a neckline that plunged to a tiny gold clasp near the bottom. The pants were loose-fitting, with a braided waistband that rode the peaks of her hips and dipped to follow the gentle curve of her abdomen. All was in shades of lavender, echoing the color of her eyes.

Only in those eyes, in their cold and implacable gaze, did her age and experience betray her. Only there did the image tarnish. But then, she thought, many men found that more appealing than innocence.

Razer was not sure whether that fact pleased or amused her, but she smiled regardless, adjusting the long strands of raven hair that framed her face and reached down almost to her breasts.

She *was* sure that she belonged here, here in one of the exclusive private enclaves of CityPrime, capital of Coreworld and headquarters of the Corporation. And especially, she belonged here in Roman's apartment. She liked seeing her reflection surrounded by the luxurious appointments of the room. It was an apartment eminently suited to a vice-president of the Corporation, and also eminently suited to Razer, whose high rank as an eliminator afforded her a status few ordinary citizens on the planet could hope to attain, no matter how much wealth they might possess. The fact that Roman had chosen her for his lover was as it should be, she thought. A mark of honor . . . an award befitting her value to the Corporation, as much as her great beauty.

"There," said Roman as he entered the room. He had changed from his suit and now wore a long black robe with corporate emblems on the lapels. "I trust I've kept you waiting long enough? I've deactivated the servant, since I know how much you detest robots."

Roman carried a tray in his hands. It bore a small

gold platter of hors d'oeuvres and a carafe of azure liquid. Two slender goblets of the finest crystal stood inverted alongside the carafe. He set the tray down on a low table near a bank of cushions arranged in the center of the floor.

As he straightened, he looked at Razer admiringly, possessively, letting his gaze rake across the full length of her form. He knew she was striking an alluring pose to please him, to arouse him, and she was succeeding. Yet her catlike smile, as always, seemed more mysterious than friendly.

"You know," he said, "even after all the times we've been together, I still never know quite what you're thinking."

Razer arched an exquisite eyebrow. With a downward sweep of her hand, she said, "If you don't know what I'm thinking, then you aren't paying attention to what I'm wearing."

He stepped closer to her. "I'm paying attention. Of all your many outfits, I like that one best. It's so difficult to conceal weapons in it."

She put her arms about him. "Really? Is that all you like about it?"

Roman gave a short, deep laugh in reply. He pulled her tightly to him and kissed her. As tall as she was, Roman was still an inch taller. He was older than she by at least two decades, but he was youthful, with an athletic build and a certain dynamic energy. Even the gray that streaked his temples seemed a decorative, aristocratic touch and not a sign of age. His angular face with its narrow jaw was flawless, and seemed almost boyish at times.

Razer broke off the kiss, looking up into his eyes through the dark curtain of her lashes. Softly, she said, "You're wrong, you know. If I did wish to kill you, I could do it without weapons. Anytime. Anyplace." The tone of her voice was sultry, the words more a caress than a threat.

She reached down and removed the small gold clasp that bound the bottom edges of her jacket. She held the clasp between thumb and forefinger, smiling as she raised it for Roman to see.

"And," she said, "you're wrong about this outfit." With that, she squeezed the clasp. A tiny injector needle soundlessly sprang into view from one end of the golden ornament, a droplet of fluid glistening at its tip. "Nerve toxin. Quick. Deadly. Untraceable. Always ready to silence whatever enemy you ask me to deal with."

Razer retracted the poison tip and casually tossed the clasp upon the table. "Not as satisfying as a high-powered beam weapon, but effective enough." She put her arms around his neck and smiled up into his cautious gaze.

Roman studied that smile a moment, then he laughed once more and kissed her even more passionately. Even though he never truly felt threatened by her peculiarly twisted sense of humor or by her reputation as a death-dealing assassin, he had to admit even to himself that the element of danger added a certain bizarre thrill to this love affair.

As the lingering kiss ended, Roman gestured toward the cushions. "Please, sit down, make yourself comfortable. You must try the food."

Razer sat where he indicated, lowering herself with feline grace, then waited as he sat down beside her. She studied the tray on the table with curious interest.

"Is that Sinaerian wine?"

"Yes," said Roman. "And it's getting harder to obtain. I don't share it with just anyone."

"I should hope not." Razer took up one of the narrow goblets and held it for Roman to pour. She watched as the clear azure liquid, slightly thicker than ordinary wines, trickled into the vessel and slowly filled it. "Are we celebrating something special?"

"In a way," said Roman. "Tonight I stand on the verge of achieving my greatest accomplishment. The University's new hyperspace drive will soon be ours."

"Are they aware of this great gift?"

"Hardly. But they will find out soon enough. Even as we speak, my agents are on their way to Avalon to steal the plans."

Razer sipped at her wine. "Quite a coup, if they succeed."

"They will. My superior, Alpha, approved the plan himself. He trusts my judgment, as much as he trusts anything." Roman savored a long sip of wine, then sat his goblet down. He put his arm around Razer and gently kissed her neck. "Once we've got the hyperdrive secret, we won't be limited to this accursed sector of space. We can spread to other worlds . . . regain our lost momentum . . . build a true empire."

He was working his way up toward her ear, and Razer let him, enjoying his touch. As she closed her eyes to shut out distractions, she said, "An empire . . . will need an emperor. . . ."

"Perhaps. But it won't be me, my darling. The Quintad still rules, and always shall. Never forget that."

"Perhaps. But even the Quintad must have a leader, and you are assistant to their highest-ranking member. Someday . . ."

"What do I need with ambition, when you have enough for both of us?" Roman turned her face toward his and kissed her full on the mouth, feeling the warmth of her lips increasing. He took the empty goblet from her yielding hand and set it next to his on the table without removing his eyes from her. "What an incredibly exquisite prize you are."

She turned to him, and they embraced. Roman could feel her pulse quickening, even as his did. The hors d'oeuvres, still untouched, and the remaining wine all faded from their immediate interest.

Long moments passed, and at first neither of them heard the tiny, urgent beeping note that sounded. Razer was the first to give a slight start of awareness, as reflexes only partially dimmed by passion became alert once more.

"What is it?" Roman said, puzzled by her abrupt reaction before he, too, became aware of the sound. Then his look became one of consternation as he recognized it, and his eyes darted to the broad metal band around his left wrist. In the black strip that cut across the band, the glowing digits which normally gave the time had disappeared, and words were forming a message that repeatedly tracked across the strip.

Razer leaned forward to see it, but the symbols were meaningless to her. "I thought I was familiar with all the known languages—"

"It's Alpha's private code," explained Roman. "Something important, something urgent, has come up. I must return to headquarters at once."

"At once?" Razer sighed deeply, angrily, her back straightening as supple muscles flexed in a dangerous way. "Someone has a disastrous sense of timing."

Roman cast a lingering, reluctant look at the voluptuous young woman who fairly smoldered beside him, then he rose from the cushions with a sigh of his own. "Sorry, darling. But I don't think I can afford to ignore a command from Alpha. I'll have to go."

Razer got to her feet in a quick motion and stood

beside him. "I know better than to try to talk you out of it. When do you think you'll be through?"

"I have no idea. The message didn't say why I'm needed." Roman paused, looking at her speculatively. "You know, I think it might be good if you came with me."

Razer smiled. "I'd already decided to go with you anyway."

"Excellent. But we'd both better change to something more appropriate for business." Turning away from her, Roman called out a word. "Closet."

Instantly, two sections of the mirrored wall began to swing open, revealing racks of clothes, mostly men's. But some garments obviously belonged to Razer.

"Shall we see who can get ready first?" said Razer. She shrugged out of her jacket and strode purposefully to the rack of clothes, then turned to smile wickedly back at him.

Roman frowned. "An intriguing bet. But you don't play fair, my darling."

"I know," Razer said with self-assurance. "I never do."

The Corporation headquarters building was a short hop by helijet from the executive apartment complex in which Roman lived. The lights of CityPrime moved swiftly beneath them as their vehicle arced through the nighttime sky of Coreworld.

CityPrime, the first site of colonization and a once-glistening showplace of transplanted civilization, showed signs of decay, but in the private enclaves and buildings devoted to serving the needs of Corporation leaders, a semblance of the old luxury still remained. The more dangerous and tawdry areas of the city could easily be avoided by members of the ruling class.

Roman's vehicle touched down upon a reserved landing pad on the roof of the enormous building that served as base of operations for the Corporation. The jets whined to a halt, the side hatch opened, and Roman stepped out onto the roof, followed by Razer. Landing lights illuminated corporate banners that flapped in the crisp breeze flowing over the high building. The smell of the polluted outside air was mildly unpleasant.

Roman wore dark slacks and a Corporation zip jacket. A short dress cloak with high standing collar, pulled hastily from the closet, shielded him from the cool air. Razer wore no cloak. A smooth, form-fitting jumpsuit of jet-black leather covered her from shoulders to ankles, throwing glints of light from every curve as she walked. Black boots and gloves covered her extremities, and a long lavender scarf about her neck fluttered in the breeze. Together, they walked briskly toward the elevators at the building's center.

A CorSec lieutenant met them at the elevator door, snapping to attention with military precision. He stood aside to let them enter.

"Good evening, sir," said the lieutenant. "There's a briefing in the meeting room on level four." His eyes flicked briefly to take in Razer, then he looked discreetly away, following them into the elevator and pressing the button. He removed his security key from the panel and waited silently as the car hummed downward.

The lighting on level four was reduced, as was normal after regular business hours. Striding quickly along, the three of them reached the meeting room in a matter of minutes. The double door was already standing open, and as they approached they could see several CorSec Guards wheeling a cloth-draped equipment cart into the room.

Roman waited as they maneuvered it inside, then entered after them. Technicians were waiting within, busily making connections with the presentation equipment used for briefings.

"All right," said Roman abruptly. "What's this all about?"

The lieutenant drew himself up to make the report. "There's been an incident, sir. About five hours ago, CorSec scanners picked up an unidentified spaceship approaching that old hulk of a starship."

"*Glory*?" Roman said.

"Right, sir. We sent a patrol vessel up to investigate. The crew radioed back that they found the unidentified ship docked at one of *Glory*'s bays, and they suspected it was piloted there by agents of the University. They went aboard to check it out. That was their last transmission."

Another CorSec officer, one who had accompanied the equipment cart into the room, stepped forward. "Sir, I was on board another patrol vessel that was sent up shortly after the first. We observed the unidentified ship attempting to escape as we made our approach."

"Did you open fire?" asked Razer.

"Of course. And we did score a solid hit. But we took a direct hit ourselves, which prevented further pursuit. Luckily, we were able to reach *Glory* and dock there. What we found inside was pretty grim."

The man pulled the cloth cover off the equipment cart and tossed it aside. Lying there upon the sterile white cart top were the blackened and battered remains of a CorSec robot. There was only the head, several arms, a charred chunk of torso, and a number

39

of unidentifiable pieces left of what had once been an effective fighting machine.

"Everyone from the first patrol group was either dead or seriously injured," said the officer. "This battle rob didn't suffer any head damage, so his batteries should have kept his memory intact. If so, he's the only survivor with more or less complete information on what happened up there."

Technicians came forward and connected leads to the snapped cable ends protruding from the robot head. Additional power from the conference-room equipment enabled the shattered robot's brain to function at more than the minimal level it now was hanging on to. In a few minutes, the hookup was complete, and the robot head came to life.

"Damaged . . . damaged . . . severely damaged," said the robot, its monotone voice coming through its own speaker and also through the audio system in the conference room's walls. "Need repair at once—"

"Report!" snapped Roman. "What happened up there aboard the starship?"

"Damaged . . ." repeated the robot. "In pursuit of suspected University agents . . . tracked one of them through the starship . . . located . . ."

"Play back your record of the event," said Roman, "beginning when you first made contact."

"Damaged . . . may not function," said the robot. But it ceased to speak, and in a moment a glowing image lit up the viewscreen at the end of the conference room.

The picture crackled with interference, but was clearly the robot's view of a corridor within the ancient starship known as *Glory*. Two CorSec Guards and another robot were in sight just ahead, and a bend in the

40

corridor was coming into view. Faint sounds could be heard from somewhere ahead.

Roman turned to one of the technics. "Can you amplify the audio on that?"

The woman nodded and made an adjustment to her equipment. Instantly, the level of sound increased. Scuffling noises, the sounds of a human and a robot walking, became apparent. And there were also voices.

". . . still a little stiff," one voice was saying.

"Exercise is good for that," said the other voice.

There was a minute's pause, then the first could be heard again. "Marinda . . . I'm Marinda Donelson."

To one of the technics, Roman said, "Check that name out. Run it through the computer files."

"Yes, sir."

Roman and Razer watched intently as the robot's point of view rounded the corner and Roddi and Marinda became visible. Then as the others began to pursue the psybot and young woman, the CorSec robot whose brain was being tapped paused by the doorway to Laboratory C. Through the open door could clearly be seen the inner hidden laboratory and its bizarre suspended-animation cabinet. The robot's vision zoomed in to gather details of the secret room. Then he turned and followed after his fellow CorSec guards.

The remainder of the stored record displayed the pursuit through *Glory*'s corridors, Roddi and Marinda being cornered in the alcove, and then, abruptly, a shattering, deafening explosion that rocked the conference room. As the smoke cleared in the image on the screen, the robot's point of view was tilted sideways at floor level. There was a view of empty corridor for a long moment, and then a brief glimpse of three figures darting down the corridor, passing through the exploded robot's field of vision. At the sight of one of those figures, Razer abruptly stiffened and drew a sharp breath.

"Vandal," she said, her lovely eyes narrowing in hatred. "That was Vandal!"

Roman still stared at the screen. "Are you sure? He was only visible for a second. Shall I freeze his image?"

"Don't bother, I'm sure," said Razer. "I'd know him anywhere."

"Well, that explains the damage, at least," observed Roman. "But what were they doing up there?"

The CorSec officer shrugged nervously. "I wish I could say, sir. But we have nothing more to go on than what you've just seen. Their ship had vanished by the time we recovered the survivors. We were able to use the undamaged ship to get back here."

Razer said, "But if, as you claim, you did score a hit on Vandal's ship, then how did he manage to vanish? Surely he would not have tried to make it to Avalon."

Before the nervous officer could reply, the lieutenant who had escorted Roman and Razer to the conference room spoke up. "I believe I can help with that," he said. "Our scanners did track a ship's descent from that sector. It appears to have been in trouble, heading for a landing here on Coreworld, somewhere in Delta Zone."

One of the technics approached from the facility's computer console, a printout in hand. "Sir, I have something on that name."

Roman turned quickly toward the man. "What is it?"

"The only listing we can find of anyone named Marinda Donelson is from a very old record left over from before colonization. According to this," he continued, glancing at the printout, "she was a doctor of astrobiology, and assistant to Dr. Fenton Diggs, a prime architect of *Glory*'s construction.''

Razer smiled oddly. ''How ironic.''

''But,'' resumed the technic, ''there's no record of her having been aboard the starship as part of the colonization crew or passenger list. Of course, our records are not complete.''

''No matter,'' said Roman, his expression suddenly very serious. ''I think I've seen enough.''

''Sir,'' asked one of the technics, ''if you're through with it now, shall we take this robot down to the lab for repairs?''

Roman considered it but a moment. ''No, scrap it. We don't need failures.''

There was a brief, shrill scream of protest from the shattered robot. But then a technic quickly disconnected the power and other cables leading to the head, and the mech fell silent, again no more than a pile of debris with a fading memory. They covered the wrecked form and began to wheel it from the conference room.

Roman nodded toward the CorSec officers. ''Thank you, gentlemen, you've been of great help. Prepare your reports, and be sure the members of the Quintad are notified in the morning.''

''Yes, sir,'' both men said in tandem, and went on about their business of straightening things up.

Roman left the room with Razer at his elbow. Walking slowly, they continued down the hall until they were out of earshot of those in the conference room.

''This worries me,'' Roman said softly. ''If this Marinda Donelson is truly a surviving original Earth colonist, she could prove to be very dangerous to our cause, and very valuable to the University. She knows the truth about Earth's history and the colonizing mission. A living artifact like her could rally others against us, and aid the University. I would hate for her to fall into University hands."

Razer smiled wickedly. "Don't worry, my love. I think I can solve that problem for you, and solve another one for myself—a problem named Vandal."

"You don't mind postponing our little celebration?"

"I mind," she said, squeezing his arm. "But not nearly as much as I would mind missing this opportunity to destroy Vandal once and for all, and to rid your mind of this new worry."

"Very well. Then I give you the assignment."

"Just provide me with the estimated landing coordinates for Vandal's ship, and give me a chance to go home and pick up my weapons."

"The coordinates we can get now from the tracking center," Roman told her. "But I'd rather you not delay getting started on this. Go ahead and draw whatever new weapons you need from our armory here in the building. I'll take care of the authorization. I want you to get started at once. I have a feeling that this is much too important to allow even one more minute to slip past."

"As you wish," Razer said. "I'll begin at once. And when I return, we'll both have even more to celebrate."

4:

DELTA ZONE

THE TWIN MOONS OF Coreworld were high in the nighttime sky over the arid and desolate region of the planet known as Delta Zone. Their light was more often than not blocked this night by the masses of clouds that scudded past, their shadows creeping across the blighted land. The wind whispered rumors of a coming storm, dry moans and warning threats, to any who might hear and pay heed. It was a place no longer warmed by the touch of humanity or the bustle of civilized society. There would be no welcome here for visitors, willing or unwilling.

A small spacecraft was revealed by the intermittent moonlight, which played across the landscape of gray crystalline sand, rolling hills, and dry desert grasses. It stood at the end of long and twisted lines etched across the sand by its own landing skids. Lines that told the story of a difficult descent and touchdown. The ship tilted sharply to one side on the uneven ground, and traces of smoke still curled upward from a charred cavity in the side of the craft.

Red emergency lights spilled their firelike glow through the open hatchway of the ship onto the sand and the three figures who stood there. As they stared at the damage, the reality of the situation was apparent to them all.

"The ship's finished," said Vandal, his voice dry and hard.

Roddi agreed. "It does look to be beyond repair."

Marinda sighed, her look as bleak as the landscape around them. "I suppose I should count my blessings, but this has been one hell of a thing to wake up to."

Looking toward her, Roddi extended a hand to her shoulder in a gesture he had seen humans use. "I am truly sorry things have been so unpleasant for you. This all must be quite a shock to your system."

"She'll face worse before this is over," Vandal said abruptly, still studying the ship. "Of all the places we might have crashed, Delta Zone is about the worst. And you can bet the Corporation will send someone out looking for us. Soon. We'd best be well clear of the area when they get here."

"In that case," said Roddi, "I had better get the T-beam radio at once and notify the University of our situation."

Vandal gave a nod of agreement. "I'll get the weapons and whatever gear we might need."

"Wait here, Marinda," Roddi instructed the young woman. "There is still a danger of explosion. I shall return in a moment."

With that, the psybot and Vandal reentered the heavily damaged spacecraft, Vandal going to the rear of the ship, where the weapons and equipment lockers were located, and Roddi going forward. Roddi went to a compact unit mounted near the control panel. He disconnected the cables hooking it up to ship's power and released the latches locking it to the bulkhead. He took time to grab a small equipment case of his own, then brought everything back outside.

Marinda stood waiting in the sand, looking uncomfortable in the dry, alien wind. "This . . . this University you mentioned. What is it? Will it be able to send someone to rescue us?"

"One certainly hopes so," Roddi replied earnestly. "The University is the organization which sent us to find you, or more accurately, to find the source of the signal. But before our associates there can begin to help, we must let them know what has happened and where we are."

The silver-blue psybot now sat the device he had removed from the ship upon a high mound of sand and flipped open its access panel. A keyboard and small screen were revealed.

Marinda watched with concerned interest as he made adjustments to the odd-looking directional antenna. "Aren't you worried the Corporation might pick up your message?"

"Not in the least," answered Roddi. He gave an irritable flick of his wrist once, then twice, trying to get his hand to work properly. "Got to repair that circuit! Anyway, as I was about to say, this is not a conventional radio, Marinda. It's a relatively new device called a T-beam transceiver. It doesn't put out signals on any ordinary radio band. It converts a message into a tiny burst of prepackaged data, then fires it straight through hyperspace, where it pops back out at its destination. It's virtually instantaneous and can't be intercepted."

"Hyperspace?" Marinda raised an eyebrow. "Mankind has finally discovered how to use hyperspace?"

"The University has," Roddi corrected. "The Corporation has not, yet. But it would dearly love to. Now, just let me tend to this a moment."

Roddi's fingers began to move across the keyboard,

slowing down only when those on his damaged arm seemed to quiver a bit. When his message of their coordinates and status nearly filled the screen, he pressed the transmit button. There was a moment's pause as the odd antenna began to glow, becoming slightly hazy near the point, then there was a hiss and a sharp ping of sound. The words on the tiny screen disappeared, replaced by the brief phrase "Message transmitted."

"There, that's done," said Roddi. "They may take a moment to respond, while they decide what to do." His head rotated toward the young woman. "The University will be very excited, I'm sure. This is truly amazing. You've actually been in suspended animation aboard *Glory* all these years!"

"Yes, since the night before we left Earth." Marinda's pretty eyes scrunched into a troubled frown. "All what years? Just how long has it been, anyway?"

"Well, just a bit over seven hundred Earth years."

"Seven hun—" Marinda's mouth dropped as her words faded to a dry gasp. In the next moment, her hands flew to her face to feel the skin there. "Oh my God! You mean I'm over seven hundred and thirty years old?" She quickly reached into both pockets of her lab smock and in one of them found the small compact she was searching for. Flipping open the case, she studied her own reflection in the feeble light.

"Well, chronologically I suppose you could be said to be that old," Roddi remarked casually. "But of course, biologically you are no older than you were when the suspended-animation process began." He leaned closer to study the young woman. "I can't be sure without adequate medical testing, but you certainly look well preserved."

Marinda gave a sigh and snapped the compact closed. "Thanks . . . I think."

"An original Earthling," Roddi said with a certain awe. "Fascinating. But I still do not understand why the chamber in which you made the journey was so carefully hidden away."

"It was hidden," Marinda replied, "because it was never supposed to be there in the first place."

"A provocative statement. Please explain."

The young woman ran a hand through her blond hair. "It seems like only yesterday, but I guess it must have been a great, great many yesterdays ago. I was an astrobiologist on Earth, working with the space program, when I was assigned to the *Glory* project. I became the assistant to Dr. Fenton Diggs, the man in charge of developing the suspended-animation system for the starship. I leaped at that opportunity, because I was one of his students in college and I thought he was a genius."

"That much makes sense. But the system used to keep you alive all those years was vastly different from the cryogenic chambers in the rest of the ship."

"Exactly," said Marinda with enthusiasm. "It was a breakthrough development that Fenton made, partway through the project. He presented his findings to the committee in charge of the program, and tried to convince them how much better it would be to use his new system rather than the conventional, crude system. But, they were too narrow-minded to approve it. They said his idea was too unorthodox, too risky. They voted him down in favor of their older, 'safer' system. In part, I think they may have figured they had too much money tied up in the first design to start over again."

"A not uncommon reaction, sad to say."

"Anyway," Marinda went on, "Fenton remained convinced of the validity of his theory and continued his tests and research. I helped him build the experimental chamber you found me in, and we secretly installed it in the back of a spare lab section on *Glory*. We concealed it with a false wall. Fenton even doctored the ship's plans so no one would notice the smaller compartment."

Roddi nodded, then inquired, "And you volunteered to test it?"

"Yes. I didn't mind being the guinea pig. I had faith in Fenton's work, and in my own work, for that matter, since I had been helping him. Not that I didn't have doubts, but the night before the ship was to leave, we snuck into the hidden compartment and he connected me inside the chamber. That's the last thing I remember before you found me."

"Remarkable." Roddi checked his screen on the T-beam transceiver. No reply was showing yet. Had his message gone through?

"Fenton went on the mission too, of course," Marinda added. "But not in a suspended-animation chamber. He was to be an overseer for the early part of the trip, just to be sure the systems were working properly. He was supposed to use one of the chambers later on, so he could reach the new star system too. And of course, he would know to revive me, once there. I . . . I guess something must have happened to him. No one else knew to wake me up."

"Well," replied Roddi, "I don't know what finally happened to him, but I do know that your Dr. Diggs lived long enough to have offspring. One of his descendants in this star system grew up to be Professor Elias Diggs, the man who invented psychogenetic robots, among other things. I do know that toward the end of *Glory*'s spaceflight, something happened. Something terrible."

"What?"

Roddi spread his metallic hands in a helpless gesture. "No one knows for certain. The records of that time were either lost or deliberately destroyed. But it seems clear there was some sort of power struggle among those on board the ship. Those that prevailed were the ones that oversaw the landing and colonization of this planet, Coreworld. The government they formed was modeled after the giant corporations of Earth, which is why it is known today as the Corporation, and for a time it worked very well."

"What went wrong?"

There was a small bleep of sound now from the T-beam transceiver, and Roddi's attention immediately focused upon the screen. Words were rapidly forming across its glowing surface.

"I shall have to explain the rest later," said Roddi. "We've received a reply."

Behind them, Vandal emerged from the battered ship carrying several large packs of equipment. He strode up quickly and looked at the transceiver's tiny screen.

"They're sending a ship?"

Roddi rotated his head to take in Vandal. "Not exactly. Their message states that they are concerned about the hazards of getting a ship both in past Coreworld's defenses and then back out again."

"Well, what then?" Vandal snapped.

"They report that a ship is available at a secret University base. But our chances of reaching it are slim. They're sending a rescue team to help us, and we are to rendezvous with them in Jonnersville."

Vandal shook his head irritably. "I don't like relying

on others. I think we could do better on our own.
There must be Corporation ships we could reach. We
could take one over."

"Possibly," Roddi agreed. "But their crews will likely
be alerted to such a possibility. Besides, the University
has instructed—"

"The University be damned," snarled Vandal. "I
may take assignments from them, but they don't own
me. Those fools sit in their pristine buildings on Avalon, spinning theories and plans, then leaving them to
others to carry out. They don't know the real world."

"Perhaps," said Roddi with polite caution. "But
you must admit their concerns are real enough. And
there is more at stake here than just our necks."

Vandal glanced at Marinda, and his frown lost some
of its stubbornness. At last he said, "Perhaps. We can
follow their plan for now. But I'm keeping my options
open."

Vandal set down the packs he had carried out and
rummaged through one of them. He pulled a spare
cloak from it and tossed it to Marinda. "Here—you
might need this. Now let's get out of here. We can't
afford to wait until morning."

This strangely grim man slung the largest pack over
his shoulder and two more across his mechanical arm.
The last one he plopped down in front of Roddi. He
paused just long enough to get his bearings from the
twin moons and the stars before setting out across the
sand.

"Don't mind him," Roddi said softly to Marinda,
scrambling to gather up his radio and gear, as well as
the pack Vandal had left him. "He's always in a bad
mood."

The young woman tugged the borrowed cloak about
her and turned the hood up against the unpleasant

breeze. "So I see. Still, he was thoughtful enough to notice I needed protection against the wind."

The psybot stared at her a moment, nonplussed. "Oh my, yes of course. Forgive me, I do not feel the wind as you do, so I did not think—"

"I wasn't criticizing you, Roddi," Marinda said hastily. "Believe me, after all you've done, I couldn't. I just meant, about Vandal, I mean . . ."

"Come on," Roddi urged with a friendly wave of his hand. He switched on his chest light. "We must hurry and catch up with him. There is much of Delta Zone yet to cross."

Just as they reached a point less than a mile away from the ship, there was a startling, gut-wrenching *whump* of sound. Behind them, their downed spaceship exploded. A fireball rose briefly into the air, then faded as flames consumed the rest of the ship.

Marinda stared in horror at it for a long moment. Then with a sigh, she turned and pressed onward.

5:
MISSION FOR CLEERA

TARNBUCKLE'S EMPORIUM WAS LOCATED on one of the wilder streets of Port Madrid, a decidedly wild city to begin with. As the name implied, the city was a port settlement and was situated on the western coast of the continent, roughly five hundred miles northwest of CityPrime. It had long been a center of trade servicing the cities of the northern outlands and the other seaport cities along the coast, as well as those across the sea. In recent decades, it had become a tarnished and squalid relic of its glory days, full of dangerous and disreputable men and women. Although the quality of its business had sharply diminished the quantity of its business had not.

Tarnbuckle's Emporium was a large shop, filled to the rafters with all manner of goods. Most were black-market items, and those that weren't had probably been obtained by questionable means before finding their way here. Everyone who came to the place was aware of that fact, but none of them seemed to care.

Moving through the cramped and dingy aisles of the shop, a humanoid robot walked with careful speed, carrying a small parcel from the back. Crafted to resemble a young woman, the robot's metallic form was a glistening design of curving white and lavender panels, overlapping at joints and flex points.

A grubby man whose look and manner belied the rich clothing he wore stood at the shop's front counter, glowering at the robot carrying his parcel. His lips and nose twitched nervously with each step she took toward him.

"Now don't you drop that package, you stupid mech," snarled the grubby man. "I've been waiting a long time for that to arrive. A very long time indeed!"

Standing near him behind the counter, the shop's proprietor allowed his eyes to narrow reflexively before forcing a businessman's smile upon his face. It was a pleasant face, with easy features and youthful vigor, surrounded by dark hair and beard.

"You have nothing to worry about, my friend," the proprietor told his customer with a carefully controlled voice. "We have nothing but the best here, and that includes the service. Cleera would never drop your shipment."

The grubby man's eyes flashed. "Cleera? Is that what you call it? Damn stupid practice, giving names to mechs. They're not pets, for pity's sake."

The robot reached them, oblivious to their words, and moved with precise steps behind the counter. Turning to face the customer, Cleera slowly lowered the parcel to the counter surface. Just before placing it there, her mechanisms jerked slightly, hesitating before continuing smoothly once more. Then Cleera stepped back from the counter and remained motionless.

"See, see that?" growled the grubby man, apparently feeling both vindicated and irritated by the near-slip. "Obviously a faulty machine. And handling my precious merchandise." He quickly unwrapped his parcel to check for damage. Beneath the outer layers of paper and polyshielding, within the foam shock buffers, rested a hermetically sealed case. Through the transparent sides could be seen a shiny new cybernetic heart pump. The labels and serial number had been scratched off. "Well, no damage done, it seems."

The proprietor glanced quickly around as his hands moved to cover the object. "I wouldn't be showing that around too much," he cautioned softly. "Not if you want to live long enough to put it to use or to resell it."

"Have no fear of that," replied the grubby man, with a smug pat of his blaster. He still cast ferret glances over his shoulder and around the shop, though, as he cautiously rewrapped his parcel. He slapped a fat envelope upon the counter and waited briefly while the money inside was counted. Then he tucked his merchandise under his thickset arm and pulled his cloak around to conceal it. With a parting nod that was only barely cordial, he said, "Good day to you, sir."

The proprietor watched silently as the man left his shop, then when he was certain that no one was within hearing range he said to the robot beside him, "I doubt he wants that for himself. He'll probably sell it to some rich man whose old unit is wearing out." Facing her, he added, "You had me worried for a moment, Cleera. Did you falter with the package just to tease that creep?"

Cleera's eyes swiveled toward him, and her video-optics lost the expressionless stare they had maintained before. "No, Josh, that's not it at all." Her voice was soft and pleasantly feminine despite its slight electronic tone. "I wasn't trying to falter, believe me. I was startled, I received a message alert."

Josh tensed a bit. "Message alert? From our people?"

Cleera nodded in affirmation, then turned slightly and put a hand to her chest, concentrating on the internal circuits she must operate. Deep within her well-sculpted form was hidden a compact T-beam transceiver, wired directly to her brain circuitry. Both it and the directional antenna were shielded to prevent scanner detection by CorSec Guards or Corporation agents, as were her psychogenetic mental circuits. As she aligned the antenna properly, she transmitted an acknowledgment signal, then waited for the message which would travel back through hyperspace to her coordinates. In a moment, that message came.

She looked to Josh quickly. "My team has been activated. The Uni is sending us on a rescue mission. I must leave right away."

"What sort of rescue?"

"An agent named Vandal, and a psybot. And someone else, as well. Their ship crashed in the Delta Zone."

Josh whistled low. "Vandal, here on Coreworld."

"You know him?"

"No. But I know of him. The man's a legend. Used to be an eliminator for the Corporation, back during the plague years. Then something turned him around and he's been working on our side. He's the best, the absolute best. But he's as good as dead if the Corporation gets him."

"I did not know," replied Cleera. "My programming must be incomplete."

Josh fondly brushed a bit of storeroom dust from her shoulder. "You're new yet. Don't worry about it. Do you need help contacting the others?"

"No. I understand the procedure. It will not take long. I . . . I'm sorry to leave you without assistance here."

"No sweat. I can manage. Besides, I'll have it a lot easier than you will, from the sound of it."

Cleera turned and started for the back room. She had reached the halfway point when she abruptly turned around to stare back at her "owner" and fellow agent. "Goodbye, Josh."

"Goodbye, you silly mech," he said with a wry, teasing look on his face. Then he added soberly, "And Cleera, don't you go getting yourself damaged or anything. Okay?"

"Thanks, Josh. You take care, too."

Between a tavern and the artificial-food-processing plant on Dockside Road stood a large warehouse. Its faded sign bore the name "Lands-End Shipping Company." Lights were on in the building, for work was always being done there.

Cleera walked cautiously toward it, keeping to the shadowy areas and doing her best to avoid attracting unwanted attention. As she reached the open doorway, she glanced once more down the street, then quickly slipped inside. She was grateful the University's message had come at night, for at this hour there would likely be fewer humans present in the building.

Though past its heyday, the warehouse was still better than half filled with stacks of crates and transport containers. A wide aisle ran down the center of the building, branching out into lateral aisles separating the storage sectors. A green-hued robot was walking down one of those aisles, looking for a spot to put away the shipping container he carried. Locating an empty place, he looked up to gauge its height. Then suddenly his tubular leg sections, which had been partially telescoped before, expanded upward until he was twice as tall. With relative ease he shoved the container forward onto the stack, then lowered to his normal height.

Not far past him, another robot was toiling. This one was dark blue, and although still basically human-oid in shape he had bulky arms and legs and a massive torso crammed with servos and power units. He was lifting an immense crate from its spot in a storage sector and muscling it onto a transport pallet.

As soon as both had completed these tasks, Cleera stepped into the light at the end of the aisle and called softly to them. "HiLo—Torb—"

Both robots' heads quickly swiveled in her direction, and as they turned to start toward her Cleera rushed forward to meet them. The bulky blue robot was surprisingly fast for a mech his size and weight.

"Cleera," said HiLo, the green robot, "what is it?"

"We have an assignment," the attractive psybot told her fellow agents. "There is not much time to explain. We must leave at once."

"Leave?" replied Torb, the blue robot, in a voice that was deep and hesitant. "Leave for where?"

"We must travel to Jonnersville, and rendezvous with several stranded agents. Then we must help them reach a ship that will take them off Coreworld."

Torb stared at her a long moment. "Why can't this ship fly to them?"

"Because there's no one to fly it," Cleera said in exasperation. "It's hidden in an abandoned University research station. There's a small detachment of CorSec Guards in the area, but they don't know about the ship."

HiLo said, "There is no other way to help these agents?"

"Apparently not," Cleera told him. "The informa-tion I've been given is that at present there is no other craft capable of spaceflight near that area. The Uni doesn't want us to steal a ship, and they think commercial vessels and military ships will be even more dangerous to approach. Besides, they suspect the Corporation has been installing a new kind of tracer beacon on every ship."

"We can be ready in a few minutes," HiLo told her. "Have you contacted Jayray and Jom yet?"

"No," said Cleera. "They're next. Is Chiron here?"

"He may still be on the dock."

"No," Torb corrected, looking past them, "he comes now."

The others turned as a pallet came into view in the aisle behind them, stacked with more crates. And in the next instant, the thing moving that pallet also came into view.

A large robot painted red and tan went rolling past on four heavy-duty wheels. Its elongated body contained the motors and power cells which drove it. At the front end of the unit rose a more or less human torso capped with a round head. Normal mech arms were attached at the shoulders, and there was a second set of auxiliary arms, much longer and heavier, installed at the front of the body. It was these lower arms that carried the pallet. Chiron noticed the three standing there and halted as quickly as he could, lowering his burden to the floor.

To Torb and HiLo, Cleera said, "You two get your things. I'll brief Chiron, and then we can make our next stop. . . ."

Across town in the so-called entertainment district, the Metal Arena featured fights and gambling. Slates of robot boxers, wrestlers, and martial-arts fighters were scheduled all night, pitting machine against machine. The fights were interrupted only long enough to clear away the broken hardware and debris between matches.

By the front entrance, where patrons queued up to buy their tickets, stood a large video display with moving images of the combatants participating this night. The names tracked across the screen; some colorful, others ludicrous. All were hype. As the image changed again, a new name crawled into view. "The Terror Twins" was emblazoned in red above pictures of two slender robots who were built and painted exactly alike. Their combat movements were a modern update of ancient Oriental fighting techniques, and they moved together with the grace of well-choreographed dancers. Judging from the odds placed on them, the two were popular and regular winners.

But it was to the rear entrance Cleera and the others went, moving through the alleyway alertly and quietly. This was the entrance for the robots and their owner-managers, so their presence here was neither noteworthy nor strange.

Cleera walked boldly to the doorway and took a step inside. Torb and HiLo were close behind her.

The arena was dark, with sharp spotlights stabbing down at the fighter's ring. Large videoscreens showing close-ups of the mayhem were suspended from the ceiling on all sides, so that every patron could see well, and a camera crew was broadcasting the events to the remaining "civilized areas" on Coreworld. Hanging over it all was a blue-gray haze of smoke and machine oil.

A human wearing plastic coveralls and carrying a portable computer tablet approached them. His sharp eyes took in Cleera, then shifted to Torb and HiLo.

"Ladies' night is tomorrow, missy," snarled the man

between teeth that clenched an unlit cigar. "You two big fellows I can use, though. Where's your manager?"

Before they could speak, two assistants hurried by with a litter. On it were the remains of an older-model robot, battered and broken beyond repair, still sparking and smoking. Cleera and the others got an unpleasantly close look at it as it moved past, and they heard the clanging clatter it made when tossed upon the junk pile behind the building.

Fighting the sinking feeling she felt deep within her circuits, Cleera said, "Are you Tobias?"

"That's my name, all right, mech," replied the human in the coveralls. "But like I said . . ."

His words trailed off as Cleera surreptitiously handed him a folded note. She and the others waited silently as the man opened it and quickly scanned the codewords printed on it. His expression underwent a subtle change, and he instantly crushed the paper into a tiny ball and stuffed it into his pocket. Looking up at the psybots before him, he gave a nod of acknowledgment.

"All right," Tobias said with a sigh. He took his stylus from over his ear and touched his computer tablet, where the list of fighters glowed. One of the names winked out, and although they could not see it from their present vantage point, it also disappeared from the advertising video display out front. "Wait here—I'll send Jayray and Jom right out to you," he told them. As he started away he shook his head slowly. "A real pity. The fans will be disappointed."

"That leaves only one," said Cleera softly, "and we shall pick her up on the way. The real trick will be finding transportation."

6:
ARRIVAL ON AVALON

THE STARCRUISER *ZEPHYR* DESCENDED toward landing pad four, stark and gleaming against the airless black sky of Avalon. A scattering of stars shone brightly in the heavens, steady and undimmed by atmosphere. Just above the nearly planet-sized moon's rocky horizon could be seen the world it circled. Logres hung there in space, large and bright and colorful.

As the starcruiser settled gently onto the pad, a boarding bridge was already swinging out to meet it, red lights flashing on the end of the docking vestibule. In a matter of minutes the bridge was in position. The seals made fast to the cruiser's hull with a sucking hiss of air pressure, and in just seconds the red lights changed to green, indicating a hard seal and full pressurization within the vestibule.

Attendants cracked the hatch and swung it out, then stepped aside to allow their passengers to debark. Those that emerged were mostly humans, but some robots were present in the group, as were a handful of Omblat travelers wearing air masks. The Omblat rarely left their native world with its rich and heavy atmosphere, as such travel was difficult for them and normally against their simple beliefs. But occasionally some would brave the journey and take advantage of the regular human flights between Nottat and Avalon.

Beneath the passengers' feet as they made their way along the enclosed bridge, their luggage moved by conveyor belt; it would be ready for them to pick up as soon as they reached the spaceport terminal. Scanners automatically checked for contraband and unlicensed weapons.

Of the humans who made their way to the terminal, two seemed less relaxed than the rest, though they made an effort to appear nonchalant. One man was of medium height and very slender, with a hawkish face from which narrow eyes peered alertly. The other man was a bit taller, beefier of build, his complexion sallow and his face knotted with muscle.

As they reached the official at the end of the boarding bridge both men produced their travel passes and identification. They exchanged surreptitious glances while the man checked their papers.

"Welcome to Avalon, gentlemen," the official said routinely, his eyes still upon the papers in his hands. "You've been on Nottat two years?"

"That's right," replied Rasp, the slender, hawk-faced man. "We've been working for a mining company there."

"Taking a little vacation, are you?"

"In a way," said Rasp smoothly. "But to tell the truth, the mine business isn't really to our liking, and Nottat is a royal pain to live on. We thought we might investigate some other possibilities while we're here."

"I see," remarked the official, checking the photos on the travel passes with the faces of the men before him. They matched, and everything else seemed in order. He handed their papers back to them and waved them through with a smile. "Enjoy your stay here, gentlemen. And good luck with your efforts."

"Thank you." Rasp and his traveling companion moved forward into the concourse of the terminal itself, and when well past the official who greeted them he turned to the other man and whispered, "Told you, Cudder . . . I told you the passes were perfect. The Corp can fake any document."

"Maybe so," replied the beefy man. "But it doesn't make me any less nervous."

"Can you imagine? That fool wished us luck with our 'efforts' here. He wouldn't if he knew what really brought us to Avalon."

Cudder gave a cautionary shush of sound and an irritable glare. "These people aren't fools, Rasp. They can make mistakes like anybody else, and they may have their heads in the clouds, but they aren't fools."

Rasp shot him a reproachful look. Under his breath he snarled, "I don't know why they ever teamed me up with a nerveless worrywart like you, Cudder. I haven't gotten this far as a field agent by being timid."

"And I," drawled Cudder, "haven't survived this long by being stupid. Come on, let's pick up our gear and get moving."

The interior of the main terminal facility was a sharp contrast to the cold monochromatic surface of Avalon. Vividly colored banners and tapestries were everywhere, radiating warmth and life and cultural vitality. Wedge-shaped planters overflowed with flowers and green leafy growth, and the clean, purified air was filled with their scent. Through the clear-walled domes which covered the terminal facility could be seen enclosed tram tubes and walkways leading to other parts of the base. What had begun years before as a special isolated campus for the University had grown into a massive complex of buildings, laboratories, hydroponic farms, civic centers, and offices. Coreworld had once ruled all within this star system, and sought to do so again, but with the Corporation's decline, Avalon was truly the heart of human civilization in this part of space. Indeed, the University was its only hope for continued survival.

Rasp and Cudder claimed their luggage and quickly crossed the terminal, heading for the tramway that would take them to the University's hotel facility. In less than an hour they were checked in and settled into their rooms. The flight from Nottat had been a long one, and their first order of business was to clean up and get a meal in the hotel restaurant. With that accomplished, the two gathered once more in the room Rasp had reserved.

As Rasp unlocked his flight case and began to remove a portable computer plotter, Cudder surveyed the room and the gleaming city beyond the viewport. His expression was introspective.

"You know," the beefy Corporation agent said after a moment, "compared to Coreworld and Nottat, this place is practically paradise."

"Yeah, sure," replied Rasp, occupied with his work as he now pulled out a microcomputer and started connecting it and the plotter to their respective power supplies. "Just don't go getting attached to this place. We gotta be out of here in a few days so we can report back. And don't forget, while this place may be all pretty and clean, the University's to blame for Coreworld's being in such a mess. It was one of their damned eggheads that invented the plague in the first place."

"So I've been told," said Cudder.

"Yeah, well, you were told right. And you'd better

start listening to what you're told, before the Quintad gets the idea that maybe you're not working for them anymore."

"I know who I'm working for. That doesn't mean I have to believe everything they say."

"It goes with the territory. Me, I've got no complaints. We pull this assignment off and we're both set for the rest of our lives, which, with what we'll be able to afford, should be a long, long time."

Rasp fell silent momentarily as he switched on the equipment and fed a roll of paper into the plotter. Then he removed the ornate finger ring he wore and began to pry out the stone. He grinned as it popped free, then carefully removed a tiny microchip from within the hollowed-out stone.

"Roman really had it figured," Rasp said admiringly as he studied the microchip. "He knew it would be risky if we tried to bring the plans for the Uni's secret research center along with us where they might be scanned in our luggage or found on us. But this way, the plans don't even exist until we get here and through customs."

Rasp inserted the microchip into an open socket on an ordinary computer card and plugged the complete assembly into the computer itself. He tapped a series of coded numbers into the unit and waited for it to decipher the data stored on the microchip. In a matter of seconds, the plotter jerked into action and started drawing, rapidly. As the paper fed out of the machine, a blueprint of the University's top-secret research facility appeared, its corridors and entrances, its security checkpoints, and its hidden labs and document-storage areas all clearly indicated.

Rasp waited until the unit was through drawing and

the rendering was complete. Then he tore the sheet off and held it up to enjoy.

"This pretty little thing is our roadmap to the secret of the University's hyperspace drive, and the riches it will bring." Rasp's eyes sparkled with greed and selfish visions. "And now, all we have to do, my faithless friend, is contact the man who will get us in."

7:
DEADLY DESERT

THE ARRIVAL OF MORNING in the Delta Zone did little to improve its looks. The gray crystalline sand glistened bright and hot all around them, rolling in undulating dunes to the horizon. It stretched ahead of them and behind them with the same dreary view, a monotonous, mind-sapping lifelessness, devoid of color and detail. Even the polluted sky above them looked dirty and dismal.

Peering through the tainted clouds, the morning sun bore down on three figures as they trekked across the sand. The wind that had harried them the night before had at least wiped their tracks from view, but it did not help cool them now.

Marinda Donelson trudged along beside Roddi, squinting into the glare and showing signs of fatigue. They had been marching most of the night, and she was tired and footsore. Her lips felt as if they were beginning to crack. She tried to moisten them with her tongue, but her tongue was more sticky than wet. She glanced over at Roddi and envied him his lack of physical discomforts.

"How much farther?" she asked softly.

"Too far," remarked Roddi with an irritability that surprised her. "Much too far! Just look at me."

The silvery-blue psybot paused long enough to hold up one of his large feet. His normal ray-protective color was gone from the lower portion. Plain metal alloy showed through.

"This wretched sand is wearing my paint off," Roddi wailed. "Much more of this and I'll be abraded away to nothing."

Marinda saw that, his exaggeration aside, the damage he complained of was real. Her envy lessened and a sympathetic smile twisted her mouth in a pretty fashion.

Roddi studied that smile a moment, then continued walking beside her. "Oh, listen to me complaining. Here you are enduring much more than I and not saying a word. My apologies, Marinda, for not answering your question in a proper manner. But the truth is, I really don't know how much farther we have to go. I'm not even sure Vandal does."

Marinda looked ahead to where Vandal marched, leading the way for them. He was maintaining the same pace, with the same barely discernible limp he always seemed to have. To Roddi, Marinda said, "Doesn't he ever get tired?"

"Oh, I'm sure he must," replied Roddi with a shrugging gesture. "But he'll never admit it." The psybot pulled a digital compass from his gear and consulted it briefly. "Still on course. I don't know how he does it without using instruments, but he does."

"Celestial navigation, probably," Marinda replied. She caught Roddi's questioning stare. "The positions of the stars and moon, or in this case moons, by night, and the sun by day. I used to be a Girl Scout, long time ago. Boy, what a long time ago."

The psybot's tone sounded puzzled as he inquired, "You served as a scout when you were but a mere girl?"

"No, it means something else, but never mind. I'll explain later. But there are other ways to find your way, too. Moss on trees, for example. Not that it would help here in this awful wasteland. I swear, Roddi, you rely too much on electronics."

"What a strange thing to say. I *am* electronic." The psybot marched on in silence a few moments more, then added, "There used to be trees here, and I rather imagine they did have moss on them."

Marinda still trudged forward. "You mean, millions of years ago?"

"No. More like ten years ago," Roddi replied. "In fact, this whole area was a forest once. There were lovely cities on the edges of it."

Marinda gave him a dubious look that swung to encompass the dreary desolation through which they marched. "Here? You're kidding."

"I would not joke about something as terrible as this, Marinda."

"But if there was a forest here, what happened to it?"

"This area—Delta Zone—is where the plague began," explained Roddi in a serious tone underlaid by anger. "A virus—a deadly virus—was discovered years ago by a scientist working for the University. He did nothing with it himself, but the formula for recreating it was stolen by agents of the Corporation. They thought they could develop it as a weapon, and they set up their own testing center at a secret facility. But their people were incompetent. They didn't take the proper precautions. The virus leaked out and began infecting plant and animal life in the area. They tried to cover it up, which only gave the virus a chance to spread even farther. Over the years that followed, it not only infected most of Coreworld, it also spread to virtually every other planet in this star system."

Marinda was aghast. "That's horrible!"

"A cure was eventually found," Roddi told her, "but not before many, many humans and other beings died, and not before the ecology of this world was wrecked, perhaps beyond repair. The food chains and ecosystems have been shattered. This planet is slowly dying. That's only one of several reasons Vandal and I work against the Corporation."

"But why don't they let the University help them?"

"Ha! I wish it were that easy. No, the Corporation has always feared and mistrusted the University, always tried to control it. There will be no cooperation with the Uni. The Quintad will see to that."

Marinda acquired a downcast look and seemed more tired than before. "It's sad, Roddi. When we left Earth, we had such hopes, such dreams for this great journey. But we seem to have brought all our worst traits along with us."

Roddi gave the young Earth woman a comforting pat. He felt a genuine need to cheer her up and reassure her. "Maybe your people did bring some bad traits with them, Marinda. But from what I've seen of humankind, I would have to say your best traits outweigh them. Anyway, I'm sure you would be pleased to know that the descendant of your own Dr. Fenton Diggs, our Professor Diggs, was the one who developed an early means of combating the effects of the virus."

"He did?"

"Oh, yes. He was in the Robotics Department of the University, and he found a way to replace infected human limbs and organs with mechanical parts. There are many people alive today because of his techniques."

"Well, that pleases me, and I'm sure Fenton would be pleased, too." Marinda dabbed at her face with her handkerchief as small trickles of sweat ran down. "I'd like to meet your Professor Diggs."

Roddi's head swiveled away from her. "Oh, I'm sorry to say that would be quite impossible. He's no longer alive."

"The plague?"

"Ah, no," Roddi replied evasively. "At least, not in the direct sense. At any rate, it does not really matter now." Roddi knew, but did not wish to say, that Professor Diggs had been killed by a Corporation eliminator . . . an eliminator named Vandal. The irony of it was that the technology created by Diggs ended up saving Vandal's life, and his realization of that fact created a lasting torment, and a desire to fight against the Corporation. Roddi knew this, and knew also that it was something Vandal did not wish to share with outsiders, least of all this young woman.

Marinda stared ahead at the grim-faced man who led them, a speculative frown on her face. "Vandal is one of them, isn't he?"

"I . . . I beg your pardon?" The psybot's tone bore a trace of worry.

"Vandal is one of the people whose life was saved by replacing limbs with mechanical ones. Isn't he?"

"Oh, yes. Indeed." Roddi sounded relieved. "Vandal is now what we call a cyborg, but it was due to combat injuries and not the plague. Please don't say anything to him about it. It would make him uncomfortable."

Marinda nodded understandingly. "I won't. And I

think he's a very brave man. I hope I have more of a chance to—"

She bit off her words as Vandal suddenly halted in his tracks and threw up an arm in a cautionary gesture. He seemed to be watching the distant horizon intently, then he abruptly whirled and ran swiftly back to them.

"There—that low spot—" Vandal directed, thrusting a hand toward a hollow between dunes. "Get down, quickly!"

The urgency in his voice made Roddi and Marinda react instantly, diving into the low spot in the sand and staying prone there. Vandal quickly crouched beside them, placing the gear he carried next to the psybot.

"What is it?" Roddi asked.

"An aircraft, heading this way," Vandal replied. "I doubt it's friendly."

Marinda watched as Vandal used his mechanical arm to bulldoze a layer of sand over Roddi's body, concealing the psybot from view. He straightened the spare hooded cloak Marinda wore so that it smoothly covered her, then spread a scattering of sand over her so that only her face was exposed, hidden within the shadow of her hood.

Next, Vandal peeled back a pocketlike flap on the leg he seemed to favor. Marinda had suspected it was artificial, and now she found her suspicion confirmed. His fingers quickly worked a release mechanism and flipped open a panel. A large device was mounted within his upper thigh. Vandal flipped several of the switches and adjusted a dial, then slapped the panel closed again. He lay belly-down in the hollow, between Roddi and the young woman, then rapidly spread sand over himself until he too was camouflaged.

They all lay quiet and motionless, hearing nothing

but the sound of the wind softly moaning across the sand. Then a new sound became evident, a high-pitched whining noise that steadily grew in volume.

A helijet came into view, bearing silver-and-black markings. It passed within a mile of their position, heading to the southwest, and kept going.

Vandal waited another minute until it had passed completely out of view before he stirred. Then he rolled the sand off his back, sat up, and brushed himself off.

Marinda found herself holding her breath and gasped suddenly as the need for oxygen screamed in her brain. She raised her head, scanning the horizon behind them. "Is it safe?"

"For now it is," Vandal replied. "I don't think they saw us." He opened the panel and switched off the device within his leg.

"What is that gadget?" Marinda could not help asking. She immediately felt self-conscious, though, as Vandal looked up and his hard eyes met her curious gaze.

"ECM gear," he answered, flipping the panel quickly closed and resecuring the flap. "Electronic Counter Measures can block most scanners. I didn't want them picking us up."

Roddi was sitting up too, shaking one limb after the other to remove the remaining particles of sand, and quickly checking for further paint damage. "That looked like a Corporation ship, all right," he said. "But it was too small to be carrying troops."

"I know," said Vandal.

"Razer has been known to fly a vessel like that one," Roddi added.

"I know that." Vandal's eyes narrowed slightly, as if

reacting to some inner pain. "I think we'd better move on."

Marinda sat up and began to brush sand off her clothing. "I could use a little water, if you still have any. If we could just rest a few minutes . . ."

Vandal frowned toward the distant horizon, back in the direction of their downed ship. Then he looked ahead in the direction they were going and sighed inwardly. "All right. A few minutes. But that's all. We should be getting close to a place where there are still some buildings standing. I don't like being out in the open like this."

"Vandal," Roddi said suddenly, "perhaps once we reach that spot, we could rest there until darkness and then continue on. I'm fine, of course, and I know you're in excellent condition. But Marinda here is not used to all this."

"We'll see," Vandal replied as he got to his feet and helped Marinda to hers. "Just remember that our lives are on the line here. Once one Corporation ship finds our crash site there'll soon be others. And, as long as we're out here in the middle of this desert with no place to hide, they won't have any trouble finding us."

8:

PSYBOTS TO THE
RESCUE

THE LARGE DELIVERY TRUCK was completely
armored around its cargo section and cab, and its
airless tires were steel-reinforced. There were gunports
facing all directions, and instead of a hood ornament
the cab had a small missile launcher facing front to
clear roadblocks and other obstacles. Its turbines whined
as it sped along the neglected highway between Port
Madrid and CityPrime, adding to the song of the tires
and the rush of air past its improvised design.

"We're almost there," said the driver, a gray-haired
man with a potbelly and a stress-hardened face. He
hunched over the wheel as he jockeyed across the
uneven road surface, his alert eyes scanning ahead and
frequently darting off to the side to watch for trouble.
His right arm was mechanical, an early model, more
practical than aesthetically pleasing. "Been a quiet
trip, so far."

In the seat beside him, Cleera glanced at the speed-
ometer. The truck was careening along at near eighty.
She was grateful they were making good time, but
concerned about the safety of driving at such a high

speed along an imperfect road. Her eyes searched the brush and occasional piles of rubble along the way, watching for nomads and hijackers.

"Are you robbed a lot, Slag?" Cleera asked him.

"Not lately. Used to be, before I got all the heavy plating on. Those buzzards know I carry goods worth a lot of money, and there are lots of places they can be sold, no questions asked." He glanced at her with what she hoped was a joking grin. "For that matter, you and the others would bring a pretty price in the right places."

"We're paying a pretty price for this ride," Cleera reminded him. "I just wish you were going farther than CityPrime."

"Yeah, well, I wish I could oblige, little lady," Slag said, "but that's as far as I go. Besides, I'm taking a big enough chance as it is. I don't mind doing a job for the University when I can—you know I'm on your side—but if the CorSec people stop my truck and find all you special mechs on board, they're gonna hit me with a lot of questions I don't have answers for. Not answers I can live with, if you know what I mean."

Unfortunately, Cleera knew exactly what he meant. She did not doubt for a minute the Corporation's willingness to kill Uni sympathizers. What she didn't know was just how far they could trust this man. He had worked with Uni agents before, but his profile indicated he might sell them out, if the price was right or if his own life hung in the balance. If there had been any other way they could have reached CityPrime they would have taken it. There simply had not been any.

Cleera looked back through the small doorway cut through the rear of the cab. Huddled together amid a jumble of crates and loose parcels of black-market items were the other psybots on her team. They had been on the road since just after midnight, and it was now a few hours after dawn. They did not need sleep as humans did, of course, but most were powered down to save energy. Energy they would need for what lay ahead.

"There it is," Slag said suddenly, gesturing toward the skyline growing on the horizon. "You'd better climb in back with the rest. Folks are used to seeing me travel alone."

Cleera gave a nod of assent and left her seat, moving carefully in the bumping truck. She sat atop a crate in the back, next to HiLo, but left the curtain open into the cab and kept her weapons ready.

Slag took the perimeter road partway around City-Prime, then turned sharply onto a street in one of the more run-down districts. He slowed his pace here, driving carefully and avoiding anything that might draw attention to him. In a matter of minutes he was pulling into a small warehouse and driving well in past the doors.

"Okay," he said as he switched off the engine and locked the brakes. "End of the line."

He opened the heavy door on the driver's side and climbed down to the floor, then walked around and unlocked the back of the truck. He keyed a switch beneath the bed of the truck, and a sturdy ramp slid out. He watched as the psybots used it to reach the ground.

Chiron rolled out first, followed by HiLo and Torb. Cleera strode down the ramp next. The last out were Jayray and Jom, the fighting twinbots. As they looked around, they saw nothing in the warehouse except empty crates and a lot of dust. Apparently it was an abandoned building Slag used occasionally for "business."

Slag locked the rear of the truck and retracted the ramp, then said, "Well, I've been paid and you've been delivered, so I guess that's that. Now I've got to see some buyers on the other side of town, so if you want to stay here before you move on, be my guests."

Without another word, Slag climbed back into the driver's seat and backed the truck out of the warehouse. It disappeared from sight, and the sound of its engine faded away.

"Not that I don't trust the man," said Cleera, breaking the silence that had settled over them, "but it might be wise if we don't stay around here too long."

"We can't, anyway," HiLo observed. "Once we get Muse we must start out for Jonnersville."

"If we can," said Torb, looking around the abandoned warehouse. "The vehicle which brought us here is gone. I feel as stranded as those we are supposed to rescue."

Cleera tried to ignore his negative words. But even she could not shake the feeling those words evoked. Stuck here on the outskirts of CityPrime, in an all too real sense they *were* stranded.

HiLo walked about slowly. He said wryly, "This isn't nearly as much fun as I imagined a mission would be."

Even though she knew he was kidding, Cleera felt mildly angered by the remark, and that helped to rally her leadership instincts. "All right, I know this hasn't been pleasant so far, and there very likely are worse things in store for us before we're through. But it was our choice to work for the University, each and every one of us. That's why we were sent here to Coreworld

in the first place. This is important—people are counting on us."

"Hey, take it easy," HiLo told her. "It was just a
joke."

"I know, HiLo. I just want you guys to know I need
your help and support, if we're going to pull this off."

"Well, you've got mine," HiLo replied.

"Mine, too," said Chiron.

Torb nodded silently, but the large blue psybot still
seemed hesitant.

The twinbots stepped forward with enthusiasm,
though. "Affirmative," said Jayray. "You can—"

"—count on us," finished Jom.

"Thanks, all of you," Cleera told them. "I appreciate it. But Jom, Jayray, you'd better do something to
change your appearance, in case we're seen."

The twinbots simultaneously looked down at their
markings. A large red triangle bordered in black was
on each of their chests, and repeated in smaller form
on each forehead. Three stripes of black ran around
each arm and leg, a marked contrast to the bright
yellow of their bodies. It was part of their professional
image as fighters.

"She's right," said Jom. "This will not do. We've—"

"—been seen on sports video," finished Jayray.
"Someone might recognize us and wonder what we're
up to."

With that, they both began to peel off the stick-on
vinyl markings. Cleera nodded approvingly and walked
to the open doorway, looking out cautiously. There
was no traffic on the streets, no pedestrians, either.
Many of the other buildings in the area seemed to be
unused and neglected, as well.

Cleera stepped out farther and looked around the
neighborhood. A block to the south of them stood a

two-story office building that looked in better shape. A small storage building and a longer maintenance wing adjoined it, and the whole complex sat at the corner of a block-sized paved lot.

A double chain-link fence ran around the paved area, and there was a small guardhouse at the gate. Security against thieves was no doubt just as important here in CityPrime as it was back in Port Madrid. That was to be expected. What made the place interesting was that several small cargo helijets were parked within the compound, their boxy shapes and side-mounted lifters making them easily identifiable. One of them could solve their transportation problems, once they'd found Muse and were ready to leave.

But, Cleera thought, with security the way it was, they could not sneak into the compound to reach a craft, and fighting their way in not only would be risky, it could endanger their mission. Unless . . .

Cleera focused on the guard at the gate, then swung her gaze to the front door of the office building at the corner. Switching her internal circuits to image magnification and enhancement, she studied the way into the building. There was a heavy door of clear armorplex, with a sturdy remotely activated lock visible. Beyond that stretched a corridor with a cross corridor intersecting it. A wall directory with labels and arrows showed the way to different departments, and at the end of the main corridor was an elevator to the second floor. She could just make out the outline of a security camera scanning the entrance corridor.

Cleera looked along the streets beside the building. Nothing of possible use could be seen there, but as her sharp eyes swept the streets to the west of them she noticed a small vehicle parked near a corner. Several mechs wearing repairmen's vests were working on what looked like a phone junction box. Cleera added that to the plan she was beginning to construct, then turned to take in once more the interior of the warehouse to which Slag had brought them.

As she studied that and each of the psybots, HiLo commented, "I trust all this silence doesn't mean you're completely baffled about what to do."

"No, I have an idea. And I think it might just work," Cleera told them. "But we're going to have to split up temporarily to do it, and the timing is going to be close."

The monorail hummed to a halt at the dirty station near the outskirts of town, and the doors slid open. A few people got out, but the cars were almost empty at this point on its route. Before the doors closed again, two figures stepped aboard the car at the rear.

The few passengers who were already on the monorail glanced up, then promptly averted their eyes. The two who had just gotten on were garbed in the all-concealing robes of the Carsonites, a religious sect made up of plague survivors who believed their horrid disease had been God's punishment for their sins. Though they had received the medical cure for the plague, they had resisted cybernetic implants and even cosmetic surgery, preferring to merely cover their wasted and disfigured bodies with robes and veils.

The two took seats in an area of the car away from the other passengers, to everyone's great relief, and settled themselves as the monorail started up. They did not speak to each other but merely sat and rode, their cloth-wrapped hands folded in their laps.

A number of stops later, at a station much closer to the center of CityPrime, the two left the monorail and descended to street level. There was more pedestrian traffic here, but still not as much as in the office sector. And here, as on the monorail, people avoided looking at the robed figures.

The one on the right leaned close to the other. "Now you see why the Uni wanted us to carry robes like this with us?" said Cleera softly, well obscured beneath the fabric.

"Yes," whispered HiLo. He had reduced his normal height slightly and hunched himself over to aid the illusion. "Do you know where Muse works?"

"Just ahead."

They continued to walk until they reached the next block, and a large building loomed before them. It housed a nightclub frequented by the wealthy and powerful members of the Corporation, those who could afford such amusements. An electric sign spelling out the name "Club Azure" ran across the front of the building, but the power was off at this early hour.

"This is it," whispered Cleera.

They walked casually by the front door of the club. The door was locked and its small window was curtained.

"It's too early for anybody to be here," said HiLo. "Everything's closed up tight."

"Muse will be here." Cleera scanned her circuits. She had never been in CityPrime before, but the information she needed about it and about how to contact Muse had been programmed into her memory. She found the experience of visiting CityPrime firsthand interesting, but from what she had seen of it thus far, she did not feel she had missed much. "We should be able to find her on the second floor."

"Then let's go around back."

They turned down the alleyway between buildings and doubled back along the rear wall of the club, walking through filth and refuse littering the alley. Finally, they located a back door with the club's name painted on it. It was heavy steel, with strong hinges. HiLo reached out and tried the handle.

"Locked, like the front. I'm not surprised."

"There's probably an alarm system," Cleera told him, "so that rules out blasting it open." She tilted her head back, looking up at the second floor. "HiLo, there's a window open up there. Do you think you can reach it?"

The psybot looked up at it, gauging the height. "It's a bit of a stretch, but I think I can."

Looking swiftly once more to be sure no one was in the alley to see them, HiLo took hold of Cleera's waist and lifted her off the ground. Then he braced his feet, locked his knee joints securely, and began extending the tubular sections of his legs.

Cleera watched the wall sliding past as HiLo grew taller, raising her closer and closer to the window above. When the green-hued psybot reached the upper limit of his leg extension, Cleera was still just short of the window ledge. She reached up, clawing for the edge.

"I can't quite make it."

"Wait," HiLo told her, "I have a bit more reach left."

HiLo began expanding his arm sections, stretching still higher. This was enough to make the difference, and Cleera grabbed hold of the window frame and scrambled inside. She glanced quickly about the room to be sure it was clear, then reached back out to secure HiLo's grasp of the ledge. He reversed the process, telescoping both his arm and leg sections as he clung to the window, pulling himself up to it. In a few moments he too clambered inside.

HiLo straightened his robes about his body, making sure all was covered once more. Then he and Cleera crossed the room.

It seemed to be a dressing room for human performers. Costumes and tables with mirrors and makeup cases filled much of the space. It would be much later in the day before anyone would show up here. Cleera and HiLo reached the door and peered out before entering the hall. The place seemed deserted.

Cleera motioned for him to follow, leading HiLo down the hall and to another part of the second floor. Faint music could be heard coming from somewhere. Dance music, lively and exotic.

As they drew nearer, they found the sound was coming from a small studio. The door was open. Cleera reached into a pocket of her robe and put her hand around the grip of a tiny but powerful laser.

The center of the studio was empty, with furniture along the sides. Posters for the club hung on several walls. Seated at a desk at the far wall was a robot, manipulating the controls of a small computer. The unit's monitor screen displayed a dancing figure, moving in time to the music. The music halted abruptly as the robot worked the keyboard with a sudden burst of enthusiasm, then sat back to watch. Once more the music played, but this time the animated figure's movements were slightly different, smoother and more refined. An artistic fluidity now showed in the movements that had not been there before. Seemingly satisfied with the results, the robot stored the data and removed the small pack from the drive, popping it into a hidden slot within its body.

"Muse?" Cleera ventured aloud.

The robot at the desk spun around quickly, rising to her feet with perfect grace despite her surprise. Revealed in the morning light streaming in the window, the robot looked for a moment like a golden statue of a woman, perfect in every detail. Even her seams were nearly invisible. She was clearly a robot made for human eyes, for there was no practical reason for her shapely form or the ponytail of spun gold that seemed to grow from her head. Her eyes looked large and exotic. They stared questioningly at the two robed figures.

"What are you doing here?" she asked, keeping her tone flat and expressionless. "The club is closed now."

Cleera removed her veil and threw back her hood. "It's all right, Muse. I'm Cleera, part of Dean McAndrews's group." McAndrews was their contact at the University, the dean in charge of Special Operations.

Muse studied them a moment longer, watching as HiLo also removed his veil and hood. Then she relaxed, striking a more casual pose. "Thank goodness! I was afraid you might be thieves." She reached behind her in a fluid movement and switched off the computer. "I was just programming a new dance routine for myself."

Cleera's head tilted slightly. "Does anyone here know you can do that?"

"Of course not. That is, no one besides the club manager, who's a human agent with the Uni. He just tells everyone he does the choreography for our shows." She stepped forward to greet them. "So at last we meet. I assume you are here because of an assignment?"

"Yes," Cleera told her. She introduced HiLo and quickly explained about the crash in Delta Zone, about Vandal, Roddi, and Marinda Donelson, and about the University's T-beam message ordering her team to assemble.

Muse nodded as Cleera finished relating it all. "I

see. But do you think we can reach them before CorSec patrols track them down?"

"I don't know," Cleera said honestly. "But we've got to try."

Muse quickly gathered her belongings into a bag and removed several weapons hidden behind a wall panel. Then she went to the desk and hastily wrote a note on a scrap of computer printout paper: "Muse in shop for repairs. Remember to arrange for replacement dancer." She mimicked the manager's handwriting perfectly and signed his initials.

"I've left a coded message for my boss, so he'll understand I've been called to duty."

Cleera extended her hand to Muse's glistening arm. "You do realize that if you go with us, you may not be able to return to this job?"

Muse looked around the confines of the studio, at the dance practice floor, at the posters on the wall. The images of her performances upon the lavish stage played through her mind. In many ways this was not a pleasant place, and yet there were pleasurable memories here. "Yes, I realize that."

"All right, then," Cleera said, reaching within her robe and producing another garment like hers. She handed it to Muse. "Here, you'll have to wear this for now. And if you know how to work the locks on the back door, it'll save us from going out the window."

Jayray drove the small telephone repair truck down the street that ran beside the office building belonging to Prime Movers Shipping. Hidden from view in the back of the truck, Jom waited by the rear door. Jayray had chosen this moment to start up because there were no vehicles or pedestrians on the street.

The two mechs who belonged with the truck had

been disabled with tiny jammer packs that paralyzed their bodies and limited minds, and were now being guarded by Torb and Chiron in a nearby alley. Circuit wires in the telephone junction box the mechs had been servicing had been pulled, interrupting service for several blocks.

As Jayray reached the corner he slowed. No windows faced this street. Luck was with them.

Jom needed no verbal order to leap out the rear door, since the mind-linked twinbots shared telepathic communications. Jom closed the door quietly behind him and dashed for the front corner of the building. Thick shrubbery grew along the front wall, and Jom disappeared behind it.

Jayray turned the corner and parked the truck at the edge of the street, directly in front of the building's door. The phone service's sign would be clearly visible to the entrance corridor's security camera, a fact he was counting on.

Jayray switched off the truck's electric motors and got out, carrying a small toolkit. He and Jom wore identical safety vests with the phone service logo on them, and both psybots had applied a vinyl stick-on number 3 to their foreheads.

Jayray marched up to the door with plodding precision, stopping just before the thick panel of armorplex. He tapped on the clear panel, waiting for a response.

"Yes?" came a voice from a small box by the door.

"Service mech," Jayray said in a loud voice with flat intonation. "There is a problem with the phones in the area and we are checking the lines. May I come in?"

There was a moment's hesitation, then there was a buzzing click as the door was unlocked by someone in the main office upstairs. Jayray pushed open the door and stepped through. As Cleera had told him earlier, the wall directory indicated that the main office was on the second floor, and he made a show of studying it. Then he marched directly for the elevator, conscious of the security camera's rapt attention.

The elevator needed work; it jerked several times as it carried him upstairs. When the door whisked open and he emerged into the office, several workers looked up at him, then continued with what they were doing.

One man, perhaps the office manager, studied him with an abrasive smirk and gestured to an equipment console near the door, where a young woman sat who seemed to be filling the duties of receptionist and secretary. "The switchboard's there. Our lines went out twenty minutes ago."

Jayray said a flat "Thank you, sir" and went to work on the console. The circuits inside were quite simple. Jayray made a show of checking through everything.

"Look," said the man with increasing irritation. "The problem has to be outside somewhere. It can't be in here."

Jayray continued working a moment more, then he stopped and looked up. "What? Oh, yes, perhaps you are right. But I have found a defective part here. I will get another from the truck."

He went directly past the man and to the elevator door, stepping inside. As the door closed he caught a glimpse of the man shaking his head and saying something that sounded like "Dumb mech." In his mind, he smiled to himself.

When the door opened on the first floor, Jayray thought, *Be ready*. He heard an answering *I am* in his mind. He walked steadily down the corridor toward the door, still carrying one of his tools in his hand. Then as he reached the door and the buzzer sounded, he instantly triggered the device he carried, which was not a tool at all but a tiny jammer. Pointed toward the rear wall, it would reduce the security camera's image to indecipherable snow.

Before the lock-releasing buzz could end, Jom leaped from out of the shrubbery and ducked through the doorway, entering the corridor and taking up a position with the door just barely open. At the same time, Jayray darted back down the corridor to the cross hallway leading to the computer room. The moment he was clear of the camera's view he switched off the jammer. To the person watching the monitor upstairs, it would appear that he had just reached the front door, when in reality it was Jom that was now leaving.

Jom stepped out the door and went to the truck to begin digging around for the part. How long he would take to find it would depend on how much time Jayray needed.

The twinbot inside went directly to the computer room. Jayray peered cautiously through the viewplex panel in the door. There was no one inside at the moment. He counted his blessings and went inside.

He knew he would have to hurry, though, and immediately went to the main computer console. The equipment was on, the menu already showing on the screen.

It took only seconds to bring up the schedule for the day's shipments and flights. There were a dozen listed, but some had already gone out earlier, and others were scheduled too late in the day to be of much use. There was one, though, scheduled to leave in a bit over an hour, with a delivery due to arrive for the flight just before takeoff. It was even heading close to the direction they wanted to go. All the proper code numbers and clearances were on the screen. He stored them away in his memory.

Next, Jayray brought up the manifest format for the printer and quickly filled in the blanks for the shipment that was to arrive, adding some information of his own. He hit the button and watched as a perfectly authentic shipping manifest spewed out of the printer.

Before he could congratulate himself, he heard the front-door lock buzz, and then footsteps. They turned down his corridor.

Oh, glitch! he thought to himself. He heard in his mind, *You'd better get out of there!*

Jayray returned the computer screen to the main menu and tore off his manifest, tucking it into a storage compartment in his leg. He swiftly went to the door and peeked through the viewplex.

A woman in a business suit was heading his way, glancing through some paperwork as she walked. She hesitated by another door, as if preparing her thoughts, then she opened the door and went inside.

Jayray slipped out of the computer room and cautiously moved down the corridor. As he did so, he sensed Jom leaving the truck and starting for the front door with the new part clutched in his hand.

Behind him, there were more sounds from the office into which the woman had gone. He hoped she wasn't coming out soon. He was nearly to the corner and the main entrance corridor, and the timing was going to be critical. In his mind, he could see Jom's point of view as the other twinbot approached the door from outside. Jom was nearly there and slowing his pace slightly to coordinate with Jayray.

Jayray paused at the corner, just out of view of the security camera, listening for sounds he did not want to hear coming from the office behind him. Jom stepped up to the door, rapped on the armorplex, and waved to the security camera.

The buzz. The clicking of the latch. The slight squeak of the door starting to swing open.

Jayray hit the button on his jammer and edged it around the corner of the hall, pointing it at the wall with the camera. He leaped into the corridor just in time to see Jom stepping into the corridor from outside. Jom tossed the phone part to him and ducked back outside, leaving the door to swing closed on its own.

The moment the other twinbot was out of view, Jayray switched off the jammer and started plodding down the corridor as if he were the one who had just returned. Just as he entered the elevator, he heard the office door down the hall open and close, followed by the door to the computer room. He had made it with mere seconds to spare.

Reaching the second floor, Jayray went to the phone console and changed the new part for the old one, just for the sake of appearance, then put the panel back in place and packed his tools away. As he started back for the elevator, he noticed the man who had spoken to him before, standing before the security monitor and tapping the case with a puzzled look. The man looked up and, seeing that Jayray was leaving, called after him.

"Hey, mech. Does it work now?"

"Your unit does," Jayray answered in a tone flat and innocent. "But there is still trouble on the lines. We will have it cleared up shortly."

The man raised his hands in a gesture of helplessness and frustration, fuming but finding no words he wished to utter. And then Jayray was gone, heading downstairs and for the door.

He wasted no time getting into the borrowed phone truck, made a U-turn, and went back the way he came, pausing long enough to pick up Jom before driving back to rejoin the others. The phone service would remain out for now. It was better that the company could get no calls in or out for the time being. Much better indeed.

A half hour later, the twinbots, Chiron, and Torb were waiting in an alleyway near the shipping company. They kept comparing notes on the time, even though they all knew their internal clocks were accurate. They were going to be cutting it very close. Perhaps too close!

Suddenly, three figures appeared at the end of the alley, three robed figures. It was Cleera, HiLo, and Muse hurrying toward them.

"Well," Cleera said as she shed her robe and folded it to put away, "did it work?"

"So far," replied Jom. "It worked—"

"—just as you planned," Jayray finished. They were both obviously very pleased with themselves.

"What about the service mechs?"

Torb spoke up. "We put them and their truck back where we found them. It should be hours before they come out of their daze."

"Excellent, Torb," Cleera said. "I'm so proud of you all."

"So are we," said Jayray jokingly. "But we must hurry! The rightful shipper—"

"—may be along soon and spoil everything!" Jom concluded.

Five minutes later, the guard at the gatehouse looked up and was startled to see Torb marching heavily toward him, carrying a sealed crate. Close behind him was Chiron, his auxiliary long arms extended, carrying an even larger crate. They stopped right before the gate, their heads swiveling toward the guard.

The human looked at them in dismay. "Where did you two come from?"

"Truck," said Torb, in his deep voice.

"What truck? I didn't see any—"

"Truck!" insisted Torb, and the sound of his voice shook the gatehouse panels.

The guard scurried out and looked at the crates. Attached to the one Torb carried was a manifest detailing the shipment, the destination, and all the proper codes and authorizations. That, and one other thing.

"Wait a minute," said the guard. "According to this, not only the crates go, but two cargo mechs, too. This is not normal pro—"

"We go!" boomed Torb.

"Okay, okay," replied the guard with a shrug. "The paperwork's all in order, so why should I care." He opened the gate and gestured toward one of the waiting helijets. "Just take them over to pad six. The ship's ready to go."

He watched them lumber through the open gate toward the air vehicle and saw the pilot and crewman starting up the engines. In a matter of minutes the crates were loaded aboard the cargo craft, and the two large psybots with them.

The guard gave a farewell wave to the pilot as the helijet lifted off the pavement and began to soar skyward. Then he went back to his routine duties and gave it not another thought.

On board the helijet, two surprise packages were getting ready to open.

9:

THE HUNT BEGINS

THE HELIJET WITH ITS silver-and-black Corporation insignia swung in a slow, wide circle around the blackened wreckage below, then briefly hovered directly above it. Fire-scorched sand blew and swirled in the craft's downdraft.

Razer was strapped into the well-padded pilot's seat, gripping the controls lightly as she studied the scanner readouts on the instrument panel before her. The wreck was cold. No residual heat was left from the fire or the engines, and there were no spots of warmth to indicate human bodies, not living bodies at any rate. The image on the infrared display barely distinguished between the wreckage and the sun-warmed sand around it. The magnetic detectors revealed no energy levels from weapons or forcefields, and the other scanners were equally useless.

There was nothing more to be learned by indirect means. She would simply have to get out and look. Razer pulled the craft back a short distance before landing so its downdraft would do no more damage to the sand around the ship than it already had. She didn't expect tracks to remain after this many hours of wind. That would be too much to hope for.

As soon as the helijet's circular feet had extended and touched down upon the sand, Razer switched off the engines. She checked her gear, pulled her proto-blaster from its special holster, and climbed out of the craft.

After the steady whine of the jets, the silence in the vastness of Delta Zone was unnerving. There was only the faint moaning whisper of the wind and the crunch of sand underfoot. Razer flinched with each footstep, for she was used to moving quietly, stalking her prey with silent stealth. No matter how carefully she walked in this blasted sand, her boots announced each step. She could do better barefoot, she thought with grim amusement, but she was not about to resort to that. Not here. Not in this place.

She had flown from CityPrime as soon as she had drawn new weapons and the craft had been readied, stopping only in Dresco City for refueling. Her search in Delta Zone had begun at daybreak. She might have found the wreckage before now if the crash coordinates had been accurate, but they were off by a good dozen miles. There were far too many incompetents among the CorSec Guards.

Razer still wore the same jumpsuit of jet-black leather she had worn when accompanying Roman to Corporation headquarters, and while it had felt good last night in CityPrime and during her long flight, it was beginning to feel warm and sticky in this heat. Her lavender scarf fluttered in the dry and dusty breeze that blew like a corpse's breath across Delta Zone.

Her senses alert, her reflexes at the point of hair-trigger reaction, she advanced upon the wreckage, protoblaster ready. Nothing happened as she approached, and as she cautiously explored the interior of the collapsed and scorched spacecraft, she began to think all aboard it must have perished. Her eyes narrowed at that thought. If Vandal was to die, she wanted it to be at her hands, and not from some accident or whim of fate.

With a hand-held scanner, Razer briefly probed the wreckage. Her beautiful face was lit by a darkly chilling smile as the device told her there wasn't enough organic residue left in the wreckage to account for even one body. What little was there was most likely the remains of food stored on board.

So, Vandal still lived. She still had a chance.

Razer left the wreckage and began examining the ground immediately around it. As she had feared, the unholy wind that blew across this fearsome place had long since obscured their tracks. There were no physical marks left that could tell her which way Vandal and the others had gone.

Razer sighed angrily. She was glad Vandal had not deprived her of the pleasure of killing him, but she was frustrated by the lack of a trail. They could have gone in any direction. Trying to guess which one seemed pointless. There was simply not enough physical evidence, and no way to know what city they might be trying to reach.

Reluctantly, she walked back to her helijet craft and reached inside, switching on the radio. It was already set to one of the reserved frequencies used by the Quintad, and its scrambler matched the configuration of Roman's private transceiver. She knew he would be waiting eagerly for news from the crash site.

She brought the microphone close to her lips and shielded it from the breeze with her hands. "This is Razer."

There was a moment or so of silence, then a resonant masculine voice came through the speaker. "Roman here. What have you found?"

"The burned-out hulk of a spaceship," answered Razer. "Which, I might add, was not even close to where your people told me it was."

"Sorry, my darling." Roman's voice was soothing but firm. "We could only track it until it disappeared below radar level. It was obviously still under some degree of control beyond that point, making it hard to be completely accurate."

Razer hesitated a moment, gathering her thoughts. She did not want to take out her frustrations on Roman. The man was not only her lover, but perhaps even more important, her superior, and a direct link with the Quintad. She would be a fool to anger him, especially when she had little progress to report.

"Yes, of course," she said at last. "It couldn't be helped. Forgive me for sounding peevish. I'm just angry with myself for not having better news for you."

"What news do you have?"

"They all seem to have survived the crash," Razer told him. "That will only be a temporary setback, of course, but the winds have blown away whatever tracks they left. It may take longer than I expected to find their trail."

"I see," Roman replied. "Well, then, perhaps I should dispatch a squad of CorSec troops to help you. I could have them there by late afternoon—"

"No," Razer said quickly. "No, I don't think that will be necessary. I'm sure I'll be able to find a way."

There was silence for a moment, then Roman's voice responded again. "As you wish, then. I have complete confidence in you, my darling. Oh, and one other thing. I've been thinking about what I said last night. If you can bring this Marinda Donelson back to me alive, I would appreciate it. We may be able to learn something of interest from her."

She frowned slightly. "All right. That's not my usual style, but for you I'll gladly make an exception in her case. I trust you've had no such second thoughts about Vandal's fate?"

There was a brief burst of static, then Roman's voice came strongly through her transceiver. "No, not at all. I wouldn't dream of disappointing you, my dear. I know just how eagerly you've looked forward to writing the final chapter to your former lover's legend."

Razer's eyes flashed. "Please don't call him that, Roman. You know how it angers me. Whatever there was between Vandal and me was long ago, when I was younger and much in awe of his record as an eliminator. Before he became a disgusting cyborg, and turned traitor to our cause. He would have been better off dead from his injuries. At least then I would have had some respect for him. The only thing I can feel for him now is loathing. I was a fool for not seeing his weakness before."

"Sorry to upset you. I only meant that I understood how important this assignment is to you. As far as Vandal is concerned, you may handle it as you wish. The same goes for his psybot companion."

"Good," Razer replied curtly. "If Vandal still has a price on his head, I intend to be the one to claim it, and that dreadful machine that follows him around will be an added bonus."

"That's a reward the Quintad will be pleased to pay, and I'm sure I can think of a bonus or two for you myself." His tone had a wicked playfulness to it that made her smile and look forward to her return. "Contact me the moment you have something positive to report. Or if you need any help."

"Yes, of course. Until then . . . ."

Razer switched off the radio and walked back to the wreckage, determined now more than ever to find some way to track her prey. She set her hand-held scanner for a more specific range than before and fanned it toward the sand around the crashed ship. She was hoping either Vandal or the girl had been injured enough in the crash to leave a traceable trail of blood. But after checking the sand thoroughly in a complete circle around the ship, she came up with no readings at all.

She walked out a bit farther in the hope of finding at least one discernible footprint to point the way, her sharp eyes searching the sand. It seemed hopeless. She knew she was only kidding herself. There was just no way—

Suddenly, her gaze riveted on a tiny speck of something as the sand blew to one side. She bent closer for a better look.

There, partially imbedded in the gray crystalline sand, was a tiny chip of something silvery-blue and shiny. Razer stared at it for several moments, then reset her scanner for material analysis and held it over the spot.

After a second's delay, the readout spelled out the results. The chip was a ray-protective metallic paint.

"Vandal's psybot," said Razer under her breath. Through her mind flashed an image of the robot running with him through a corridor of *Glory*, just as the CorSec robot fighter had recorded it. A silvery-blue robot. Perhaps the vile machine had one redeeming quality after all. Perhaps it would lead her to Vandal.

Razer quickly adjusted her scanner to the frequency

of that particular metallic paint and fanned it toward the general direction the first speck seemed to indicate. A hard smile lit her face as tiny blips appeared on the display, scattered here and there in the sand before her, stretching away in a definite direction. At last, a trail she could follow!

She hurried back to her helijet and climbed aboard. Hastily she strapped herself in and fired up the engines. She recalibrated the onboard scanners to match her hand-held unit, sealed the hatch, and lifted off, watching her readouts and moving steadily in the direction Vandal, Roddi, and Marinda had gone. Though not flying at anywhere near top speed, the helijet would not take long to catch up with people traveling on foot.

In a luxurious office deep within Corporation headquarters, Roman switched off his radio equipment and closed the decorative panel of his ornately fashioned desk. A monitor circuit would alert him if another transmission on that frequency came for him.

Roman turned and leaned back in his tall, well-upholstered chair. "Everything seems to be going quite nicely," he commented to himself. "But you are not as clever as you think, my darling Razer. 'Disgusting cyborg' indeed."

He reached into a drawer of his desk and pulled a fresh vial of liquid from a case. Then he pulled open his jacket and shirt and exposed a portion of his chest. As he pressed his finger into the space between his second and third ribs, a seam miraculously appeared in what had looked to be normal flesh. The seam expanded, outlining a small panel, which now swung open. Cybernetic mechanisms were visible inside. Roman slipped the fresh vial of rejuvenation fluid into place after removing the empty one from the injector device that slowly fed the fluid into his bloodstream. With the change completed, he resealed the utterly realistic synthetic flesh on his chest and adjusted his clothing.

"If you only knew, my love. If you only knew. . . ."

10:

CREACHERY AND CREASON

IT WAS EVENING ON Avalon, and though the sky was as black and star-filled as always, the stars seemed brighter without the daytime glare of light upon the moon's surface. Artificial light kept the campus complex and connecting tramways illuminated, and beacons atop each dome and the surrounding lunar peaks pulsed in warning to shuttles and other spacecraft.

Within one of the domes, in a restaurant popular with University students and staff, Rasp and Cudder sat at a table near the back. Their meals were mostly eaten, and the row of empty cups before them attested to the beverages they had already consumed.

Rasp fidgeted and toyed with the remaining food on his tray, throwing furtive glances toward the front of the restaurant. "I don't think he's coming," he snarled beneath his breath, not so much to make conversation as to vent his own frustration.

"It's been an hour," Cudder agreed. "He's late, all right. But he may have a good reason, so let's give him a chance. Try to relax, Rasp."

"Sure, relax. Without this guy, we can't do our business here."

"Then we've got nothing to lose by waiting," Cudder said.

"Listen to this," Rasp muttered. "Mr. Worrywart here is telling me to relax."

Cudder slowly swirled the drink in his cup, looking at the tiny whirlpool it created. "I didn't say I wasn't worried. I just know how to do it quietly. No sense attracting attention we don't need."

"Attracting attention? You mean as if it wasn't enough that two guys who just flew in from Nottat are spending their first night sitting here lingering over fast food? You think that's normal?"

"So, maybe we're looking to pick up women. Lots of people hang out at places like this. Look over there. The people at that table were here when we came in. So just settle down. You want another drink?"

"No, I don't want another drink. I'm—" Rasp paused abruptly as his eyes fixed upon a middle-aged man who had just entered the restaurant. His face was familiar from the photo Roman had shown them, and there was something about his nervous manner that seemed to confirm it. "Hey, I think this is him now."

"See? What did I—"

"Just let me handle this." Rasp caught the man's eye and gave a subdued wave. He struck a casual pose as the man approached their table with a questioning look. "Evening."

The man gave a hesitant nod of greeting. "Mr. Rasp?"

"Just Rasp is enough. You're Dixon?"

"Yes." He swiveled a stool from the wall and joined them at the table.

"We were getting worried, Dixon," Rasp told him

calmly. But it was the kind of calm that held an underlying threat.

"I'm sorry I'm late." Dixon shifted uneasily in his seat and kept his voice low. "But it couldn't be helped. At the last minute my supervisor asked me to help her finish putting some files away, and then I missed a tram heading over here."

"You're here now," Cudder told him. "That's all that matters." He glimpsed Rasp's irritated look from the corner of his eye, but chose to ignore it. "Listen," he said cautiously, "we don't have to worry about surveillance cameras or bugs in this place, do we?"

Dixon shook his head reflexively. "No. There are plenty of security measures in the secret research sections, but nothing like that out here in the public areas. The University doesn't believe in doing things like that. It's a matter of high principle."

Rasp gave a crooked grin and raised his drink. "Let's hear it for high principle." He took a long sip from the cup and set it down. "Have you got what we need?"

Dixon blanched slightly, as if facing this moment was unpleasant for him. "Yes, yes I do." He glanced around briefly, then reached into the inner pocket of his jacket. He produced an envelope, held it for a moment in his hands, staring at its blank outer surface, then pushed it across the table to Rasp and withdrew his hand.

Rasp pulled it closer to him, raised the flap, and looked inside. There were a dozen pieces of folded paper with printing on them, and between the folds were two identification badges bearing the University seal and phony staff names.

Rasp studied them, then said, "Very good. These will get us inside?"

"Inside the main complex, yes," Dixon answered. "Inside the security section of the research wing, no."

Rasp leaned forward, his eyes narrowing. "What do you mean, no? Your part of this is to provide us with access."

Dixon squirmed a bit, his eyes avoiding Rasp's steady gaze. "I can only give you access to the complex itself, which is normally closed to outsiders. I don't have access to security badges for the research section. I'm only a records clerk, after all. By all rights, I should have been promoted to supervisor long before now, and then I'd have a higher security clearance, but things haven't gone that way."

Cudder flashed him an approving smile. "That's quite all right, Mr. Dixon. I'm sure our employer appreciates a man of your obvious talent and experience."

"Thank you. And . . . and make no mistake. Those will help you get close to the area you want. And I was told that you do have information on the precise layout of the research section."

"Yeah," said Rasp peevishly. "Yeah, we've got that."

"Well, tomorrow morning should be your best chance. There are delegates visiting from University facilities on the other planets. I've added your names—the names on those badges, that is—to the computer listing of visitors. You won't have any trouble getting past the outer checkpoints. All you'll have to do is break loose of the group and do whatever you people do to get past the security scanners in the research wing."

"Right," said Rasp, still frowning at the contents of the envelope.

"Also," Dixon added, "there's a printout of the

110

day's schedule of events, and information on the current guard procedures, in case that might help you."

"It will help a great deal," Cudder told him warmly. "We appreciate your efforts." He looked to Rasp. "Isn't that right?"

"Yes, indeed," Rasp said grudgingly. He put the envelope into his jacket pocket and pulled out a small folder. He slid it across the table and placed Dixon's hand on top of it. "This is for now. There'll be more later, once we've gotten the information back to our people. They must approve final payment, you understand."

"Yes, yes, of course." Dixon put the folder away without looking inside, nodding as he slid back from the table and got to his feet. "That's quite all right. It's not just the money, after all. And, good luck tomorrow."

"Thanks," Rasp said with mechanical cordiality. "It's been a pleasure meeting you, Dixon. I'm sure our employer will wish to continue doing business with you."

The man smiled nervously, but seemed pleased. Then he turned away from the table and made his way back to the front of the restaurant, disappearing out the door.

"It never is," Cudder said softly as he watched him leave.

Rasp looked at him oddly. "What?"

"It never is just the money," Cudder told him. "Not with guys like that. Come on," he added, pushing up from the table and downing the last of his drink. "Let's get out of here. We've got to do our homework and get some rest, if we're going to be ready for tomorrow."

11:
TERROR IN THE SAND

THE SUN WAS NEARLY overhead, bearing down unrelentingly upon the gray and dismal sands of Delta Zone. Only the dry wind which blew constantly across the rolling dunes kept the desert from becoming chokingly hot. The wind was as much an enemy as a friend, though, sucking moisture from human eyes and throats and pummeling the skin with airborne grit. It was nearly as harmful to machines.

Roddi gazed forward, a jacket from one of the packs incongruously covering his arms and back, the hood pulled awkwardly over his head to protect his sensory devices. He stood beside Vandal, staring at the cluster of ruined buildings which lay ahead.

"Looks quiet enough," Roddi observed.

"Looks can be deceiving," Vandal replied. He was studying the complex of structures in greater detail with the aid of binoculars. "But I don't see any sign of CorSec Guards."

Marinda Donelson blinked in the glare and wind, uncertain how much hope the ruins offered. "Not much to look at, is it? What did it used to be, a small city or something?"

"Not quite," said Roddi. "Do you remember,

113

Marinda, when I told you about the secret facility where the Corporation accidentally released the plague virus that did so much destruction?"

"Yes." Marinda's eyes widened with realization. "You mean . . ."

Roddi nodded. "Those ruins were that facility."

"And that's where we're going?"

"It is if we want shelter," Vandal said without looking at her. "There isn't anything else in Delta Zone. Not in this part of it, anyway." Vandal put away his binoculars and picked up the packs he had set down. "Besides, we're still in the middle of this damned desert. That leaves a lot of ground to cover, and our time is running out. I'm hoping there's enough hardware left around the facility to build a few powered gliders. It may be the only chance we have of getting out of here and reaching Jonnersville."

"What a choice," said Marinda, a look of mild horror setting her features. "Certain death in the desert, or a visit to plague city."

"Come on," Vandal ordered, "let's get moving."

There was no more than a quarter mile of rolling dunes between them and the facility's ruins. It would be a short walk after the distance they had covered. Vandal and Roddi started forward at a steady pace, while Marinda followed with somewhat less enthusiasm.

They had covered about half the distance when the sand dunes near them began to change in a way that could not be explained by the wind's steady flow.

"Vandal . . ." Roddi began.

Before he could finish the question, the answer revealed itself with frightening suddenness. With an explosive spray of sand, something big and metallic raised itself from the shallow depression in which it had been resting. The windblown sand had covered it and concealed its shape, but that sand now cascaded from its shiny surfaces.

The warrior robot was built in the shape of a scorpion, with four walking legs and two forward-mounted arms fitted with large pincers. While a real scorpion would never be much larger than a hand, this one was as large as a truck. A segmented, flexible tail curved up over its back, and mounted at the end of it was a giant laser.

To make matters worse, the mechanical creature was not alone. Twenty yards on either side of the glistening metal monstrosity stood two others shedding their concealing sand and swinging their laser-equipped tails up into fighting position.

If there was any doubt as to their purpose or intentions, that doubt evaporated as a high-powered laser beam seared from the tail of the middle scorpion warrior. The thing unleashed a second beam an instant later.

Roddi was already diving to the right, and Vandal dove to the left, propelling Marinda with him. They were barely clear of the spot of sand when it exploded into a cloud of charred and fused particles.

Marinda hit the ground with a dull thump that partially knocked the wind out of her. As she raised her head she saw Vandal rolling away from her and twisting himself around and up into a crouching position facing the nearest of the scorpion warriors. She shot a worried glance to Roddi, who had gone in the opposite direction. She was relieved to see her psybot friend unharmed, if only for the moment, as he also scrambled to get into fighting position.

Vandal leveled his protoblaster and fired three shots in rapid succession. The intense particle beams sizzled through the air, one striking the side of the scorpion, one hitting the tail, and the last hitting the pincer on the near side. Vandal frowned as each shot struck home—struck home and did nothing more than darken the surface and raise a small spray of tiny fragments. He saw that Roddi was having even less success with his laser.

"Roddi!" he called out. "The things are shielded with densepak armor beneath their paint. Don't waste your shots!"

In the next instant Vandal had to leap from his crouching position to avoid a searing ray shot. It missed by the narrowest of margins, and Marinda gave a small scream and started scrambling herself.

Vandal hit and rolled, an idea occurring to him even as he moved. He aimed at the small, dark face of the battle mech and fired, hoping to destroy the eyes.

The thing was pivoting on its legs, starting to turn toward him, as his protoblaster flashed. But its robot brain, limited though it was, must have calculated the angle of his weapon and guessed its target, for in the same instant the deadly particle beam stabbed out a small panel of densepak armor shot up several inches from a slot directly before the eyes, shielding them from the beam. It left the mech without vision, but only temporarily, for the panel dropped out of the way in the next moment.

Vandal took a quick look around. The other two scorpion warriors were starting to advance toward them to join their fellow creature in battle. His packs containing most of his weapons were lying in the sand some distance away, where they had fallen after his hasty lunge away from the first laser strike. He swore under his breath, cursing his own lack of alertness.

The first scorpion warrior was pivoting toward him, balancing its great bulk upon its clawlike legs and moving somewhat slowly. Vandal saw the laser turning in his direction, but it hesitated before it was fully aligned with him. That was a limitation, Vandal realized suddenly. Though the weapon was in a good firing position, elevated high upon the tail, it still had only about a thirty-degree field of fire. That meant the whole machine had to be facing the target it intended to hit.

"Marinda," Vandal shouted, "move to your left!"

He was pleased to see that she did so promptly, and he scuttled in the same direction himself, staying in a low crouch. He caught up with her as they both moved out of the scorpion's firing angle. That would help buy them a little time.

Roddi was circling back in the direction Vandal had taken, attempting to reach the fallen weapons packs. Just as he was about to grab for them, he caught a glimpse of the second scorpion warrior swiveling its laser toward him.

"Oh, glitch!" he muttered, and continued to run. A beam seared the air near him mere moments after. Still moving, he pulled free a small sling case from his pack and with quick but careful aim flung it toward the others. "Vandal! Try these! Grenades!"

Vandal's attention shifted to the moving object at the sound of the psybot's voice. He saw it sail through the air in a high arc, heading his way, the case's long strap spiraling as it flew.

Unfortunately, that arc carried it directly in front of the first scorpion warrior, and it saw its flight as well. The pincer on one of its front arms extended, servos whining briskly, and neatly closed around the case, trapping it.

Vandal, seeing this, wasted no time yelling, "Roddi, down!"

Gary Alan Ruse

As he saw the psybot diving to the ground, Vandal pushed Marinda forward into a shallow spot in the sand and covered her with his body. In the same swift motion he leveled his protoblaster at the grenade case and fired.

A ball of fire erupted with thundering force as the high-explosive grenades were detonated by the proton beam. The scorpion's pincer blew apart with the force, leaving only a frazzled stump where the arm had been. Shrapnel from the shattered pincer rained along the scorpion's sides, but did little damage to the armored shell.

"Come on," Vandal snapped, helping Marinda to her feet and steering her forward. They covered another twenty feet, then dropped into another shallow depression facing the side of the first scorpion. "Wait here," he told her. "Don't move unless you're drawing fire."

"Okay by me," she replied, then watched in alarm as Vandal leaped up and darted directly for the side of the scorpion warrior in what looked like a suicide attempt. "Hey!"

The huge machine attempted to swing around toward the position where Vandal had been and where the young woman still was, but its ponderous movements could not match the cyborg's speed.

Vandal reached the scorpion and darted between its center two legs. He ducked low and with his knees bent ran directly under the belly of the metal monster.

Roddi, in the meantime, had gotten to his feet again and was running toward Marinda, even though this path carried him across the field of view of the scorpion. Having noticed Vandal's discovery, Roddi leveled his laser at the battle mech's eyes and fired a series of hasty shots timed to keep the small armored panel popping up and down in front of the scorpion's eyes, hindering its vision as it attempted to line up a shot.

Vandal emerged on the other side of the thing, straightening only slightly as he slipped between the legs on that side and sprinted toward the weapons packs beyond. He quickly scooped up the straps with his mechanical arm and had just cleared the area when a blast struck from the second scorpion's laser. Going back the way he came, he darted beneath the first battle mech, twisting through the moving forest of legs, and reemerged on the other side.

Roddi reached the spot where Marinda lay sprawled in the shallow depression and hunched down beside her, rummaging through his weapons pack. "Here, take this," he said, handing her a ray pistol and continuing to rummage for something else. As he searched, he said, "I hope you're not planning on staying here?"

She looked at him oddly. "But Vandal said—"

"I know. Let me guess. Vandal told you not to move unless you were drawing fire, right?"

"Yes."

"Well," said Roddi smoothly, "unless I miss my guess, that should happen right about . . . now!"

A cloud of charred sand shot up into the air a few yards in back of them as a ray beam hissed in from the third scorpion warrior. Marinda let out a yelp of surprise and scrambled up out of the depression after Roddi. They both were running toward the ruins, and as Roddi rotated his head back to check he saw Vandal catching up with them.

"Ah, good, Vandal," Roddi said as they joined up, still running for their lives. "I trust you have something in mind for those dreadful machines?"

"I do if we can reach those buildings alive. Do you still have the smoke grenades?"

"Yes." Roddi began digging through the pack he was carrying. "Somewhere . . . oh yes, I think these are the ones."

He handed two to Vandal and kept one for himself. They armed the grenades and flipped one in the direction of each scorpion warrior. The devices hit and popped loudly, spewing out great clouds of billowing smoke. Roddi drew three more from his pack, and he and Vandal dropped those only a short distance behind them as they ran. A second wall of smoke began to rise, blocking everything behind them.

They reached the edge of the ruins and began to slow, cautious lest guards or some other threat await. But as they edged deeper past the outer row of buildings they saw no dangers, human or other.

Vandal directed them around the corner of a low wall of thick stone. There was some shelter here, and more a short distance away. There was also a clear view of the smoke-filled sector where the three scorpion warriors remained hidden from view.

Marinda sat down wearily and leaned back against the wall, breathing hard. "Say what you will about the desert," she gasped. "At least out there, there wasn't anybody, or any *thing*, shooting at us."

"There would have been, soon enough." Vandal crouched behind the wall next to her, peering over the top and watching for the metal monsters to emerge from the smoke.

On the other side of Marinda, Roddi also crouched, ready to continue the fight. "Well, I must say, this has certainly been a most unpleasant surprise. What do you think those things are doing here?"

"Hard to say," Vandal replied. He began pulling

weapons from one of the packs. "Probably some experiment. It appears the Corporation has still been using this site to test its weapons."

"On us?"

Vandal shook his head. "If this place was currently staffed, there'd be guards swarming around us by now. I think they just left those scorpion mechs behind and we were unfortunate enough to stumble into their range and activate them. There are probably more buried in the sand all around this place."

Marinda sighed heavily. "It's always good to know things aren't one hundred percent hopeless. Just ninety-nine percent."

Vandal popped a small warhead into an airjet launch tube. Reaching down to the lower portion of his mechanical leg, he exposed a panel and flipped it open. A power outlet and switch were beneath it.

The airjet load launcher had a power cable wound up on a reel, and Vandal pulled this out and connected it to the power outlet in his leg. A soft purr of sound came from the launcher as its compact air compressor began building pressure in the chamber beneath the firing tube. Vandal lined up several loads where he could reach them quickly, then looked once more over the top of the low wall.

"They're coming," he said grimly.

Tired as she was, Marinda flipped over and knelt close to the wall, peeking above the edge of the stone barrier. She saw one of the large scorpion warriors step through the dense wall of smoke and emerge into the bright sunlight. The second and the third machines soon followed, and all were advancing steadily upon the ruins. More specifically, they were advancing toward the exact spot in the ruins where she and the others were hiding.

"Oh, my," she said softly. "And I bet they're plenty mad, too."

"Not really," Roddi said absently, getting his ray pistol into position. "That level of artificial intelligence is much too primitive to allow real emotions. They've merely been programmed to kill us. Doesn't make any difference to them."

"Thanks." Marinda shot him a pouting glare. "You're a real morale booster."

"Listen up," Vandal snapped. "I want you two to keep shooting at their eyes. I need their shields up as much as possible."

"Right," said Roddi.

"Uh-huh," Marinda replied, studying the ray pistol in her hand. The thing was heavy and unfamiliar, quite unlike any gun she'd ever seen, though its basic shape and arrangement of grip, trigger, and barrel were similar. She pointed the weapon over the wall and pulled the trigger twice. Nothing happened. She looked at the side of the device. "Uh, is there a safety on this?"

Roddi fired several times at one of the advancing robots, then swiveled his head in her direction. "Yes, right there near your thumb. Just push it up and over, and—"

There was a loud, buzzing burst of noise as a beam flashed from Marinda's gun. It vaporized a large chunk of wall in the building next to them.

Roddi ducked, then sighed inwardly. "—and do try not to squeeze the trigger at the same time."

Her face scrunched into an apologetic smile. "Sorry!" Then she turned and started firing over the wall, at first awkwardly. But as she began to get the feel of the weapon, its weight and balance and the way its sights worked, she started gripping it more steadily and taking better aim. Soon her shots were hitting as close as Roddi's.

By this time, though, the scorpion warriors were returning fire. Laser beams were flashing overhead with sizzling regularity. Some were striking the wall behind which they crouched, cutting away at its stone. It was a thick wall, but it could not block those fierce rays indefinitely.

The scorpions were still advancing, even though their laser shots were limited to those moments when their vision shields were down and they could actually see and target on something. As they drew near, Vandal adjusted the sights on the airjet he held braced against his shoulder and waited for the battle mech he was aiming for to raise its shield. The instant he saw that shield starting up, he squeezed the trigger.

The storage chamber promptly released the air compressed within it, and with a muffled *whumph* the load was propelled from the launcher tube. Hurtling through the air, the blob of sticky material softened as air friction heated it. It hit squarely in the face of the center scorpion warrior, just as its camera shield was about to lower. The sticky goo plastered the shield and completely covered the head of the battle mech, imbedding itself in every nook and cranny, sticking to every surface and holding tight. As the scorpion tried to lower the armor shield before its eyes, the gluelike mass held fast and kept the shield raised, effectively blinding the robot.

"A tangler load," observed Roddi with surprise as he continued firing. "What an interesting choice."

Marinda frowned. "It is?"

"Tanglers are normally an antipersonnel weapon, used to immobilize humans and the like," Roddi told her. He ducked as a ray strike from the second scorpion blasted the wall near him. "Quite an inspired idea. Shall we try it again, Vandal?"

"Soon as the air pressure's back up." He glanced at the gauge on the side of the airjet. The needle was steadily rising toward the ready mark. Vandal grabbed a second tangler load and popped it into the launcher tube. "Keep firing," he told them.

Roddi and Marinda did their best to hinder the remaining two scorpions' vision with ray fire. They were pleased a moment later when their efforts were rewarded and Vandal launched the next tangler load. This one sped toward its target with equal accuracy, striking the face of the second battle mech and completely covering it. Now this unit could no longer see, either.

Both scorpion warriors slowed their pace, walking erratically. Their pincers attempted to pull the sticky mess free.

"Hooray," exclaimed Roddi. "Two down and one—"

"And one's going," Marinda said, pointing furiously.

Vandal had already noticed. The third battle mech had turned away from the path the others followed and was going around to one side. Vandal checked the airjet. It was not fully pressurized yet, and even if it had been, he didn't have a clear shot at the scorpion's face. In another moment it would be completely shielded by the building to their right.

"It's gotten wise to our tactic," said Roddi. "Perhaps their intelligence isn't quite as primitive as I thought."

"I think we'd better find a new position," Vandal told them. His airjet finally reached the pressurization mark, and he pulled the power cable free, not wanting it to impede the movement of his leg. Vandal dropped the third tangler load down the launcher tube and grabbed the rest of his gear. "Back this way," he shouted.

The three fell back a short distance, moving across what must once have been a roadway. They passed between two buildings that were still reasonably intact and darted behind one of them to reach the corner, taking up a position behind the tumbled stones of a collapsed wall. From where they were they could still see the two scorpion warriors they had succeeded in blinding. It now seemed that success would only be temporary.

"Oh, glitch!" said Roddi. "Look at that, would you? They are indeed smarter than I thought."

It took only a moment to see what he meant. Both battle mechs had ceased their efforts to pull the tangler mess from their faces, and had angled their tails forward as far as they would go. Short bursts of laser fire were coming from each tail's tip, directed at the sticky goo covering their eye shields.

"Oh, no!" Marinda gasped. "If they burn through that stuff, we're right back where we started."

"Not quite," Vandal replied with grim assurance. He reached to his gear and picked up a small cylindrical device with a lens at one end and a socket at the other end. He slid the socket over the tip of his metal index finger, pushing the cylinder back until it snapped in place. He made a fist with the rest of his fingers and thumb, so that his hand resembled a gun with a silencer.

He held that arm out straight, gripping it with his right hand and depressing a concealed button near the elbow. Latches within the arm snapped and released, and a narrow panel running from elbow to wrist popped open. A servo whined madly, raising a small, single-shot missile launcher.

Vandal picked up a missile from the padded case in

his pack. Carefully, he inserted it into the launcher and made certain the electrical contacts were lined up.

"Thermite warhead?" Roddi inquired.

"Good guess." Vandal raised his arm in the direction of the first scorpion. The mech was cutting through the last portion of sticky mess plastered over its face. In seconds it would be clear.

Vandal pointed his index finger at the monster's laser-tipped tail. A targeting beam flashed out, finding its mark and holding it. With a sudden hiss of sound, the missile launched, shooting away from Vandal's arm.

Arcing high at first, the small missile soon reached its peak and angled down, homing in on the spot of light from Vandal's targeting beam. If he could only hold it steady until the missile reached that target—

The missile slammed into the tip of the scorpion's tail, exploding on contact. The high-powered incendiary ignited instantly and began to burn through the armor and metal structure, dropping flaming fragments down into the battle mech's face, scorching the camera shield and spreading along the seams. Sparks flew as the laser weapon short-circuited and dropped from the tail.

"I think we can consider that one disabled," Roddi said.

Vandal was reaching for another missile as the exhaust smoke from the first still curled and eddied about his arm. He picked it up and checked it before inserting it into the launcher.

Marinda's pulse was pounding. They had a chance to beat these things and escape with their lives, but still she worried. She looked behind her, searching the buildings, ruined or standing, for other places to take shelter should they have to fall back once more. There were more than enough, but she hoped the battle would not last much longer.

She was about to look back toward the second scorpion when something caught her eye. Something small moved, just at the edge of her vision, near a ruined wall behind them and to the right. Something, but what?

Marinda blinked, rubbing her eyes and wiping the sweat from her forehead with the back of her hand. She stared at the spot where she thought she had seen the moving thing, and began to wonder if the heat and her fatigue had finally pushed her to the point where she was hallucinating. For that matter, everything she had seen and been through thus far was perilously close to hallucination anyway. She half hoped she was still sleeping, in her suspended-animation chamber on *Glory,* or better yet, back on Earth, in her bed. If only this were all one strange and terribly long dream.

Something moved again, and this time she was sure she was not imagining it. Whatever it was, it was hunched over and mostly hidden behind a crumbled wall. She had a glimpse of brown and white—soft, dull, and dirty colors that did not seem like those of a robot or machine. She prayed it was not some alien beast, dangerous and hungry, stalking them while their attention was diverted by the scorpion warriors.

"Vandal, I . . ." she began, then hesitated.

"What?"

She glanced over and saw he was busy loading his missile and checking the position of the second scorpion. Looking swiftly back to the crumbled wall, Marinda saw the top edge of the thing as it hesitated near an opening. She shifted her position slightly, readying her laser so that she could fire toward the open space the moment the thing revealed itself.

And then it did, darting out through the opening with surprising speed. It loped silently across the clear area behind them.

Marinda almost fired out of pure reflex. But she did not. She relaxed her trigger finger and raised the gun, staring with surprise and relief as a young boy ran for the building on their right. He was dressed in rags, and their dusty colors and his shaggy hair had been what created the impression of a lurking animal. He glanced toward them as he ran, and his frightened eyes met Marinda's gaze. He kept running, disappearing into the doorway of the building.

"A boy—" Marinda said abruptly. "I just saw a little boy!"

"Out here?" said Roddi in a skeptical tone, still facing forward. "That hardly seems likely."

Vandal glanced quickly back and saw nothing. He returned his attention to the scorpion warrior and his aim.

"Well, I did see him." Marinda hesitated a second longer, then got to her feet and started running for the building. She reached the open doorway in seconds, caught her breath, and peered cautiously inside.

She did not see the child, though. There was an old table, long and dusty, with benches beside it. Several metal cabinets stood along one wall, their doors hanging open. Cans and boxes of food were scattered on the table and the floor, some of them opened and empty. A can suddenly hit the floor, somewhere off to her side, making Marinda jump before it rolled into her range of vision.

Then even as she smiled at her own nervousness, the boy suddenly darted from his place of concealment in the room and ran out through the door, brushing past her so quickly he almost knocked her over. Carrying a large sack filled with scavenged foodstuffs, he headed back in the direction she had seen him come from.

"Wait!" Marinda called after him. "I won't hurt you."

From the corner of her eye she saw Vandal and Roddi turn in her direction. Then, with frightening abruptness, a flash of intense light hit the building directly behind the cyborg and his psybot companion. The sizzling hiss of the ray beam passed straight over her head on its way.

Roddi whirled toward her. "Marinda! Look out!"

She stepped a bit farther from the building and looked up, the hairs already rising on the back of her neck. There behind her, coming around the building and looming above her, was the third scorpion warrior. Its right pincer was spread wide open and reaching out to crush her in its metal grasp, while its tail laser was aiming for Vandal and Roddi.

Marinda threw herself to the left, out of the way of the huge claw. She hit the ground and rolled, stopping on her back and firing her laser directly at the thing's nasty face.

Just as it snapped up the shield before its eyes, Vandal fired. The monstrous thing was so close that the tangler load's sticky blob struck it in the face as a solid sheet instead of spreading strands. It immediately sealed the eye armor closed.

Vandal and Roddi were moving quickly out of the way, lest the thing fire another shot where it remembered them being. They motioned frantically for Marinda to join them.

She got to her feet and ran only too gladly. When she was clear, Vandal swung his mechanical arm up and fired his missile directly at the battle mech without even bothering to use the targeting beam. At that distance, he could not miss.

As flames erupted over the scorpion, Marinda caught up with the others. She was breathless and a bit giddy with excitement.

"Hey," she said proudly. "Not bad reflexes for a seven-hundred-year-old broad, huh?"

"Very nice indeed," agreed Roddi. "But let's congratulate ourselves later. That was Vandal's last thermite missile."

"I glimpsed that boy you saw," Vandal snapped abruptly. "Where did he go?"

Marinda pointed the way. "Over there, I think. But why?"

"Because if he managed to get into this place, alone and unarmed, then maybe—just maybe—he can show us how to get out."

12:
ESCAPE ROUTE

MARINDA JOGGED ALONGSIDE RODDI and Vandal as they headed in the direction she had seen the strange boy take. Behind her she could still hear the thrashings of the severely damaged scorpion warrior, and her nostrils were still clogged with the odd metallic smell of burning thermite and armor. Off to the south she caught sight of the second scorpion, its vision mostly restored, starting to advance once more upon the ruined facility and the three targets it wanted to destroy. Three targets that desperately wanted to stay alive.

"Vandal," she gasped out as she ran, "what if the boy isn't alone?"

"For that matter," speculated Roddi, "what if he isn't unarmed?"

Vandal gave a quick, negative shake of his head. "No. That kid had 'loner' written all over him, even from what little I saw of him. He's either a nomad or a scavenger from one of the devastated cities near here. And if he had a weapon, he'd have been carrying it. Even if there are other people here with him, I still want to know how they got into this place."

Roddi glanced toward the edge of the ruins where

the second scorpion warrior stalked, and beyond that, to the distant horizon. "How far behind us do you think that Corporation helijet is?"

"Not far enough," Vandal said grimly.

They reached the building where Marinda thought she had seen the boy go. The doorway stood open and beckoning, a shaft of raw sunlight spilling inside to illuminate part of the floor and a wedge-shaped slice of the wall. There were fresh tracks in the dust and windblown sand upon the floor. Small tracks, close-spaced leading out and farther apart, indicating a running stride, leading back in. This had to be the right one.

Vandal led the way up to the door, his blaster in hand but held nozzle up. He stopped at the door-frame, alert and listening, then he ducked low as he swung around through the opening and crouched just within.

He kicked up a thin cloud of dust as he entered, and there was still a slight swirl of dust hanging in the air farther back in the room, indicating someone's recent passage. There was little else here except some old, broken furniture and refuse scraps. Part of the ceiling had fallen in toward the back, letting another shaft of sunlight cut through the room.

Roddi cautiously followed Vandal, with Marinda close behind him. "I don't see him," Roddi said.

Vandal's hard gaze searched the floor. There was less dust in here, farther back from the door and the wind, but there was still enough to make out faint tracks. They led around the corner into an angled extension of the room that was still out of sight.

Vandal started toward the corner, moving quietly. He motioned for the others to follow. They advanced cautiously toward the hidden area, uncertain what might be waiting there. Marinda peered warily past Vandal's shoulder, hoping the boy would not run again or put up a struggle and be hurt. As they rounded the corner she saw that her concern was needless, or at least premature.

This part of the room was as empty as the first, and it did not take her long to see why. In the far corner, near the floor, a small section of the wall had crumbled, leaving a gaping hole that led outside. As they hurried to it, fresh tracks could be seen in the dust and sand that had blown through the opening.

"He's smart," Vandal said, stooping to glance through the hole and looking both ways along the street behind the building. "He's avoiding the open areas, so he can't be seen as easily."

"Yes," agreed Roddi. "He certainly seems to know his way around here."

"Like a stray cat," Marinda said absently, a thoughtful frown on her face. "Vandal, when I saw him run past me, he had a sack of food in his hand that should last for weeks. If he's been living here awhile, taking advantage of what the last people here left behind, then the only reason he'd want to gather up that much food now is that he's planning to leave."

Vandal nodded. "Our fight with the scorpion mechs probably convinced him it was time to move on. All the more reason to find him quickly."

Marinda knelt beside Vandal, seeing something that had escaped her notice in all the excitement. There was a small streak of blood on the left side of his face, near an old scar that ran vertically above and below his left eye. "You're bleeding," she said, reaching out to his cheek.

He pulled away slightly, still intently watching the

street beyond. "Don't worry about it. One of the ray blasts sent a chip of stone flying. I've been cut worse."

"You should still put something on it," Marinda urged. "In a place like this—"

"Later," Vandal snapped. "Look, there he goes!"

Marinda jerked her head to where Vandal pointed. She saw the boy rise from behind some rubble and turn to run toward the building beyond. He had apparently been watching to see if his pursuers were still on his trail, and finding they were, had decided not to linger there any longer.

Vandal darted out through the opening in the wall. Marinda ducked through next, leaving Roddi to scramble awkwardly through after them. As they ran after the boy they saw him turn before reaching the doorway and head along the side of the building, keeping to the shadows. They crossed the street and chased after him.

There was still no sign of any vehicles, and not much in the way of usable hardware left behind. However the boy had gotten here, he seemed to be the only key to the mystery.

"This way," Vandal said, somehow managing to keep an eye on the frantically scurrying boy.

They ran through the shadows along the side of the building and turned in the direction Vandal indicated. Ahead of them, the boy darted across an open area near the center of the deserted complex and disappeared into the doorway of a building that had been boarded up, slipping lithely through the narrow gap between two boards.

Marinda had started to sprint after him when Vandal abruptly grabbed her by the waist and pulled her back into the shadows. "Hey—" she started to protest. Then her words were stilled by the look of deadly seriousness in Vandal's eyes. He put a finger to his lips and jerked his head toward the ground not far in front of them. A shadow was moving slowly across it. A shadow cast by something very large that stalked humans.

Marinda immediately recognized the characteristic curve of the tail with its bulging laser pod at the tip. The second scorpion warrior was searching for them, and there was no sense in helping it find them.

Vandal waited a moment, but was clearly growing impatient. Too long, and they might lose the boy completely and have to search the entire complex for him. Finally, his blaster ready, Vandal leaned carefully forward and looked around the corner toward the shadow's source.

Beyond the far end of the building he saw the scorpion warrior, moving slowly down the street. It was not as near as he had expected; its shadow had been cast by light reflected from the shiny panels of a solar collection tower. The scorpion was facing away from them, but was heading for the building they had just exited. If it could see tracks as well as a human, it would not have any difficulty following them.

"Come on," said Vandal softly. "We'd better try it."

The three moved as quickly and quietly across the open area as they could, reaching the boarded-up building. But the narrow gap the boy had squeezed through was too tight for adult humans and a comparably sized psybot. Vandal grasped the second board from the bottom with his metal hand and pried it loose. He climbed through the enlarged opening, shifting the position of his weapons packs to fit through. After Roddi and Marinda had followed him, he put the board back in place and pushed the nails in well enough to hold.

They looked around. There was less light reaching into this place with the windows and doors boarded up as they were, but it was clear this was a larger building than the other they had entered. There was more furniture here, desks and chairs and file cabinets, with a layer of dust that suggested long disuse and neglect. Several tables had fittings and cable connections for test equipment no longer present.

Roddi took it all in with interest, recording what he saw for possible use later. The University might want the data. "Do you think this was here during the original plague-virus experiments?"

Vandal looked it over quickly, wiped a finger through the dust to gauge its depth. "Maybe. But it's been used more recently."

There was a sudden squeak of sound that brought their attention sharply to one side of the room. A door there moved a bit, swinging slightly more closed.

Vandal gestured to the others, and the three of them strode silently to the door. If there was no outlet from this next office, if there was no broken wall, then this was as far as the boy could go. But would he yield to them his secret?

Vandal put his hand on the door, listening for any sound that might signal danger. Then he gave the door a forceful push that sent it slamming against the inside wall.

Marinda almost screamed as she glimpsed what stood just beyond the door. Something tall and horrible and only vaguely humanoid faced them, its large and glistening eyes staring at them, its snout dark and ugly. What was worse, there was not just one of these ominous beasts facing her, there was a small army of them!

Marinda staggered back a step, clutching at her throat. Roddi put a steadying arm behind her.

"Wait," the psybot told her. "I think this may not be as bad as it looks. Vandal?"

The cyborg agent lowered the pistol he had brought up to fire, breathed a heavy sigh of relief, and nodded affirmatively. "Anticontamination suits," he said simply.

Marinda looked closer, still a bit shaken by the experience, but more than a little angry with herself for being so easily startled. Then she thought back over the day's events thus far and decided she had been thoroughly primed for a bit of well-justified fright.

She could see now that the things before her were not creatures, or even robots. What she had mistaken for eyes were only the lens pieces of the facemask, the snout merely a rubbery air-filtration unit covering the area of the nose and mouth, not unlike a conventional gas mask. The suits were made of a material stiff enough that the body of each stood out as if filled by a person wearing it, and all were hanging, not standing, from metal racks she had not seen at first.

They stepped into the narrow room. There was no sign of the boy here, but while one end of the room was walled off, the other had a door of metal and thick armorplex.

"He must have gone through here," Vandal snapped, leading them on in that direction.

The door proved to be the outer hatch of an airlock built into the end of the room. It had been left open for some time, judging from the deterioration of the seals around the edges. A control panel built into one wall was inactive, with no power showing on its readouts.

There was no second door leading out of the airlock,

but an opening yawned up from the floor. Stairs spiraled down it into darkness.

Vandal considered a moment, then faced the others. "Well, do you want to chance it?"

"May as well," Roddi replied, cocking his thumb toward the streets outside the building. "We seem to be running out of places to go out there. Not to mention time."

Marinda shrugged. "Sure, why not? At this point, we don't have much to lose. Do we?"

"I'm glad we agree," Vandal said, and started down the stairs ahead of them, his protoblaster held ready.

The stairs continued straight down a good thirty feet, illuminated only by what little light filtered in from above. The steps ended upon solid flooring, metal from the sound of it, and the three found themselves in another airlock very much like the one upstairs. A strange, sickly-orange light poured in through the open hatch, coolly artificial compared to the harsh desert sun.

Vandal stepped out first, followed by Marinda and Roddi. The air here was quite pleasant after the blazing heat aboveground.

"I can't say much for the building," Marinda said in awe, "but it sure has one heckuva basement."

The underground chamber was easily twice the size of the building that sat over it on the desert sands. Though the sides of the chamber were dark, pools of orange light spilled down from fixtures scattered here and there throughout the place. Cables ran from them to a central circuit box where a pipe rose up to the surface, presumably connected to solar power collectors aboveground.

Two sets of tracks ran across the floor of the chamber, one set running off to the far end and disappearing into a tunnel, the other running in almost, but not quite, the opposite direction and disappearing into an identical tunnel. There was no car on the first set of tracks, but there was one on the second. An extra vehicle sat off on a spur that connected both.

There was something else down here as well. A rasp of sound caught their attention and drew it to the small, streamlined car resting on the second set of tracks. The sliding canopy panel that served as both door and part of the vehicle's roof was jerking back and forth, but not fully opening.

Vandal ran for the car, leaped from the low platform which ran alongside the tracks, and disappeared around the far side of the sleek vehicle. There was a small yelp of protest, followed by a string of obscenities uttered in a voice ill suited for such foul language.

Reappearing around the side of the shuttle car, Vandal strode back toward Roddi and Marinda with the scruffy boy in tow. The boy still clung to his bulging bag of scavenged foodstuffs, fearful it might be taken from him. His small face glared defiance with each forced step he took.

"Where was he trying to go?" Marinda asked.

"Back the way he came, no doubt," Vandal replied. "And he's inadvertently shown us a way out of Delta Zone."

"Two ways, actually," Roddi corrected. The silvery-blue psybot had his digital compass out and pointed it first down one and then the other section of tracks. "This one to our left heads due north. The one to our right heads southeast."

Vandal squinted as he visualized a map of the continent. "Kezos City lies due north of here, about a hundred miles from the coast. That would take us roughly in the direction of Jonnersville. The other track must go to Port London, on the east coast."

"I have nothing in my programming about this," Roddi said in a perturbed tone. "The Corporation must have built this hidden shuttle system as a means of getting to and from their research facility without attracting attention."

"Well, I'm glad they did," replied Marinda. "Can we use one of these cars to get out of here?"

"Let's check the power cells in that spare car," Vandal said. "If it's still got enough of a charge we'll push it onto the tracks for Kezos City. If not, we'll have to use the other one."

It took only a few moments to reach the car and slide its door forward. Vandal reached in and flipped the power switches on. The lights and display panel came on instantly. After a few more seconds the read-outs reported the car's status.

"About three-quarters power," observed Vandal. "Probably as good as or better than the other car. Let's get it over on the track."

The three of them started pushing the car forward, and thanks to its lightness, had little trouble moving it once they had it rolling. Switches guided the car onto the right set of tracks, and in a matter of minutes it was ready.

"There, let's get the gear inside." Vandal looked quickly around, frowning in sudden realization. "Where's that boy?"

Marinda looked about in mild alarm. "He was just with us a minute or so ago, when we were pushing."

There was a sharp click behind them as the door panel closed on the other shuttle car. Vandal started toward it at once, but before he could reach it, the car's motors whined to life and the car shot down the tracks, picking up speed. In a moment it reached the tunnel on the southeast side of the chamber and disappeared from view.

Marinda and Roddi caught up with Vandal as he stopped, their own pace slacking off as they saw the futility of pursuit. Marinda was crestfallen.

"I'm sorry. I should have kept a better eye on him."

"We all should have," Vandal replied, in a tone that told her he blamed himself more than her. "He may be better off in Port London, though. We're not going to be the safest people to be around, wherever we are. And I planned to send that car off anyway, just to keep anyone pursuing us from knowing which way we went."

"Well," said Roddi, "he looks like a tough little ragamuffin. I'm sure he'll manage."

Vandal stepped up to the boarding platform and glanced into the alcoves and storage areas behind it. "Let's see if there's anything we can use here before we go. I doubt there's any food our young friend missed."

They quickly checked the area, finding a few porta-lights and power cells, and a dozen disposable coveralls sealed in clear plastic. But as they suspected, no food. It was unlikely food had ever been stored in this part of the facility. There were, though, several water containers that had been left behind, their seals still intact. The dates on them indicated they had been there less than a year. They were a most welcome find. As they checked the last large alcove, Marinda found something else of immediate interest.

"A shower!" she cried as she recognized the familiar arrangement of spray heads, piping, and stalls. "Oh, Vandal, I want a shower so bad. I'm hot and I'm tired, and although I hate to admit it, my deodorant was just never meant to last seven hundred years and a trek through the desert."

Roddi eyed the tanks above the shower stalls. Their labels indicated they held water with various chemicals added. "It seems to be an antibacterial, antiviral rinse, no doubt intended for technicians and workers leaving the area. I suppose it couldn't hurt. In fact, it might even be a good way to get the dust off my outer shell."

Vandal considered it, weighing the time delay and possible risk against their continued discomfort. The pleading look in Marinda's eyes, the endearing pathos of her bedraggled appearance, should have no weight in the cold and logical decision-making process of a professional like himself. Should not, but . . .

"All right," he agreed at last. "But make it quick."

There were two sections of stalls, placed back to back, with swinging doors providing some privacy from about knee height to shoulders. Vandal and Roddi took the far side, leaving Marinda with the other section to herself.

Marinda wasted no time in hanging her borrowed cloak on a hook, kicking her shoes off, and stepping into the stall. She pulled the lever on the wall valve and let the water spray over her, drenching her hair and clothes, washing the sweat and gray sand from them. Only then did she peel off her garments and quickly bathe beneath the spray. The water smelled funny, vaguely reminding her of the pet shampoo she used to wash her dog with, but it was at least moderately cool and felt refreshing.

Those memories, inadvertently conjured up by the chemical smell, brought tears to her eyes as she realized that both her dog and the close friend she had entrusted it to were long dead—a part of history that was tiny and insignificant in the grand scheme of things. That made them no less vivid or poignant to her now. As the tears mingled on her face with the shower spray, she wondered how much Earth had changed in her absence.

Marinda cut off the water flow and wiped the water from her eyes. There were no towels anywhere in sight, and she suddenly wondered how she was going to dry herself. As if in answer to her thought she suddenly heard Vandal's voice, and the abrupt sound of it made her jump.

"There's a button in the stall, near the doors," he told her. "Push it to dry off."

Marinda realized that Vandal had not read her thought after all, he had merely heard the water turn off in her stall. She also realized that she had taken longer than she thought, for Vandal and Roddi were apparently already through.

She found the button where he told her it would be, a waterproof switch beside the stall doors. She hesitated a second, then gathered her courage and reached out to press it.

There was an immediate hum of sound directly above her and a rush of warm air flowing down. Marinda glanced up and saw a large blower suspended from the ceiling above her stall. In fact, there was one above each stall, she noticed. Filters covered the air intakes on each, and on the one above her she could see a light grid that glowed a stark electric blue, unpleasant to look into. From what she knew of space medicine she suspected its purpose was to sterilize the air blowing down on her, destroying whatever organisms might be present.

In a bit over a minute her skin was completely dry, her hair nearly so. She switched off the blower, not wanting to delay them any longer than she already had. She bent to pick up her garments.

"Oh . . ." she said as she gingerly raised them. "My clothes are going to be wet for a while." She was just debating with herself whether to put them back on wet or take still more time by using the blower to dry them when Roddi suddenly appeared in front of her stall. Robot or not, she caught herself wondering just how much of her he could see past the narrow swinging doors.

"Here, miss," Roddi said, his tone a bit flatter than usual as he extended a thin package over the top to her. "Vandal asked me to bring you this."

Marinda quickly took it, calling out, "Thank you." Roddi turned and left the area. It was one of the disposable coveralls they had found minutes before.

She tore open the clear plastic package and pulled out the one-piece garment. It was white, made of some sort of synthetic material that was lightweight and soft. She stepped into the coveralls and fastened the closures on the front. The fit was a bit too loose and the pantlegs were too long, but she rolled those up enough to clear her ankles and decided this was no time to be concerned about making a fashion statement.

She quickly transferred her personal belongings from the pockets of her clothing to the coveralls, then pushed out through the swinging doors and stepped into her shoes. Grabbing the cloak off the wall hook, she ran toward the shuttle car, dodging small pools of dirt and grease on the floor.

Vandal and Roddi were already there, loading the water containers on board. Vandal, too, was wearing white coveralls, and Marinda noticed they fit him much better than her. She also found herself wondering for a moment, from both a personal and a professional standpoint, just how well his cybernetic limbs were blended into his living flesh at their various points of attachment. But she knew she would have to respect his privacy just as much as he had respected hers.

Vandal turned as she approached, reaching for the wet garments she carried. "Here, let me take those."

Marinda watched, puzzled at first, as he proceeded to tie them securely to a handrail running around the sides and back of the vehicle. Then she saw what he had in mind. He planned to let the flow of air past the moving shuttle dry their clothes for them. His own garments were already fastened there.

"All right," said Vandal when he was done, "now let's get out of here while we still can."

They climbed into the shuttle car and pulled the door closed behind them, latching it securely. Then they slipped into the first row of seats, just behind the controls. There was another row behind them, where they stored their gear. The seats were cushioned and had high backs to support their heads, leaning back at a slight but comfortable angle.

Vandal reached forward and powered up the car, waiting as the readouts came on fully. Then he pressed the start button and the shuttle whined into action. In mere seconds it crossed the tracks that headed north along the chamber floor and darted into the tunnel at the end.

Darkness swallowed them up, and for a moment Marinda was frightened, uncertain about the wisdom of plunging headlong into the unknown. Then she noticed a small screen built into the panel before them, displaying a red-tinted image of the tunnel as it stretched out for miles ahead. This would alert them to any problems on the track, she felt sure.

"Vandal," she said suddenly, "back in the desert,

you and Roddi mentioned something about the pilot of that aircraft or whatever it was that seemed to be searching for us. You thought it might be someone called Ray, or Ray something?"

"Razer," Vandal replied, and there was an odd quality to his voice as he uttered the name. "But I'm not sure it was her."

"Her?" Marinda said. "Then it's someone you know?"

"Not as well as I thought I did." Vandal's tone was dry and bitter, and he remained silent for a long moment before speaking again. "She's an eliminator for the Corporation, as I used to be, not so very long ago. And she's very good at her work."

"Eliminator." Marinda frowned uneasily. The word had a very unpleasant taste to it. "That sounds like—"

"Exactly what it is," Vandal replied. "I suppose a better name for it is 'assassin.' The Corporation likes to think of the eliminators as its elite group of problem-solvers, but the problems always turn out to be people the Corporation doesn't like, and the solution is always to kill them. It's a job I was trained for since childhood, and there was a time when I was the best—a time when I took pride in the fact."

Marinda found it hard to believe this man could ever have been a cold-blooded, remorseless killer. His fighting skills had been well demonstrated in the past two days, but she could see in his manner, and in his brooding, pain-haunted eyes, that this was not a man who enjoyed killing. He was simply doing what he had to do, and paying a personal price for it. And though she was sure Vandal would be reluctant to admit it, Marinda had sensed an unmistakable kindness and decency in him.

On her other side, Roddi leaned forward and studied the readouts on the panel before them. "How long, do you think, before we reach Kezos City, Vandal?"

"Three, four hours, maybe longer," Vandal told him. "Hard to be sure without knowing the exact mileage and the speed of this thing. At least the trip will give us a chance to rest. We may not get many."

Marinda settled back into her seat, fully conscious for the first time since reaching the research facility of just how tired she was. The shuttle car swayed rhythmically as it rolled rapidly along the rails. Closed snugly around them and shrouded by darkness as it sped through the tunnel beneath the desert sands, the shuttle had a cozy quality to it that was a welcome relief after all the discomfort she had experienced thus far. She felt clean again, and comfortable, and for now at least, safe.

Marinda felt sleep drifting over her, and as she shifted in her seat she twisted slightly to lean toward Vandal, cradling her head against his right shoulder. She felt a dim sense of pleasure at finding that shoulder to be real and warm, and not machinery. Within seconds she was sound asleep.

Vandal stiffened slightly at first as he found the young woman snuggled against him. But as he studied her, she looked like such an innocent child, a frightened, exhausted child, that his expression softened.

He reached over with his left hand to brush aside the damp blond hair that had fallen across her face, then as he did so his expression stiffened once more. Vandal held up that hand before him, seeing the glints of instrument light reflecting off its shiny metal palm and fingertips. He closed his eyes as tightly shut as the fist he now made of the hand that was not flesh and blood, only steel and servos and microchips.

On the other side of the car, Roddi saw that expression with photoreceptors tuned to the reduced light level. He thought he understood, at least to some extent, what his friend was going through. He had hoped to get away from the whole subject of Vandal's past with his question about their estimated arrival time, but clearly he had not succeeded. Perhaps there was no way to avoid it, with so much of the unpleasantness not just a memory, but still a very real part of his present and his future.

Roddi looked at the girl snuggled against his friend's side, wondering if perhaps she could be the key to unlocking the man's troubled soul. Razer's pursuit of them, if indeed she was following, did not help matters any.

Something else troubled Roddi briefly. Though he could not quite grasp this strange comfort humans found in the physical closeness of another of their kind, he nevertheless felt a strange and inexplicable sense of hurt over the fact that Marinda had not even considered falling asleep on *his* shoulder. He was a friend, too, after all. Was he not? And he had saved her life, too. Had he not?

Finally, Roddi decided to power down for the remainder of the trip and conserve precious energy. Important areas of his mind and operating system would stay alert for trouble, should there be any. He sincerely hoped there would not.

Above the desert, the Corporation helijet drew closer and closer to the deserted research facility. At the controls, Razer checked her scanners for confirmation that the trail of microscopic paint chips did indeed lead here, even though she knew there was little doubt at this point. The telltale specks were fewer and farther apart by now, but there were just enough resting beneath the surface of the sand to show up on her scanner display and assure her she was still tracking them.

"Ah," she said to herself as her glistening eyes came up from the scanner display and noticed the damaged hulk of the first scorpion warrior outside the base's perimeter. "Vandal's handiwork, unless I miss my guess."

She slowed the craft, switching the scanners to human-detection mode and beginning a wide swing around the complex. From forty feet above the sand she soon spotted the next damaged scorpion machine, and even though it indicated another small defeat for the Corporation, such was her hatred of robots—all robots—that she could not help but smile at the sight of its smoldering form.

The last scorpion came into view, still plodding through the inner complex and searching. Suddenly it became aware of Razer's helijet and paused in its tracks, turning toward her. Razer saw the laser weapon at its tail swiveling in her direction.

Almost at the same instant, the path of her aircraft took her over the eastern perimeter of the complex, activating three more scorpion warriors beneath the all-concealing sands. They rose into view, adding their own deadly threat to that already posed by the one within the complex.

Razer started to arm her weapons system, but then, with an unpleasant twist of her mouth, she thought better of it. Reaching for a device installed near the radio transceiver, she flipped it on and pressed a button on its front panel.

A coded signal was sent from the device, identifying the craft as belonging to the Corporation. Instantly, the three scorpions on the eastern perimeter settled back down into their shallow depressions, flattening their segmented tails and waiting for the windborne sand to cover them once more. The battle mech within the complex resumed its search.

Razer found the base's landing pad and let the downdraft of her jets blow away the coating of sand. Touching down, she switched off the engines and started to reach for the radio controls to contact Roman. Then she remembered that he had said to let him know when she had something positive to report. She had found them—that was positive news, wasn't it?

Perhaps, but not as positive as being able to tell him that Vandal and his miserable psybot were dead, and that the girl that so intrigued Roman was in her hands. Now that would be news.

Razer decided to wait, forgoing the pleasure of contacting Roman for the time being. After all, hadn't she just told him the night before that pleasure delayed was pleasure enhanced?

She checked her holstered pistol and slipped out of the straps which held her securely in the seat. Then she grabbed extra weapons and power packs, popped the hatch, and climbed down to the ground. A thin smile spread across her face as she thought just how near her long-awaited moment must be.

15:

TROUBLE IN TROY

CLEERA HELD THE CONTROL yoke steady in her hands as the helijet cargo craft flew high above the hilly and desolate terrain below. They had been flying for several hours since leaving the outskirts of CityPrime, and had been in command of the aircraft since shortly after takeoff. Cleera rotated her head back to the cargo hold directly behind the cockpit area. Like most craft of its type, it had an altitude ceiling low enough that it did not need pressurization, and so there was no solid divider sealing off the cockpit. She saw the shipping company's pilot and copilot, still sitting on jump seats in the back, still securely tied and gagged. She did not like feeling responsible for their discomfort, but the fact that they worked for a division of the Corporation helped ease her conscience a little. Besides, no harm would come to them.

Cleera looked back to her instruments and the bleak landscape moving below them. It was early afternoon, and although there were troubled clouds drifting by overhead, there was enough bright sunlight to reveal the ground and blighted foliage clearly.

Humanity had always been spread thin upon Coreworld, collected mostly in the few dozen major cities, chosen for their resources, coastal location, or scenic appeal. While the areas between those gemlike cities had once been filled with lushly verdant foliage and a variety of animal life, there was little beauty to be found there now. What plants and animals were left struggled to survive amid the plague-decimated ecology.

HiLo sat in the copilot's seat beside Cleera, with Muse, Jayray, and Jom occupying jump seats immediately behind the cockpit area. Chiron and Torb were strapped into place in the rear of the craft's cargo bay, having boarded behind the crates they used to carry the rest of the psybot team into the vehicle.

Something had been troubling Cleera for much of the flight. Indeed, it had been troubling her since the previous night. Now with HiLo next to her and the steady whine of the helijet engines helping to keep their conversation private, she decided to broach the subject.

"HiLo," she said softly, "you've worked with Torb almost since you got here on Coreworld, haven't you?"

"Yes, he arrived only a week after I did." The green robot with the telescopic arms and legs studied her a moment. "Why?"

"Well, I thought you must know him better than I, and I just wondered . . ." Cleera hesitated a moment before continuing. "Torb seems, well, unfriendly toward me, and I don't understand why."

HiLo glanced back to where the large and powerful psybot stood strapped in place. "I can't say for certain, Cleera. But I think he may resent the fact the Uni chose you as team leader."

"But I had nothing to do with the choice. I didn't especially want the job, but Dean McAndrews seemed to think it would be the best arrangement."

HiLo gave an understanding nod. "Yes, and I think

he was right. I'm sure he and the others at the Uni had their reasons. From what I've learned, the process that creates psychogenetic brains is unpredictable. The human technicians can create us, but they cannot really control what we become. So we have to be evaluated— our capabilities, our personalities, our whole mental profile. It stands to reason that some of us are better suited to some jobs than others."

"Perhaps," replied Cleera. "But I don't want Torb to resent me, or to feel that I'm trying to boss him around."

"Why not?" said HiLo, with a humorous quirk to his voice. "That's your job, boss."

"Don't be a wise guy." Cleera appreciated his attempt to cheer her up with a joke, but the matter had brought up a deeper issue that was even more unsettling. "You know, HiLo, sometimes it's a bit frightening being what we are . . . psybots, I mean. Knowing we've been created by humans. Just machines, as they call us, but being able to think and feel and wonder about things. We're almost human, but not quite."

"Yes, I know what you mean," HiLo told her. "Sometimes it is unpleasant to think about. But even so, we are still beings, even if we're not organic beings as humans are. They have their advantages, we have ours. Besides," he added with a knowing laugh, "from what I've seen so far, being human is a bit frightening for them at times."

Muse leaned forward at that moment and called into the cockpit. "How long until we reach Troy?"

Cleera checked the instrument readouts and the computer-generated map on the panel display. "About ten minutes."

They flew on in silence for another minute or so, then there was a pop of sound from their transceiver and a voice suddenly came through the headphones Cleera and HiLo wore. Both psybots adjusted the devices to fit as well as possible over their own audio receptors, but wished a direct-patch cord had been available.

"PMC-7, come in, PMC-7," said the voice on the transceiver. "This is the Prime Movers branch office in Troy calling."

Cleera looked to HiLo with an alert and questioning glance. "This could be a problem. These people must know the regular pilot's voice."

"True," HiLo agreed. "And our voices aren't exactly normal. Still, if we don't respond . . ."

"Do what you can," Cleera told him. "At least your voice is deeper than mine."

HiLo picked up the microphone clipped to the center of the control panel and pried off the front of the case. He broke loose one of the wires soldered to the transducer element, then held it in place with his thumb. Reaching to the radio controls, he proceeded to flip off the automatic frequency hold and turn the tuning knob slightly. This altered the pitch and sharpness of the man's voice in Troy as he repeated his message, and would blur the sound of their outgoing reply as well. Only then did he respond to the call.

"Troy branch," HiLo transmitted in as human a voice as he could manage, occasionally using his thumb to slide the loose wire across its contact to create static, "Troy branch, this is PMC-7. We read you, but we are heaving some radio difficulty."

"Yes, PMC-7, you do sound a bit garbled here," replied the voice in their headsets. "Any other problems with your flight?"

"No," HiLo transmitted, glancing at Cleera. "Everything is fine so far. Any problem with our landing there at Troy?"

"Conditions here are okay," said the voice. "But there seems to be some confusion back at your home base. Something about a shipment not put aboard."

HiLo hesitated a moment. "I don't see how that can be." He made more fake static with his thumb. "We loaded everything that was listed on our flight manifest."

"Maybe so, but about an hour after you left another shipment arrived, with an identical manifest number. Your office has been trying to check it out with the supplier, but they've had trouble with their phone service."

"Probably some sort of paperwork foul-up," HiLo told the man. "You know how it is. Anyway, we just deliver them. You guys can straighten out the details later. We should be there shortly."

"Right, PMC-7. Over and out."

HiLo hung the partially disassembled microphone back on its clip. He looked to Cleera once more. "Will we be there shortly?"

"If you're just asking about arrival time, yes," Cleera replied. "But if you're wondering whether we should still go there, I think the answer is no. At the very least, they know something is wrong with the shipment. They'll have people out to the landing pad to check it as soon as we touch down. And if they suspect there's more of a problem than that, then we may find CorSec Guards waiting as well." Cleera shook her head in frustration. "Drat! I was hoping we could land there long enough to refuel and be on our way."

HiLo leaned toward her to try and read the gauges. "How much fuel do we have left?"

"Nowhere near enough to reach Jonnersville," she

told him. "And fuel won't be easy to find between cities."

"Is there anyplace else in Troy we can land and refuel?"

Cleera cut her forward airspeed to give them a little more time to think, then she looked to the computer map and tapped in a command asking for other fueling locations to be shown. In a moment the general map of the area vanished, replaced with one detailing the city of Troy.

"There are two other places," Cleera said, studying the map closely. "One is a small base on the western edge of town, where a detachment of CorSec troops is stationed."

"I think we can rule that one out," HiLo replied.

"The other is a fuel-processing plant on the eastern side of the city. It's probably where most of the helijet fuel comes from."

HiLo considered it a moment. "It's a possibility. If they have fuel trucks there we could land near one and use the hose."

"There's another possibility," said a voice behind them. Or actually, two voices behind them, for during the radio communication, Jayray and Jom had come forward to the cockpit.

Cleera turned to them. "You have an idea, guys?"

"We could run a scam on them," said Jayray. "Fly high enough for their radar to pick us up heading for the fuel plant, and then—"

"—drop beneath radar level," Jom took over, "and head for the CorSec base. While their troops are over at the fuel plant looking for us, we can load up the helijet."

"Not bad," Cleera replied. "But I think there are two many unknown elements in that type of approach.

How do we know the guards would be called promptly? If they are, would they take all their forces, or leave some behind to protect the installation? Besides, someone could see us flying in that direction and alert them."

There was a note of dejection in Jom's voice as he said, "So you do not think—"

"—it would work?" Jayray finished, equally downcast.

"It might," Cleera told them. "And I really do appreciate your suggestions, guys. Believe me. But in this case, I think the risks are too great. Our only real choice seems to be the fuel plant."

"Well, okay," said the twinbots.

Cleera pushed the control yoke forward and angled the craft down, steadily losing altitude. "You're right about avoiding radar detection, though. We don't want them noticing we're changing direction."

She studied the position of the fuel plant relative to Prime Mover's branch location and turned the control yoke slightly. As the helijet cargo ship banked toward the east, Cleera held it as low to the ground as she safely could, skimming the rolling foothills.

Troy was well in view now, and as the aircraft began its swing around the outskirts of the city those aboard could make out details of the large settlement. Troy seemed to be a mostly industrial city, located near mines and oil fields. Factories outnumbered offices and private homes, though dormitorylike residences were visible on the grounds of individual plants. Trucks and conveyor tubes fed ore and other resources into the city at a steady rate, though it looked as if the streets had once handled much more traffic than they did now.

"Look," announced HiLo with a jab of his finger

157

toward a complex rising ahead to their left. "That must be the fuel plant over there."

Cleera nodded in agreement. "I see it." Her steady gaze probed the area ahead, taking in the cluster of storage tanks and the tight maze of processing equipment. "Let's check it out."

She guided the helijet in closer. She could see that the refining plant took up perhaps a third of the complex, the storage tanks at least another third. There were large open spaces between everything, and roads created geometric patterns throughout the facility. A small one-story building was situated at the far end of the property, and was likely the office.

Cleera saw a number of trucks within the compound. Some were parked in a lot just off the main roadway. A few were being filled at a pumping station by the center storage tank. Something else caught her eye, though, and she leaned to point it out to HiLo.

"There are two landing pads over there," she said. "It looks as if they're prepared for cargo or military aircraft. And I think I can see a refueling pump next to each pad."

"Could be," HiLo replied. "It's pretty far away from the tanks and the plant."

"Probably to lessen the risk of a crash and explosion," Cleera commented. "Better for us that it is distant from the work areas."

"But a bit more easily seen, out in the open," cautioned HiLo.

Cleera hesitated only a moment longer, then said, "I'm going in. That landing pad on the right should be partially hidden from the office's view by the last storage tank. If we don't waste time fueling up . . ."

Cleera turned the control yoke and eased it forward. The cargo craft skimmed in low over the uneven terrain, crossing the perimeter road and clearing the fence which surrounded the fuel plant's property. The craft swung briefly up into a stable hover directly over the landing pad, then descended until its landing skids were fully resting on the ground.

"Quickly, now," Cleera said, throwing open the hatch and scrambling down to the ground.

HiLo was out at the same moment, moving swiftly for the fuel pump just past the edge of the pad. He reached it and started to unreel the hose, then saw that the reel was held immobile by a small lock. There was no time to look for keys or to attempt picking the lock, so HiLo merely grasped it in his hand and twisted sharply until the lock snapped.

He took hold of the end of the hose and started pulling it toward the side of the helijet, where Cleera was already opening the access panel to the fuel tanks.

HiLo slid the nozzle into place. "Shall we leave an IOU or just charge it to the Corporation?" he joked.

Cleera started to respond, but her words were cut short by a searing ray beam that crackled just above their heads. The beam was followed instantly by a snarling shout, somewhere behind them.

14:

VANISHING ACT

"HALT! DO NOT ATTEMPT refueling! Do not attempt escape or offer resistance!"

Cleera and HiLo whirled toward the voice and saw five CorSec Guards approaching from around the side of the nearest storage tank. There were four robot guards led by one human officer, and all were well armed and exceedingly dangerous-looking. They had been out of sight until now, and judging from the officer's blunt commands they had been expecting trouble. Expecting them.

It took only a second to size up the situation. If they gave up now and allowed themselves to be arrested, their lives would be lost as soon as the Corporation was through interrogating them, and their mission would be lost as well. Vandal and the others would truly be on their own.

Cleera made her decision. She raised her hands in the air, palms open and empty. In the next instant she activated circuits within her arms that caused tiny panels to pop open near her wrists and in the centers of her palms. Special mirrored disks snapped into view in both palms, angled to reflect the laser beams now flashing up from each forearm. It all happened in a heartbeat, and twin beams of deadly energy shot from her hands before any of the CorSec Guards could respond.

The human officer took a hit in his gun arm, just below the shoulder. His weapon clattered to the ground as the arm went limp and blood coursed from the wound.

The second beam struck the nearest robot guard, blasting a chunk of armor plating loose from its boxy torso, but not disabling it. Its own ray weapon flashed in answer.

Cleera was already moving aside as the beam scorched the air near her. It hit the right front helijet engine and burned deep within it, destroying the turbine and igniting fuel that spilled out into the housing. Smoke and flame began to pour from the engine like a volcano awakening.

Calling into the craft, Cleera yelled, "Everyone out! Get the crew out, too!"

HiLo, meanwhile, had ducked low and moved to one side. Disengaging his right hand and its power core from the end of his arm, he snapped it into a clamp on his hip to hold it securely out of the way, then reached to his waist, where panels were swiveling around, bringing clips of loads into view. With his left hand he grabbed a load and dropped it into the open tube of his right arm. HiLo aimed at the battle robot firing at Cleera and popped a round squarely at it.

The load whizzed out across the distance between them and hit the area of weakened armor that Cleera had struck. Detonating on impact, the concussion load virtually disintegrated the metal beneath it, and a spray of fragments and debris burst from the back of the robot. The battle rob staggered sideways, then toppled to the ground with a heavy smashing sound.

The other guards scrambled forward, seeking cover in a low ditch running between the road they had just crossed and the landing-pad area. They opened fire with their own beam weapons.

Things had happened fast within the aircraft, too. At Cleera's command, Muse reached into the cockpit and flipped switches opening the rear cargo hatch and extending the ramp. Chiron rolled out quickly, producing protoblasters and laying down a barrage of withering rays to help cover the exit of the others.

Torb emerged next, his heavy bulk providing a shield as Jayray and Jom carried the bound pilot and copilot out. Muse left the craft last, carrying what gear was left aboard.

"So much for our transportation," muttered HiLo as the helijet engine continued to burn.

"We'll have to abandon it," Cleera replied. The delicate-looking lavender-and-white psybot had retracted her palm mirrors now and was firing her lasers with her arms straight out, both hands bent up to keep them clear of the burning beams. She was moving with HiLo around the end of the aircraft and back away from the CorSec guards. "We'll find something else, if we can just get away from here!"

HiLo reached to his left waist clip and grabbed two more loads. Dropping one down his arm launcher, he rapidly lobbed it at the ditch where the CorSec Guards were. Immediately reloading, he lobbed the next round slightly farther along the ditch.

Smoke billowed as the loads struck the ground and detonated. All-obscuring smoke, laced with tear gas. The tear gas would have no effect on the robot members of the guard, but would further disable their human officer.

Cleera reached the spot where the pilot and copilot

were. Jayray and Jom were at work freeing their bonds, and Cleera quickly began removing their gags.

"You mechs are crazy!" gasped the copilot as soon as his gag was free. "First you tie us up and take over our ship, then you untie us."

"Shut up, Will," the pilot snapped, throwing an angry look in the direction of the smoke-filled ditch. "Those fools from CorSec don't care if they kill us, too."

Cleera looked around quickly, then as the last packing straps were removed from their ankles, she steered the two men toward the far side of the aircraft. "Head for the plant! Run, if you want to save yourselves!"

The pilot and copilot needed no further encouragement, stumbling forward on legs stiffened from confinement, then gaining speed as adrenaline surged through them. They rounded the cargo craft and were on their way toward the plant before the next barrage of ray fire erupted from the thick cloud of smoke along the ditch.

Cleera let out a shriek as a beam caught her in the leg, charring a fist-sized spot on her thigh and sending a brief curl of smoke up along her torso. "HiLo, I'm hit!"

The green-hued psybot grabbed for her as she tottered toward him. He put his left arm around her, then leveled his right arm toward the smoke and fired the load within it. It was another concussion round, and though it seemed to hit something in the murky smoke cloud, he could tell from the sound of the detonation that it did not hit anything solid enough to do much damage.

Another ray beam flashed, exploding the open end of HiLo's launcher arm. He swung around, positioning

Cleera behind his own body, and tried to move them both out of the line of fire.

"Fall back," Cleera shouted. "They're using scanners to see us!"

Even as she said it, more rays shot out, striking the ground near their feet, striking the side of the cargo craft, burning through the air near their heads. The psybots moved as quickly as they could, trying to place themselves on the far side of the helijet to obtain whatever cover they could. But once the CorSec battle robs emerged from the ditch the psybot team would be unable to hide for long.

Cleera leaned on HiLo, limping along with her damaged leg bent unsteadily beneath her. As she tried to see if all her team were able to move, she caught a glimpse of Torb, not falling back but moving instead toward the aircraft once more. "Torb, what are you doing?" she wailed.

The immense blue psybot lumbered on to the side of the ship. "Stopping them," he said.

Torb braced his huge feet solidly against the ground, reached out, and put his hands on the helijet's fuselage. Digging his powerful thumbs in through the lightweight metal shell, he gripped the support beams within and began to lift.

His mighty servos straining against the load, Torb slowly raised the aircraft a foot off the ground, two feet, four feet, higher. In another moment he had it over his head, and suddenly his servos and pressure pistons were shoving forward, propelling the craft sideways through the air on a final brief flight.

The ship caught ray fire as it hurtled forward, then disappeared into the cloud of murky smoke. An instant later there was a horrendous crash as the helijet smashed into the ditch.

As the reverberations echoed through the facility, bits of battle rob hardware and aircraft wreckage tumbled out of the smoke, bouncing across the hard landing pad. Then, unexpectedly, the flames from the damaged helijet engine flared and gushed violently up into the air, spreading sideways along the length of the ditch.

HiLo realized at that moment that the dull sound of his last concussion load had not meant a miss. The round had struck the fueling pump solidly enough to break the valve and send highly flammable aviation fuel gushing out onto the ground and into the ditch.

A wall of flame knifed up through the cloud of smoke, slicing it down the middle and adding more billowing coils of blacker smoke to that which was already there. Fire-alarm bells rang all over the facility, adding to the confusion.

"Chiron," Cleera called out, "pick up Torb. We need you to take us out of here."

The wheeled, centaurlike robot instantly complied, rolling up to where Torb stood and extending his heavy-duty lifting arms. Stepping back onto those arms, the bulky blue psybot positioned himself for balance, hunched down, and grabbed hold securely. Chiron lifted him far enough to achieve ground clearance, then rolled back to the others.

HiLo had already disengaged his damaged forearm section and thrown it aside, replacing it with a new unit from his pack. He snapped his right hand back in place and lifted Cleera in his arms.

Gently placing Cleera upon the horizontal portion of Chiron's back, directly behind the long psybot's upright torso, HiLo climbed up behind her. He reached down and gave Muse a hand as she swung up onto

Chiron's back, then watched to be sure Jayray and Jom made it as well.

"We're all on," said Jayray. "You may—"

"—leave when ready," finished Jom.

"Easy for you to say," muttered Chiron, turning his wheels and angling for the perimeter road under the weight of his multiple burden. He turned at the corner and accelerated down the long stretch of roadway running past the fuel-storage tanks.

They caught glimpses of heat-shielded firefighter mechs rolling out of the plant and heading for the blazing ditch. Cleera hoped the fire would not spread any farther. There was a good chance it could be contained. As she watched the thick column of smoke rising into the sky she wondered if it was visible from the other side of town, where the Prime Movers office and CorSec base were located. She also could not help wondering what their chances were now. Somehow they would have to avoid capture and find some other way of reaching Jonnersville if they were to continue their mission.

An empty CorSec vehicle came into view ahead, parked by the side of the perimeter road, bristling with weapons and communications equipment. If the human officer or any of the battle robs had survived the fire and reached the radio, or pursued them, it would not help matters any.

"Chiron," Cleera said as she clung tightly to him. "Can you take out that CorSec transport?"

"I'm carrying quite a load as it is," Chiron protested.

"No—I meant 'take out' as in disable or destroy."

"Sure," he replied, swinging a protoblaster toward it and taking aim at the interior, where armor did not protect the controls and communications gear.

But before he could fire, Cleera abruptly yelled, "Wait, stop! Don't fire!"

Chiron slowed, rotating his head back to look at her. "Are you sure it was just your leg that got hit?"

"Leave her alone," HiLo scolded. "She knows what she's doing." He leaned close to Cleera's audio receptor and whispered, "Don't you?"

"I hope so," she said softly. "It's just that I had another idea. Maybe we can use it."

She had Chiron halt alongside the vehicle, then she turned to Muse and the twinbots. "Do you think you can drive that thing?"

"Easily," said Jom. Jayray added, "We're fully vehicle-qualified."

"Then you three take it and lead the way," Cleera instructed them.

The twinbots and the exquisite golden psybot dismounted and ran to the transport. Muse slipped into the back while Jayray and Jom checked the controls for booby traps. They found a security lock on the main control panel, but disabled it and started the engine.

Backing up in a tight arc, Jayray pulled the vehicle in front of Chiron. He hesitated a moment as he spotted a CorSec uniform jacket and cap on the floor in front of the seat. He slipped it on and pulled the cap low over his eyes, then gunned the engine and started off down the road with Chiron following at the same speedy pace.

They reached the end of the perimeter road in a matter of minutes and turned right. The gate and a small guardhouse stood before them.

Jayray could see the man inside the guardhouse staring up at the billowing column of smoke rising over the far side of the complex. The man's eyes shifted to take in the approaching CorSec vehicle racing toward the gate, with what looked like a second vehicle close behind it. Jayray waved frantically for the gate to be opened, still maintaining his speed.

The guard jumped from his seat and grabbed at the switch on the control box just in time. With a soft whine of power the gate started rolling back, opening a gap which just cleared the transport's sides as it careened through without waiting for the gate to open fully. The second blur of motion out the gate was Chiron, with Torb, Cleera, and HiLo hanging on for dear life.

The guard stared after them for a long moment, a puzzled look on his face. Then he pulled the switch to close the gate and returned his worried gaze to the smoke and flame behind the row of storage tanks.

"Not bad," said HiLo. "But that CorSec transport is eventually going to attract the wrong kind of attention."

"I know," Cleera replied. "I'm not planning to use it all the way to Jonnersville, just a little while longer. We're going to need something more enclosed, anyway."

"Sounds reasonable. Any idea where we might find something like that in Troy?"

Cleera rubbed at the charred spot on her damaged leg. "It may not sound very leaderlike, but at the moment your guess is as good as mine. I think the best thing we can do is head away from this area as fast as we can, and avoid the center of town." She turned toward him, and her voice acquired a warmth it sometimes lacked when she was preoccupied with the responsibilities of leadership. "And thanks, HiLo, for everything back there."

"We're a team, aren't we?"

"Yes, we certainly are." She hesitated, her tone

becoming sober. "But if we can't repair my leg I won't be much use to the team. You may have to leave me behind and go on with somebody else in charge. I—"

"Hey," HiLo interrupted, "we're not just machines you can throw away when something gets broken. We're better than that. At least, I think I am. And I know you are. Besides, I'm sure the damage is repairable."

Cleera looked forward once more. "I hope so. This doesn't look like the sort of place I'd want to spend a lot of time."

"Well," said Muse, "it's not pretty, but it's functional. You want to try it out?"

Cleera looked down at the spot on her leg where the laser beam had cut into it. A round patch of metal sheeting had been set in place with epoxy to cover the hole. Beneath it, Muse and HiLo had repaired the limb's control circuits and welded a brace across the damaged internal supporting structure with a tiny acetylene torch.

Cleera had not wanted to watch as they worked on the leg. Even though she knew full well what she was and how her various systems operated, she still felt ill at ease seeing her inner workings exposed to view. Seeing the raw metal and cables and circuit boards laid open beneath what had been a beautifully painted outer surface was just so—the only word she could find in her programmed vocabulary was "dehumanizing," and that of course was inappropriate.

At that moment, the sound of a helijet grew overhead and everyone listened, wondering if it was a CorSec ship looking for them. It continued on, and the engine whine faded in the distance.

The psybot team had taken refuge in a deserted

vehicle-repair garage at the southern end of town, choosing as they had done in CityPrime a neighborhood with few people around to notice them. The place was greasy and dirty, with a few tools and parts left behind. It was anything but comfortable, but it did at least offer them shelter.

With HiLo's steadying hand, Cleera got to her feet, still gazing sadly down at the ugly patch on her thigh. "Everything was so nice and new," she said softly. "Josh would be angry with me."

"Take a few steps," Muse encouraged her.

Cleera did as she was told, and found the leg now held her weight with ease, as it had before. She moved forward and back several times, then balanced on her other foot so she could flex the leg. Finally, she seemed satisfied with the results.

"The feedback from it feels a little different, somehow," she told them. "But otherwise it works just fine. Muse, HiLo, you both did a great job. Thank you."

"Our pleasure," said Muse. "Believe me, if there's one thing a dancer knows the importance of maintaining, it's the legs. That little cosmetic problem you can solve the next time you're back on Avalon."

"Avalon!" Cleera said with a start. "I'm glad you reminded me. I need to contact the Uni and give them an update. Perhaps they've heard something from Vandal, and haven't been able to reach us because they don't know where to aim the T-beam."

Using her internal gyroscopic circuits, Cleera positioned herself so that her built-in antenna focused on the point in space where Avalon and the University facility were located. Then she quickly formulated her message and beamed it into hyperspace. A minute passed before the return message was received and made itself felt in her mind.

She turned back to Muse and HiLo. "All right, that's done. I've let them know what's happened so far, and they're pleased we've covered this much ground already. No further word from Vandal and the others yet, but when they do make contact the Uni will let them know we're on our way and getting closer."

"We're not getting closer right now," Torb said abruptly.

Cleera shot him a questioning look. There was a critical edge to Torb's remark, and she found it both irritating and hurtful. "We will be," she said firmly. "That's the next order of business."

HiLo put the repair kit back in his pack and said, "I saw a truck yard on the way here. We could go back there after dark."

"Yes, I saw that, too," Cleera replied. "But I'm not sure we can afford to wait until dark. The CorSec Guards are going to be searching the town for us. Besides, I would rather not steal a vehicle from a business if we can possibly avoid it. We commandeered that cargo aircraft and that turned out rather badly."

Torb lumbered forward. "Are you blaming that on me?"

Cleera shook her head. "No, Torb. You did what you had to do, and I'm sure you saved our lives. The fire was an unfortunate accident. It's nobody's fault. I just want to limit the amount of destruction we do along the way."

Jayray and Jom were standing by a window in the back wall of the garage, looking outside. Jayray turned and called over to the others, "Hey, you might want to come look at this."

Chiron, who was keeping watch near the front, stayed where he was, but Cleera and the rest walked back to join the twinbots. They cautiously peered through the greasy, dirt-streaked window.

There was a parking area, empty of course, behind the garage building itself. Beyond that ran a street partially shaded from the afternoon sun by a long factory building with peeling paint and broken windows. It was what stood parked at the end of that street that had aroused the twinbots' interest.

A long transport truck that looked none too new was at the corner of the block, emblazoned with colors once garish but now faded. Painted with an artful hand were banners with ornate lettering flowing across them, and a scroll-like border around the edges of the truck. There were flowers and rainbow-hued birds, glowing suns and sly, winking moons, blue comets and green stars, and a host of strange fantastical creatures not likely to have been seen on any known planet. Arcing high across the long side of the truck's elaborately painted paneling was a row of tarnished gold-and-black letters which proudly proclaimed this name:

DR. ARCANUS & HIS TRAVELING AUTOMATED MAGIC SHOW!

Words on a banner beneath this advertised the show as a "Wondrous Cornucopia of Magical, Mystical, Mechanical Marvels, Certain to Thrill and Confound Even the Most Jaded of Spectators!" There were other words on the truck of a similar nature, and even in their present faded state their grandiose spectacle dwarfed and overshadowed the small figure stooped by the vehicle's rear wheels.

"What a bizarre vehicle," said Torb.

"What a wonderful vehicle," was Muse's response. "Especially if it can get us out of here."

"Yes," Jayray replied. "Exactly what—"

"—we were thinking." Jom pointed to the man bent by the rear wheels, one of which was off its axle. "But he does seem to be having trouble."

HiLo remarked in a humorous tone, "He must be running low on magic. From the looks of it, he could certainly use a mechanical marvel or two right now."

"Yes," said Cleera as she studied the situation. "Perhaps he can at that."

The man continued to work even as their footsteps came up behind him, struggling with the wheel, grunting mightily and cursing under his breath. Then he suddenly became aware of the presence of someone—or something—near. He threw a glance over his shoulder, then quickly rose to standing position.

Tall, gaunt, white-headed, he seemed old at first, almost frail. And yet a certain energy appeared to crackle beneath his skin and flash from his eyes. He raised an eyebrow as he looked at Cleera, HiLo, and Torb standing close to him. Then he looked both ways down the street and peered as if wondering who else was with them.

Cleera spoke first. "Do you need some help with your truck?"

The old man glanced cautiously once more in all directions. "Maybe." He studied Cleera and the other two with a cold and discerning eye. "And just who might you three be?"

"Friends," Cleera told him. "Friends who could use some help as well as give it. Perhaps we can assist each other?"

The man rubbed his chin thoughtfully. "Depends on what kind of help you need. And on what kind of help you can give. Do you think you can fix a broken wheel?"

HiLo looked at the wheel on the ground and measured it visually. "I think so. There are still some wheels and hardware in the garage back there."

"I don't have a jack," added the old man.

"That is no problem," replied Torb.

"Well, then," said the man, "if you can get this decrepit conveyance rolling once more, I, the great and world-renowned Dr. Arcanus, master of illusion and mechanized prestidigitation, shall be in your debt, and do here and now give you my solemn word that I shall help and assist you and your friends in any way that is practically possible and reasonably convenient."

Cleera gave a small laugh, and there was a smile in her voice as she said, "I don't see how we could turn down a deal like that. But we'd better hurry. HiLo, go get what you need for the repair."

"Gladly."

HiLo returned in a matter of minutes with a new wheel and a handful of nuts. Working quickly, he removed the firm-core tire from the old wheel and secured it around the new one. Then with Torb raising the truck slightly, HiLo slipped the new wheel in place and spun the nuts tightly upon the threaded posts. He checked the remaining wheels and tires to be sure there were no other breakdowns imminent. Although the truck was not in great shape, he found that it was at least roadworthy.

"There," HiLo told him when he was done. "It's ready to roll."

"Miraculous," Dr. Arcanus replied. "Truly miraculous. I thank you for your help."

"And you will help us?" Cleera asked. "We need transportation to Jonnersville."

"Jonnersville?" Arcanus rubbed his chin. "Why, yes, I suppose that would be a suitable city for my next public performance. Troy has certainly shown a remarkable lack of cultural cognizance and appreciation for the higher arts. Yes, I can take you and your friends to Jonnersville."

Cleera extended her hand to him. "Excellent." To HiLo she said, "Go and get the others."

Arcanus abruptly froze in the midst of his handshake, watching HiLo run back to the garage. "Others? There are more than the three of you?"

"Only four more," Cleera said. "And I assure you, most of us take up relatively little room."

Arcanus smiled wryly. He concluded the handshake and gave a courtly bow. "Very well, then. Dr. Arcanus does not go back on his word. And I must say it is a pleasure to meet such a delightful psychogenetic robot."

"You know, then?"

"My dear young automaton, how could I be who I am and not know? I assume, then, that you are here on behalf of a certain well-known educational institution, and that you are in some kind of trouble?"

"You assume correctly. Do you still want to help, even under those conditions?"

"Why, yes, of course." Arcanus raised his hand in a graceful and mildly theatrical gesture. "I have no great love for the powers that be on this planet. A bit of adventure might be fun at this point in my life. If caught, I can always plead feeblemindedness. But tell me, what made you think you could trust a stranger like me?"

Cleera pointed to the garishly painted truck behind him. "I knew that whoever was responsible for that was gifted with both imagination and a flair for the dramatic. From what I have seen, humans loyal to the

Corporation tend to be a fairly boring and uninspired lot."

Arcanus laughed heartily. "Well said, my metal friend. Well said indeed. Now we had better see about making room in the back of my truck." He hesitated as he saw Chiron, Muse, and the twinbots returning with HiLo. "Quite a lot of room, it seems."

Because of their size, Chiron and Torb waited out of sight between the truck and the building while the other psybots investigated the truck's interior. Dr. Arcanus led the way between the magic-show props which filled the cramped cargo area. There were flats and sets and curtains, and a shabby proscenium arch, broken down into sections, for a makeshift stage. Stage lights were clamped to metal pipes running back and forth overhead, and there were control panels, electrical generators, pneumatic lifts, and trapdoors.

There were also the standard magical props—trunks and cabinets, skinny little tables with frilly covers, flashy boxes of chrome and acrylic, and other special gear, all looking a bit knocked about and travel-worn. The most dilapidated of all the things stored within the truck were the principal performers in Dr. Arcanus's show.

The collection of robots—perhaps twelve in all—looked old. Even antique, by modern standards. The paint was chipped on most, with rust showing through here and there. On some, arms hung by the barest of connections, and on others, the eyes were crossed, or falling out of their sockets.

HiLo stared at it all in dismay. "Dr. Arcanus, how long has it been since you've upgraded your equipment?"

"A while," he replied. "Quite a long while, actually. I once had the finest of equipment, and I played all the big cities. Even visited some of the outlying worlds. But . . ." He sighed, seeming to wilt a bit as memories flooded back. "But then the plague years came and conditions got worse. Survival became more important than entertainment, and my income suffered for it. I couldn't afford new equipment. Do you have any idea how much new robotic parts cost these days? Well, yes, of course. You must."

Cleera took it all in—the props, the old and broken-down robots, and Arcanus himself. Then she said, "Perhaps we can help you out in a way that will aid us all. But we will have to make some room back here."

"All right," replied Arcanus. "There are some things here I can get rid of, even a number of these unrepairable robots. I've only hung on to them for purely sentimental reasons, and in case I needed to sell some of their parts for food money. Yes, there are at least four or five that are beyond saving, whose parts are worthless. Those I can leave behind."

"That would work out well with what I have in mind," Cleera said. She picked up a ragged piece of canvas from a case beside her. "HiLo, we can put this tarp over what we remove from the truck and let Torb or Chiron carry it over to the garage. There should be enough room for us."

She now turned to the twinbots. "Jayray, Jom, on that CorSec transport, did that security device have provision for alerting their base?"

"Yes," Jayray answered. "There was a standard alarm and tracer-beacon circuit."

"Which we disconnected," Jom added.

"Good," Cleera replied. "Do you think you could reconnect it, and quickly rig up some way to operate both it and the drive controls by remote control?"

After a moment's thought, Jom said, "Why, yes.

That's easy enough. Actually, we saw a remote-drive-control unit already in the vehicle. It would not take—"

"—much work to splice the alarm circuit into one of its functions," Jayray finished enthusiastically.

"That will be your job, then, while we get things ready here," she told them. "And Muse, since you know about show business, perhaps you can help Dr. Arcanus decide how best we might fit in here. If my idea works, we could just be on our way."

The garishly painted truck rumbled along the road, heading for the city limits of Troy. There was only one road going southwest, and there was little cover. That was why they could see the CorSec roadblock for at least a mile before they reached it.

Dr. Arcanus put the brakes on gradually and slowly pulled to a halt before the temporary barricade. Opening the truck cab's door, he stepped down to the ground and smiled at the approaching CorSec Guards.

"Good afternoon, gentlemen. What's the problem here?"

"Who are you?" demanded one of the two human guards. Two CorSec battle robs stood waiting by the barrier itself, their weapons ready.

"The one and only, world-renowned Dr. Arcanus," he said with a bow. "Master of illusion and—"

"Some sort of stage act," interrupted the other guard. "Where are you heading?"

"Why, to my next performance, of course," Arcanus replied with a grand flourish. "I have a number of engagements lined up in various cities. Perhaps you fine gentlemen have seen my wondrous show during one of its performances here in Troy?"

"No," said the first guard. "Let's have a look in your truck."

179

"Why certainly, gentlemen. I am at your service."

Arcanus led them around to the back of the truck, past the ornately painted sign panels describing his show, and reached up to struggle with the latches. "Excuse me—I am not quite as young as I used to be," he apologized. Then at last he succeeded in releasing the doors and slowly tugged them open.

The two CorSec Guards stretched up to peer inside, studying the stage props and gear within the truck. Then their eyes fell upon the dozen or so robots mixed in with the other items. The first guard stepped up on the tailgate rung and climbed inside.

"Let's check this out," he told the other man.

The second guard and Dr. Arcanus followed him up into the truck's interior, and they stood in what little space there was near the back. Arcanus continued to smile, but glanced quickly about the truck, hoping they had forgotten nothing.

Torb and Chiron were still hidden from view behind some stage flats and a large cabinet. Most of the remaining psybots were in plain view, though, mixed in among Arcanus's own robot performers.

The first guard used the cramped aisle to step back into the truck. He looked at the silent robots sitting or standing there on either side, and noticed the dilapidated condition of most of them. "There are some real junkers in here. Do any of these things really work?"

"Yes!" enthused Arcanus, then with a shrug he added, "Well, most of them do, some of the time."

The guard's eyes came to rest on HiLo. The green psybot was seated upon a crate, and had smeared a fine coating of dust and grease over his normally shiny surfaces. HiLo quietly released latches within his elbow joint. His lower arm fell off and clattered onto the floor of the truck.

The guard shook his head in disgust and moved on, past two more of Arcanus's own machines. He next stopped before Jayray. "What about this one—does it work?"

Jayray was standing still, wearing long strips of gray patching tape as if his housing were cracked. He found himself exerting considerable effort to resist the temptation to throw up his hands in the guard's face and yell "Boo!" as he had seen human children do. A warning voice in his head from Jom reminded him just how foolish that would be.

Arcanus, as if sensing the potential for disaster, moved forward along the narrow aisle and reached Jayray's side. "Why, certainly. Allow me to demonstrate."

Arcanus reached behind Jayray's back to an imaginary button and said, "There, I've activated it." Nothing happened at first, and the ancient-looking showman gave Jayray a whack on the shoulder.

Jayray lurched forward and blurted out, "Thank you, ladies and gentlemen. And now, for our next act . . . act . . . act . . . act . . ."

Arcanus gave him another whack, then as the psybot leaned back and fell silent he shrugged apologetically to the guard. "A minor technical problem, I assure you."

The guard gave a dismal grunt and turned to look elsewhere. As he did, Cleera reached down to the sheltered area next to her and activated the remote-control device the twinbots had brought with them from the CorSec transport. She flipped a switch, and back in the garage the vehicle's lights came on and the engine started. Wired across those lights was a line to the alarm and tracer circuit, and both began functioning as well. Cleera imagined that guards manning radio equipment at the CorSec base would be jumping out of their seats with the signals abruptly coming in.

Next she pressed buttons causing the transport to shift into forward drive and accelerate. A tiny videoscreen in the remote-control unit gave her a view ahead of the transport, and she successfully steered it out of the garage and down the street, in the opposite direction from where they now were. She could not see them, but knew that an assortment of Arcanus's unfixable robots now sat in the seats of the vehicle as if actually in control. Illusion is everything in a magic act.

A moment later, an alert signal buzzed from the CorSec vehicle parked by the barricade. A voice blared over the radio: "This is Command Headquarters. The criminals have been located. Repeat, the criminals have been located. All units proceed to South Sector Five at once."

The first guard jerked around at the sound of the radio message and hurried back to the rear of the truck. "Come on," he told the other man. "We're wasting our time here. What we're looking for is back in town."

The men hastily climbed down from the truck and started for their vehicle. Arcanus followed, farther back, calling after them.

"Gentlemen, is it all right, then, for me to be on my way?"

"Yes, you old fool," bellowed the first guard as he and his fellow soldier threw the barricade into the back of the vehicle. "You can take your rolling rubbish heap and get out of here!"

The battle robs got in last, and then the vehicle started up. It sped off down the road to the city, raising a cloud of dust behind it.

"Old fool, am I?" muttered Arcanus with a broad grin. "There's no fool like a young fool, I always say."

He hurried around to the back of the truck once more, moving with less difficulty this time. Looking inside, he announced, "They're gone!"

Still working the switches of the remote-control device, Cleera made the CorSec transport angle down another street and accelerate even more. It took no more than a minute for another transport filled with guards and weapons to come into view ahead. She swiftly worked the controls and sent the vehicle she commanded turning wildly away from it.

The tiny videoscreen showed flashes of ray fire scorching past the decoy vehicle as it sped along. Then there was an abrupt and terribly intense flash, and the remote-control unit's screen went dark.

Two seconds later, a muted, thundering BOOM ebbed out from the city, from the part of town where the chase had been. Seconds after that, a small fireball rose skyward over Troy, trailing smoke and raining debris.

"So much for that," said Cleera, switching off the remote-control unit and moving to join the others. "Now I think we'd better get out of here. Jayray, I think it might be good if you ride up front with Dr. Arcanus. That way, if there's trouble, Jom can let us know back here."

"Right, Cleera," agreed the twinbots in tandem.

Arcanus was already closing and latching the rear doors. As he hurried forward to the cab, HiLo reattached his dropped arm and approached Cleera.

He braced himself against one of the props as the truck started forward. "You did just great," he told Cleera.

"No," she said. "We all did."

"How soon, do you think, before they catch on?"

"Never, if we're lucky," Cleera told him. "Maybe a few hours, if we're not. In the meantime, all we can do is hope for the best, and head for Jonnersville as fast as we can."

15:

SECURITY BREACH

SUNLIGHT STREAMED INTO THE main dome of Avalon's University complex, unimpeded by clouds or atmosphere, and would have been even more intense were it not for the filtering layer coating the dome material. Its warmth, its angle, the crisp shadows it cast compared to artificial light, all announced that day was beginning on the airless moon of Logres.

Birds in the complex's several small aviaries also announced the fact, their exotic songs and cries filling the air. Food facilities in the area added the pleasant smells of breakfast, and there was an awakening quality to the flow of people into the campus center.

Some of those people were gathering in the spacious lobby of the University's main complex. Wearing normal business attire, or in some cases modified ethnic costumes from their various planets, all the members of the group had identification badges fastened to their clothing.

Rasp and Cudder were no exception. Both wore the badges supplied them by Dixon, and both were dressed in what they hoped was proper academic attire for the event. Of the two, Rasp looked less comfortable in his disguise. Cudder resembled an overgrown athlete turned middle-aged coach and professor.

"I don't like this," Rasp said under his breath as he stood in line with Cudder. He shifted his shoulders uneasily in his jacket and glanced at his reflection in a glossy pillar next to him. His hair had been combed neatly back, and the sight of it brought a smirk to his lips. "This kind of masquerade isn't my style. My talents lie in more, how shall I say, direct methods."

"How well I know," Cudder softly replied. "Try to think of this as a challenge. A way of expanding your professional horizons."

"You can expand your horizons if you want to, but me, I plan to retire after this project."

Cudder sighed inwardly. "We'll see."

The line they were in steadily moved closer to a registration table, positioned beneath a banner welcoming the visiting delegates. As they moved forward again, an attractive young woman with long brown hair came into view. She was wearing a perky bright-yellow business suit with a University staff badge. She finished with the person in front of them and turned to face Cudder and Rasp.

"Hi!" she said, a warm cheerful smile lighting up her face. "Welcome to Avalon. My name's Jenna."

Rasp forced a smile to his lips and nodded. Cudder smiled back warmly, his muscular face actually becoming somewhat pleasant.

"Pleased to meet you, Jenna," Cudder replied. "I think you'll find my friend and me listed together— Derwent and Oglethorpe?"

The young woman checked the display on the computer tablet she held cradled on her arm. "Yes, I see your names here. You're Mr. . .?"

"Derwent," said Cudder. "My friend is Oglethorpe."

Rasp flashed an icy glare toward his partner, then jerked the look away as Jenna glanced up from her screen. He smiled benignly.

"Well," said Jenna. "I'm glad you could both make it. Are you new with the organization?"

Cudder nodded pleasantly, remembering the cover story provided in Dixon's information. "Yes, we recently joined the survey station orbiting Anostus."

"How interesting," Jenna replied, and made it sound as if she meant it. "Just let me read your badges and you'll be all set."

She lifted the reader wand from her tablet and quickly scanned across the dark strip running horizontally along the bottom of each of their identification badges. Her computer tablet made a series of fast, high-pitched bleeping sounds and then spewed out a slip of paper with printing on it for each man.

"Here," Jenna told them, "just give these to the woman at the registration desk and she'll give you your briefing folders. It was nice meeting you, and if I can be of any help during the conference, just ask."

Rasp and Cudder moved on to the table and presented their slips of paper. After they were given their folders they stepped over to a table where pastries and coffee were placed for the delegates.

Rasp picked up a pastry, scowling at it disdainfully, and grumbled, "I hate perky broads."

"Who, Jenna? She's a nice kid." Cudder picked up a cup of coffee and sipped at it. "Besides, the type you like won't be found around this place."

"You got that right." He glanced at the various delegates in the lobby. All were busy talking to friends and associates, or being introduced to others. None were close enough to hear their conversation. "At least the stuff Dixon gave us got us in this far."

"Yeah," replied Cudder, examining his badge closely. "And that thing Jenna did with her computer wasn't just to assign us briefing folders or register us, although I'm sure it did that as well."

"What do you mean?"

"That scanner checked the coding on our badges against the University's own computer records, just to verify we're on the up and up. Dixon did a good job of it."

"He should," Rasp grunted, "for what we're paying him."

Cudder ignored the remark and went on. "I'd be willing to bet that our badge codings are now entered into the security computer, along with those of the other delegates Jenna checked in. That means scanners throughout the facility will be able to tell if a delegate is straying from the areas open to the conference and entering a restricted area."

Rasp shook his head. "Swell. That means these things are good enough to get us in, but will keep us from going where we want to go. It also means their security system can keep track of us every step of the way. What kind of help is that?"

"It beats standing outside, trying to break into a well-protected system. Besides, although these things can be a hindrance, they can also be exploited. If we stash them in some auditorium during a speech, or slip them into some other delegate's pocket, then that's where the security system thinks we are."

"Yeah." Rasp's eyes began to twinkle at the possibilities. "And if we appropriate the badges from some staff people here, we can move around as we please without setting off alarms. Cudder, I may have been wrong about you. You've got a good head for these things."

"Thanks," Cudder replied with lukewarm appreciation. "Now, we're going to have to pay attention to the badges people are wearing. Look, ours and the other delegates' are white with orange trim. Jenna's badge was silver with red trim, and I think I saw someone on staff that had a completely gold badge."

"So, they're color-coded as well as scanner-coded," Rasp said. "The big shots can come and go as they please."

"Yes. And probably so can anyone who happens to be wearing or carrying one of their badges."

Rasp was silent for a moment. Finally he said, "All right. We've memorized the layout of the complex, so we shouldn't have any trouble finding our way to the research section. All we have to do is play along, find out what we can about where the conference activities are and who has access to the restricted areas, and then make our move."

Cudder opened his briefing folder and flipped through the papers inside. The conference schedule caught his eye. "We can start with this," he told Rasp. "Look, there's even a diagram showing where the meeting rooms are located."

"How thoughtful of them." Rasp smiled, making his narrow features look especially weasel-like. "All we have to do is superimpose the rest of the layout on this to see how close we can get to the research area. Then"—he smiled more broadly, but it was a hard and wicked smile that spoke of dark, murderous thoughts— "we can make use of some of my special talents."

A short while later, Dean McAndrews looked up from his desk computer screen as a splash of bright yellow entered his peripheral vision. He smiled reflexively as his assistant, Jenna, breezed into his office with a cheery wave.

"Back again," she said. "Sorry to disturb you."

He flashed her a wry look. "Maybe I should have signed up for this conference myself. You know, I only lent you out to the Advanced Studies Department because Dr. Westfield practically got down on his hands and knees and begged me for 'that charming young lady who's so good with people.' "

She rolled her eyes. "Had I but known how much of my time this thing would take . . ."

"How's it going so far?"

"About average for these things," Jenna replied. "Lots of work. Lots of nice people. A few strange people. Some that are a little of each." She scratched her head, glancing down at her computer tablet. "Only thing that puzzles me is that I thought I had been told to expect two hundred and thirty-seven delegates. We seem to have two hundred and thirty-nine."

McAndrews looked back to his computer. "There are always last-minute additions or cancellations."

"True. Oh, well. I probably got the numbers confused." Jenna walked over to her desk and opened the lower drawer. She took out her purse and slung its strap over her shoulder, then glanced at McAndrews's computer screen as she started past him. "Hear anything new about Vandal?"

"No, and I'm getting worried. I've got a report there that came in a short while ago from Communications. A T-beam transmission from Cleera."

"Good for her. And shame on Vandal. Just like a man not to remember to call."

McAndrews glanced up with a bemused look. "Umhmm. But this could be serious, Jenna. They're in the desert, which is bad enough to begin with. And I know the Corporation must have forces out looking for them."

Her smile faded, and she leaned forward to put a hand on his drooping shoulder. "I know that. And I'm just as concerned as you are. I just thought I could cheer you up a little. Look," she said softly, "you know how good Vandal is, and you of all people should know how good Cleera and her team of psybots are. They'll make it. All of them."

"I know they're good. I also know how stubborn Vandal can be. But you're right. They've got a better chance than most would have, under those conditions. We also have our ace in the hole, if it comes to it."

"The Prometheus?"

McAndrews nodded. "But we'll cross that bridge when we come to it. Now, you'd better stop trying to prop up an old sourpuss like me and get back to your guests."

"Please! Don't I deserve at least a little break from all that smiling and handshaking?" Jenna gave him a hug and started for the door. "I'll check by again a little later, okay?"

"I'll count on it," he told her warmly. He waved as she left the office, then returned his attention to the report on his computer. He could not help thinking that Westfield was absolutely right. Jenna was good with people.

He frowned slightly as another thought intruded. Jenna was not only good with people, she was also seldom wrong about facts and figures. It seemed unlikely she had made a mistake about the number of delegates in attendance. And if she was right, was the discrepancy something he should be worried about?

16:

CITY OF DEATH

MARINDA AWOKE WITH A start as a shriek of sound cut through the silence. She jerked fully upright in her seat and looked quickly about, trying to see where she was. It took a moment for her vision to clear, and for the lights and shadows around her to take shape and become recognizable as the shuttle car's interior. Now, in addition to being alarmed, she was also disappointed. She had been dreaming about Earth and her friends there, and those comforting images faded as the cold reality of where she was, what she had been through, and how much danger she was still in came flooding back.

The shrieking sound came again, but this time it was softer, more muted. It seemed to surround them.

"What's wrong?" Marinda asked.

"The brakes," Roddi replied. "They need work. Probably a little stiff."

Marinda rubbed her arms and stretched. "Aren't we all." She glanced at Roddi in the faint illumination of the shuttle car and found the psybot's familiar appearance and voice comforting. Then as the brakes shrieked again she felt a strong sense of deceleration. "Why are we stopping?"

Vandal's dry masculine voice came from her other side. "I think we're about to reach the end of the line."

"Kezos City?" Marinda's eyes went to the glowing red screen on the panel before them. There did indeed seem to be some sort of opening ahead in the tunnel, but she could make out no details beyond that. She stretched again. "How long have we been riding in this thing?"

"Oh," said Roddi, "about five hours, fourteen minutes, and a dozen or so seconds, as of the moment you asked."

"I slept longer than I realized," Marinda said with a sigh. "I seem to be making a habit of that. Well, at least we're finally reaching civilization. What's Kezos City like?"

"I wish I knew," replied Roddi. "Have you ever been there, Vandal?"

"Not in a very long while." The cyborg agent seemed unusually grim. He reached for the weapons packs. "We'd better be ready."

The shuttle car continued to slow as it neared the portal at the end of the tunnel, then in a few minutes it passed through the portal and emerged in the chamber beyond. At least, the image on the small glowing screen indicated they had. It was hard to be certain otherwise, for the chamber had no lights at all. Unlike the one beneath the research station in Delta Zone, this chamber was a pit of total darkness.

They felt the shuttle car come to a halt, and the motors became quiet. The place was dark and silent, with only a small amount of floor on either side of the shuttle illuminated by its interior lights.

"Apparently," observed Roddi, "they don't have

any solar batteries hooked up at this station, and the regular power is switched off."

"If there is any," said Vandal. He took one of the portalights and aimed it out the shuttle window, thumbing the switch on.

The spot of ghostly light crept along the floor and up the wall as Vandal slowly turned the portalight to encompass as much of the chamber as he could, first from one side of the shuttle car and then the other. The beam revealed a low boarding platform and a spiral stair leading up to the ceiling, but there was no airlock here, no showers and no second rail line running out. From this station there was only one place to go, one place to come back from—Delta Zone. There was one other difference, as well. At the far end of the chamber, opposite the side where the spiral stair rose, a simple ladder ascended to what looked like an air vent high overhead.

There was no sign of people, CorSec Guards or anyone else. Indeed, there was not even a place for them to hide here.

Vandal released the latch and slid the door back. "May as well get out."

He stepped outside, the portalight still in his hand and a ray pistol ready. As he disappeared around the side of the car, Marinda approached the open door, looking into the murk. Roddi came up beside her and turned the other portalight on.

Marinda noticed the hand Roddi held the portalight with was steady. She leaned around to look at his damaged shoulder. "Did you repair yourself while I was asleep?"

"Only partially," the psybot told her. "I plugged in a new control circuit for my arm, which stopped most of the tremor and malfunctioning. A better job will have to wait until later."

"Why didn't you wake me? I could have helped."

"Ah, well. You needed your rest, and anyway, I'm afraid my internal workings are rather boring compared to my sparkling personality."

Vandal came back around the corner and thrust Marinda's clothing into her hands. "Here—there are some wrinkles where they were tied to the handrail, but they're dry now. You can change in the car. Roddi, maybe you can find something to do out here?"

"What? Oh, yes, of course. Excuse me." He eased past Marinda and joined Vandal outside, muttering, "Not that it really makes any difference to me, mind you."

Marinda smiled to herself and took her garments to the rear of the shuttle. She noticed a narrow door in the back wall of the passenger compartment and discovered it opened into a tiny, cramped lavatory, not unlike those she had seen in commercial airliners back on Earth. After she had changed, she combed her fingers through her hair and touched up her face. Then she rolled up her coveralls for possible future use and tucked them into one of the packs.

Marinda picked up the remaining two packs that Vandal and Roddi had not yet removed and went to the doorway to peer cautiously out. She saw Vandal was already changed and was checking his weapons and gear. She stepped on out and put the two packs down beside the others. The air felt noticeably cooler outside the shuttle car, and as she went back for the water containers she put Vandal's spare cloak back around her.

Vandal stepped in past her and cut the power on the control panel. The interior lights and readouts faded, leaving his portalight the only source of illumination. "All right, let's go."

Playing the beams before them, the three advanced across the platform toward the spiral metal stairs. As they started up, the sound of their footsteps echoed harshly through the large and empty chamber.

They reached the top of the stairs and emerged in a dark room. Playing their beams around it, they saw unpainted concrete walls, tables with old and dusty equipment, and a number of crates with faded shipping labels.

"Looks like the cellar of some large building," said Roddi.

Vandal turned and swept his light along the other side. "It also looks like we're not going to get out this way."

The others saw what he meant. They had seen no doors anywhere else in the room, and Vandal's beam revealed what was left of a set of stairs leading up to the rest of the building. But the stairs were now impassable. Part of the upper wall and ceiling was collapsed, with heavy concrete beams and rubble completely blocking the steps and spilling down onto the cellar floor.

Marinda frowned at the damage. "It's as if a bomb hit this place."

"One probably did," said Vandal, drawing them back to the spiral stairs. "We're going to have to try another way out."

"Wait." Marinda hurried down the stairs, trying to keep up with him. "What do you mean, one probably did? A real bomb?"

Vandal did not slow any, directing his words over his shoulder as he descended. "Yes, a real bomb. Back in the plague years, fighting and food riots broke out in some cities. And not all the weapons were in the hands of the CorSec Guards."

"How terrible."

"That's not the worst of it. The panic got so bad in one city that a small nuclear weapon was inadvertently set off. Even now there are some cities that have never recovered from the destruction and the horror. Cities that fell into barbarism."

Marinda arched an eyebrow and glanced overhead. "And Kezos City?"

Vandal did not reply. He reached the bottom of the stairs and led them across the floor of the broad chamber, his portalight throwing a long oval ahead of them. Once on the far side, he paused at the base of the ladder and directed his beam up along the rungs to the narrow opening high overhead.

"If it's not blocked," said Vandal, "we may be able to get out this way."

Marinda tilted her head back farther and farther to take in the length of the climb. "Oh my, I've never been excessively fond of ladders."

"Frankly," Roddi muttered, "climbing them has never been very high on my list of favorite activities, either."

"Come on," Vandal commanded, slinging the pack straps well back upon his shoulders and starting up the ladder.

"Oh well," Marinda sighed. "I suppose it's better than staying down here in the dark."

"Don't worry," Roddi told her, adjusting his own pack straps. "I'll follow you, in case you slip."

Marinda started climbing, and hoped sincerely that she would not slip, for she doubted that the well-intentioned psybot would be able to catch her and hold on to the ladder himself. The image of them both flailing together through the air on a collision course with the floor was just too grim to dwell upon, so she concentrated on wrapping each sweating palm around the appropriate rung and placing each foot securely.

The ladder was every bit as tall as it looked, and even after they reached the ceiling and entered the narrow opening there, they found there was still another fifteen feet of ladder to traverse within the tube-like air vent itself. This at last yielded access to a small room, apparently at ground level, for a faint light came in through frosted windows at the front and back.

Vandal and Roddi switched off their lights and looked around. There were two shelves on each side wall, one low, the other higher. A long box sat upon each, and there was no paint on the plain stone walls. Air from outside came in through slits near the roof.

Marinda frowned oddly at the spartan look of the place. Not that she had expected an air vent and emergency exit to have anything more to it than this, but it did seem unusually plain. It also seemed vaguely familiar.

Vandal moved to the door and found a heavy-duty latch. There was also a small device, apparently triggered by the door's opening, with wires running down to conduit in the vent tube.

"An alarm sensor?" Roddi ventured.

"Yeah," Vandal replied, throwing the bolt on the latch. "But there's no power to work it, and no one to hear it anyway. Let's get out of here."

He could see nothing through the frosted-glass panel, so he pulled the solid metal door open. It creaked on hinges much in need of oil. Peering out, he quickly scanned what lay outside, then, opening the door wider, he slipped out with his pistol drawn and ready.

Roddi followed him out, with Marinda close at his

heels. An eerie breeze swept over them, stirring their cloaks and rustling small bits of debris upon the ground, then fading as quickly as it had begun.

It was dusk, and the fading light revealed a setting that was in its own way as bleak and forlorn as the desert had been. Black ironwork fences formed small rectangles, and row upon row of stone markers stretched in all directions. Miniature Greek temples and plain boxy structures dotted the hilly terrain, with paths winding between.

Her eyes widening in realization, Marinda whirled about and saw what the small building they had just emerged from truly was. A crypt!

"This is a cemetery," she said abruptly, and she found her own words as chilling as the revelation.

"Welcome to Coreworld," Roddi observed with dry wit. "One delightful place after another. How ironic that they should have chosen a graveyard as one of the access points to their plague-virus-testing facility."

Vandal pointed to a nearby building whose entire eastern half had been demolished. It appeared to have been an office and mausoleum. "That must be the main entrance, where we tried to get out. A stray bomb must have got to it."

Marinda pulled her cloak tighter about her. "Do you think we could manage to leave here before it gets any darker?"

"You're a woman of science," Roddi said playfully. "Surely you're not worried about ghosts?"

"Well, no, but . . ."

"There are worse things than ghosts here," Vandal grimly observed. "Come on, we'd better head into town and see if there are any working vehicles left."

Marinda was eager to do just that, and was pleased

to find Vandal in agreement. His cryptic words about "worse things" were not at all reassuring, though.

They started down the slight incline from the crypt and took the path which seemed to lead most directly to the front gate. There were no trees in this place either, only holes in the ground where trees might have been. Marinda thought this especially sad, since it looked as if this might have been a lovely place once, as cemeteries go. She was surprised to see that the plague virus had left the grass untouched. But as she bent to take a closer look she was repelled to find that the green she had mistaken for grass was only some horrid form of mold or fungus, covering the dirt.

The air here was damp and cool, a contrast to the desert environment so far behind them now. Tendrils of mist floated about them, swirling with their passage, ghostlike and disturbing. There was just enough light left that they could see their way without using the portalights, and more than enough darkness lurking behind the crypts and marker stones to conceal . . . unthinkable things.

"I swear," Marinda grumbled nervously as she strode quickly along with the others, "if I hear a wolf baying I'm going to set a new record for the hundred-yard dash."

"Wolf?" inquired Roddi.

"Oh, never mind."

They reached the main gate and left the cemetery, taking the roadway that led into town. They finally had to use their lights to see the path they were following. Along the way their beams revealed several pits by the roadside, huge scooped-out depressions with fire-blackened earth. Puddles from a recent rain lay at the bottoms, only partially concealing the jumble of bones which filled them.

Marinda stared in mute horror at the sight, imagining the scene years before as plague-wracked corpses were thrown into the flames. Was this what Vandal had meant by "worse things"?

As the buildings of Kezos City drew near, their silhouettes loomed before them against the darkening sky. There were no lights shining in the windows and no sounds of any kind. No voices, no music, no laughter. No people in the streets, hurrying home to dinner or going out for an evening's entertainment.

Kezos City was a ghost town. Ominous and dead, a relic of the past.

Their footsteps echoed from the walls of the office buildings and high-rise apartments as they traversed the highway running through the center of town. Some of the buildings showed signs of combat, with fire and ray damage. Rubble from collapsed walls closed off some streets. There were ornamental planters and whole parks that were plague-blighted. Faded and broken signs hung outside shops and offices and theaters, speaking of commerce and life and activities that no longer existed. In a way, this city was far more terrible than the desert.

Roddi rotated his head in all directions. "Much as it pains me to report this, so far I see no sign of any vehicles, working or otherwise, anywhere in the area."

Vandal nodded grimly. "Probably driven out by people trying to escape the sickness or fighting, or stolen by looters."

"And," Roddi added with a note of quiet urgency, "it also pains me to report another disturbing fact. We are not alone here."

"Are you sure?" Marinda asked, her eyes desperately trying to make out details in the night-shrouded city.

"Well, I certainly wish it were otherwise," said Roddi softly. "But my sensors indicate other moving forms besides ours, all around us."

"I was hoping I would be wrong about this place," Vandal replied.

"What should we do?" Marinda asked.

"Keep moving," Vandal told her. "Maybe whoever or whatever is out there will keep away from us."

They covered another block, walking briskly but not running, checking side streets and probing shadowy areas ahead of them with their portalight beams. There was still nothing in sight to suggest trouble. Faint sounds of movement became more pronounced, though, seemingly coming from all directions. They were half-way down the next block when a sound behind them alerted them to danger.

Vandal spun around first, his light beam stabbing through the darkness a moment before Roddi's joined it. Revealed in the glow was a group of men and women emerging from a shop thirty feet behind them. There were fifteen or twenty, with unkempt hair and grimy clothes. All wore harnesses with a variety of weapons ranging from simple knives to laser pistols. All had a hardened, hungry look more threatening than words. The words came next.

"Get 'em!" shouted one of the men, pointing violently at Vandal, Roddi, and Marinda.

Vandal reacted instantly, firing two searing ray blasts into the pavement directly before them. As debris and smoke sprayed up, sending the people diving for cover, Vandal turned Roddi and Marinda in the opposite direction and started them running. He fired three more quick shots to further scatter and confuse the group, then started running himself.

Marinda threw a worried glance over her shoulder,

then, as Vandal caught up with them, she gasped, "Who are they?"

"Nomads," Vandal said quickly. "They travel the uncivilized areas, stealing whatever they can and preying upon unguarded cargo shipments."

"Murderers and highwaymen," Roddi added with more than a trace of discomfort. "They would gladly dismantle me and sell my parts to the highest bidder. Of more immediate concern to you and Vandal, I have even heard rumors that some of them may be cannibals. Suffice it to say, they are not at all nice people."

They ran down the street, still hoping to find some form of conveyance that might take them from this place. Behind them came the sounds of pursuit, running feet and raucous outcries. And worse, ray blasts punctuated the noise as the band of nomads chased after them.

"We're silhouetted in our own light flare," Vandal snapped. He immediately switched off his portalight, as did Roddi.

They ran on in darkness a few minutes more, then Marinda stumbled, tripping on a crack in the roadway and gasping as she went down to the hard pavement. Vandal was at her side in an instant, getting her to her feet and putting an arm around her, hurrying her along.

"How can you see?" she asked him, regaining her breath.

"One of my eyes can see infrared light," he told her. "Roddi has a built-in infrared beam."

Marinda remembered the long scar on Vandal's face, running across the area of his eye, and realized that he must have sustained an injury that caused the loss of that eye. The cybernetic replacement was so real-looking that she had not guessed its nature. It pained her that so much had happened to Vandal, but there was little time now for such thoughts. Marinda concentrated on running, and was grateful for Vandal's strong arm about her for support in the darkness.

Another beam seared past them, and the footsteps seemed to be drawing closer. Vandal slowed and halted, giving a short, whispered command to his psybot companion. Digging into one of the packs slung over his shoulder, he withdrew two small objects and hurled them in the direction of their pursuers. Roddi did likewise.

"Close your eyes," he said near Marinda's ear.

The objects ruptured as they hit the pavement, exploding into blinding white light that filled the street with its glare and created a wall of vision-blocking brightness. Vandal steered Marinda and Roddi toward a narrow side street, and the three darted down it and were well out of sight long before the flash bombs were exhausted.

They raced along the side street in a new direction, then upon reaching the corner Vandal directed them east once more, parallel with the main road.

"This way," he said. "Before we turned back there I had a glimpse of something up ahead. Something I want to check out."

Their footsteps echoed softly as they ran along the street, past deserted offices and storefronts, but the sound was well masked by the nomad gang's noisy confusion. Vandal, Marinda, and Roddi covered a block, then another and another. Four blocks passed, then in the middle of the fifth an alleyway offered a narrow path to the main street.

Vandal slowed them, raising a hand for caution. Carefully, so quietly that not a sound was made as they advanced, the three moved along the alley and

crept up to the corner. Vandal peered around the edge
of the building, looking a short distance back down
the street, for his route had taken them just past
whatever interested him.

Marinda looked past the corner also, breathing hard
from their run and the fear which chilled her spine,
struggling to keep the rasp of air through her nose and
mouth from becoming audible. At first she could see
nothing where Vandal was looking, then her night
vision improved and she calmed enough to look more
closely. She could make out a number of odd, trucklike
vehicles parked along the street. Their outer surfaces
seemed to be lumpy and cluttered, and she thought
she could smell dust and grease and a variety of unpleasant odors emanating from them.

She was also aware that two, possibly three men
guarded these vehicles. They were looking down the
street in the direction of the other nomads, their backs
to her and Vandal.

Marinda strained to make out the gang farther down
the street. They seemed to be milling about in confusion, splitting into smaller groups and checking the
side streets near them. She was pleased they did not
yet realize how far their prey had gone.

Leaning close, Vandal whispered softly, "Stay here
with Roddi."

Marinda opened her mouth, but before she could
reply, before she could ask what he planned or tell
him to be careful, Vandal had slipped soundlessly
away from them and disappeared among the dark
street's deepest shadows. She knew he wanted one of
the vehicles parked there, but the odds seemed stacked
against him, with three armed nomads guarding the
area and the rest of their number not more than a few
blocks away. She strained to see where he was, how

close he was getting, but the cyborg agent had vanished as if he had been swallowed up by the cracked, neglected pavement.

Marinda took a step back from the corner, whispering to Roddi, "How can he take on three guards without alerting the others? It's too dangerous."

There was no reply from the usually garrulous psybot. Marinda turned. "Roddi?"

She gasped violently as firm hands grabbed her, and another hand clamped over her mouth with startling, wrenching force. Marinda glimpsed a large number of darkly clad figures swarming about her and Roddi, their faces obscured by hoods. Roddi was limp and awkward, apparently disabled, though she could not guess by what means.

Marinda felt herself being dragged backward, nearly lifted from the ground, her arms pinned and helpless. The hand that muffled her cries was swathed in coarse fabric, mittenlike and stinking. The foul odor of it and its abrasive pressure against her face was as much an affront as her captivity itself.

She and Roddi were being moved rapidly and with amazingly little noise toward an alcove in one of the two buildings which formed the alley. She had seen nothing before when they had come this way, and obviously neither had Vandal or Roddi. Now she found herself being pulled through a concealed doorway and into even greater darkness.

She heard the door close behind them as they made their way inside, heard the scuffling sounds of their feet against the hard concrete flooring. She was pulled, jostled, tugged along despite her struggles. It was like falling sideways, out of control. It was like some horrid nightmare.

Vandal! her mind cried out, again and again. But the word could not escape her smothered lips.

They crossed a long room, then turned abruptly and started down a flight of stairs. She felt her heels thumping and bumping along the risers as she tried to maintain some measure of control over her movements, but it was hopeless. She might as well struggle against the currents of some raging river.

As they reached the bottom of the stairs and emerged within a cellar, light washed into her straining eyes, light that was golden and flickering. Marinda glimpsed torches in the hands of several more of these strange attackers, burning with an oily yellow glow and illuminating the cellar with eerie effect.

The yellow glow illuminated her attackers as well, and Marinda drew a sudden sharp breath through her nose as torchlight spilled into several of the men's hoods, revealing their faces. At least, she thought they must be men. It was difficult to tell.

Marinda was reasonably sure they were human, anyway. Certainly they had once been. The faces were frightening to look at and horribly disfigured by disease. It looked as if the flesh had melted and decayed in spots, cheeks sagging away from eyes, noses twisted and collapsed, mouths distorted into perpetual grimaces that exposed rotting teeth and jawbones. Other places were puffed into great, sickening lumps of bloated tissue, and the men's skin was an unhealthy grayish brown.

She felt her stomach twist at the sight, and realized with awakening horror that the cloth-wrapped hands that gripped her and covered her mouth were surely as horrid as the faces she could see. Even knowing the desert she had crossed had once been a forest, it had still been difficult to grasp the full significance of the plague and its effects. What she saw before her fear-widened eyes removed all lingering doubts.

Marinda and Roddi were half carried, half dragged to the far side of the cellar. Upon reaching the wall, the group narrowed their formation once more and passed through a crude doorway chiseled through the concrete. Wooden planks with dirt protruding around the edges filled the gap between the first wall and that of the next building over. Clearly, a passageway had been cut between the two cellars, linking the buildings belowground, and it appeared that path continued.

Still moving quickly through this second cellar, their captors took Marinda and Roddi into yet another building, the torches trailing smoke and wisps of flame in their hurried progress. Where were they going? What could they want with their two captives?

Marinda did not know, and was not even sure she wanted to know. All she was certain of was that she desperately wanted to be free of these horrible creatures.

Somewhere behind her on the street above, she knew that Vandal must be attempting to steal a vehicle. She hoped he would be successful, but she feared he would not be able to find them down here. He might not even know where to begin looking. And if he did, could he find them soon enough?

Marinda struggled again with all her strength, tried to break free and reach the weapon Roddi had given her. But she simply could not move, could not resist the strong grip of those who rushed her forward to what she feared would be her doom.

17:
THE BROTHERHOOD

MARINDA LOST TRACK OF how many buildings she and Roddi were taken through by their captors, and had no idea exactly where in the city she might be. The pace through the underground levels was too frantic, too frightening. She suspected, though, that they had changed directions several times, crossing beneath streets and ending up many blocks away from the initial point of capture.

They seemed to be in the belowground parking garage of a large office building, and the robed men swiftly took them to the stairs, forsaking their subterranean route. Torches burned here in crudely made holders fastened to the walls, providing fair illumination but bestowing an almost medieval look to the place.

Past the first floor, past the second and third, too, the group continued to climb until they reached the fourth level. Only then did they leave the stairs and start down the main corridor heading into the heart of the building. Here they slowed their pace, beginning a solemn and orderly march, their prisoners securely in the group's center.

Now that there was better light and she could actually walk on her own, Marinda looked to her psybot friend with concern. Roddi was still being half carried, half dragged by the horrible hooded men. She noticed a device, small and strange-looking, affixed to the back of his neck, near the base of his head.

She was not certain, since her training had been primarily in the life sciences, but she knew enough about computers and electronics in general to suspect the device was some sort of jammer which had a paralyzing effect on robots. It was crudely made, but it obviously worked well enough to put Roddi out of commission. She hoped he could recover once it was removed.

As the men continued to march them along, Marinda glanced into the offices along the hall, seeing by what light reached into the cubicles from the passing torches. They no longer resembled ordinary offices at all. Most of the furniture had been removed and the rooms were being used for storage, with much of the space being taken up by long troughs made of sections of air duct. What lay in those troughs could not be seen, and even if it had been day instead of night, no light from outside could penetrate these rooms, as the windows had been heavily painted over.

They reached the end of the corridor and turned right. Then after a short distance they stopped before a set of closed double doors on their left. One of the men at the front of the formation, perhaps in charge of the group, opened the doors. He moved slowly, with a sense of ceremony, as if this were a special place they were about to enter. Marinda found this distressing. She was sure that "special places" frequented by men like these would be unpleasant at the very least and almost certainly dangerous.

The group entered the room, which proved to be a

large meeting chamber. It was windowless, being interior to the building, and its concrete walls were painted black. Torches stood at angles from sconces along the walls, and a row of the same troughlike stands Marinda had seen in the offices stretched down each side of the huge room. Another trough stood at the far end of the room, where curtains hid the wall or whatever lay behind them.

Parting slightly to create a path down their midst, the group halted in the wide center aisle. The man Marinda had guessed to be their leader strode back toward them. He flashed a malevolent glare at her, then turned to Roddi and jerked the small device from the psybot's neck. The man walked back to the front of the group, approached a small table just before them, and struck a crude gong fashioned from heavy iron pipe.

Roddi, meanwhile, sagged as the men around him released their grip. Those holding Marinda also let go of her, moving away to leave the two standing in the center.

Marinda went to Roddi's side, holding his arm securely, attempting to steady him. "Are you all right?" she whispered.

"No, I'm not all right," Roddi snapped softly. "I've been shaken about and jammed by something, and I can barely sort out which motor circuits are which. That is not at all the proper way to handle a delicate machine, I can assure you."

Marinda smiled wanly. "Well, I'm glad to see your speech circuits are still functioning."

"I suppose I deserve that," Roddi replied. "Forgive me for not asking how you are."

"I'm okay," she whispered back. "But I'd be a lot

better if I were somewhere else. Who are these . . . people?"

"Actually, I haven't the slightest idea. At first glance I thought they might be Carsonites, but now I think not. I suppose they may be survivors of this city who have developed some bizarre post-plague society. This place certainly has all the trappings of a religious cult."

"But how can they live here?" Marinda said, her eyes rolling to take in everything. "What can they possibly find to eat? Or do I really want to ask that?"

"I think you're probably safe in that regard. Look in those troughs."

Marinda glanced cautiously over to the nearest one. There was more light here than there had been in the offices along the way, and the robed men were not so close as to block her view. She could just see inside the trough. It was filled with a thick layer of some lumpy substance that looked spongy and rubbery, with rounded protuberances that bore a vague resemblance to mushrooms. But not an appetizing resemblance.

"That," she whispered, "is food?"

"Some form of edible fungus, from all appearances," Roddi said. "It may even explain their survival here. Fungus is one of the very few life forms not affected by the plague virus. That discovery was what eventually led to a biological cure for the disease."

Marinda stole a glance down to where she had stored her weapon, but it was gone, removed no doubt by some of the hands which had grabbed at her during the frenzied march here. Another glance told her that Roddi was also weaponless, and that their packs were being held by several of the hooded men.

Abrupt movement at the end of the room caught her eye, and Marinda looked up to see yet another robed man step through the curtains and take up a position facing the group. She saw the others give a slight bow of respect to him, and then the man she had initially taken to be the leader spoke up and addressed his superior.

"We have found these violators, Wise One," the man said, his speech distorted by his facial deformities. "There are more outside, near the Denheim Building."

"Nomads?" inquired his superior.

"Yes, the others. These, I am not sure." The man held aloft the small jammer device. "You were right, Wise One, this does weaken the robots."

"Good. But we will need more power cells. And more parts."

Marinda thought she felt Roddi flinch at that remark, as she gripped his arm to steady him. She marveled at these humans before her, more than mildly horrified. The man who spoke with the "Wise One" sounded as if his mind had been partially eroded by the disease, and although their strange diet had seemingly arrested their illness, it had done nothing to help their plague-rotted looks. It had somehow made them physically powerful, for the men who had dragged them here at such an energetic pace were anything but frail.

"We are not nomads," Marinda said abruptly, with an assertiveness that surprised her. "We were stranded, and were just trying to reach another city. You have no reason to fear us. And no right to hold us this way."

Roddi leaned closer to whisper, "Careful, Marinda. Remember that this is not a place bound by laws or decency."

The heads of the hooded men turned to face them, especially Marinda. The gaze of the man addressed as "Wise One" fell fully on her now. His cold eyes narrowed within a face that was less disease-scarred than the others but almost equally unpleasant.

"Whether or not you are a nomad is of no concern to us," he told her in a voice that carried easily through the room. "You are still an outsider, and outsiders have no rights in Kezos City. But you are right about one thing. We have no need to fear you."

There was something malevolent in his tone and in his look that sent a shiver down Marinda's spine. With less confidence she said, "Then . . . then why not let us go on our way and leave your town? We mean you no harm."

The leader's stern gaze swept the others in his group. "See how they would use words to deceive us? Never place your trust in outsiders. Never! It was outsiders who brought the plague to our city. It is outsiders who come to steal and to kill."

"But we are not like them," protested Marinda.

"Indeed not," added Roddi. "I have nothing at all in common with that unsavory bunch down the street."

"Silence!" commanded the leader. To his followers he said, "They were carrying weapons, were they not? They are violators, are they not?"

All heads nodded, and a chorus of fervent, slurred yesses rang out. Now that there was a better opportunity to observe, Marinda could see that some of these men were missing arms, and some had replaced a rotted leg with a crudely made artificial one. Whatever their handicap, it had not impaired their speed.

"Trust not these strangers," continued the leader. "True trust lies where?"

"The Brotherhood," chanted the others.

"Who gave you life, when the plague wracked your bodies and death was at hand?"

"The Brotherhood."

DEATH HUNT ON A DYING PLANET

"Who sustains you, and gives you freedom from disease?"

"The Brotherhood," again came the chant.

"And who gives you strength, to take what is rightfully yours?"

"The Brotherhood!"

Raising a handful of the vile fungus growth from the trough at the front of the room, the leader said, "Remember always that it was the Brotherhood that found the means of survival, that sheltered you and gave you purpose."

Another chorus of yesses, even more fervent than before. There was an almost maniacal energy crackling through the crowd. Most of the hooded people were rocking back and forth from one foot to the other, like children with barely contained emotions.

"Cheerful little bunch of lunatics," muttered Roddi.

"They're pathetic," whispered Marinda, with a stare that was as sickened as it was frightened. "And they're very dangerous. How are we going to get away?"

"My circuits are getting back to normal, so I should be able to fight them off now that they don't have the element of surprise in their favor. They did not search me carefully. I still have a hidden pistol—" His words ceased as his hand went to the compartment where he kept the small laser weapon he always carried. The panel was hanging open. The compartment was empty. "Obviously I spoke too soon. But never mind that. I activated a built-in tracer beacon some minutes ago. As soon as Vandal finds us gone he will track us here."

"If it isn't too late," Marinda replied.

At the front of the room, the leader seemed to be drawing strength from the energy he had generated among the crowd. His eyes were aglow with visionary zeal.

"The outsiders would destroy us, if we let them," he told his followers. "But we shall not let them. They think they come here to take from us, but it is we who shall take from them."

He gestured quickly, and his followers instantly moved to narrow the path running down the center of their midst. Rough hands reached in to grab Marinda and Roddi once more, pushing them forward into the grasp of new hands, moving them to the front of the room. Pushed by a multitude of hands, or remnants of hands, all swathed in coarse cloth to conceal the eroded fingers, the stumps, the twisted bones, they ran a grim gauntlet of horror.

Even though their captives were struggling, the strength of these hideous survivors was impossible to fight. Roddi and Marinda found themselves conveyed to the front, brought to the very feet of the leader and pushed to their hands and knees. Marinda let out a gasp as her hands brushed the hem of the man's robe, exposing a pair of feet shaped from blocks of wood and metal braces.

As her eyes rolled up to meet his steady, malevolent gaze, the leader bent down and took hold of her shoulders. His grip was painfully strong, and with a slow and forceful motion he raised Marinda to her feet and held her arms pinned to her sides. He stared for a long moment into her frightened eyes, then let his gaze take in her form.

"Yes," he said with a sibilant rasp, "you and the other violators have much to offer us in payment for your crimes. So very much. Such . . . fine, healthy limbs."

"You're not suggesting—?" Roddi said in horror.

Without releasing his grip on Marinda, the leader turned his chilling gaze on the silver-blue psybot. "You too shall serve our needs, robot. There are many of us among the Brotherhood. For some even cybernetic limbs would be a blessing."

As Roddi started to spring from his kneeling position to attack the man, a half-dozen hooded followers seized him. They held him secure, his servos whining helplessly against their combined strength.

"Come," their leader told them, "let us take these violators to the holding area."

Marinda and Roddi were forcibly taken to the curtained area at the end of the room. A narrow space was revealed behind the curtains as several of the hooded men held them aside. One door led to an office seemingly fitted out as living quarters for the leader, and another door yielded access to a flight of stairs. It was the stairs to which the captives were led, and the members of the Brotherhood filed along with them.

It was a short trip this time. The holding area proved to be on the next floor up, in another large conference room similar to the first. But while the one below was for meetings and ceremonies, this one clearly had a different, darker purpose.

One half of the area was set up as an improvised operating room, with medical gear, transplant equipment, and operating tables apparently taken from the city's hospital. Surgical tools and anesthetics had been gathered, and though torches now lit the room, gas-fed emergency lights waited for use. Something else waited for use as well.

The other half of the room was fitted with several cages, and rows of shackles ran along one wall. All of this was clearly designed to hold prisoners—prisoners or involuntary organ and limb donors. In Kezos City, there seemed to be little or no difference.

As Roddi was forced into one of the cages and their packs were placed on a shelf, the leader maintained his grip on Marinda. He faced his lieutenant with a stern command.

"Take your men and return to where the nomads are. Alert the other posts. Use whatever means you must to capture the violators. But I want you to take as many alive and uninjured as you can. Do you understand?"

The man nodded fervently. "Yes, Wise One. I shall do as you wish."

"For the Brotherhood."

"For the Brotherhood." The man bowed, then turned on his heel and hurried out, leading a large portion of his followers with him.

The leader now turned his full attention upon the girl who struggled unsuccessfully within his strong grip. His horrid face was chokingly close to hers, his probing eyes taking in everything about her lovely face and form. With lowered voice, he spoke to her.

"For you, I may just delay your final punishment. You have much to offer alive and intact."

Marinda's gaze burned angrily into his. "You should live so long!"

He let his hands slide down to her wrists and raised them over her head, forcing them back into waiting shackles fastened against the wall. As he latched the first device in place the long sleeves of his robe fell back. Marinda saw with frightening clarity that one of his arms was healthy and pink from his gloved hand to just past the elbow, while beyond it was the same grayish brown as his diseased face. An ugly scar and a double row of surgical stitch marks ran around the arm at the border of the two types of flesh, explaining the difference wordlessly, horribly.

The leader saw the look on Marinda's face and knew what she was thinking. "Yes," he told her with soft menace, "you are not the first violator to serve our needs here. Nor will you be the last."

He reached across her to secure the second shackle. Before he got it fully within his grasp an intensely bright ray beam cut through the gloom and struck him in the side of the head, passing through with a weird corona of light that lit up his eyes with its deadly glow. His jaw dropped slack as pink-tinged smoke poured from his nostrils and mouth. In the next instant, the horrid man dropped at Marinda's feet, utterly motionless, and smoldering.

Marinda's head jerked around toward the room's doorway, hope burgeoning in her look and in her voice. "Vandal?"

"No such luck, my dear," Razer announced in a honeyed voice, mocking and dangerous. "But he's next on my list, just as soon as I find him."

18:

RAZER'S EDGE

FIRING A BARRAGE OF lethal rays into the remaining group of Brotherhood men, the beautiful Corporation eliminator advanced into the room, heading for the end where the two captives were held. Moving with lithe and agile steps amid the confusion her surprise attack had created, she rapidly picked off the now leaderless followers one by one, ducking knife thrusts and laser blasts that seemed impossible to avoid.

"Oh, glitch and double-glitch," said Roddi softly. "That's Razer."

"You mean, the one who . . .?" Marinda began, stunned by the sudden appearance of the ruthless Corporation killer she had heard about. Stunned also by how beautiful she was. Marinda thought at the time Vandal had spoken about Razer, limited though his remarks were, that their relationship must have been more than professional. It was there in his voice, in his look. Now it was easy to see why he, or any other man, would have been attracted to her. Easy to see why he might still be in love with her. And yet, how could he love a woman who so coldly and mercilessly killed, who in fact wanted to kill him?

Marinda snapped out of her momentary shock and

frantically worked the latch on her shackled hand with her free hand. It came loose, and slipping clear of it she stepped over the leader's body and ran to the cage where Roddi was imprisoned.

Roddi was already trying to work the door from the inside, to no avail. "It's locked, Marinda."

She found a set of keys on the floor where one of the slain Brotherhood men had dropped it. Scooping it up, she tried first one, then another key. The third one released the latch, and she jerked the door open. As she turned away from the cage she saw Razer approaching swiftly.

"I don't understand," Marinda told her warily. "Why are you rescuing us?"

"Rescue?" Razer gave a brief and wicked laugh. "Frankly, Miss Donelson, I'd sooner leave you to these maggots. But the Quintad wants you for their very own, and so they shall have you." Her hard eyes flicked toward Roddi. "However, they did allow me the pleasure of disposing of this bit of junk."

Razer abruptly leveled her beam weapon squarely at Roddi and fired. The sharp hiss of its beam rose above Marinda's sudden, gasping "No!" and resounded through the room. Surprisingly, the beam did not hold on its target. It deflected slightly, passing near the startled psybot without striking him, and vaporized a portion of the cage behind him.

Razer glared angrily at the pistol in her hand. "Damn weapon misfired. I should have gotten my own."

At that moment, off to the side, one of the fallen robed men stirred, mortally wounded but still alive for the moment. Still alive, and filled with vengeful purpose. Struggling to raise his laser into firing position, he took aim at Razer and pulled the trigger.

At the last instant the man's arm twitched in a

sudden spasm of pain, and his shot went high as his hand pulled back. The laser beam struck the ceiling just past Razer's head, bringing down a shower of tiles and part of the suspension grid which held them. The debris crashed down on Razer as she threw her arms over her head to protect herself. The end of the grid toppled a metal shelving unit over onto her, knocking her to the floor.

Marinda and Roddi wasted no time in grabbing their packs from the shelves behind them. They darted past the spot where Razer struggled beneath the heavy shelving unit and ceiling debris, heading for the door and freedom. But freedom was not quite yet at hand. Three more Brotherhood men appeared at the door, blocking their escape, and those already in the room who had taken cover when Razer attacked began to rise and draw weapons.

One of them advanced on Razer as she tried to free herself. Her weapon had been knocked from her hand, just out of reach. She saw the man advancing, a long dagger in his upraised hand, and clawed frantically at the pistol just beyond her grasp. It seemed hopeless.

Suddenly there was an explosion of motion at the doorway. The third man who had just entered behind the first two jerked erect, taller than he had seemed, and kicked out mightily into the back of one of the other robed men. He instantly did the same to the second man, and both were sent flying across the room with bone-crunching force.

Vandal tossed back the hood of the robe which had disguised him. Fixing his steely gaze on the man poised to plunge his dagger into Razer, he raised his proto-blaster and fired twice rapidly. The first beam vaporized the dagger. The next beam struck the man's midsection and dropped him to the floor, a smoldering heap.

Vandal fired several times at the other members of the Brotherhood who still posed a threat. Those he missed were sent scattering, trying to find a way out of this death trap. His eyes darted back to Razer as Roddi and Marinda reached his side. A look that was hard and bitter and questioning burned in those eyes.

Razer met his steady gaze with a look of utter contempt and defiance. Her great beauty seemed inflamed by the powerful emotions boiling within her.

"What do you expect, Vandal? Gratitude?" she snapped. "Fool."

With a superhuman lunge she dragged herself another few inches free of the debris which held her and snatched her beam weapon from the floor. Swinging it around with frightening speed, she fired directly at Vandal's heart.

With a sizzling hiss the beam flashed out. And as before when she had aimed at Roddi, the beam missed, seeming to angle slightly off a true trajectory. It scorched its way across the large room and incinerated a piece of medical equipment in the surgical area.

Razer cursed beneath her breath and aimed again, but her targets were already ducking through the doorway, out of sight. She considered firing through the wall in the direction she thought they were moving, but from the corner of her eye she glimpsed several hooded figures moving closer and reluctantly turned her attention on them.

Out in the hall, Roddi said, "With all due respect, I don't think we need to hang around any longer on her account, do you?"

Vandal's tone was chilling. "No. Come on."

He led them at a dead run down the hall, reaching a

different stair from the one Roddi and Marinda had used in ascending to this floor. Vandal paused at the doorway a moment, listening intently, weapon poised. Then he whirled through the opening and checked the area before beckoning the other two. .

As they hurried down the steps, Vandal said, "Roddi, turn off your beacon. We don't need it now."

"Oh, yes, quite right," the psybot replied, mentally switching off the internal device. "Lucky for us you were able to track us here."

Vandal checked his hand-held tracer unit to be sure the signal was indeed off. "Lucky? I suppose," he said tersely. "Not so lucky that Razer scanned it too."

"Oh my," Roddi exclaimed softly, realizing that the very signal which had brought Vandal had also brought the Corporation eliminator to this building. "But to be within range, she must have already followed us to this city."

"A good guess," Vandal said. "With only two rail lines out of Delta Zone, she had a fifty-fifty chance of hitting the right exit."

Marinda trotted down the steps close behind them. "Maybe her heart's not really in this. She did miss both times she shot at you two."

"Well, it wasn't for want of trying," Roddi asserted. "In my case I can assure you she was aiming straight for me. As she said, her weapon must have misfired."

They continued down the stairs at a breathless pace until they reached the ground floor. There Vandal held them back a moment, just within the doorway, as a small group of Brotherhood members ran along the corridor, heading for the front of the building. He waited until they were well past and around a corner before motioning the others on. Before he stepped out into the hall he pulled the hood of his appropriated robe over his head.

The three hurried down this new corridor toward the back of the building, then slowed as they reached the corner. A short distance down the cross corridor, a guard was posted by the rear door. Vandal led the way, his head tilted down to keep his face in shadow, striding at a calm but purposeful pace. Marinda and Roddi followed single-file behind him.

The Brotherhood guard nodded in greeting as Vandal approached. Vandal stepped by him, then quickly turned as the guard reacted to the sight of the two "violators" behind him. Vandal brought his normal hand down in a sharp chopping strike to the base of the man's neck and the guard fell to the floor unconscious.

Roddi bent to help Vandal lift the man, and they carried him out the door. They left him in a dark corner of the alley outside, then headed off in the opposite direction.

Softly, still fearful she might be heard by someone, Marinda asked between breaths, "Where are we going?"

"Just a short distance," Vandal replied. "This way."

They cut around the corner of another building and started down the street. Parked there along the darkest side was a vehicle, barely visible in the night.

As they reached it, Marinda saw that it was essentially a small truck, old and battered-looking. Small openings had been cut in the sides for windows, and a patchwork of ropes and netting ran over most of it. Much of the surface was cluttered with small pouches and an absurd assortment of stolen and found hardware, all securely tied onto the ropes and nets. Something that looked like a rolled-up tent was strapped to the top, next to a cylinder that appeared to hold a liquid of some kind. It struck Marinda as being a bizarre cross between an old-fashioned gypsy wagon and a junkyard on wheels.

"One of the nomad trucks?" Marinda asked. "Then you were successful. How did you get past those guards?"

Vandal hesitated, looking at her as if he read more in her question than the mere words implied. "I didn't kill them, if that's what you're thinking."

"I didn't mean . . . I just wondered—"

"They had another problem to worry about at the time. A different unit of the Brotherhood discovered the nomads that had been chasing us. The nomad guards left their vehicles to help out. All I had to do was pick one and drive it away."

Roddi opened one of the doors. "Anything that will get us out of this city is fine with me."

Vandal helped Marinda into the vehicle, then went around to the driver's side as Roddi climbed in and closed the door. He started the engine as sounds of conflict came from a short distance back.

Vandal slipped the truck into gear and eased forward, slowly at first, seeking to avoid noisy clatter from the hardware on its sides. Then he gradually accelerated down the street.

Marinda settled back into the seat. It was hard and lumpy, and the whole truck smelled of old sweat and grime, but compared to being shackled within the Brotherhood's surgical ward, with the threat of death and dismemberment hanging over her, this was a very comfortable place indeed.

"Do you hear something?" Roddi abruptly said, cocking his head to one side and rotating it a bit.

"Like what?" Marinda asked.

But the question proved pointless in the next moment. A steady whine became audible, growing in intensity.

"Helijet!" snapped Vandal.

"Razer," Roddi said with a weary sense of alarm. He craned his head out the window in the door beside him, looking back at the building they had left.

Suddenly, at the top of the office building, a small cluster of lights came on and began to rise above the roof. The aircraft hovered a long moment in the air, then tilted abruptly and began to swing toward them.

"So that's where she parked that thing," Roddi observed. "I think we're in serious trouble now, Vandal."

"Maybe," came the cyborg agent's laconic reply. "Maybe not."

They had not traveled a full block before the first ray beam flashed down at them, burning a spot in the street before them. If it was intended as a warning shot it was wasted effort, for Vandal merely swerved around it and increased his speed.

He began steering evasively, swinging the old truck from one side of the street to the other, and not in any predictable pattern that would allow Razer to place a shot where she expected him to be. Careening down the street, Vandal turned the corner and swung wide onto a cross street, narrowly missing a light pole.

More beams flashed down toward them, each striking close but none actually hitting their vehicle. Vandal continued his wild driving, staring forward while Roddi kept his gaze skyward.

Marinda stared wide-eyed at the street ahead, wishing she could see in the dark as well as Vandal apparently could. Then suddenly she perceived something large and black looming against the indigo sky, something that stretched across the roadway before them.

It came more clearly into view as they sped toward it. It was an overpass of some sort, meant to carry traffic in a day when Kezos City had still been vital and filled with people. Now it was just an architectural relic. And maybe a brief moment's shelter?

The helijet was just a short distance behind the truck now, flying a good fifty feet above it. Vandal reached the overpass in the next instant and hit the brakes, sliding the vehicle to a squalling halt directly beneath the overpass's farthest edge.

Opening the door on his side, Vandal stepped partway out of the truck and braced his gun hand against the top of the truck for support. Sighting along his protoblaster, he aimed at the sky just beyond the edge of the overpass, at the point where the helijet's trajectory should carry it.

In a moment the aircraft's lights became visible, passing above the overpass and still in pursuit of the vehicle that was expected to emerge on the other side—a vehicle that was now well behind the point of aim for the aircraft's weapons.

Vandal adjusted the position of his protoblaster ever so slightly and squeezed the trigger. A beam crackled in a brief burst of energy, searing upward through the sky and blasting into the left rear helijet engine.

He leaped back into the truck and slammed the door, then turned and headed back down the street he had just come along, even as debris from the ruined engine rained down. Reaching the end of the block, Vandal turned down another street, disappearing from sight.

Razer's helijet spun in an awkward spiral, tilting down in the back as it lost flying power on that side. Under limited control, Razer was steering it toward the only clear landing area nearby, a plague-blighted park within a block of the overpass.

Continuing away from the area as fast as they could, Vandal, Roddi, and Marinda heard the sputtering whine of the remaining helijets fade and then still altogether. But there was no sound of explosion or impact.

"Well," said Roddi, "she didn't crash."

"No," Vandal agreed grimly. "But she won't be flying out of there again. Not without help, and not anytime soon."

He drove in silence to the edge of the city, moving at top speed for the old truck. He located the main highway that ran northeast to the coast, and vowed to himself to put as many miles between them and Kezos City as he possibly could.

19:
MYSTERIOUS MAGICAL TOUR

"AH," SAID DR. ARCANUS with great pleasure and an expansive gesture of his hands. "What a perfect day for a performance."

It was midmorning now. Cleera and her psybot team had been traveling with Arcanus all night, with Cleera driving much of the time while the elderly showman napped. They had covered the miles between Troy and this city without incident, arriving a few hours earlier. At last they had reached their intermediate destination, their meeting place.

Jonnersville.

Cleera repeated the name in her mind. She stood near Dr. Arcanus in the vacant field next to what had once been a large shopping center and now had just a third of its shops working. Jonnersville had been only a name to her before, a goal she must reach to fulfill the first part of her mission. Now that she was here, it was more. It was a place, a real place, with people and buildings, and most of all, the normal things one might expect to find in a city. But somehow, filling in the gaps made this place no less frightening than when it had only been a dark and brooding name in her mind.

She envied Dr. Arcanus's enthusiasm. He seemed to find this new adventure very much to his liking, looking forward to the next performance as if it were no more dangerous than an ordinary show. If it was not just an act, his zest for living was certainly something to admire.

"Do you think we can make this work?" Cleera asked.

"The show?" said Arcanus. "Why, yes, of course we can. With the specialized skills of you and your friends, and my own immodest talents, I see no reason to worry. It will be a magnificent, stupendous performance. A once-in-a-lifetime event!" He finished his flourish and looked at Cleera with a wry smile and a shrug. "Then again, it may be a complete and utter flop. But why think negatively? Besides, I doubt our audience will be expecting all that much."

Cleera immediately felt better, if only because Dr. Arcanus's irrepressible good humor was contagious. She gripped his arm fondly and told him, "Well, no matter what, I happen to think you're magnificent and stupendous. And you've been more help to me than you can imagine."

Arcanus's look became more serious, almost fatherly. "Being a leader is not always easy, is it?"

"For me, it's never easy."

"Well now, that surprises me," said Arcanus. "You certainly seem to be very much in control of things. And from what I've seen, you have a good mind for plans and, shall we say, nefarious schemes."

There was something about the way "nefarious" rolled off his tongue that pleased her. He imbued words with such delicious drama. "Thanks for the compliment. But there are still times when I wish someone else were in charge. It's just that it's my job, and I want to see it done right."

"Ah, the mark of all truly great leaders. A good balance of self-doubt and determination. It's the leaders who have no doubts that cause all the trouble in this world, or any other."

Cleera laughed and nodded in understanding. She saw Torb and Chiron moving more of the stage equipment into place, and she started away from Arcanus. "Well, I'd better go help the others if we're going to be ready for the afternoon show."

"Don't forget to send someone around with the posters and circulars. There can't be a show without an audience."

"Already attended to," Cleera called back over her shoulder.

As she reached the area where the others worked, Cleera sought out HiLo and Muse. "I sent a T-beam transmission to the Uni a little while ago," she told the two psybots. "I let them know we reached Jonnersville and briefed them about Dr. Arcanus."

"That must have been a hard message to compress," HiLo said wryly. "Have they heard from Vandal yet?"

"Yes. They told me that Roddi sent a transmission during the night. The three of them made it safely out of Delta Zone and some place called Kezos City. They're on their way to Haddock, just across the bay from here. They may be there already."

"Great," Muse replied. The golden robot with the dancer's figure shifted the carton of stage props she carried and held it more securely. "Maybe we should try to meet them there instead of waiting for them to reach us."

"I know what you mean," Cleera said. "It would be

easier than just staying here and going through this charade. But the Uni still wants us to meet here. They say further instructions will be sent at that time."

Muse shrugged. "I guess they have their reasons. Anyway, I'm kind of glad. This show should be fun."

"I agree," said HiLo. "Besides, it gives us a cover story, so we don't have to be running or hiding for a little while."

"True," Cleera replied, glancing toward the large blue psybot as he moved past. "But I'm not sure Torb is enjoying this. I think it's time I had a talk with him."

"Do you want me to go along?" asked HiLo.

"Thanks for offering. But I think I had better do this on my own."

Cleera left HiLo and Muse to their work, following Torb across the field as he carried a ticket booth they had assembled earlier. She waited as he set it down, then approached him.

"How is it going, Torb?"

He straightened up. "Fine. We'll be done soon."

"Have you talked with Muse about your part in the show?"

"Yes." His tone was flat and a bit stiff, though not unfriendly.

"Torb," Cleera began uneasily, "do you dislike me?"

The big blue psybot looked at her fully now. "No. Why?"

"Because you don't seem happy with this situation. You act as if you resent the fact the Uni made me the team leader. Do you resent it?"

Torb was silent a long moment. "No. It's not that so much. And it's not really you, Cleera. You are good at this. I'm realizing that more now than I did at first. It's just that . . ."

"What?"

"It's just that it seemed to me that the University took it for granted that I could not be a leader. You know—'Torb is big and powerful, but he's not intelligent enough to do anything important'—that sort of thing."

"Oh, no, Torb," Cleera protested. "They couldn't think that, or else they would never have recruited you for special missions."

"I mean, I have full intelligence capabilities, and my programming is as adequate as anyone's."

"I know that, Torb. We all do." Cleera paused a moment, gathering her thoughts. "Tell me, do you think Muse is any less capable, or unintelligent?"

"Well, no."

"Or HiLo, or Chiron? Or Jayray and Jom?"

"No. They're all smart."

"I think so too," Cleera told him. "But the Uni didn't pick any of them either, and I would hate for any of them to feel they had been slighted because of it. I don't know why they picked me, and I don't really think it matters. Not as much as how we all get along. Maybe it's just some sort of test—maybe the Uni wants to see how we work together as a team."

Torb inclined his head slightly. "Maybe."

"Besides, we all really do need each other. We don't fit in so well with the standard mechs, and most of the humans, especially on this world, are very uncomfortable around us. Some hate or fear us. We're about all we have for friends."

"I know," Torb replied. "For a long while, HiLo and Chiron were the only ones I could really talk to." A smile seemed to come into his voice. "Did you ever try striking up a conversation with a standard cargo mech? They're only programmed for moving things. If what you're saying doesn't have the words 'pick up,' 'put down,' 'carry,' or 'storage bay nine' in it, they just stand there looking at you."

Cleera laughed. "Sounds like some of the store mechs I've seen. I guess we shouldn't laugh at them. They're doing what they were built for. It just makes me feel like an outsider at times."

"Yes. Me too." He glanced toward the stage, where Chiron still labored alone. "I know you're in charge, Cleera, but maybe we should get back to work."

"I think you're right. We should," Cleera agreed cheerfully. "And Torb, anytime you have ideas, or you think there's a better way to do something, I do want you to let me know. I can't guarantee I'll always agree with you, but I would like your input."

"Fair enough. Just listening helps."

By early afternoon, the stage had been fully assembled and the tentlike walls erected to keep out the nonpaying customers. Benches were set up before the stage, and a fortune teller's booth was ready nearby, with Muse garbed in something approximating traditional gypsy costume. Some of the benches were already filled, and people were trickling in at a slow but steady rate.

Jonnersville was only slightly smaller than Troy, but was not as industrial. One of the civilized cities, it had enough Corporation-supported businesses and virus-controlled hydroponic farming to maintain an adequate standard of living. Even so, tickets for the magic show had been priced low enough to fit within most people's budgets. This was partly to attract a large crowd and partly to make the show appear pedestrian enough to discourage wealthy Corporation executives from attending. As the time for the matinee show drew near, the crowd grew larger.

Behind the curtains, Cleera and Dr. Arcanus waited, peeking out through tiny openings. Cleera studied the people on the benches with mixed feelings.

"I'm glad we're drawing a good audience for you," she said. "But I'm also a little nervous. I'm not a performer like Muse, or even Jayray and Jom."

"You'll do fine," Arcanus told her. "Just remember—you're carrying on a great tradition that's centuries old."

She looked away from the hole in the old and slightly tattered curtain. "Now you are making me nervous," she said with a laugh. "Tell me, how did you ever get involved with this sort of thing?"

"My grandfather came here as a young man on *Glory*, the old colonizer ship. He was a research scientist, professionally, but his hobby was magic, and he brought with him a number of books on all the great stage magicians and their tricks. He was so enthusiastic about it, showing me all sorts of tricks and things when I was growing up, that I became interested in it myself. It was the showmanship of legerdemain that appealed most to me, and robots were just becoming popular, so I updated the old tricks with new technology and 'Dr. Arcanus' was born."

"Then Dr. Arcanus isn't your real name?"

"Oh my, no. It's merely a stage name, drawing from the old word 'arcane,' meaning occult or unknown. It seemed fitting for a magician. I won't tell you my real name, though," he said with a laugh. " 'Twould spoil the grand illusion, I fear." As he continued to gaze through the peephole at the crowd outside, his expression grew more serious. "There's something I will tell you, though. Some of the audience we're drawing we could well do without."

"Oh?" Cleera turned back to the opening closest to her and peered out. "Oh."

Besides the average folk gathering for their performance, about a dozen CorSec Guards had just entered the enclosure and were taking seats near the back. They were wearing uniforms but seemed to be carrying few weapons, and their manner was casual.

"Maybe they're just off duty and looking for a little entertainment," Cleera suggested.

"Let us hope so, my dear. Let us hope so." Arcanus abruptly consulted his watch, then said, "And now you'd best have Jayray return from the ticket booth and tell Miss Muse to put away her crystal ball. Matinee time is upon us, and the show, as they say, must go on."

A fanfare of recorded music burst from speakers at the corners of the stage, and the crowd settled down, shifting upon their benches, ready to be entertained. The curtain rose, with the sound of squeaky pulleys masked by the loud music.

The stage seemed empty at first. Then there was a great puff of smoke near the center and Dr. Arcanus appeared within it. He wore a tuxedo, the jacket of which sparkled with dazzle crystals from one of the moons of Coreworld. Worked into the design were silhouette moons and stars and various magical symbols. It was a modern-day sorcerer's robe. His mane of white hair was neatly combed, and with his height and trim build, he was quite an imposing figure.

"Ladies and gentlemen," said he, his eyes alive and dancing with energy, his long-fingered hands striking a graceful gesture. "I am Dr. Arcanus, and I welcome you all to the one, the only, Traveling Automated

240

Magic Show. I and my robot troupe are here for your amusement and amazement. Our goal is to delight and to baffle you. And now, as my two lovely assistants join me, let the show begin!"

As he spoke the last line, Cleera and Muse came onstage from the wings, wearing sparkling bands of sequins at their wrists and ankles and around their necks. They kept their movements precise and a bit slow, trying to look like ordinary mechs as much as possible. They had had to modify many of Arcanus's standard tricks, since few of his own robots were working properly, and Cleera hoped they all had learned their routines well.

"For my first illusion," continued Arcanus, "I shall acquaint you with a bit of stage history. A great magician of centuries past, named Harry Houdini, once caused an elephant to disappear before an audience's very eyes. Now, an elephant was a very large beast weighing many hundreds of pounds, and there are none here on Coreworld. But I think I have devised a reasonable substitute."

The magician secretly pressed a button on a remote-control device hidden within his coat sleeve. Power winches in the wings began raising the second curtain at midstage. As it rose, a startling sight was revealed behind it.

Torb was standing there, his bulky legs spread wide, powerful arms raised. Then the curtain lifted fully, and it could be seen that he held the long wheeled robot, Chiron, above his head. As murmurs went through the crowd, Torb slowly turned and lowered Chiron carefully to the stage floor, directly behind him. Torb lumbered forward several steps closer to the front of the stage, plodding heavily, emphasizing his power and weight. He stopped alongside Dr.

Arcanus, his squat head slowly turning to survey the audience.

"Behold the mighty cargo mech!" boomed Arcanus with high drama. "I had him demonstrate his strength for you so that you may be assured he is real and solidly built, and no mere shell. Now watch, and wonder!"

With that, Arcanus gave a slight nod of a signal to Muse. The golden robot moved gracefully to the wings and immediately returned with a length of sturdy cable. One end ran overhead to the center of the stage framework, out of sight behind the proscenium arch.

A square metal framework with curtains hanging down on all four sides slowly came into view, descending from the overhead framework. As it was lowered, the curtains enclosed Torb, touching the floor and hiding the massive robot completely from view.

Cleera and Muse moved around all four sides of the enclosure, making sure there were no gaps in the curtain and that the folds of cloth were hanging right. At a gesture from Dr. Arcanus, not to mention the touch of another secret button, spotlights now illuminated the enclosure and Chiron a short distance behind it. Torb's massive shadow clearly showed on the front curtain of the cloth cubicle.

As Cleera moved out of the way, Muse took the free end of the cable back to Chiron, then she too stepped aside. A synthesized drumroll began, and Chiron began pulling the cable, winding it up and slowly raising the enclosure into the air. Nothing could be seen under it where Torb had been standing, but the familiar bulky shadow still showed on the front curtain.

When at last the enclosure was raised a full ten feet above the stage, Chiron stopped pulling the cable and held it steady. Dr. Arcanus walked across the area where Torb had been, making an expansive gesture with both hands.

"See?" said Arcanus. "Vanished before your very eyes!"

Murmurs, whistles, and catcalls surged through the audience. People pointed energetically at the curtained cubicle, where Torb's shadowed form still showed.

Dr. Arcanus leaned forward with a frown, listening to the crowd, then turned to follow the direction of the pointing arms. He stared up at the enclosure and the shadow, which only a blind man could fail to see.

"What?" he said disdainfully. "You think that large and heavy robot did not disappear at all, but is still within the enclosure up there?"

There was a chorus of yesses from the audience, and a few jeering remarks. Arcanus gave a pained and disappointed look.

"Well, then let us just see," he boomed, "for I promised you magic, did I not?"

Arcanus gestured at the curtained enclosure, and something miraculous happened. With a flash of light and a loud report of sound, the curtains abruptly fell from the metal framework. The soft, translucent cloth fluttered to the stage floor and lay in flat folds there, leaving nothing overhead except the top of the metal framework. Torb was nowhere in sight, and there was nothing which could conceal him.

There was a collective gasp from the audience, then roars of approval and applause. Arcanus smiled broadly, as much to himself as for the crowd, then quickly gathered the cloth up and tossed it offstage.

"And now, for my next illusion," Arcanus addressed the crowd, feeling even more confident, "I have something a bit different up my sleeve, so to speak. It is something I call Matter to Energy to Matter! Ladies, if you please. . . ."

Muse and Cleera had retreated to the wings at the same time Chiron left the stage, and they now returned, each pushing a large cabinet in, one from the left, one from the right. The cabinets were raised on clear plastic legs, with casters beneath them. Before Muse and Cleera positioned them on either side of the stage, they rotated the tall and boxy cabinets so that all sides could be viewed. Then they opened the door on each, revealing the empty interiors.

"As you can readily see," thundered Arcanus, "each cabinet is like the other, and there is nothing at all in either one of them."

Coming from backstage, Jayray now made his appearance, wheeling out a bizarre contraption with flashing lights, mounted atop a pedestal. He positioned it roughly between the two cabinets, at center stage, then connected a glowing cable to the cabinet on the left. Jayray pointed the odd device at the cabinet on the right, then approached Dr. Arcanus and stood at attention.

"May I now have a volunteer from the audience?" the old magician called out sharply.

There was a soft undercurrent of voices among the crowd, then some good-natured pushing in one of the back rows. A young CorSec trooper rose, amid encouragement from his friends, and started reluctantly forward to the stage.

Cleera kept her eyes locked straight forward and maintained her stiff pose. She inwardly tensed at the sight of the uniformed man approaching them. It seemed an innocent enough thing, a young human responding to a dare from his friends. But it made her feel no less nervous performing before such a potentially dangerous group. She glanced briefly toward Arcanus, but the experienced showman seemed unfazed by this development. Either that, or he was actually enjoying the element of risk.

"Good," said Arcanus as the trooper reached the stage. "I see we have a brave man here, a stalwart youth, ready to risk life and limb for the sake of science!"

The young trooper laughed and shook his head. He started to take a step back.

"What?" inquired the magician. "You mean you don't wish to become famous as the first human being to have his atoms torn apart and shot through space, then reassembled once more?"

The trooper shook his head vehemently this time, laughing nervously.

"Well, I cannot say that I blame you. But you can assist me in another way, my lad." Arcanus produced a pen and a pad of blue paper from his coat pocket, handing it to the trooper. "Now, merely write a brief message or statement on a piece of this paper—something you will recognize as your own."

"Yes, sir." The young trooper thought a moment, then scrawled something across the paper. He tore the sheet off and folded it.

Arcanus handed him an envelope of matching color and said, "If you will be so good as to slip your note into this envelope, seal it, and write your signature across the flap, just so that you may later verify that your note has indeed remained sealed . . ." He watched as the young man did as instructed, then he motioned for Jayray to step forward. "Now, my lad, please place your note in the hand of my robot assistant here, since he will be taking your place in the transferral chamber."

The trooper did so, watching the yellow-hued psybot

take the note, turn, and step into the large cabinet on the left. The man looked back to his comrades with a sheepish smile.

"And now," Dr. Arcanus boomed, "we are ready to begin!" He gestured at Jayray, who stood rigidly still within the cabinet. "As you can see, my robot helper is now in place within the transferral chamber, this young gentleman's note tightly clutched in his hand." Arcanus bent to wave his arm beneath the cabinet. "And as you can also see, the transferral chambers are elevated upon transparent legs, with a clear view beneath them. There is no possibility at all of leaving the chamber—by ordinary means. The same is true of the other chamber. Now watch, and wonder!"

Arcanus closed the door to the cabinet in which Jayray stood, then crossed the stage and closed the door on the other cabinet. He went to the strange-looking device standing between the two large cabinets as Cleera and Muse waited at either end of the stage.

The magician checked the alignment of the device with great care, sighting along the top edge and taking aim at the exact center of the cabinet on the right. He next checked to be sure the cable connection to the device was secure.

This was not science, nor even mere showmanship. The purpose was to take time—time needed by Jayray and Jom for their parts in the illusion.

Dr. Arcanus switched on the device. Lights blazed into life around its edges, and around the edges of the cabinet on the left. Swirling, flashing, pulsing with ever increasing intensity, the lights moved in a pattern that suggested movement away from the first cabinet, flowing toward the odd contraption manned by Arcanus.

Then the lights on the first cabinet went out, those on the device becoming brighter. With startling abruptness a laser beam, or what appeared to be one, flashed from the device and struck the second cabinet. Instantly, lights began pulsing around that one. Then they, too, faded away.

"Matter . . . to energy . . ." thundered Arcanus, gesturing to the first cabinet, then to the device, then finally to the second cabinet, ". . . to matter!"

With that, the door to the cabinet on the right swung open. Jom stepped out and down to the stage floor, clutching the duplicate envelope in his hand and looking exactly like Jayray.

Arcanus quickly walked to the first cabinet and threw open the door. It was empty, since Jayray was in the hidden compartment. Arcanus strode back to the young trooper and motioned for Jom to give him the note.

"Examine the envelope, my lad," Arcanus told him. "Is that your signature?"

The CorSec man studied the telepathically traced signature carefully. A trained expert might have seen the difference, but he did not. "Yes, it is."

"Then tear it open and examine the message!"

The trooper ripped the edge off the envelope and extracted the note. Opening it, he quickly read the words written on the paper and saw the familiar handwriting.

"Now tell me," said Arcanus majestically, "is that not the very same message?"

The man gave an enthusiastic nod and waved the paper at the audience. "Yes, sir, it sure is!"

Wild applause burst from the audience. Everyone knew there had to be some trick to the illusion, knew it deep down. But being baffled was simply too much fun not to enjoy it.

The trooper returned to his friends. Jom walked offstage with the transfer device, and Muse and Cleera wheeled away the two cabinets. As soon as they were clear, Chiron rolled onstage, carrying a narrow platform with a coffinlike box atop it. He deposited it carefully, then rolled back out of sight.

HiLo walked out to stand beside Dr. Arcanus, near one end of the platform. The magician indicated him with an overblown introductory gesture.

"And now, another of my mechanized assistants will help me with yet another variation on a classic stage illusion, using what you might say is"—he smiled wolfishly—"the cutting edge of technology."

Arcanus circled the platform and box, showing it off, then he pressed a button on the platform's side. Servos drove the top of the platform up and over, raising the box to an upright position with one end on the stage floor. Arcanus opened the lid of the box and gestured for HiLo to enter.

HiLo's head rotated around to take in the box. As if knowing what was coming, he shook his head negatively. The effect was comical, eliciting chuckles from the audience.

Arcanus gave a stern frown and gestured once more into the box, his pose full of severe authority. He was in charge here, and would not be swayed.

His movements showing some reluctance, HiLo turned and stepped over to the box. There was just enough room for him to fit inside. Turning again, he backed into it and gave a small, mechanical farewell wave to the audience.

Arcanus immediately slammed the lid and pressed another button on the platform. The top and the box tilted back over and came to rest in the horizontal position once more.

Cleera appeared from the wings now, pushing out a large laser on a rolling stand. Muse brought a thick-paneled laser baffle from offstage and positioned it behind the platform. While this was happening, HiLo, quite hidden from view, was lowering himself through panels in the bottom of the box into the platform top itself, which was actually deeper than it seemed, thanks to clever surface decoration. There he waited, hoping no one had miscalculated what was to happen next.

Cleera positioned the laser in front of the platform, a third of the way from the end. She locked it in place and stood to one side.

"Thank you, ladies," said Arcanus with a courtly bow. Then to the audience, "And now, dear patrons, allow me to show you a different slice of magic history!"

Arcanus switched on the laser. Its burning beam flashed out, passed above the top of the box, and was stopped by the baffle behind the platform. With a devilish look to the audience, Arcanus now cranked the laser lower, so that the beam cut straight through the box. It stopped just short of the surface of the platform top, since pins set into the laser stand prevented it from descending any lower. He switched it off.

With Cleera's assistance, Arcanus repositioned the laser a third of the way down from the opposite end and raised it. Then he repeated what he had already done, making another burning cut through the box. This done, he switched the device off again and Cleera wheeled it away.

Moving behind the platform, Arcanus picked up metal barriers and slid them into the burned grooves. They passed through, all the way to the platform top.

Arcanus tapped on the box. "Are you all right in there, my friend?"

A slow rapping came back. "Good," said Arcanus, and he grasped the middle section of the box and pulled it back. He allowed it to crash heavily upon the stage floor.

Cleera and Muse came forward and at the magician's direction pushed the two remaining portions of the box together with a resounding clunk. They retreated again, and Arcanus winked wryly at the crowd, much to everyone's amusement.

Now Arcanus yanked the metal barriers free and dropped them on the floor as well, creating enough clatter to hide sounds of motion within the platform and box. He pressed the button to activate the servos once more.

The platform top began tilting up, raising the now abbreviated box to vertical position again. As it whined to a halt, coming to rest on the floor, the magician gestured at it with mystical intent.

"Now," he said, "let us see what we have left."

Arcanus reached out and opened the two lid pieces, standing aside. A roar went up from the crowd.

HiLo emerged from the remains of the box, his arms and legs telescoped to their innermost limit, so that he stood at barely half his normal height, looking dwarflike and stumpy. He made a show of looking at the damage done, then he proceeded to chase Arcanus around the stage with short, waddling steps.

Cleera remained rigidly motionless through it all as the audience's laughter continued for a full minute. She glanced at the CorSec men at the rear of the crowd, but they were laughing just as hard, seemingly enjoying themselves and not showing any signs of suspicion.

She was glad, very glad, that their little show and cover identities were working so well thus far. She only hoped Vandal and the others were finding equal success in their efforts, and that a rendezvous would be possible soon.

20:
RASP'S DILEMMA

"WE'RE GETTING NOWHERE FAST," Rasp complained to Cudder. "We've been checking this place out since yesterday, and we're still no closer to finding what we came here for."

They were in the lobby of the University's main complex, moving between groups of conference delegates and keeping to themselves except for occasional smiling nods to others that they met. It was only a few hours after Dr. Arcanus's matinee performance on Coreworld, but on Avalon it was morning, and the second day of the special conference.

"What do you expect?" Cudder said calmly, keeping his voice as low as Rasp's grumbling. "The way this thing has been scheduled, it just hasn't been possible so far. Besides, if this place was easy to crack, Roman wouldn't have needed specialists like us to do the job."

Rasp gave a shrug of grudging acceptance. "Yeah, maybe so. But I don't like hanging around here any longer than I have to. We came here for results."

"I don't like it either," Cudder replied, glancing about the large room and at the mass of delegates gathered there. "We've managed pretty well so far, but sooner or later, someone is going to ask us to explain our work on the Anostus survey station, and we're not going to be able to fake an answer. Our background material is thin enough as it is."

"I'm not worried about that," said Rasp. "We can always hit them with something like 'I'm terribly sorry, but we're involved with a research project that we're not allowed to discuss freely at this time.' That should work. I'm just tired of making polite small talk with these eggheads."

Cudder gave a reluctant nod of agreement. Although he wouldn't want to admit it to Rasp, he had found most of the people here quite likable and interesting. He would like them even better if he did not feel so out of place. "Let me see that map again."

Rasp glanced about briefly to be sure no one was close enough to observe, then he opened his conference folder to the back section. Well secured there was the folded map of the University complex their Corporation-supplied computer drafter had made as soon as they arrived on Avalon. Carefully drawn onto that map was the layout of the conference activities for both days, indicated in different colors.

Cudder shook his head slowly. "Today's schedule takes us a little closer than yesterday's, but still not close enough."

"It'll be close enough for me, just as soon as I can get a staff badge or two to get me past the security sensors."

"I'm just trying to keep the element of risk down to a minimum."

"Yeah, well, risk-taking goes with the job," replied Rasp. "Maybe you're getting too soft for this line of work, but I'm not."

Cudder's eyes narrowed in a dangerous way, but he

only paused and said, "Let's not argue. The delegates are starting to move out to the first session. We'd better get going."

The two Corporation agents mixed in with the flow of delegates as they filed out of the lobby into the main corridor. It was a relatively short walk back to the part of the complex where the auditoriums and conference rooms were located, and the drone of conversations continued along the way.

Easels were set up before each room, bearing placards describing the conference topic. A few delegates went immediately to specific rooms while the rest remained engaged in their chats. Then at last they began to drift into the rooms, dividing themselves into interest groups. As the crowd thinned, a familiar figure became visible.

The young woman with long brown hair was standing near the center of the room, her computer tablet on her arm. She was wearing a green outfit, and her manner was as cheerful as ever.

Rasp held back a bit as the crowd thinned still further, then he tapped Cudder with his knuckles and started toward the girl. "Come on—I think I see our chance."

"Rasp—" Cudder started to protest, but Rasp was already heading away from him and he had to hurry to catch up. He thought he knew what his partner had in mind, and he did not like the idea. Maybe Rasp was right; maybe he was getting soft.

"Well, good morning, gentlemen," Jenna greeted them. "How do you like the conference so far?"

"Well, we think it's just marvelous," Rasp replied with a slick and oily effusiveness. "Have you got a moment?"

"Sure," said Jenna, though she seemed a bit taken aback. "Is there something I may help you with?"

"Why yes, I believe there is." Rasp moved close to her, his conference program held open as if he planned to show her some item on the agenda. But as she looked down at it she saw protruding beneath the edge a small and very nasty-looking weapon, its nozzle against her side. As her pretty eyes went up to his in a look of alarm, Rasp added in a low, menacing voice, "Not a sound, and no quick movements. This little prize doesn't make any noise, but it can kill you very quick and very sure, and no one will ever know how or why."

Jenna glanced at the weapon again. There was every reason to believe from its appearance, and from the tone of the man she knew as Oglethorpe, that he was deadly serious. She looked to the other man, who had called himself Derwent. He had seemed so warm and friendly, but he was obviously part of this, too. She had the fleeting impression that his look was more one of concern than menace. She looked back to Rasp.

"What . . . what do you want?"

"Just a bit of help," he told her, with a quick glance to be sure all the delegates were gone. "And some of your expert knowledge." He started her moving forward down the cross corridor, away from the conference rooms, keeping the weapon's nozzle at her side and hidden from view. "Let's go this way, Jenna. You don't mind if I call you Jenna, do you? Of course you don't. Now, first of all, I want you to tell me where there's a room near here. An empty room where we won't be disturbed, so we can have a nice little chat. And no tricks. Tricks will only get you killed. Understand?"

Jenna nodded silently. She led them down the corridor, moving carefully with the ever-present threat of the weapon at her side. Then after a few moments, she indicated a door with a solid panel on her left. The word "Staff" was lettered on a small plaque near eye level.

"It's a private meeting room," she told them. "It can be locked from inside."

"Excellent," said Rasp, looking it over thoroughly. "You're doing just fine, Jenna. Just fine."

He nodded toward the door, and Cudder moved to open it. It was what she'd described, and it was empty. There was no one in the hall to notice their entering, and they did so quickly. Rasp closed the door behind him and locked it, forcing the girl toward the small table at the room's center.

"Take a seat," he told her, "and put that gadget flat on the table."

Jenna sat in the nearest chair and placed the computer tablet before her. She looked around at Rasp as he stayed close beside her.

Cudder strode up to Rasp's side and whispered to him, "We should have considered all our options before committing ourselves this way. We—"

"Quiet. Just let me handle this," his partner told him. "You gave me the idea for this anyway." To Jenna, he now said, "That gadget of yours—you've already used it to input our badge numbers into your security system. Now I want you to feed it some new information."

"What kind of information?"

"I want you to change our status," Rasp replied. "Change it so we're not just delegates, but some sort of VIP types that are to be given special consideration. I want to be able to enter the restricted section without these setting off alarms."

"But I can't do that," Jenna protested. "It's just not—"

"Possible? Sure it is. I've been keeping an eye on you. I can tell you've got clearance yourself, and it didn't take me long to notice you're in tight with the big shots around here. So I know you can do it."

Jenna sighed deeply. "It won't be easy."

"Easy? You want easy?" Rasp said. "Dying is easy. Living takes a little work. Now demonstrate some of that hidden talent of yours. And don't try anything cute. You alert the security system to us, or set some kind of electronic trap in the computer, and people start coming after us, we'll start taking out everyone in sight. Maybe some of your friends. You don't want that, now do you?"

A mixture of fear and anger flashed across her lovely eyes. "No. I don't want anyone hurt."

"Good. Now go ahead and tell your fancy computer a pretty little lie about us."

Jenna looked from one man to the other, then reluctantly set to work on the computer tablet's controls. It took several minutes for her to access the main security line, use her private codes to enter the system, and then enter the data required to do what Rasp wanted. As assistant to Dean McAndrews, she did have the authority to issue special authorizations to visit the restricted wing, even though she would not normally do so unless McAndrews had so requested.

"Okay," she said at last, her tone nervous and guilt-ridden. "It's done."

Rasp looked over her shoulder at the tablet's printout. "Are you sure?"

"Yes," Jenna replied flatly. "You've both got clearance now to the security area. But not without a staff member with you. Sorry, it's the best I could do.

258

Anything else would have triggered a lot of automatic checks and questions by the system."

Rasp frowned at first, then smiled to himself in a frighteningly evil way. "Well, now, I'm sure we can find a way around that little obstacle."

He reached around her and removed her security badge, holding it in his hand. Then he raised his weapon until it pointed at the back of Jenna's head.

"No!" Cudder said abruptly, and there was a commanding power in that single word.

Rasp looked in his direction and saw that Cudder had his own weapon trained on him. The look in his eyes was grim and unwavering. "What do you think you're doing? We don't need her now, and we sure don't want to leave her behind to bring trouble down on us."

"No, I said," Cudder repeated. "We may need her as an escort. Those badges may be encoded to work only if the right person is wearing them. Besides, there are ways she can be immobilized later, other than killing her."

Rasp glared at him, seething with barely controlled anger at this challenge to his authority. "Look, what do you care, anyway? She's one of them."

Cudder stared at the girl, her fragile innocence tearing through him. The image of his young wife and daughter, neither of whom had survived the plague, flashed through his mind after years of being safely buried away. The original horror of that time, and the belief that the University had been responsible, was what had aligned him with the Corporation in the first place. But that same painful image now forced him to challenge Rasp with murderous resolve.

"As I say," Cudder told him, with a calm that was unreal, intense, determined, "I think the smart thing is to take her with us. Maybe she can help us get past the human guards. Maybe I have plans for her myself. You've run this your way so far. Now humor me."

It was not a request. Rasp stared at him a moment more, glancing at the weapon pointed his way. He sighed and lowered his weapon, then handed the badge back to Jenna.

"All right," Rasp told Cudder, his eyes narrow and burning despite the smile in his voice. "Sure. Anything you say, my friend. Makes no difference to me, really. But let's get going. The sooner this is all over with, the better."

21:
ACROSS THE BAY

IT WAS LATE AFFTERNOON when the nomad truck pulled to a halt just outside the city called Haddock. The battered and often-patched vehicle was even dustier from its journey than when it had left Kezos City, but it had gotten them here, and that was what mattered. It was well off the road now, and Vandal parked it for the moment beneath the sheltering branches of a small cluster of trees. There were at least some trees in this area that were unaffected by the plague.

Marinda sat on the front seat between Vandal and Roddi. She was staring down at an open can of food in her hand, part of the provisions they had brought with them from the ship, pushing bits of the stuff around with a metal spoon, without much enthusiasm. Finally, she put some of her thoughts into words.

"I'm sorry to see there's been such little culinary progress in the last seven centuries."

Roddi's look took in the can, and he hastened to explain, "Oh, those are merely survival rations. They are not representative of regular food, insofar as I understand it. But they are fully nutritious."

"I know, I know," she replied with a heavy sigh and a look as wistful as it was tired. "But what I wouldn't give for a steak right now, and a baked potato with cream cheese and chives, and some buttered carrots. And a salad. Oh, how I'd love a salad. A nice tossed salad, with some nice fattening dressing, and gobs of croutons."

Marinda fell silent again, and there was something in that silence and in her slightly strained talkativeness a moment before that caught Vandal's attention. He turned toward her with a questioning gaze.

"All right," he said softly. "What's wrong?"

She did not answer for a moment, chewing her lip. Then finally she said, "I was just wondering . . . how long is the incubation period for the plague? How long between exposure and the first symptoms?"

"Why do you ask?"

Her eyes, now moist around the edges, flicked up toward the cyborg agent with a flash of irritation. "Why? For heaven's sake, Vandal, I'm no fool. I must have been exposed to it by now, after tramping through Delta Zone and being in Kezos City. And I just wanted to know how long. How long before the symptoms show up?"

"It varies," Vandal replied, his own words cautious. "It may take a few days, maybe a few weeks, or even longer." He placed his normal hand against her forehead for a moment. "You don't feel feverish."

"You may not even get it, Marinda," Roddi told her. "The organism may have become dormant in this area, or mutated into a less virulent strain. And anyway, there is a cure for it, now. Once we get you to the University, you won't have anything to worry about, I assure you."

"I know," she said. "At least, I hope I know. It's just that seeing those people in Kezos City kind of got to me. It was all so horrible."

The cyborg agent was staring through a pair of binoculars, scanning the city before them. "Right now, we'd best be thinking about how we're going to get into town and across the bay without attracting attention. It might be wise if we leave this truck here and continue on foot. It's just a ten-minute walk, and the people of Haddock won't trust anyone showing up in a nomad truck."

"How true," Roddi observed. "Also, Razer may have radioed ahead, telling them to be on the lookout for such a vehicle."

Marinda thought of a new concern. "What about us? Up till now we haven't had to go through a civilized town. There must be a description of the three of us circulating, at least among the CorSec people."

"Probably," said Vandal. "Wouldn't hurt if we split up. I think you and Roddi should go into town without me, then we'll meet once we're all there. I'll tell you what I've got in mind. I also think we'd better change our appearance."

Haddock was a coastal town, like some Marinda had seen on Earth if you discounted the minor differences in building construction and materials and the slightly alien landscape. She kept expecting things to be more futuristic, more strange, but she realized that the people who had journeyed to Coreworld in the suspended-animation chambers aboard *Glory* had been Earth people. They had slept through the long journey and had brought their own cultural and artistic tastes with them; in fact, they had clung to them in the midst of a strange new world where many things dear to them were forever lost. It was only natural. She felt the same tug in that direction herself. She also knew that despite technological advances, there are some things that just do not change radically even in the course of a few centuries.

Marinda glanced through the viewplex door of the shop she had spent the last fifteen minutes in, then as she saw no sign of trouble she stepped outside with what she hoped was nonchalance. The street seemed quiet enough. In fact, it was all remarkably normal and familiar, after what she had been through.

Marinda walked down the street in the new dress she had bought. It was a simple design, but was well crafted of some glittery synthetic and showed off her figure nicely. It was red, and she had added a matching pair of dress shoes. Reversing her borrowed cloak with its black inner lining gave her a striking outfit. Her blond hair shone from a washing in the stream they had passed that morning, and for the first time since landing on Coreworld she felt good about her appearance. With her old clothes and her joggers stuffed into her shopping bag, she looked like a different person.

Marinda turned the corner and started down the sidestreet. There in the shadows waited Roddi, guarding their packs. The psybot had done a bit of changing himself, adding several stripes and geometric patterns from his disguise pack's precut sheets of adhesive vinyl. Once stuck down, the purple designs resembled painted markings of the sort used for personal servant mechs, and even with his silvery-blue paint showing he looked different enough to make identification difficult.

As Roddi saw the young woman stop before him he looked her up and down, then said, "Marinda, you look very nice. Very nice indeed." His gaze lowered to take in his own modifications. "I'm afraid we clash, though. Perhaps I should have used different stickers."

"You look fine," she told him. "In fact, you're kind

of cute with those markings. Makes you look almost like you're wearing a tuxedo."

"Perhaps," he replied unenthusiastically. "Frankly, I've never thought of myself as the butler type. But I suppose one does what one must in difficult circumstances. Well, how much change do you have left?"

"Change?"

Roddi stiffened a bit. "Oh, no, you can't mean that you spent all the money I gave you. I really wanted to buy a spare power cell for myself, just in case, and there should have been more than enough—"

"I'm teasing, just teasing." Marinda handed him the Corporation currency she had left from her purchases. "See? I still know how to shop for bargains. Now we'd better go meet Vandal."

"I quite agree. Fortunately, the docks aren't far from here."

Marinda frowned. "I still don't understand why he wants to travel by boat. Wouldn't one of those funny aircraft be faster?"

"A helijet?" asked Roddi. "Yes, of course it would be faster. But there's a much greater chance of CorSec personnel or Corporation executives traveling on the few commercial helijets that operate between Haddock and Jonnersville. Even if we don't sit together, someone might recognize Vandal."

"Makes sense. Well, the sooner we get started, as they say . . ."

Roddi bent to pick up the various packs that had been sitting on the sidewalk at his feet. As he straightened, he extended one to Marinda.

She looked at it, hanging there from his hand. "Me? You want me, dressed like this, attended by a servant mech, to carry a travel pack? Wouldn't that look suspicious?"

"You're right, of course," said Roddi glumly, placing the pack's strap over his shoulder with the rest. "But I think you're enjoying this entirely too much."

Marinda laughed lightly. Turning on her heel, she hooked a finger through the air in a beckoning gesture. "Come, Jeeves."

The hydrofoil tied up at the dock was good-sized, easily capable of carrying eighty to a hundred people. It looked as if only half that number were boarding it, though, and the company's second docking facility looked so neglected it was obvious it was no longer in use. The schedule posted at the small ticket office showed ships commuting between Haddock and Jonnersville only twice a day—early in the morning and late in the afternoon. Roddi had given Marinda most of the currency he had left to buy their two tickets, and they now were heading up the boarding ramp, with Marinda leading the way before her diligent servant.

As they started around the ship's outer deck, Marinda paused by the rail, her alert eyes scanning the dock and the people approaching the boarding ramp. Her brows knitted in a troubled look.

"I don't like this," she whispered. "Shouldn't we have waited, to be sure Vandal gets on?"

Leaning closer in what seemed a routine bow of respect, Roddi softly replied, "He wanted us to go ahead and board, regardless. I'm sure he'll make it."

"I hope you're right," Marinda said. She continued to stare with concern at the boarding ramp and the steadily diminishing crowd that filed up it into the ship. "But we're running out of time, and I don't see him yet."

"Perhaps he boarded ahead of us," Roddi told

her. "Come on, let's go into the enclosed area where it's more comfortable and I can store these packs. It wouldn't do well to stand out here and attract attention."

With reluctance Marinda tore herself away from her vantage point and turned for the hatchway leading into the vessel's interior. She threw one last worried glance toward the dock, then moved toward seats in an area not heavily occupied by passengers. She watched as Roddi slid the packs into storage space beneath the seats, then sat down and crossed her arms in an anxious, impatient pose.

Marinda glanced up and saw that Roddi was still standing close to her, his posture stiff and mechanical. She realized he was maintaining his cover as a servant mech, for he had not been told to do anything since putting away the packs.

Attempting a bit of acting, she said in normal volume, "Oh, do sit down, you silly mech. I don't want you rocking about once we get under way."

Roddi gave a slight nod, then turned and smoothly seated himself next to her. "Thank you, madam," he said in a flat tone, then much softer he added, "Very good, but don't overdo it."

"I'm new at this," she whispered. "Give me a break. Besides, I'm still worried about Vandal."

"Well, try not to show it. Smile a little. No, on second thought, you'd better not."

She gave him a funny look. "Why do you say that?"

"Because," Roddi said very softly, "if you smile, looking as terrific as you do in that outfit, we'll have far too many men coming over here, trying to start something."

Marinda could not help smiling at that. Her mouth crinkled pleasantly, then wryly, and she looked away.

She picked up a magazine left behind in the seat next to her and glanced through it, not wanting to look as if she was having a conversation with a robot.

"That was a sweet thing to say, Roddi," she said softly. "Thank you. And thanks for caring enough to want to cheer me up. You're really quite a friend."

"That pleases me very much, Marinda. I'm never quite sure whether Vandal thinks of me as a friend or merely as a working associate. I know him fairly well, but sometimes it's hard to know what he's thinking."

"Yes," Marinda said meaningfully. "It is."

At that moment, there was a sound from the dock as the boarding ramp drew away from the side of the ship. Then with a rumbling whine and a slight shudder of vibration, the hydrofoil's engines started up.

Marinda tensed in her seat, turning to look out the windows, then looking once more at the passengers who half filled the ship's interior. "We're leaving," she exclaimed softly. "I wish I knew for sure if he made it."

"Relax," Roddi said calmly.

The hydrofoil steadily pulled away from the dock, leaving Haddock behind. Marinda was almost sorry to go. The town had been the first nearly normal place she had seen since awakening, and although she was certainly aware of the urgent need to leave Coreworld, whatever lay ahead was unknown and more than a bit frightening.

When the ship reached open water, its turbine impellers roared up to full power. As the hydrofoil picked up cruising speed, it smoothly lifted out of the water and rode solely upon its pontoon foils, becoming not only more stable, but also very fast.

"How long will it take us to reach Jonnersville?"

Marinda asked Roddi, still pretending to read the magazine in her hands.

"About three hours," the psybot whispered back. "Which will put us there around eight o'clock this evening."

"And that's where we meet the rescue team?"

"If all goes well, which I most certainly hope—" Roddi's words quit abruptly. Though his head had remained motionless, his eye lenses had been slowly scanning the ship's interior, methodically searching the faces of the passengers within his field of vision. Now he focused directly on one of them. "Marinda," he whispered, "don't make a big show of looking, but do you see that fellow over there, just getting up?"

She raised her eyes above the top of the magazine and glanced in the direction Roddi indicated. There was a man getting up, all right. Someone who had been seated in the front corner, facing away from them. He turned down an aisle and took another seat closer to the middle. As he settled himself there, he glanced in their direction.

Marinda thought she recognized him, but the cloak was gone and his face looked different. He was wearing different trousers, and his torso and arms were covered by a bulky, nondescript jacket. A soft cap covered the top of his head, concealing much of his hair, and he had a mustache. He carried a large pack, which he now pushed beneath his seat.

Marinda saw the man look her way again, and this time he winked. She immediately winked back, then suddenly her momentary sense of certainty wavered.

To Roddi, she whispered unobtrusively, "That is Vandal, isn't it?"

"It had better be. Otherwise, you may have just asked for some company you don't really want."

She looked toward Roddi, who was now staring straight ahead, then back to the man across the way. The fellow was reading something himself, or pretending to, and Marinda noticed he wore gloves—to hide a metallic hand? It must be Vandal. Feeling peeved, she looked back to her magazine.

"You . . ." she muttered sideways. She felt like giving Roddi an elbow in the ribs, but of course he didn't have any ribs and she would only injure herself against his hard body shell. "You knew all along it was Vandal, didn't you? You must know all his disguises."

"Sorry," the psybot said softly, barely able to contain his amusement. "I couldn't resist getting even for that business about the packs. Anyway, now you can relax."

"Wise guy." Marinda smiled to herself and shook her head. She glanced again toward Vandal, who was still occupied with his newspaper or whatever it was. Apparently he intended to sit apart from them to avoid the appearance of their traveling together. Fine, she thought. She could understand that. But she did not plan to let the entire trip go by without finding an opportunity to speak with him.

Marinda glanced at the clock on the ship's forward bulkhead. It had been over an hour since they had left the dock at Haddock.

She looked over at Vandal just in time to see him rise from his seat and pull his pack free from beneath it. She hoped that he might be heading over to join them, but that hope died in the next moment as Vandal went aft and placed his pack in one of several dozen coin lockers there. She watched him go next to the hatchway that led to the upper deck.

"Roddi," she asked softly, "what's Vandal up to?"

The psybot had been partially powered down, conserving energy, and took a moment to respond, straightening in his seat and leaning closer to her. "I suspect he's just tired of sitting still and wanted to walk around. I wouldn't worry about it."

"I'm not," Marinda told him, getting up quickly. "Watch our things, okay?"

"Wait," Roddi said, and was about to protest more when he realized that he could not afford to call attention to himself by actions unbefitting a common mech. He decided to stay in his seat for the time being and let things take their course.

On the upper deck, Marinda reached the top of the stairs and stepped through the hatchway. This was an observation area sealed in by viewplex windows and roof, to protect against the high-speed flow of air created by the craft's swift progress. There were seats here, but at the moment there were only a few passengers making use of them, all up near the bow. She looked about, trying to see where Vandal had gone. Darkness was falling, and there was only the dying sunlight and the faint bluish glow of scattered deck lights to illuminate her way. Finally she saw him, standing by the starboard side just past the middle of the ship. Trying not to look as if she was heading his way, she did exactly that.

Marinda walked casually past him and paused at the handrail a few feet beyond. Turning toward him, she studied his face. At this distance there could be no doubt it was Vandal. She could even make out the faint outline of the scar on his forehead and cheek, though it seemed to be covered with makeup.

She smiled at him as she leaned against the rail. "Hi," she said, keeping her voice low. "Think it will hurt anything if I'm seen talking with you?"

Vandal's eyes cautiously swept the deck. "I suppose not."

"You really look different," Marinda told him.

"So do you." Vandal studied her with a look that was difficult to decipher, taking in the details of her new outfit before his eyes once more met hers. "So, were you getting restless down there, too?"

"Sort of. After all the running and everything, I thought it would be nice to just sit and relax, but I guess I'm still too nervous."

Vandal said nothing in reply, but his questioning gaze seemed to doubt her words. He was not the easiest person in the world to make conversation with.

"I . . . I guess that's not the whole truth," Marinda said finally. "Part of the reason I came up here, maybe the biggest part, is that I just needed to talk with you."

He leaned against the handrail in a casual pose and looked out at the waters of the bay as if enjoying the view. "You're not still worrying about the plague, are you?"

"No . . . well, at least not quite as much as before."

"Then what is it?"

Marinda hesitated a moment. "I guess maybe I'm a little afraid of what will happen next. I mean, after we leave here and reach your friends on Avalon."

"They're not really my friends," Vandal said, a bit stiffly. "But you don't have to worry about them. They'll see to it you have whatever you need, and help you adjust to things as they are now."

Marinda looked away, watching the darkening waters that seemed to isolate them from everything. "That's not quite what I meant. What I was wondering was, after we get there and I get settled in, what

272

happens with you and Roddi? Do you guys just go off on another assignment somewhere?"

"That's our job. Whatever needs to be done."

"Is that all this has been? Just a job?"

Vandal turned to her, his face an emotionless mask. "It's been different from most, I have to admit."

Marinda looked into his gaze, awkwardly, reluctantly. "You're not . . . you're not making this easy for me, you know that? What I'm trying to say, Vandal—what I've been wanting to say—is that I think I'm falling in love with you. Maybe that sounds crazy, considering the short amount of time we've known each other, but we've been through so much, and it's just the way I feel, and now . . . and now I'm afraid once we get out of this I may never see you again."

"Marinda," Vandal said quickly, grasping her shoulders with his strong hands. "Look, in the first place, I'm sure Roddi and I won't be dashing off right away. We're not going to throw you in among strangers and disappear. I'm not much for friendships, or any other kind of relationships for that matter, but we'll be around."

"Vandal, I—"

"Let me finish," Vandal cut her off. "In the second place, it's just like you said—you've been through a lot in a short time. You were awakened in different circumstances than you expected. Difficult circumstances. Everything's strange to you. None of your friends are around anymore. For what it's worth, Roddi and I have been the only constant and friendly element you've seen so far. It's only natural you'd feel something, but it would be a mistake to think—"

"No, don't try to tell me what my feelings are. I'm not just some silly schoolgirl, Vandal. I've had enough psychological training to know there's some truth in

273

what you're saying, but I also know enough about myself to be sure there's more to this than just a reaction to stress. My feelings are real."

Vandal lowered his eyes. "Trusting feelings can be dangerous. And that's something I know for sure. Besides, you've got to face reality. What's the point of getting involved with me? Where's it heading? You know who I am—what I am. I'm not . . . I'm not even a complete man anymore. Forty percent of me is hardware. Forty percent! Do you have any idea what that's like, Marinda? What it's like dealing with that? Living with that? Day after day? I tried to kill myself once, after the operations, when I found out what I'd become. The only thing that's kept me going since then has been my determination to destroy the Corporation. It's what I live for."

"There are other things to live for," Marinda told him. She reached out and touched his face. "And as far as your damned hardward goes, I'm not worried about that. When it comes right down to it, Roddi is a hundred percent hardware, but I still care about him."

"That's fine," Vandal replied, "for friendship. But love is something else. You're a healthy young woman, Marinda. You shouldn't be wasting yourself on a freak like me. You wouldn't really want to be loved by, or make love to, a cyborg."

She let her delicate fingers come to rest upon his hand, his mechanical hand, as it continued to grip her shoulder. "Why don't you let me decide that, when the time comes? Unless you just don't find me attractive, or . . ." Her lips twisted up in a wry quirk of a smile. "Or unless you have something against older women. I mean really older."

His expression softened into a smile that was only slightly cynical. He removed her hand from his and gave it a pat. "You're more than attractive enough, especially tonight. But we'll talk about this later. Right now, we still have a lot ahead of us. Surviving—getting to safety—that's the important thing right now."

Marinda nodded soberly. She could not deny his logic, but this was not the answer she had wanted. "All right. Just remember what I've said, and give things a chance."

On impulse, she lurched forward and kissed him, then gave him a hug that was imperative and tremulous, her face buried against his muscular chest. Then she turned away and hurried back to the stairs.

Alone by the rail of the observation deck, Vandal watched her go, then turned once more to the sea. His face again became a stone-hard mask, brooding and grim. He shook his head once, sighing, and stared into the encroaching darkness with eyes as pained as they were troubled.

Below, on the main passenger deck, Marinda returned to her seat and settled there beside Roddi. She wiped at the moisture threatening to well up in her eyes.

Roddi swiveled his head toward her, studying her for a moment. "Are you all right?" he whispered.

"Yes. Sure. Just fine." She pulled her cloak about her, huddling within its warmth and concealing her pretty new dress. "Well, maybe not fine, but I'll be okay. It's just that sometimes my emotions get me into situations that only seem to turn out awkward and hopeless, and I just make a fool of myself. Can you understand that?"

"Yes," Roddi said quietly, looking away from her and wondering if his own feelings were only the delusions of an electronic mind. "I believe I can. . . ."

* * *

At exactly that moment in the city of Haddock, Razer stood by the open hatch of her damaged helijet, one foot on the ground and the other raised upon the boarding step. She reached in and grabbed the microphone from its clip by the radio, then threw a dismal glance behind her at the crew that worked so feverishly on her craft.

The helijet was parked on the landing pad outside the operations office of a small CorSec detachment on the eastern side of town. The helijet engine Vandal had disabled was gone. Razer had cut it loose in the park in Kezos City after sealing off the fuel lines leading to it. Minus the engine's weight on that side of the ship, the remaining three engines had been able to support the rest of the aircraft at a reasonably stable angle. It had taken her many more hours to reach Haddock than it should have, limping along at low altitude and at slow speed, and landing often to allow the overtaxed remaining engines to cool. But she had made it, on her own, and she considered that well worth the price of delay.

Technicians positioned a replacement engine pod where the missing one had been and worked quickly to connect it. Others busied themselves with the task of refueling the craft. It would soon be ready, though not a moment too soon to suit Razer.

Looking back to her radio, the beautiful Corporation eliminator switched on the power. The unit was already set to the special Quintad frequency and Roman's scrambler code. She thumbed the button and spoke into the microphone.

"This is Razer. Are you there, Roman?"

There was a momentary pause, then Roman's voice came back through the receiver. "Yes, my darling.

276

I've been eagerly awaiting your next report. Where are you?"

"In Haddock—I've just arrived," she replied, glancing back at the CorSec crew again, not really caring whether they heard her lover's informal greeting. If anything, it gave her added status. "I've had some trouble with the aircraft, but it's being worked on now. I was able to track Vandal and the girl to Kezos City, and from there on to here. I'll be resuming the search again in a matter of minutes." Her eyes flashed at the work crew to emphasize the point.

"From Kezos City to Haddock?" Roman's voice responded. "Interesting. There was a disturbing matter yesterday, involving a group of mechs apparently taking over one of our company's cargo helijets here in CityPrime. It landed in Troy, as scheduled, but it seemed they had the intention of refueling it and heading elsewhere."

"Mechs? Hijacking a helijet?"

"Obviously not ordinary mechs. I think we can safely assume they were the psybot variety, operating on the orders of the University. They've not been caught yet, though it seemed some of our troops in Troy had destroyed them. What intrigues me is the fact that this group and Vandal's group appear to be converging on a central point."

"Haddock?"

"Or Jonnersville," Roman told her. "There's really very little else in the area along that path."

"Jonnersville," Razer said, her eyes narrowing. "That might make sense at that. There's a hydrofoil service operating between the two cities. A ship left just a little over an hour ago. I can check with the ticket office, see if anyone like our group of three boarded it. If so, they've got a slight head start, but I think I can still get in the air soon enough to reach Jonnersville about the same time."

"Excellent. I am confident you are close to success. I look forward to your resolving this matter, and to your speedy return."

"As do I. Just try to keep the assistance to a minimum, please. I really don't want anyone cramping my style. Some overzealous rookie could ruin everything."

"I'll do what I can," Roman told her in a pleasant but firm tone. "But I can't make any promises. Alpha is adamant about this matter, and I must follow his wishes to the letter. You do understand, don't you?"

Razer gave a peevish sigh and frowned. "Yes, I understand. Do what you must, as shall I. Over and out."

She switched off the radio and tossed the microphone onto the seat. Then she drew her protoblaster and checked the sights to be sure they were still properly aligned.

"This time, Vandal," she said softly to herself, "I won't miss."

22:

PERILOUS
RENDEZVOUS

"THEY'RE HERE," CLEERA said abruptly, stiffening as she stood beside Dr. Arcanus at the side of the stage. They were between illusions, and the other psybots were moving apparatus for the next trick into place. "Vandal and the others are here."

Dr. Arcanus looked toward the audience gathered for their evening performance. "Here?"

"In Jonnersville," Cleera corrected herself. "They've just arrived and sent a T-Beam message to the Uni for relay to me. I have their coordinates, at least for the moment, and they've been informed of our location."

"Are they going to try to meet us here?"

"No. McAndrews wants us all to gather at another place. I've just been given the location."

Arcanus gave a sober nod, his alert eyes surveying the crowd. "Just as well. We seem to have even more of our friends in uniform out there tonight than at our matinee performance."

"Yes, so I've been noticing."

"I'd like to think it's all due to word-of-mouth advertising in praise of our show," said Arcanus, "but

I'm afraid it's more likely the authorities have gotten suspicious about recent events in Troy and are starting to put things together."

Cleera studied the people in the well-filled open-air "theater." Mixed in with the ordinary citizens of Jonnersville were a very large number of CorSec Guards, officers and soldiers alike. They were divided into small groups of men scattered throughout the audience, but there was something about them that still looked organized and purposeful. If that was not enough to worry about, Cleera noticed one other significant difference between these men and the guards who came to the earlier performance. These men all wore weapons.

"I hope you're wrong," Cleera told the magician. "I hope we're both wrong. But I'm afraid that's too much to hope for, under the circumstances." She shifted her worried gaze back to center stage. "Look, the Ghost Chamber illusion is ready—we'd better get back out there."

Arcanus arched an eyebrow gravely, tugging at his white gloves to smooth their fit. "Indeed we had, my pretty metallic miss. The show must go on, as they say, if only to give us time to think."

At that moment, Vandal, Roddi, and Marinda stood in a narrow alleyway between buildings not far from the hydrofoil service's dock facility. Roddi was packing away the small T-beam transceiver unit he had just used to make contact with the University and, indirectly, with Cleera's group.

"I'm glad we're finally this close to the rescue team," Roddi said with enthusiasm.

"As far as I'm concerned," complained Vandal, "we'd be better off if the University would just tell us where this ship of theirs is. We've made it this far. I don't see why we need anyone else's help."

"I'm sure they have their reasons," Roddi replied. "Do you think we'll have any trouble finding the rendezvous point?"

"No. I know this town well enough to locate it." Vandal turned to Marinda, who had been silent much of the time since they docked in Jonnersville. "Are you ready to go?"

She looked around in his direction, but was having difficulty making eye contact. "Yes," she told him. "After the truck ride to Haddock and the boat ride here, I'm unusually well rested. I . . . Vandal!"

Marinda suddenly dove forward, pushing the cyborg agent aside. Almost at the same moment, a beam from a protoblaster tore through the air just above their heads, melting a chunk of wall behind them.

Vandal wrapped an arm around Marinda even as he ducked with the force of her push, pulling her along with him behind an old truck parked near the mouth of the alleyway. Finding cover there, they hunched low alongside the truck. Vandal's head whipped around, trying to determine Roddi's fate. He could see the psybot a dozen feet behind him, taking shelter behind an empty crate large enough to conceal him. He was safe for the moment, but there could be no doubt that a beam weapon would soon burn through such a crate. There could also be no doubt as to the wielder of that weapon.

"Razer?" ventured Marinda.

"Safe bet," replied Vandal.

The hissing throb of another blast shattered the stillness as a beam struck the rear of the truck, scorching its way through the metal paneling and sending a spray of glowing fragments flying. The beam continued on to the wall beyond. Obviously the truck was no better protection than the crate.

Vandal had his own pistol out and ready. Putting a staying hand on Marinda, he hesitated a second, then quickly thrust his head and gun hand around the rear edge of the truck, knowing Razer would expect him at the front. He fired off two swift shots, then drew back instantly.

Even as he pulled back, a beam caught the rear of the truck, barely a foot above his head, forcing him to duck below a shower of charged embers. He caught a glimpse of his attacker, but took no satisfaction in being right.

Razer knew she had missed again, even before the beam struck. She could tell from the angle. The curse she was about to utter froze on her pretty lips as Vandal's two shots struck the pavement near her feet, kicking up debris and forcing her to leap backward.

Behind the truck, Vandal reached into his pocket and extracted something. To Marinda he whispered, "Get ready to run." He looked toward Roddi and, seeing that he had the psybot's attention, gave a quick hand signal. Then, bending low, Vandal hurled a handful of tiny devices beneath the truck and into the street beyond.

Razer was just straightening from her leap, trying to take aim at the spot where she thought Vandal would be behind the truck, not caring a great deal whether the girl was in the way or not. But before she could pull the trigger again, the thumb-sized devices Vandal had thrown onto the street erupted in a series of light flashes of blinding intensity. The beautiful eliminator threw up an arm to shield her eyes, but it was too late. Dazzling spots danced before her, even with her eyelids tightly shut. There was also a barrage of noise from the tiny devices, making it impossible to aim at a target by the sound of footsteps.

Roddi instantly rose from behind the crate and darted toward the truck, running at full speed. As he passed the open space, he ventured a look at Razer, tempted to fire at her while he had the chance. He knew Vandal had chosen not to fire a killing shot, and so he did not wish to do so either. Besides, there was something vaguely unsporting about it, and shooting humans, even a human as nasty as Razer, was a loathsome thing for him. Roddi caught up with Vandal and Marinda as they started running from the truck, and he tried to place himself as an extra shield between the young Earth woman and Razer.

Keeping pace with them as they rounded the corner and headed down a side street, Roddi commented, "I do wish that woman would stop showing up uninvited. She makes life very difficult."

Vandal gave a grunt of agreement. "In every sense of the word."

At Dr. Arcanus's Traveling Automated Magic Show, yet another illusion was under way. The rear curtain was raised to reveal a backdrop of the deepest black, a dark and somber background that matched the black flooring extending to center stage. An ivory framework with sculpted curves and straight top, resembling a bench or bizarre bed, stood at center stage, its intense whiteness making it leap out against the ebony gloom behind it.

Positioned at either side of the stage, near the audience, stood oddly shaped pots of roiling vapor, spilling cloudlike mists to the floor. Behind the pot on the left was Cleera. Muse stood motionless behind the pot on the right.

Dr. Arcanus strode quickly into view from offstage, came to a halt between the two vapor pots, and addressed the audience. "And now, ladies and gentlemen, for our last illusion, I proudly present my interpretation of another classic feat of legerdemain, using one of my lovely mechanical assistants. For your pleasure and puzzlement, I give you—the Levitation!"

Looking toward Muse, Arcanus seemed to activate her with a magical gesture. He waited as she turned stiffly and walked to him, then took her hand and displayed her to the audience. The lovely psybot's glistening gold body sparkled in the combined glow of the various spotlights, throwing glints of light with every movement.

Arcanus led her to the ivory framework with slow, deliberate steps. Upon reaching it he stopped Muse at one end of the framework, her back to it. With a glance and a wink to the audience, he proceeded to gesture at Muse's face with his long, expressive fingers, as if hypnotizing her.

Acting on cue, Muse slowly closed her metal eyelids, feigning sleep. Then she very mechanically lowered herself to the platform and reclined upon it. In a moment she was in the proper position, stretched out and rigid as a board, supported by the ivory framework at key points along her tall, well-sculpted body.

As the recorded music began to build and become more dramatic, Arcanus gestured magically at Muse's "sleeping" form from the side so that he did not block the audience's view. Slowly, ever so slowly, Muse began to rise from the platform, inching upward, floating steadily higher.

She reached a point roughly ten feet in the air and stopped, seeming to hover there. Arcanus quickly grasped the end of the ivory framework and pulled it aside, propelling it offstage on its casters as Jayray assisted from the wings.

Returning his attention to the floating robot, Arcanus now walked beneath her, his arms extended to both sides, demonstrating that no machinery held her up. Then with a raised finger and an arched eyebrow, he said, "Ah, I see there are yet skeptics among you. I must prove there are no wires holding my pretty assistant in the air. Very well, I shall, ah . . . rise to the challenge."

Cleera was already stepping to the wings, to pick up a large golden hoop roughly a yard in diameter. She returned with the hoop and handed it to the gaunt magician.

"Thank you, my dear," Arcanus said in a booming voice, then in a tight-mouthed whisper he added, "Is everyone ready?"

"Yes," Cleera said softly, adding with a glance toward the audience, "and so are they, I'm afraid."

Arcanus's alert gaze swept the audience. As Cleera had indicated, a number of the CorSec Guards had left their seats and quietly taken up positions near each side of the stage, as well as at the entrance to the theater area. Others were scattered along the soft tent walls to head off an escape there.

"We may as well proceed as planned," Arcanus whispered, then as Cleera moved to the edge of the stage, he tapped the hoop on the stage floor and held it up for the audience to view. In a loud voice, he proclaimed, "As you can see, I have in my hands a solid ring of metal. Now watch as I prove to you there are no wires or supports of any kind."

Dr. Arcanus stepped to a spot just below Muse's feet, turned the hoop sideways to the audience, and raised it over his head. He slowly moved it over her feet, passing the ring around the golden psybot.

What he could see from his position but the audience could not was that standing directly behind him was HiLo. Cloaked all in black, the extendable psybot was virtually invisible against the black background and flooring. The contrast of bright light shining on Muse's glistening body made it even harder for him to be seen.

HiLo held his arms out before him, his hands beneath Muse's back and legs, holding her in the air. He was extended to near his maximum height, swaying slightly from side to side and moving his arms up and down just a bit, to add to the illusion that Muse was truly floating.

As Dr. Arcanus moved the golden hoop around Muse's horizontal form, his right hand secretly slid a tiny tab protruding from the hollow ring. A portion of the ring at the back telescoped within the outer section, allowing enough space between the ends to slip around HiLo's arms. The break was concealed by Muse's body, and Arcanus quickly slid the piece closed again as soon as he passed HiLo's other arm.

Arcanus swung the hoop around and down as applause came from the audience, then gave it a roll that carried it offstage. He bowed briefly, then with a sly wink and a raised hand, he abruptly stepped forward, turned, and threw an expansive, magical gesture at the floating robot.

There was a bright flash of light, and in the next instant Muse had disappeared, totally gone from view. More applause and cheers came from the audience, who did not know how simply a disappearance could be accomplished with an explosive burst of flashpowder and a black cloth dropped swiftly into place in front of Muse.

Arcanus bowed deeply. The curtains swept in from the wings at his remote command, completely closing off the stage from view.

As the applause continued, several groups of CorSec Guards started for the steps at the sides of the stage. But they abruptly halted as the curtain was drawn open again. The men looked back to their officers, who unobtrusively motioned for them to wait.

Dr. Arcanus stood at one side of the stage, taking his curtain call. Arranged in a line across the stage were his "mechanical assistants," Cleera, Muse, HiLo, Torb, Chiron, and one of the twinbots. Arcanus took a long bow, seeming to enjoy the applause, then he turned and extended his hands toward his assistants, as if presenting them for audience approval.

Cleera bowed first, somewhat mechanically, taking her time, followed by Muse. Each of the psybots in turn took a bow, until at last the twinbot on the end took his. As he straightened and the applause finally began to die out, the psybots all turned their heads toward Arcanus.

The elderly magician cast an amused look toward the audience, then he suddenly made one last great magical gesture taking in all those upon the stage. To the audience's delight and awe, all of the robots, and Dr. Arcanus himself, instantly began to shimmer and dissolve, fading away to nothing without moving from the spot on which they stood.

There was more wild applause, and some members of the audience rose to their feet. Some of those rising, however, were CorSec officers, who looked at the stage with alarm rather than admiration or wonder. They quickly gestured for their men to advance upon the stage.

The soldiers were up the steps in a matter of seconds, searching for some clue as to where and how the troupe had vanished. They could see the outline of the main trapdoor Torb had used in his disappearance, but clearly it could not account for them all. Nothing else could be found except for a number of small boxy devices on the stage floor, each positioned exactly where a member of the magic act had been standing. A thin power cable connected them all and ran offstage.

Up till now the audience had thought the soldiers merely part of the show and had greeted their frantic searching with laughter and more applause. But it became clear they were not acting, for some had weapons drawn. As the applause faded to a worried hush, another sound could now be heard.

Somewhere beyond the tent walls of Dr. Arcanus's theater came the muffled roar of a truck engine, speeding away, and the fading sound of an old man's laughter.

Galvanized to action, the CorSec officers called to their men, hustling them all to the exit and their vehicles beyond. The movements of the startled crowd, however, impeded their plan and slowed them down.

In the truck that was so swiftly leaving the area, Cleera was at the wheel, checking her rearview mirror for signs of pursuit. Dr. Arcanus and Muse were beside her, and the rest of her psybot team were in the back.

"This thing moves pretty fast without all the stage equipment in it," Cleera observed. Then with an apologetic glance to Arcanus she added, "I'm sorry we had to leave everything behind."

"Nothing to worry about," Arcanus told her. "Equipment alone does not a magician make. It was old anyway, and needed replacing. Besides," he added, giving a pat to two bundles in his lap, "I did manage to save some keepsakes, and, of course, today's receipts!"

Vandal, Marinda, and Roddi turned down yet another street, keeping to the shadows, running as fast as they could. In this part of town there were no restaurants or entertainment facilities to bring traffic into the area. Whether that was a benefit or a hindrance remained to be seen.

Suddenly, Vandal halted, motioning for Roddi to stop as well, and grasping Marinda, who, in her haste, almost ran past him. He directed them to an inset entrance beneath a building's overhang, a place swathed in darkness and offering shelter from several sides as well as from above. As they waited there, breathing hard, Vandal tensed and listened alertly.

In the next few seconds, Marinda heard it, too. The distinctive whine of a CorSec helijet grew louder, heading their way. Razer!

Vandal reached for the upper thigh of his artificial leg. The slacks he wore as part of his disguise were also made with a special flap providing access to the panel within the limb, and Vandal had it open in an instant. He switched on the ECM device fastened within and motioned the others to flatten against the alcove's back wall.

In the next moment the craft came over the building across the street from them, its engine whine growing louder and its searchlight probing the area. The helijet hovered directly above the street for a long while, sending its beam up and down the street, illuminating the building entrances and the alleyways, searching . . . searching.

The spot of light swept past the building where they were hidden and went on, then abruptly doubled back, probing the alcove with its brightness. Marinda gave a slight gasp, quiet and tense. The overhang above them and the angle of the helijet worked in their favor. The beam reached most of the way into the alcove, but stopped short of their feet by mere inches. They could not see the helijet from where they were, and so Razer could not see them. The Corporation eliminator was probably using the craft's scanners as well, but Vandal's electronic countermeasures would interfere with any signals that might give them away—they hoped.

Finally, after mere moments that seemed an eternity, the beam and the helijet moved on. It moved down the street and crossed over a row of buildings, its sound growing fainter.

Vandal waited another few seconds after it was gone before turning off his equipment and refastening the panel and flap. "Come on," he told Roddi and Marinda, "let's head this way."

Dr. Arcanus's truck sped along the street, blocks away from the shopping center and the site of the magic show. Cleera drove with determination and continued to check the rearview mirror for any signs of trouble. She could see that one of the rear doors to the truck was still open, hanging out from the back and swaying with the truck's motion. There had been no time to secure it after the other psybots boarded, and she hoped it would not cause any problems.

"That was quite a closing illusion," Muse said suddenly as they rolled along. "Lucky for us we had taken the precaution of recording that holographic version of the curtain call. It gave us time to escape."

"Not luck, my dear Muse," Arcanus told her. "Just Cleera's good planning. She anticipated everything."

Cleera smiled to herself, but in the next instant something she saw in the mirror caused her smile to fade. "Perhaps not everything. . . ."

A CorSec troop car came sharply around the corner behind them and began pursuit. Apparently some of the soldiers had been able to get out of the theater and reach a vehicle. So far, it was the only one she saw.

"Trouble?" Arcanus asked.

"Some of our friends in uniform, I'm afraid." Cleera swerved as she saw one of the men in the troop car bring a pistol out through the window and aim at them. Her timing was perfect, for a ray beam scorched close along the truck's side in the next instant. To the others, Cleera shouted, "Hang on!"

Cleera swerved once more as she glimpsed the soldier trying to aim for another shot. Another ray burned past them. Cleera drove the truck faster, but doubted she had a chance of outrunning the troop car.

In the back of the truck, HiLo and the others had been aware of their predicament from the first moment the troop car turned onto the road behind them. Swaying with the truck's lurching motion, they tried to stay upright. Torb and Chiron, with their heavier weight and wide stance, were the most stable.

"Torb," HiLo snapped, "back me up here, okay? I'm going to try to hit that thing."

HiLo immediately went prone on the floor of the truck, pointing a beam weapon out the back and attempting to aim at the troop car. He got off two quick shots, but both missed. He tried again, more carefully, and still missed. Try as he might, between the movements of the truck and the evasive maneuvering of the

CorSec vehicle, his gun was always pointing just slightly off the mark.

Standing just behind him and remarkably steady, Torb decided to draw his own pistol, or perhaps a missile launcher. He suddenly gave a grunt of impatience and looked overhead. There above him ran the long metal pipes upon which the stage lights were clamped during travel. Reaching up to one of them, Torb wrenched it from the roof and faced the open back of the truck. With one mighty motion of servos and drive pistons, he hurled the pipe directly at the pursuing vehicle.

Whether the driver of the troop car swerved into its path through misjudging its flight or Torb's aim was perfect mattered little. The long pipe struck the front end of the vehicle dead center. The impromptu lance tore through the hood and the vehicle's turbine, then continued into the pavement and became imbedded.

Pinned to the roadway, the car stopped instantly with a shuddering crash. Its occupants did not, their momentum propelling them against the dash and windshield. They fell back, dazed and bleeding.

"There," said Torb as HiLo rolled over and looked up at him. The bulky blue robot gave a heavy shrug. "Saves ammunition."

Cleera saw the vehicle fading from view as they sped away, and thought she could guess who was responsible. She made a mental note to compliment Torb on his quick thinking and good aim.

She turned at the next corner, then turned again in her original direction to make it harder for other CorSec pursuers to spot the truck. She slowed somewhat, not wanting to risk turning over.

"Are we getting close to the rendezvous point?" asked Arcanus.

"Yes, sir, we are," Cleera replied grimly. "But not as close as I'd like us to be."

"I knew I should have changed shoes," moaned Marinda, bending down and rubbing her ankles. "Do I have time to put my joggers back on, or should I wait until we get to where we're going?"

"We're there," replied Vandal.

From the sheltering darkness of an alleyway on the west side of town, Vandal peered at the old building across the street. It was a two-story structure, filling half the block, and its windows and doors were boarded up. In fact, they looked as if they had been boarded up for years.

Marinda straightened and peeked around Vandal's shoulder, staring at the place. "Is that the rendezvous point?"

"Yes," said the cyborg agent.

Marinda sighed. "Not a lot of glamour in your line of work, is there, guys?"

Vandal started across the street. "Come on."

The three moved quickly over the roadway and reached the sidewalk on the other side. Vandal started for the door near the center of the building, then immediately reconsidered and led them to the end of the building nearest them. Light from the street fixtures did not reach here as strongly, and there was a window with a few boards that had already fallen out of place. With a quick glance up and down the street, Vandal made sure no CorSec patrols or passersby were in the area, then he pried loose one of the remaining boards and checked the window behind it. The viewplex panel had already been broken out, probably by thieves or derelicts, or perhaps some storm-blown debris. Whatever the cause, they had access, and it was better to wait inside, out of view, than to remain on the street.

Vandal went inside first, checking out the dark interior with a small infrared light. Then he turned to help Marinda inside, lifting her through the opening and setting her down lightly upon the hard concrete flooring.

Roddi climbed through next, activating his own infrared beam and scanning the area. "Not much to look at, is it?"

"Especially not for some of us," Marinda said.

"Oops, sorry." Reminded that Marinda had no provision for seeing infrared, Roddi stepped away from the window and switched on his regular chest light.

The interior of the building was empty, or nearly so, with no interior walls. What looked like an office was set in one corner, the space created by divider panels that did not reach all the way up to the high ceiling. A few broken pieces of lumber littered the floor. Over on the far end were a number of large empty crates and a rusting power generator that looked as if it must weigh several tons.

Marinda raised a skeptical eyebrow. "You're sure this is the right place?"

"Oh, yes," insisted Roddi. "This is the location given us in the University's message. The other agents are to meet us here."

"Well, I hope they make it soon," said Marinda, kicking off her dress shoes and slipping into her joggers. "Do you guys mind if I change back to my old clothes? This outfit's not made for running and climbing."

"Better make it fast," said Vandal, standing at the window and looking out between the boards. "I think the others are here."

Marinda hastily fastened the straps on her joggers

and turned back to the window. Peering through the opening, she saw nothing at first. Then as her gaze grew more discerning she spotted what appeared to be a large truck stopping in the alley they had just left. The cab of the truck was facing their way, but Marinda could not make out who was inside.

"You're sure they're not CorSec people?" Marinda asked.

"I'm sure."

As Roddi joined them at the window, he agreed. "Yes, I can see two robots and a white-haired human who fit the descriptions I was given." He watched as Vandal signaled to the truck with his infrared light, then saw more of the psybot team coming up the alley from the rear of the vehicle. "Oh my, some of them are going to have a hard time fitting through this window."

Vandal jerked his head around, aiming his infrared light behind him and searching for another entrance away from the street. He found it in the side wall, where a wide delivery door gave access to the alley running beside the building.

He quickly pointed it out to Roddi. "Come on, let's see if we can get that open. The sooner they're all off the street, the better I'll like it."

Marinda waited near the window as Vandal and Roddi ran to the delivery door. There was just enough light slanting through the window to create a small pool of glow at her feet, and she used this to sort out the garments in her bag. Then she removed her cloak, slipped out of her dress, and hastily put on her jeans and lab coat. As she finished buttoning her coat, she took a last, lingering look at the pretty red dress that had done so much to raise her spirits and give her the confidence to express her feelings to Vandal. With a sigh, she neatly folded it and put it away in the bag on top of the fancy shoes.

A sudden rasp of sound made her jump, then she realized that it was the wide delivery door being lifted. Marinda fastened the cloak about her and grabbed the bag, then hurried off to join Vandal and Roddi at the door.

Marinda arrived in time to see the first members of the rescue party step through, their looks tentative and cautious. She imagined her own expression was no more confident. And as they continued to enter the old building, she was surprised that all but one were robots.

"I'm Cleera," the lavender-and-white psybot introduced herself, "and these are my friends." She quickly introduced the members of her team, then came at last to the one human in their midst. "And this is Dr. Arcanus, the stage magician who helped us get here. You must be Vandal?"

The cyborg agent nodded impatiently, then tersely indicated those in his group. "Roddi . . . Marinda Donelson."

Marinda smiled at these newcomers. They seemed friendly enough. But as she took in Cleera's pretty appearance and Muse's breathtaking looks, she could not help thinking she had changed back to her bedraggled old outfit a bit too soon. "Hi," she said weakly.

"Look," snapped Vandal, "I don't know about your group, but we've got CorSec trouble not far behind us."

"Same here," Cleera told him.

"Then let's not waste time," Vandal replied. "Do you plan to use your truck to take us to this secret base, wherever it is?"

Cleera shook her head. "No. In fact, we've already

unloaded everything from the truck that we want to take with us.''

Vandal frowned hard. "Then how?"

"Our transportation is right here, if my information is correct."

"Here?" said Roddi skeptically. "But . . . this place is empty!"

"Not as empty as it looks," said Cleera. Gesturing at the wide delivery door, she told them, "I suggest we close that. We don't want to be disturbed."

Vandal considered it briefly, then nodded in agreement. He and several of the others pulled the door down, trying to make as little noise as possible.

Cleera turned on a light of her own and strode toward the other end of the spacious building. "This property once belonged to the University," Cleera told them. "Back when its base was still here on Coreworld, before the trouble with the Corporation began. The University used it as some sort of equipment storage facility for a number of its research stations."

"Yes," replied Vandal as he and the others followed along. "I remember Jonnersville was one of the Uni centers, besides CityPrime. But how does this help us?"

"Well," Cleera continued, "the information I just received in the last T-beam transmission concerned a research installation the University had on Trasker's Island. It's about five hundred miles northwest of here. Though it started as a legitimate research facility, the University foresaw the trouble with the Corporation, and was able to install equipment there which it secretly used for intelligence gathering, even after the Uni relocated on Avalon. And since the Uni people anticipated that they might need to escape, they also hid a spaceship on the island, large enough for all Uni personnel. It's still there, waiting to be used."

Roddi continued to sweep his light around the place. "Well, that's certainly good news. But this building doesn't appear to have been used by anyone recently, let alone the University, and I don't see the connection."

"It hasn't been used lately, I admit," Cleera replied. "When the problems with the Corporation first began, the Uni transferred ownership of this building to a private shipping company, on paper at least. But it remained a University facility. And the Uni provided a means for its personnel here and others in the area to reach the island base."

Cleera stopped and angled her light beam at the floor. She and the others had traversed most of the building as they talked, and now they stopped at a spot roughly thirty feet from the far wall.

"Beneath this part of the floor," Cleera told them, "there's a specially equipped cargo helijet, sitting on a lift that will raise it to ground level. The only problem is, when the last Uni personnel closed down the facility, they decided to hide the access panels with those."

Standing directly in front of them, on top of the section of flooring Cleera had indicated, were all the heavy wooden shipping crates and the immense rusting hulk of the abandoned power generator.

"That's not the only problem," Vandal announced grimly. "What Cleera hasn't mentioned, and what I know from my own experience, is that Trasker's Island is now a CorSec weapons-testing center. And the University wants us to try to reach a spacecraft right in the middle of that?"

"Yes," Cleera said, in an apologetic tone. "They told me the only other place you might find a craft with the necessary range would be the main CorSec base, near CityPrime, and the security precautions there would make it impossible. There's a much smaller contingent of soldiers stationed on Trasker's Island. The three of you might not make it on your own, but with the rest of us backing you up . . ."

Vandal shook his head, his face a stone mask. Finally, he said, "Doesn't look like we have much choice, does it?"

"I'm afraid not," replied Cleera. "Now we'd better do what we can to get this mess cleared away from the floor panels."

Torb lumbered forward. "Come on, Chiron. I see why they needed us."

The boxy blue robot walked around to the far side of the old power generator and positioned himself in a proper lifting posture. His servos straining, he only succeeded in raising his side of the huge device a few inches off the floor. It was not only heavier than it looked, it was awkward as well.

Rolling up to the opposite side, Chiron extended his heavy-duty lifting arms beneath the edge and began lifting that end. With both psybots working together, they managed to half-carry, half-drag the heavy piece of machinery away from the access panels in the floor.

HiLo and the others did what they could with the smaller crates, moving them aside, and Torb and Chiron tackled the remaining large ones. In a few minutes, everything had been cleared away.

From the distance came the sound of sirens, cutting through the night's stillness with growing clarity. CorSec troop cars were drawing near.

"Cleera," said Vandal abruptly, "you do know how to activate the lift?"

"Yes." Cleera ran to the wall and began searching for a hidden control panel whose location she knew only by description. "What I don't know is if the secret power feed to the lift is still connected."

After a few frantic moments she found the spot she was looking for and pressed in upon the wall. Plaster cracked around the edges of the concealed panel as it flexed inward. Cleera grasped the lip of the door and wrenched it open. Revealed inside were two switches, separated by a row of numbered buttons.

Cleera flipped the top switch on, then hesitated, reviewing the sequence of numbers she had been given—the code needed to operate the lift mechanism. Then, confident there had been no error in her reception and storing of the information, she rapidly punched that series of numbers into the device. Her hand poised on the lower switch, the lavender-and-white psybot wondered if it would still work. She flipped it and hoped for the best.

There was an agonizing moment of silence in which it seemed she might have made a mistake, or that the power was dead and their work clearing the floor panels was in vain. Then a deep, muffled sound of servos whining ebbed up from somewhere beneath the floor.

"Stand clear, everyone," Cleera called out.

The whining sound droned louder as the large access panels in the floor suddenly rose, dividing from the middle and hinging outward. The twin panels that looked like concrete when they were level with the rest of the floor were actually thick sheets of metal, well braced with reinforcing girders along their lower surface. They swung away from the opening, revealing a large pit reaching down fifteen feet or more, lined with concrete walls.

A cargo helijet roughly the size of the one Cleera and her team had flown to Troy was coming up into view, elevated by a lift platform. A power cable was plugged into a connector slot in the craft's side, and plastic dust protectors were wrapped around the four helijet turbines.

Outside, the sound of the sirens grew louder. It would not take the CorSec Guards long to spot the truck, and once that was found, they would begin searching the immediate area.

"Ah," said Dr. Arcanus admiringly, "there's nothing like a good old-fashioned trapdoor."

Cleera joined the others, and as she neared the old magician she said, "You are coming with us, aren't you?"

Arcanus considered a moment, then cocked an ear toward the sirens. "Why, yes, my dear. I would be delighted to accept your kind invitation. I think I've outstayed my welcome on this shabby planet."

As the lift slowed to a halt, level with the building's floor, Vandal rushed forward to remove the protective cover from one of the engines. Roddi got the other one on that side of the craft, and the twinbots hurried around to the other side to remove those.

Cleera unplugged the power cable and checked the anti-evaporation seals on the fuel tanks. Everything seemed in order. "Let's get aboard, quickly!"

HiLo opened the rear hatch so the two large psybots could board. Then as he started toward Cleera and the forward hatch, he saw lights flashing through some of the building's windows, and around the edges of the wide delivery door. "Yes," he added to Cleera's command, "very quickly!"

Vandal whirled to appraise the situation, saw the trouble, and knew there was little time. He propelled Marinda toward the open hatchway. "Get in there and strap yourself down. Cleera! Roddi! Get that thing powered up, now!"

Cleera was not about to argue. Escape was the crucial thing. She and Roddi leaped into the craft and moved behind the controls, flipping switches and listening as the turbines began to spin and then sputter to life.

Dr. Arcanus and Muse quickly boarded after them, moving to the middle of the ship near Marinda. Behind them, Chiron rolled up the boarding ramp into the craft and locked his wheels. Torb still lingered outside, watching for trouble he knew would come.

And come it did, in the very next moment.

Beam weapons flashed outside, shattering one of the windows. The front door of the building crashed open as CorSec Guards burst through, their weapons drawn. A moment later, a horrible crash rang through the huge building as the wide delivery door was smashed inward.

A dozen CorSec men and battle robots entered through the wide door, flashing their searchlights toward the helijet. "Wait!" an officer's loud, abrasive voice rang out.

Vandal answered with a barrage of rayfire, striking several battle robs and one of the humans. Near him, HiLo brought up his own weapon and began firing, and the twinbots and Torb triggered their weapons, setting up a blistering volley that illuminated the building like an indoor fireworks display.

"We've got full power!" Cleera's voice screamed out over the din of weapons.

"How are we supposed to get out of here?" Vandal snapped.

"A section of the roof opens," Cleera told him. "The controls are on the wall."

Vandal fired more shots, glancing quickly at the wall on the far side of the craft, then returning his gaze to the enemy before them. "Controls, hell!"

Straining upward, he searched the roof for the section that opened, and found it. Raising his protoblaster, he fired four successive shots at the latch mechanisms the glow of rayfire revealed.

Particles of scorched metal rained down, then with startling suddenness the roof section swung in and slammed against the wall. The dark sky showed through the rectangular opening.

"Now," said Vandal, "if we can just get a chance to take off."

Torb eyed the pattern of CorSec Guards approaching from the delivery door and stepped behind a huge crate sitting empty on the floor, its front removed. Bracing his feet, he placed his big hands against the back and pushed forward with an explosive burst of power.

The heavy crate slid across the floor as if it had wheels and power of its own. It headed directly for the group of soldiers and robots, moving faster than they could dodge it.

Slamming into the group, the crate's open front end scooped them up and carried them with it, passing through the wide doorway and crossing the alley to smash against the opposite building wall.

Torb fired shots at the remaining troopers by the front entrance, then the bulky blue robot hurried up the ramp and entered the helijet behind Chiron, pulling the hatch closed.

"Go!" Vandal told HiLo and the twinbots, motioning to the craft.

Jom said, "We're not leaving—"

"—without you!" Jayray finished.

"You got that right," Vandal snapped, backing up as he continued to lay down a wall of rayfire that kept the CorSec Guards from attempting shots of their own. As he reached the craft he saw from the corner of his vision that the three psybots had safely boarded behind him.

Stepping into the hatch, he stood within the opening, still firing. "If you can fly this thing," he bellowed, "do it!"

Cleera answered with a tug on the thrust controls that lifted the helijet from its platform and sent it skyward with a loud whoosh. Vandal fired off one last burst of shots, emptying his weapon's power pack. Then he ducked back within the ship and pulled the hatch closed just as they cleared the building's roof and soared into the sky above Jonnersville.

Roddi vacated the copilot's seat, making room for Vandal as the cyborg agent entered the cabin. The psybot quickly took a jump seat directly behind the flightcrew seats.

Vandal slipped into the copilot's seat and strapped in. "There'll probably be CorSec aircraft after us soon."

"If they know where we are," replied Cleera. Her hand went to the console before her, and she rapidly flipped a series of switches. Instantly, the sound of the helijet turbines dropped to a muffled whisper and equipment indicators glowed to life on the panel.

"This craft was outfitted with engine silencers," Cleera told Vandal. "Also some ECM gear. But the main feature is a circuit which activates a string of underwater transmitter buoys reaching in a line from the coast to Trasker's Island. They create a kind of electronic tunnel. As long as we stay within their range, CorSec radar won't be able to tell where we're heading. With luck, they won't even know we're landing on the island."

Vandal stared at one of the panel's computer screens. He could see a generated map of the whole area, including Trasker's Island. Glowing symbols indicated the positions of the jamming beacons—the path their helijet must follow to avoid detection. He glanced at another readout, then nodded approvingly.

"Good," he commented. "I see our running lights are off, too."

Cleera gestured at the duplicate set of controls in front of Vandal. "Do you want to take over?"

"Maybe later," the cyborg agent replied. "Right now, you seem to be doing just fine."

Cleera smiled inwardly, then twisted the control yoke and applied forward thrust, bringing the craft in a sweeping arc that carried it swiftly away from the building and the CorSec Guards below, heading for the shore and into the night.

25:

SPIES WITHIN

THE SUN WAS DIRECTLY above the many-domed University complex on Avalon. It was the noon hour on this portion of the airless moon that orbited the planet Logres. There were hundreds of people walking along the paths between campus buildings and plazas where the restaurants and shops were located. From all outward appearances, it was a perfectly normal day. Things were neither normal, nor perfect, though.

Within a windowless room in the University's research department, deep inside the restricted section, Rasp and Cudder continued their work. With Jenna's unwilling aid and their newly acquired security status as VIP guests, they had succeeded in penetrating every security checkpoint so far.

The room in which they labored was a storage area, half filled with surplus file cabinets, unused desks and chairs, and an assortment of old computer equipment. After locking themselves into the room, the two Corporation agents had spent the past several hours there, carefully and quietly moving things away from the wall to the right of the door. Desks were now stacked one atop the other along the rear wall; the cabinets and other equipment lined the wall to the left of the door.

They had been working on something else in that time as well.

Jenna sat in an office chair off to one side, watching them with an intent, worried look. A gag was tied over her mouth, her hands were secured behind the chair back, and her ankles were tied to its base. The position was uncomfortable, especially after several hours, but it was not her comfort she was concerned about.

She watched as the two men continued to work on the wall they had cleared. The man she originally knew as Oglethorpe, though she had since heard him called Rasp by the other man, had attached a number of devices to the wall. They were small things, carried into the University complex in his coat pockets, and cables now connected them together.

Now Rasp and the other man were busy applying a thick line of some grayish goo to the wall in a rectangular pattern roughly two feet by four feet. There were glistening flecks in the gray goo, and though she could not be sure what the purpose of the line was, she had an idea.

As they worked, their backs to her, Jenna's gaze quickly went to her computer tablet, which was sitting on top of a box of computer printout paper. If she could manage to get to it somehow—press the right keys—perhaps she could summon help before it was too late. She glanced back at the two men and was unnerved to find Rasp staring at her with a cold, hard look after noticing the direction of her glance.

Rasp abruptly straightened from his work, turned toward her, and strode to the corner where the girl was bound. "Don't even think it!" he snapped.

Jenna half expected to be struck, so dangerous was the look in Rasp's eyes. But he did not touch her, reaching instead for the computer tablet and carrying it well out of her reach to the far side of the room. She looked to the other man, whose real name she did not know. There was concern in his eyes, but his expression was otherwise hard to decipher. He had come to her rescue once against Rasp. Would he do so again, if her life was threatened? Perhaps. But she knew that counting on a Corporation agent for help was risky, perhaps even ludicrous.

"I still think keeping her alive is a mistake," Rasp complained as he returned to the wall.

"She got us in here, didn't she?" replied Cudder, finishing the line of grayish material so that it made a complete loop. He capped the dispenser tube and returned it to his pocket. "And she's going to get us out of here, too."

Rasp consulted his watch. "It's almost time. Let's get the wires connected."

Each man now took a length of thin cable from the floor and tied one end of it to a large disk with an eye at the back. Then, they applied gel from a tube to the disk's surface. They pressed their disks against the wall, near each upper corner of the gooey gray rectangle.

Rasp quickly wiped his hands on a rag he had found in the storage room. He glanced once more at Jenna, his mouth twisting into a cruel smile.

"You're about to witness history being made," he told her. "You know what's on the other side of that wall? Do you know what's just inches away from us? Do you?"

"Rasp . . ." cautioned Cudder irritably.

"Oh, that's right," said Rasp. "How inconsiderate of me. I forgot that the little lady is having trouble talking right now. But I do want her to know just how much of a help she's been to us."

Cudder looked at him grimly, wondering whether to attempt to stop him or just let him talk. It would be hard to shut him up—maybe even dangerous, to himself as well as to the girl and their mission. He had not worked with Rasp very often, but often enough to know the man was slightly unstable, always close to the edge. Cudder was sure Rasp was trying to intimidate the girl solely to get even with him for saving her life, for challenging his authority. Perhaps it was better to let him talk and vent some steam.

"You see," Rasp continued, addressing Jenna and pointing at the wall behind him, "that wall right there separates us from the restricted research files, where all the top-secret info is stored. All the paperwork and things. All the good stuff. We couldn't go walking in there even with you along, but this way, we just sort of cut through the red tape."

He walked up to the devices attached to the wall and began switching them on. "These little gizmos are lined up with sensors built into the wall. They jam those sensors, so your fancy security system doesn't know anything's wrong. You see, we know the schedule for the personnel here. We know the file room closes down every day from noon to one, because all the clerks are at lunch. But while they're away, we're going to open it back up so we can do a little research of our own. And we're not going to use the door."

As Cudder picked up the rest of their tools, Rasp pulled something from his pocket that looked like a slender writing instrument. He twisted the upper half a full turn, and imbedded the point of the device in the trail of gray goo at the top of the rectangle. He immediately backed away toward the other wall and averted his eyes.

Cudder went the other direction, toward the girl. He took up a position in front of Jenna, his back to the wall. Softly, he told her, "Don't look at it directly."

As she averted her eyes, she saw the room abruptly brighten. Cudder's body was a silhouette against the intense light from the wall. Even the residual glow was unpleasant.

At the wall, the line of gray substance had been ignited by the timer-fuse. Burning with white-hot fury, with no more than a slight hiss of noise, the incandescent line etched its way through the wall paneling like acid through sheer cloth.

In a moment it was cut completely through. The rectangular wall section shifted suddenly as the last bits of the edge gave way, then swung back away from the wall. Suspended by the cables glued to it and the ceiling, it did not fall to the floor.

As the glare of light faded and only an emberlike glow remained around the cut edges, Jenna looked up. Cudder moved away to join Rasp by the opening, and Jenna caught her breath as she saw the file cabinets and storage systems of the restricted library showing through the hole in the wall.

"Ah, now there's a pretty sight," said Rasp, looking inside. He scanned the interior with a hand-held sensor detector. The readouts were all zeroes. He stepped through the opening. "Seems clear. All right, Cudder, it's time we got what we came here for."

At that moment, Dean McAndrews was sitting at his desk, which was covered with pages upon pages of printouts. Since the previous day, when Jenna had casually mentioned she thought there was a discrepancy in the number of delegates attending the conference, McAndrews had obtained lists of all the delegates and sent T-beam messages to their respective planets and stations asking for background information. He had received most everything he had asked for by yesterday afternoon. Reading through it all was another matter. He was not even sure exactly what he was looking for, and with the more urgent business of Cleera's rescue mission on his mind, he had made little progress.

Wondering if his assistant might have found out anything on her own, McAndrews reached for his phone and tapped in the number for the conference center. He heard the receiving unit buzz over the line several times, then a woman's voice came over the speaker.

"Conference center."

"Adela, this is Dean McAndrews. Is Jenna handy? I need to ask her something."

"Jenna? Isn't she with you?"

"Obviously not, Adela," said McAndrews, mildly perturbed.

"I mean, I just assumed she had gone back to your office to help you with some work. I haven't seen her since first thing this morning when we began today's session. I can page her, if you like."

McAndrews frowned, rubbing his chin, then he replied, "No . . . that's okay. She's probably just busy with something else. I'll reach her later. Thanks."

"Anytime. Bye."

McAndrews picked up a pen and rapped it rhythmically upon his desktop for a moment, deep in thought. Then he swung around to his computer console and called up the interoffice-message screen. Sometimes Jenna left word for him if she was going to be working in another part of the complex, or if she had personal business to take care of somewhere.

He quickly scanned through several screens of information, but found no message. He was about to switch the console off when his eyes fixed upon his name and his special authorization code number, buried in the lines of data that indicated a message to the central security computer. He looked at the date and time, and knew he had made no such order.

McAndrews queried the security computer about the details of the order, and watched with growing concern as the words changing the status of two conference delegates and granting them access to the restricted area spelled themselves out across his screen. This tied in with what Jenna had said about two extra delegates. And only she could have input the command, for she was the only person other than himself who knew his private code. He knew she must have flagged the command just so a record of it would show up on the message screen and catch his attention. And now she was missing. The implications were alarming, frightening, for more reasons than one.

McAndrews rose from his chair, reaching for the button on his desk that would signal a complex-wide security alert. Then his finger froze over the button. He withdrew it hastily.

An image flashed through his mind, a terrible image, of what might happen to Jenna if she was still in the intruders' hands when the alarm sounded. If they panicked, she could be killed.

McAndrews grabbed for the phone instead, hurriedly punching in the number for the security chief's private line. His fist tensed and flexed impatiently as the phone rang repeatedly. Then he was rewarded with the sound of a familiar voice at the other end.

"This is McAndrews," he told the chief quickly, imperatively. "I think we've got a serious problem. . . ."

24:
CREACHERY FOILED

"THERE THEY ARE," SAID Dean McAndrews, still out of breath from his run down the corridor to the security center. "There's two of them, as I thought."

He was standing alongside Chief Greeley, the head of security for the University complex, and pointing at a large monitor screen in the console before them. There were other monitors on either side of this one, full-color screens into which signals could be piped from any of the hundred or so surveillance cameras placed throughout the restricted sectors of the massive facility. The image showing on the screen came from a small camera over the desk in the foyer of the restricted file room.

The camera's view through the clear inner door of the foyer showed Rasp and Cudder going through one of the file storage units. Behind them could be seen the scorched hole in the wall through which they had entered.

Chief Greeley stared hard at the image. "What do you think they're after?"

"It can only be one thing," McAndrews replied. "The plans and data for the hyperspace engine. I just wish I knew if Jenna is all right."

315

"Obviously they used her to gain access to the area," Greeley said, "and then cut their way through the storage-room wall. I'd like to know who gave them the information on the sensors in that wall."

"This camera—why didn't anyone notice them cutting through?"

Greeley sighed ruefully. "We don't normally monitor the file room when it's closed. That's a policy that's going to change, effective immediately!"

McAndrews squinted at the image on the screen. "Can you zoom in on that hole in the wall, without attracting their attention?"

"Sure—it's a silent model. Why?"

"I thought I saw something, but can't be sure."

Greeley reached out and pressed a rocker switch marked "Zoom In/Out." Instantly, the image on the screen began to change, the background drawing nearer, the foreground disappearing off the edges. Soon the scorched hole in the wall filled the screen.

"There!" McAndrews exclaimed with a jab of his finger. "Look at that. It must be Jenna."

Greeley bent closer to study the screen. Just past the edge of the hole he saw something that looked like a girl's leg, tied to part of a chair. As he frowned in concern, he suddenly saw the leg move, as if struggling to slip free. "Yes, you're right. And she's still alive."

"Thank God for that. The question is, how do we keep her that way, and stop those men?"

"I've already got security guards stationed in the corridors just beyond that area—I sent them as soon as you called me—I could have one team stationed outside the door to the file room, and send another in through the storage-room door. If they approach from that side, entering through the hole in the wall the

316

same as the spies, they could prevent those two from heading back that way."

"Maybe," replied McAndrews, frowning at the screen. "And maybe a small war could erupt in there, too. A stray shot from a laser or beam weapon could go right through that wall and hit Jenna. We could lose some of your men too, and a lot of hard-earned data in the room."

Greeley nodded. "I know. There is a chance that could happen. But we're going to have to do something, and there's not much time."

"Maybe . . . maybe it would be better to let them take what they want and leave the room the way they came in."

Greeley flashed McAndrews an odd look. "You mean just give them the hyperspace engine? Look, sir, I know Jenna means a lot to you—I care about her safety myself. But—"

"What I'm saying is, we might have a better chance at them in the corridor, where we can control things a bit more."

"How do you know they won't kill the girl before they leave the storage room?"

"I can't be sure, but it just wouldn't make sense," McAndrews told him. "I can't believe those two are planning to try to fight their way out of here once they've got the plans. Jenna's their ticket out of there, one way or another."

"All right," said Greeley. "Maybe we can try it that way. But how are we going to protect Jenna if they stay close together?"

McAndrews's brows knitted in thought as his mind raced. "I think there may be a way. Come on. I can get what I need from a lab on the way, and you can tell your men to get ready."

Greeley grabbed his weapon and a piece of equipment from the surveillance console. Then he and the dean bolted from the office and ran down the corridor toward the restricted section.

In a research office across from the storage room, a group of young security guards waited behind the closed door. They wore laser armor over their torsos and special helmets to protect their heads. Each man had a radio link with Security Command, and the officer closest to the door held a portable monitor which displayed a surveillance camera's view of the hall outside. Their weapons were armed and ready.

In a meeting room in the opposite direction down the corridor waited a similar group, identically equipped. Another group waited at each end of the cross corridor just past the door to the storage room, out of sight around the corner. And yet another group waited in an elevator farther down the hall, holding the car on that floor, the door closed. All other personnel had been quietly steered out of the area; at lunchtime there were not that many anyway.

In the file room, Rasp was quickly flipping through a sheaf of papers from a classified file marked "Prometheus Project." His thin lips formed a twisted, greedy smile as he scanned the contents. He did not have to understand the data contained within the file to know its value.

Cudder said, "Is that everything?"

"Yeah," replied Rasp. "Everything we're gonna need for a life of luxury." He slipped the thick stack of papers into a folder and tucked it into his shirt. "Okay, let's get out of here. I want to be out of the building and on my way to the spaceport before the staff returns and finds the little door we made."

Cudder followed him back to the storage room and stepped through the opening. He immediately went to Jenna and began untying her. "You just stay calm and see this thing through, okay? All you have to do now is escort us back through the security checks."

"And then what?" asked Jenna as Cudder removed her gag.

"And then we leave you tied up someplace where your friends won't find you for a few hours, and we'll be on our way. Right, Rasp?"

The slender Corporation agent flashed a thin smile. "Yeah, sure. No problem at all."

Jenna did not like his look or the tone of his voice. She felt certain that if it was up to Rasp, she would be dead as soon as they were far enough away from the complex so that they no longer needed her. For the moment, though, there seemed little else to do but play along.

Cudder helped her to her feet and straightened her jacket. He brushed at her cheek where the gag had twisted strands of her long hair out of place. His gaze was trapped for a moment by her soft, fearful eyes, and he smiled awkwardly, almost apologetically.

"Let's go!" snapped Rasp, slipping his coat back on and checking to be sure the bulge of stolen documents did not show. He pulled his small pistol from its hidden holster and tucked it into his belt where he could get it quickly. Looking at the girl, he patted the weapon. "And just don't go getting any ideas about making trouble for us. What I told you before still applies."

Jenna nodded in understanding, but said nothing.

Listening at the door for a moment, Rasp opened it carefully and peeked out. The hall was empty. Opening it wider, he motioned for Cudder and Jenna to follow, staying close to the girl and maintaining his threatening look.

In a lab a few doors down from the storage room Chief Greeley stared at the screen of his portable surveillance console. He watched as Rasp, Cudder, and Jenna stepped out into the hall. "They're moving!" he told McAndrews. "Go for it!"

McAndrews had a white lab smock on instead of his usual business coat, its sleeves rolled up past his elbows. An ID badge identified him as a lab technician, and he had purposefully messed his hair up a bit. In his hand was a thick envelope. He looked at it soberly, nodded to Greeley, and stepped out into the hall.

Starting down the hall with what he hoped was a casual stride and an unworried expression, McAndrews headed toward Jenna and the two Corporation agents. He saw Rasp and Cudder turn slightly at his approach, and he put on a big smile as if just recognizing Jenna. He hoped she would respond properly, and that he had not misjudged his plan.

"Hey, just the person I want to see," McAndrews called out, waving at Jenna. "You can save me a long walk to your boss's office. I'm having a working lunch today and can't really spare the time."

Rasp tensed a bit, but remained motionless. He and Cudder put on polite smiles and acted like the VIP guests they were supposed to be. Jenna stared at McAndrews, her mouth about to drop open in surprise and recognition. She sensed immediately that she must go along with whatever role he was playing in this dangerous situation.

McAndrews reached them and extended the envelope to Jenna. A large seal had been stuck across the front, with the words "Classified Data" printed upon it.

"Here, give this to McAndrews for me, will you? It's the latest results on the new engine tests. I think he's been holding his breath waiting for these."

Jenna glanced at Rasp to see if he was going to protest, but he seemed to suspect nothing. She reached out and took the envelope. "Thanks. I'll . . . I'll make sure he sees it as soon as possible."

"Well," said McAndrews with a silly grin and a cheery wave, "wish I could stay and chat, but the work just never ends around here. Thanks for your help."

With that he turned and headed back to the laboratory door, with never a backward glance. Just walking off and leaving Jenna there with two potential killers was the hardest thing he had ever done, but it was essential to the plan. He hoped Jenna understood his message.

McAndrews stepped into the lab and closed the door behind him. Giving a nervous sigh, he moved quickly to Greeley's side and stared at the portable surveillance monitor. "If this doesn't work . . ." he started, but did not finish the thought.

In the hallway, Rasp and Cudder resumed walking with their reluctant escort. Rasp looked quickly around, looking for signs of trouble. There were none.

"Give me that!" he snarled softly, pulling the classified-data envelope from Jenna's grasp. As he held it in his hands he added, "This may just be a bonus, for Roman and for us, too."

Rasp bent up the tabs on the back of the envelope and raised the flap. Pulling it open slightly, he peered inside at the thick stack of papers. Cudder stepped closer to him, and farther away from Jenna, to see also. Jenna held her breath, closing her eyes.

In the lab, watching the image of the three on the monitor, Greeley said, "Now!"

Beside him, McAndrews squeezed a button on a small transmitter device. His eyes were riveted on the monitor screen's image.

From the envelope in Rasp's hands came an abrupt explosion of vapor as powder sandwiched between two of the papers was ignited by a tiny receiver chip and power cell. The vapor sprayed up into Rasp's face, a sharply stinging mist, burning his eyes and choking his nose and throat. Some of it flew into Cudder's face as well, but a lesser amount.

Greeley triggered his radio link and shouted into his headset mike, "Move in!"

Things happened very quickly. Doors burst open and University security guards in battle gear came charging out, closing in on Rasp and Cudder. Jenna, who had avoided most of the disabling cloud, staggered back from the vapor, trying to get away.

Rasp was coughing, choking, seething with anger as tears ran down his face. "You little—this is your doing!" he snarled in Jenna's direction. His hand went to the pistol in his belt and pulled it free, and he swung it toward the girl.

A ray shot burned through Rasp's hand, making his fingers fly open in pain, dropping the gun. Cudder, meanwhile, had hurled himself in front of Jenna, protecting her from what he thought would be his partner's vengeance.

The University security men swiftly converged on the three. Four of them roughly grabbed Rasp, wrestling him to the floor and holding him there. Four others grabbed Cudder, pulling the beefy Corporation agent away from the girl. One of the men started to hit him.

"No," Jenna protested sharply, "don't! He tried to help me. It's okay. Don't hurt him, please."

The man refrained, nodding. The guards moved Cudder toward the center of the corridor.

Cudder glanced back at Jenna and gave her a wan smile of appreciation. Then he averted his eyes. He looked capable of throwing all four guards away from him, but he offered no resistance.

McAndrews came rushing up, with Greeley close behind. As the security chief went to supervise and congratulate his men, McAndrews went to Jenna.

"Are you okay?" he asked.

Jenna threw her arms around him in a fierce hug. "Yes! I'm fine. I was so afraid when you came out and handed me that envelope. I thought they would suspect something and shoot you. You were taking quite a chance."

"I was more worried about the chance I was taking with your life," McAndrews told her softly. "But I was afraid if I didn't try, you might be . . ."

McAndrews's words trailed off, and he returned the intensity of her hug. Then he stepped over to where Rasp was held on the floor and ripped open the agent's shirt. McAndrews grabbed the packet of hyperspace documents and handed them to Greeley.

"Here," he told the security chief. "I'd appreciate it if you saw these are put back where they belong."

"My pleasure, Dean."

McAndrews turned back to Jenna and put his arm around her, walking her down the hall. "Let's go back to the office. I'll have lunch sent in and you can take a break after all this excitement."

"Sounds good to me," she replied.

"Have you heard anything more from Vandal or Cleera?"

"Yes, and I'll give you a complete report. I just hope their efforts there turn out as well as ours did here."

25:
ISLAND OF DOOM

"AND YOU CAME HERE on *Glory*?" Dr. Arcanus was saying to Marinda as they sat in the pull-down webbing seats of the cargo helijet. "An original colonist from Earth. Remarkable. Truly remarkable. Why, you must have known my great-great-grandfather. He would have been about your age then."

Marinda gave a nod and a shrug, for it was indeed likely. It nevertheless gave her a very strange feeling to be discussing a contemporary of hers with one of his descendants, and a none-too-young one at that.

Only darkness showed outside the windows of the helijet. They had been flying over water since leaving Jonnersville two hours earlier, and it was now nearing midnight. Marinda had tried to sleep for a while, but could not. The webbing seat was not terribly comfortable, and there had just been too much excitement, too much ongoing tension, for sleep. Instead, she occupied herself by talking with Arcanus and the psybots, bringing them up to date on what they had gone through to reach Jonnersville. And they had told her how they managed to get there. The conversation had become an exuberant exchange of words, with the release of pent-up feelings from describing the events that had been so fearful.

But while the fears of the past had been dealt with, the threat of the immediate future was quite another matter.

Marinda fidgeted in her seat for a moment, then abruptly rose. "I'm going to go see how much longer before we get there," she told the others.

She had to watch her step as she walked, hanging on to whatever she could, to keep her balance. There was enough buffeting from air currents outside the craft to keep its flight from being perfectly smooth. The steady drone of the engines was loud, and had been so for most of the flight. Cleera had switched off the engine silencers once they were well away from Jonnersville, gaining more power and speed with the turbines in their normal mode.

Marinda reached the doorway to the cockpit and looked inside. She saw Cleera and Vandal at the controls, with the cyborg agent flying the craft for the moment. Roddi rotated his head toward her at the sound of her approach, motioning for her to step in.

"Hi," she said, giving Roddi a pat on the arm as she moved alongside of him to stand behind the pilot's and copilot's seats.

"Making new friends, Marinda?" inquired Roddi.

"Yes. But not forgetting old ones," she replied, smiling warmly at the silvery-blue psybot. Looking toward Vandal she asked, "How soon will we be there?"

"A matter of minutes," said Vandal. He glanced around at her, searching her eyes for a long moment. He seemed to feel uncomfortable about what he found. Looking back to the controls he added, "You'd better strap yourself back in. We should be landing soon."

Marinda thought about heading back to her seat in

the main compartment, but after spending so many hours apart from Vandal and Roddi she was reluctant to leave. Spotting the unused jump seat behind Cleera's seat, Marinda quickly slipped into it and fastened the seat belt. She flashed an independent, slightly smug smile at Vandal, but his eyes were on the instruments.

At that moment, an electronic tweedle of sound came from the instrument panel. Cleera bent toward the readouts and screens with sudden concern.

"Oh no," she said. "We've got a problem."

"What?" Vandal's eyes jerked toward her, then to the display screen to which she pointed. He frowned at what he saw there.

On the display that showed the computer-generated map of the area the island now took up most of the screen. One of the glowing symbols was flickering, even fading completely away for long moments. Of the dots of light that made up the line of jammer beacons shielding their flight, the last one—the one nearest the island—no longer held steady.

"Is it the display that's not working or the beacon?" asked Vandal.

"It must be the beacon," Cleera replied, her tone worried. "After not being used for so long, it's a wonder more of them didn't malfunction."

Vandal reached out and switched the engines to silent mode. He pushed the control yoke forward, nosing the craft down until the instruments indicated it was flying barely above the water's surface.

Slowing the helijet's forward speed, Vandal said, "Will this thing's ECM gear prevent island radar from picking us up?"

"Maybe," said Cleera. "And maybe not. I wish I could say for sure, but there are too many variables. The gear on this ship must be several years old. If the

Corporation is using the island for weapons testing, the systems there are probably state-of-the-art."

"Then we'll just have to hope for the best," Vandal said dryly.

Cleera punched up additional information on the display screen, watching as new symbols spread across the map. Pointing at them, she said, "There's the original site of the Uni's research base, and that's the location of the hidden spacecraft over there. I've stored the coordinates in my memory."

Vandal nodded, keeping the control yoke steady in his strong grip. "Good. Stand by to back me up, just in case. We're almost in range."

Marinda tensed in her seat, straining forward to see. Vandal seemed to be looking through the windshield more than at the controls, and Marinda assumed he was seeing the island by infrared light. She could certainly see nothing in the darkness.

All that changed in the next instant. Distant lightning had been visible in the clouds far ahead of them for some time. Now there was a series of bright flashes in the sky a few miles ahead, illuminating the nearer clouds.

Silhouetted against the clouds and the unheard storm's flickering blue fire, a great and forboding island loomed before them in the night. Mountainous in spots, it completely dominated the horizon, looking more like the coast of a minor continent as they approached.

As the lightning faded the island vanished from view, plunged back into darkness once more. But its brief glimpse had been enough to make it seem an unwelcome place.

Marinda cringed. "That's where we have to go?"

Roddi nodded. "Perhaps it looks better in the daylight."

"Delta Zone didn't."

As the helijet rushed toward the shore, faint lights became visible ahead. There were no real cities on Trasker's Island, but the pattern of lights indicated at least a small settlement. It indicated something else as well.

"Vandal!" shouted Cleera as a warning tone bleeped from the instrument panel. "We're being scanned! There's a shore battery ahead!"

No sooner had the words been uttered than flashes of light came from just ahead and to the right. Rays blazed past, with more on the way.

"Cleera," Roddi asked, "did your programming tell you how much armor this ship has?"

"Yes," said Cleera. "Not enough!"

Vandal twisted the control yoke violently, swerving the craft to the left, as another burst of rays narrowly missed them. The rushing crackle of air being ionized by the beams reverberated through the ship.

In another moment the beach was moving beneath them, then the rocky land just beyond. The glow of lights revealed a scattering of buildings, and CorSec Guards could be seen in the open areas, running for cover.

"Missile!" Cleera called out sharply, seeing the flame of its launch even as the panel readouts indicated its trajectory. Cleera flipped on power to arm the helijet's add-on weapons pod and grasped the control stick, taking aim. With the targeting grid placed squarely over the oncoming missile, she fired a quick burst.

At the last moment before reaching them the missile exploded, erupting into an expanding ball of flame that brightened the night sky. Vandal jerked the controls back and around, trying to climb over and away from the explosion, and only partially succeeding.

The helijet tore through the outer fringe of the flame and smoke as it arced away from the area, buffeted by the shock waves and brightly illuminated by the intense glow. There was also a horrid, staccato sound of metal against metal, striking, tearing, smashing. A sound they felt as much as heard.

Shrapnel from the detonated missile raked the underside of the helijet. The bits of flaming debris ripped jagged lines along the craft's bottom paneling and tore through systems beneath the surface.

"We're losing power," Vandal announced. "We're going to have to put it down somewhere. Brace yourselves!"

The craft skimmed low over several more buildings as its turbines sputtered and began to slow. It was barely under control, rushing on its momentum as much as engine power. Steadily losing altitude as it left the CorSec detachment behind, it flew a weaving course between hills and stands of trees, passing only scant feet above rocky ground and dark land. It managed to maintain airspeed and flight for a few more minutes, covering another several miles, then as a large patch of level ground came into Vandal's view he pulled sharply back on the control yoke to direct thrust down and forward.

The landing was abrupt and mildly jarring, but far more gentle than it might have been. Silence swept over them as the engine whine stilled.

"Everybody out!" Vandal commanded. He flipped off all the power switches and released his seat belt.

Roddi was already up, helping Marinda release her belt and get to her feet. The helijet was tilted slightly, but at least they were still upright.

As Vandal opened the forward hatch for those in the cockpit to get out, HiLo was squeezing past Torb and Chiron to reach the rear door latch. He had it open quickly and extended the ramp as far as possible.

In a matter of moments the eight psybots and three humans were outside, gathered in the darkness. Away from the CorSec base there was only the faint moonlight peeking through holes in the cloud cover for illumination. The jutting peaks of the central mountains rose high to the north, ominous and threatening.

"We're going to have to get away from this area," Vandal told everyone.

"Yes," Cleera agreed. "I'm sure there will be troops out soon to investigate." She got her bearings, then pointed toward the northeast. "The ship we must reach is in that direction."

"Has everyone got his gear?" Vandal asked, waiting as everyone checked to be sure. When all had signaled that they had, he said, "Let's get moving then."

They set out across the uneven terrain, walking as quickly as they could. Vandal was in the lead, with Roddi and Marinda close behind him. Dr. Arcanus, Cleera, and the rest of the psybot team followed. As they walked, HiLo worked his way up alongside Cleera.

"How's the leg holding up?" HiLo asked the pretty lavender-and-white psybot.

"Fine so far," Cleera told him. "You and Muse did a good job on it."

"The technicians on Avalon will do a better job, once we get there."

"Yes, if we get there," said Cleera softly.

They covered the next half mile with relative ease, keeping to the lowland areas and trying to avoid coming in sight of the CorSec base. There were trees and other types of plant growth present, but so far, no sounds of birds or other animals on this strange island.

There was only the sound of distant thunder from the storm still off to the north.

Marinda was sharing the glow from Roddi's chest light, careful of her footsteps on the uneven ground. "Did the plague kill off the animals here, too?" she wondered aloud.

"I don't think so," Roddi replied. "It's a very large island. Most likely the animals have just been scared away from this area by the weapons testing."

"But except for the research installation and the CorSec base, nobody's ever lived here? Is there something wrong with this place?"

"No, not really," the psybot told her. "But colonization began at CityPrime and spread out along the continent. The cities were all located in spots chosen for their resources or accessibility. With only a limited number of people, it just was not practical for anyone to settle here."

The group came to a low hill, and upon reaching the crest, Vandal abruptly halted. The others gathered behind him, looking ahead at what he indicated.

Revealed by the faint moonlight, a series of structures stood on the southern end of the clearing stretching before them. What appeared to be portions of buildings and some freestanding walls were arranged in geometric patterns, divided by several streets and alleys. But there were no lights here, nor any other sign of people.

Marinda said, "I thought you told me no one ever lived here."

"That's too small to be a city," Vandal replied before Roddi could answer. "Cleera, could that be part of the old University facility?"

Cleera studied the strange layout, searching her memory for anything that might explain it. "Perhaps, but if it is, the Uni didn't give me any information about it. And according to my calculations, the spacecraft is still some distance ahead, in the mountainous region beyond the clearing."

"It looks like ruins," Marinda ventured. "Maybe the CorSec troops built it and then blew it up."

"Well," said Vandal, "whatever it is, it looks quiet enough now. Come on, let's get moving. But stay alert."

They started down the slope of the hill, advancing upon the edge of the clearing and the oddly scattered walls that stood in their path. The grass and other plant growth ended at the perimeter of the area, leaving only patches of dirt and gravel in those places not paved or enclosed by walls.

Moving forward into the tiny ghost town, Roddi looked around him. "Vandal, some of these walls have taken ray damage, judging from the blackened areas. Perhaps Marinda is right."

Slightly ahead of him along the path, Vandal was noticing this too. He frowned at the sight of the walls. The damage troubled him, but the walls' very design disturbed him as well. They did not seem like ordinary building walls. And their arrangements seemed vaguely familiar.

"You know," Marinda observed, "this reminds me of a movie set I visited while still on earth. Not real buildings, just false fronts, with the walls propped up in the back—"

She bit off her words, gasping violently as lights suddenly came on all around them, illuminating the walls and building sections, the streets and narrow paths. It was as if the ghost town had suddenly sprung to life.

Vandal ducked, his weapon in hand, looking quickly

to the right and to the left. Roddi stepped closer to
Marinda, his own pistol drawn, and as Cleera moved
Dr. Arcanus to the center of her group the other
psybots were also readying for an attack.

But as the moments dragged on, no attack came.
There was no sign of CorSec Guards, human or robot.
No sign of anyone at all! No sound, no alarms . . .
nothing stirring at all. There was only the continuing
and unnerving intrusion of lights amid the dark calm
of this place. And somehow, that fact alone was
unsettling.

"If nobody lives here," whispered Marinda, "then
who turned on the lights?"

"It may be automatic," replied Vandal. "Our walking into the area may have activated the lights. But I
don't like it either. We might be better off going
around the long way than through here."

"I agree," said Cleera.

Still cautious, they turned and started back the way
they had come. They had taken no more than a half-
dozen steps when something abruptly moved in front
of them.

A dark robot swung out from around the corner of a
building section just before them, moving with startling speed. Marinda screamed even as Vandal whirled
toward it and fired.

There was a small explosion as Vandal's beam hit
the robot, spinning it away from them, back around
the corner. It halted in its movement, gave a thudding
bounce, and swung partway back toward them.

Vandal fired again out of pure reflex, then frowned
as he saw the results. His second shot struck the robot
as well, doing damage, but the thing did not collapse.
Though the robot looked normal in most respects,
Vandal could now see that its legs were not moving,

and its feet were not touching the ground. A long support arm, painted flat black, came from behind its back and continued on out of sight around the edge of the building. Now Vandal knew why this all looked vaguely familiar.

"This is a firing range," he snapped, loud enough for the others to hear. "Some sort of training ground for CorSec Guards. I used to practice on one, years ago."

Another robot abruptly darted out from the opposite side of the street. Roddi responded quickly, even cheerfully.

"Firing range? Let me get this one, Vandal!"

The silvery-blue psybot fired a burst from his own pistol, striking the robot form a bit above center. Sparks and bits of armor debris flew out from the spot, and the robot moved back from the impact. Then it did something surprising. Its arm swiveled up. A pistol in its hand blazed. The ray beam burned through the air and hit the edge of Roddi's shoulder, deflecting upward and leaving a scorched mark.

"Hey!" Roddi shrieked. "You didn't tell me they shoot back!"

"They didn't use to," said Vandal grimly, firing a blast of his own that destroyed the target robot's weapon.

As that threat was dealt with, new ones began to appear. Two miniature weapons bunkers thrust up through the loose gravel on either side of their path, scattering rayfire in their direction.

Without a command, everyone turned and started back along the path that ran through the length of the firing range. As the weapons fire behind them continued, Vandal turned them off the first path onto another, leading them around the corner of a false building that shielded them from the miniature bunkers.

They were in the middle of things now. The automatic system, once activated, was not about to quit the job it was programmed for.

A red-hued battle rob popped up into view behind a window near them. It leveled four weapons at them simultaneously.

Cleera cocked both hands back, firing twin laser beams from her wrists. HiLo and the twinbots opened fire with their pistols, and the battle rob disappeared in a blistering barrage of fire. Whether it was destroyed or had merely dropped back down to await its next use they could not tell.

The group was running now, hoping their speed through this deadly maze would help them. But they were also aware of the dangers of moving too quickly.

"I wonder," gasped Marinda as she ran beside Roddi, "how many . . . of their trainees . . . live long enough . . . to graduate!"

Her psybot friend kept his eyes alertly on the streets and buildings around them. "Oh, I rather imagine this is more for advanced training than for rookies. Or perhaps for trying out new defensive equipment. Which makes it more dangerous to us."

"Wonderful," groaned Marinda.

Behind them, Dr. Arcanus stumbled and started to fall. Chiron was following him closely, and the large wheeled psybot caught the gaunt magician in his long lifting arms and carried him along.

They reached an intersection of streets amid the short block of phony buildings and started across it. The psybots and humans had made it most of the way in the next street when rayfire erupted behind them. Cleera and HiLo looked back and saw that a manhole cover had suddenly risen several feet on a supporting framework, and a simple robot made to resemble a man was beneath it, angling weapons at their backs.

As alarmed outcries arose, the group split down the middle, seeking refuge along the sides of the street and attempting to bring their weapons into play against this new threat.

In the next moment they saw Torb, who had been lagging behind the group because of his bulk and slightly slower movements, handle the matter in his own way. Since the manhole mech had popped up almost directly in Torb's path, the heavy blue psybot merely took a slight hopping step and came down with both huge feet squarely on top of the manhole cover.

With a squeal of rupturing pneumatics and a loud scrunch of crushing metal, the manhole cover was immediately level with the roadway once more. Bits of flattened hardware protruded from the edges, and a thin trail of smoke from shorted circuitry began to rise through the openings as Torb stepped off and continued along behind his comrades.

The group turned along another pathway, still led by Vandal as he tried to take them through to the other side of the firing range and to safety. Whichever way they turned, the potential for danger seemed high. The best bet seemed the shortest, straightest route through, and that was exactly what Vandal was attempting.

Looming ahead of them now was a canal, narrow but filled with water. The path they followed led to a metal bridge wide enough for even Torb and Chiron to cross, reaching across the canal to the far side. It seemed sturdy and well braced, but beyond these fine qualities it was quite simply the only way to get where they wanted to go.

Vandal started forward, leery of any easy path, and indeed of everything in this dangerous place. He had almost reached the bridge when there was a sudden turmoil in the canal itself.

Water sprayed up in a bubbling froth on both sides of the bridge as two metallic monsters that had been reclining beneath the surface now rose to vertical positions. They faced each other, the bridge between them, brandishing weapons whose nozzles now erupted with spitting, gushing flame.

Twin jets of fire rushed out, turning the water in and around the nozzles to steam. The flames met in the middle of the bridge, splashing together and fanning out like colliding streams of water. The inferno completely blocked the path across.

Roddi said, "I don't think they want us to leave yet."

Vandal leveled his protoblaster at the robot on the left side, firing repeatedly at both it and the flame weapon. The shots were being absorbed by densepak armor, though. To cut his way through would deplete his pistol's power cell. Vandal was about to reach for another weapon when the twinbots moved past him.

"Wait," said Jayray. "This looks like—"

"—our kind of challenge," finished Jom.

With that, the twinbots ran forward, heading not for the bridge but toward the edges of the canal nearest each flame robot. With powerful, springing cartwheels, Jayray and Jom launched themselves into the air simultaneously. As they sailed forward, each did a handspring off the top of each flame robot's head.

The mechanized flamethrowers responded, tracking the moving objects as they approached and extending the thrust of their fire streams in an effort to reach the spinning twinbots. Each flame robot aimed at the twinbot opposite it, and as Jayray and Jom sprang off the top of each robot's head, the rush of flame ended up engulfing the flame robots.

As Jayray and Jom landed safely on the other side, the two huge robots standing in the canal continued to bathe each other's heads in their respective firestreams. For a moment it seemed they might destroy each other, but then a built-in safety circuit apparently cut in and the robots lowered their flame streams and cut their intensity, so that they merely blocked the bridge once more.

"Well," observed Roddi, "at least two of us got across."

Vandal said, "A thermite missile might work, if we had one."

"I wonder," Marinda thought out loud. "This is probably cheating, but . . ."

She took her small laser and aimed at the spot where Vandal had been standing when the robots emerged from the canal. Marinda fired a series of random shots into the ground, kicking up dust as each beam hit.

Suddenly, her last shot kicked up something other than dust. Sparks and smoke erupted through the narrow hole, exposing metal and wiring. An instant later, the two flame robots turned off their streams of fire and settled back into the water with loud splashes.

Marinda looked back at the others and shrugged. "I just figured there had to be a sensor to activate them in the first place."

"Excellent thought, Marinda!" exclaimed Roddi. "Sometimes we overlook the obvious."

They moved swiftly across the bridge, which was still warm from its close proximity to the flames. Vandal and Roddi used their own pistols to probe the ground just beyond the bridge, and a thin column of smoke soon arose, confirming their suspicions about a sensor on the other side. Now they could safely reach Jayray and Jom and continue. Reunited with the twinbots, the group wasted no time in heading for the perimeter and the clearing beyond. The only thing left in sight was a boxy panel with glowing numbers displayed across its face.

Marinda stared at it as they passed. "What's that thing?"

Roddi gave it a studious glance. "Perhaps it's our score."

His words were no sooner spoken than the range scoreboard abruptly lifted itself upon concealed legs. A stubby head rose from the top, and arms swung out bearing weapons.

"Oh, glitch," said Roddi. "Not another one."

As the device prepared to fire, Muse called out sharply, "Allow me."

The golden psybot with the dancer's form stepped forward and twirled once with startling speed. As her hands whipped around, Muse hurled several tiny objects she had produced seemingly from nowhere.

The devices, star-shaped with a thick bulge of circuitry at the center, stuck into the surface of the scoreboard mech with staccato impact. They instantly discharged electrical energy, sending blue lightning crawling across the mech's surface.

Rocking back and forth, the scoreboard shuddered with a violent spasm as its circuits and mechanisms were disabled. It sank back to the ground, arms hanging limply and its display lights sputtering out.

Vandal rushed the group beyond the perimeter, and they were finally clear of the area. His eyes turned toward a storage shed where range equipment could be seen. Behind them, the lights of the range winked out, quietly awaiting its next use.

"Cleera," Vandal said to the psybot team leader, "I think you'd better contact the University—tell them what's happened. After our landing, and setting off this thing, I've a feeling it won't be long before the Corporation knows where we are."

Cleera nodded in agreement. "I'm afraid you're right."

"And while you're doing that, there's something over in that shed I want to check out." The cyborg agent looked grimly back toward the horizon. "Then we'd better get ourselves out of this area just as fast as we can."

It was late afternoon at the University complex on Avalon. Dean McAndrews looked up from his computer console as Jenna entered his office with several folders in her hand.

She laid them on his desk. "Chief Greeley sent over these copies of the interrogation reports on the two Corporation agents. He said the one called Cudder has been cooperating, and shows at least some potential for rehabilitation. The other one—Rasp—is quite another matter."

"Yes, that doesn't surprise me." McAndrews looked at his pretty assistant a minute, still grateful things had worked out as well as they had. "It did surprise me about Dixon. He's been arrested, of course, for his part in getting those two into the complex. Apparently his resentment about being passed over for promotion got the best of him."

"It's a shame," Jenna agreed. She walked around behind McAndrews's chair and massaged his shoulders as she glanced at his computer screen. "What are you slaving over now? Some news about Vandal and Cleera?"

"No," replied McAndrews. "No further word from them yet. I've just been tracing Rasp's and Cudder's movements, their cover files, any other potential contacts. Just tying up the loose ends, so we know what we're dealing with."

"Good. I'll be glad when it's all over and we can relax." She checked her watch. "I could say the same about the conference, too. It should be ending in another hour or so."

"You mean I can count on having a full-time assistant again?"

Jenna flashed him a wry smile. "Is that all I am to you? Someone to file your reports?"

McAndrews turned in his chair and took her hand in his. His tone serious, he said, "I think we both know better than that. Especially after today."

Her eyes sparkled, her smile becoming self-conscious. "Yeah. I guess we do at that."

An urgent bleeping sound came from the computer console, drawing McAndrews's unwilling attention. His eyes moved to the screen as the message screen appeared.

"It's Communications," McAndrews told Jenna. "They've received another T-beam transmission from Cleera."

As the scrambled data began to fill the screen, McAndrews remembered the decoding sequence and punched in the seven-digit number. Instantly, Cleera's message was unscrambled and scrolled across the screen.

Reading the message over McAndrews's shoulder, Jenna said, "This is bad, isn't it? Even if they don't have any more trouble reaching the spacecraft, the CorSec troops know they're in the area."

"Yes," replied McAndrews. "That's what worries me. I was hoping they might at least reach the ship before the Corporation was alerted. so they would have a head start into space."

"You think they could be intercepted before they get far enough away from Coreworld?"

McAndrews gave a nodding frown. "I'm afraid there's a very real danger of that—a very real danger indeed." He switched the screen off and glanced at his watch, deep in thought. "You know, I don't think we have a choice any longer."

"The Prometheus?"

"Yes." McAndrews grabbed the phone and dialed a classified number. As someone answered at the other end, the Dean said, "This is McAndrews, authorization code 4-D. This is a mission alert, repeat, mission alert. I'm leaving my office now."

Jenna watched him hang up the phone, her already worried expression deepening. As his eyes swung up to meet hers, she said, "You're going along?"

McAndrews got up from his chair and slipped into his jacket. "I have to. I've got too much at stake in this not to be there for the outcome. I put Cleera's team together, and I activated them. I'm even indirectly responsible for Vandal's and Roddi's being seen there in the first place."

Jenna walked him to the door and nearly collided as they both tried to step through at once.

McAndrews looked at her strangely. "Where are you going?"

"With you," she said firmly.

"Jenna, I think it would be better if you didn't. The ship's still experimental. The risk—"

"The risk is no greater for me than it is for you. I'm flight-qualified, and I have a stake in this mission, too,

343

especially if you're on it." She straightened the lapels
of his jacket and pulled his tie up from its slack position. "Besides, you said you wanted a full-time assistant, didn't you?"

McAndrews sighed deeply, the corners of his mouth
twisting into a smile. "You're not going to let me get
away with anything, are you?"

"Nope."

He motioned her toward the door. "Let's not waste
time, then."

A high-speed tramway carried them out of the main
University complex and away from the cluster of domes,
whisking them through a clear tube across the gray,
cratered surface of Avalon. Even the lights and wide
landing pads of the spaceport dwindled in the distance
as they arced in a gradual curve toward their destination.

Far from the populated areas, the tramway abruptly
disappeared into a mountainous ridge at the edge of
an immense crater. Harsh sunlight was replaced by
cool artificial light, and the tram slowed to a halt
within a safety airlock.

McAndrews and Jenna disembarked and stepped
through the airlock hatch. A crewman met them at the
entrance to the control center, handing McAndrews a
folded flightsuit.

"The young lady will be needing one, too," McAndrews told him.

"Yes, sir. Right away."

As the crewman went to get her a suit, Jenna walked
through the control center, looking at the dozens of
consoles with their myriad of winking lights and readouts. She had been here dozens of times before, with
McAndrews or representing him, but she was still
fascinated with this place, and with what lay just beyond
its outer walls.

Jenna paused by a triple-layered viewport that opened onto the floor of the huge crater's interior. There was another crater floor, a false one, roughly five hundred feet above the true bottom. The false crater floor housed a hangar beneath it.

It was what was being readied within that hangar that fascinated Jenna most. A spacecraft, easily four hundred feet in length, waited, connected to the control center by a boarding bridge. Unconventional in design, its lines were angular and lean, with only the triple dome bulges of the hyperspace engines extending above and below the sleek framework amidships. There were smaller standard engines at the rear, but it was the generators that were the heart of the ship. From there, energizer tubes ran fore and aft, creating the power grid necessary to penetrate hyperspace.

The *Prometheus*—the first of a new breed of ships that would carry humankind farther and faster than it had ever gone before. And more were being readied even now.

"Here, miss," said a voice behind her.

Jenna turned. It was the crewman, back with her flightsuit. "Thanks," she told him, and headed for the ready room.

Ten minutes later, she and McAndrews had changed and were hurrying across the boarding bridge to the ship. They entered through the airlock, emerging within a brightly lit corridor. It took them another minute to reach the vessel's flight deck.

The consoles reminded Jenna of the control center she had just left, only these were trimmer in design. As they approached the few seats unoccupied by crew techs, a young man wearing the insignia of the University's Exploration Corps turned to face them. It was

Isaacs, captain of the *Prometheus*, the man McAndrews had called.

"We're ready, Dean," Isaacs told him. "All systems are powered up and functional."

"Great. How long will it take us to reach a rendezvous orbit around Coreworld?"

"Through hyperspace? About two hours."

"Then let's get underway at once," McAndrews told him with a grim look. "I have a feeling that won't be a moment too soon."

26:
BATTLE FOR FREEDOM

"OVER THERE," SAID CLEERA, pointing cautiously and keeping her voice low. "We must reach that cave. It's where the spacecraft is hidden."

The rest of her psybot team and Vandal's group were peering out from concealment, hidden by dense foliage at the base of the mountains. It had taken them nearly half an hour to reach this spot after leaving the CorSec firing range behind, but dawn was still many hours away. The mountain towered high on their left side, a dark gray mass against an angry sky. There were still occasional flashes of lightning, nearer now than before, but no rain yet fell.

"The cave?" said Vandal, his voice dry and humorless. "It figures."

Marinda and Roddi and Arcanus, and all the rest that had made such a perilous journey to reach this spot, stared across the wide gap between their hiding place and their destination. They could see the edge of the cave in the mountainside some forty yards ahead, revealed by the cloud-filtered moonlight and the intermittent lightning.

Seeing it was one thing. Getting to it was another. The cave entrance was fifty feet from a low building near the mountainside, an old building, flanked by newer, thick-walled bunkers. Surrounding it all, and extending to the side of the mountain itself, ran a barbed-wire fence in a rough semicircle broken only by a high gate.

There were guards, too. Most were battle robs, but there were a few humans visible as well, wearing the garb of CorSec troops. Some were stationed at guard posts, others in a high guard tower near the center of the base. Still more patrolled the perimeter of the fence. Lights illuminated the cleared ground around the base, making it impossible to approach undetected, and the mountain face was too sheer to attempt reaching the cave entrance by that route.

Cleera said, "The main building was part of the original University facility. But not the rest of it. Looks like the CorSec Guards are using this for storage now."

"Explosives, probably," Vandal told her. "Doesn't pay to keep them in the main facility, where the troops are."

Roddi studied the layout of the place, the defenses, the guards. "I think I understand now why the Uni thought we might need help getting in there."

Close to Vandal's side, Marinda asked, "Do you think they've been notified that we're on the island?"

"It's a safe bet," the cyborg agent replied. "I doubt if they leave their lights on, way out here, unless they're expecting company."

"That makes it even harder," said Cleera. "I don't suppose there's any other way than a direct frontal attack?"

Vandal shook his head. "No. I don't see that we have many options. I'm glad we brought that stuff with us from the range."

Strapped to Chiron's sides were several long panels

of densepak armor, taken from the storage shed at the firing range. There were a number of smaller pieces of the heavy shielding as well.

Vandal reached into his weapons pack and brought out a fresh power cell for his protoblaster. Next he produced a missile gauntlet like the one Marinda had seen him use during her rescue aboard *Glory*. Detaching his metallic hand, he locked the gauntlet in place over his lower arm and connected the control contacts, then reattached his hand to the end of the gauntlet.

Vandal told them, "Our best chance is if I circle around from the other side and attack from there. When they pull their forces over there, the rest of you can charge from this side and break through the perimeter."

"No," Marinda exclaimed softly, her hand going to Vandal's shoulder with fear-strengthened grip. "That would be suicide. I won't let you do that."

Vandal's look was grim. "It's not for you to say, Marinda."

"Isn't it?" she whispered defiantly. "I'm the whole reason you're here. The reason you're in this mess. And I'm not about to let you kill yourself just to save me and the others."

"There's got to be a better way, Vandal," Roddi agreed. "Even with your considerable skills, it would be very difficult for you to rejoin us under that arrangement, and I would hate to try to reach the cave without our best fighter."

"Yes," interjected Cleera. "And I'm not sure my programming is up to operating a spacecraft."

Vandal looked at the two psybots as if doubting their words. But he knew there was at least some truth to what they said.

"Forgive me for intruding in areas outside my field,"

Dr. Arcanus spoke up suddenly. "But might there not be some way to make the guards *think* the attack is coming from the other side, without actually dividing our forces?"

"A bit of misdirection?" said Muse.

Vandal considered it a long moment. "All right," he said at last. "Under the circumstances, I'm open to suggestions. There are some things we can do, if we time it right."

Ten minutes later, they were ready. Chiron stood just behind an opening in the foliage, facing the small camp. He held two long panels of densepak armor side by side in front of him, the lower edges braced upon his long lifting arms, and his short arms gripping support bars on the back. They created a wide shield before him that would be difficult to penetrate.

Cleera sat astride his back, with Dr. Arcanus behind her. She checked to be sure Arcanus was holding his own small shield of armor, then turned to look at Vandal. "Okay," she said. "I guess this is it."

Vandal gazed at each of the others in turn. All nodded in affirmation, their expressions sober. Turning to Marinda, Vandal said, "All right. Get ready, and stay close."

"Count on it," Marinda replied, a nervous smile on her taut features. As Vandal started to move away from her, she reached out and took hold of him, pulling him toward her and planting a quick kiss on his cheek. "Just for luck," she told him.

His face was only near hers for a moment after that, one eyebrow skeptically arched and his mouth set in a tight line. But Marinda thought she saw fleeting emotions displayed in his expressive eyes. It was only a glimpse, but it made her feel less awkward about their conversation on the ship from Haddock, and it strengthened her resolve.

Vandal quickly stepped forward now, securing his weapons pack so that it would not impede his movement. Roddi handed him the load launcher, fully pressurized and ready.

The cyborg agent brought the weapon to his shoulder, looking through the sights and taking aim at the clearing on the opposite side of the camp. He waited a long moment, then as a distant rumble of thunder rolled through the sky, he squeezed the trigger.

With a dull pop of sound, a projectile was launched from the tube in a high arcing trajectory. It sailed invisibly through the dark sky and landed exactly where he had aimed.

It erupted with a flash of intense light as it struck, then began to spew out great clouds of smoke in all directions. The billowing waves of vapor showed in the floodlights' glow beyond the camp, looking as if it might be hiding an onrushing assault.

From their place of concealment, Vandal, Cleera, and the others could see the guards come sharply alert within the camp. Several of them on the far side of the perimeter, unnerved by the sudden explosion and smoke, began firing their weapons into the cloud. This further enhanced the impression of an attack, and other guards rushed toward that side of the camp.

"Now!" Vandal said.

Muse stepped up to the open area and sighted quickly upon the side of the fence facing them. The golden psybot whirled once, twice, hurling several of the small, star-shaped devices.

The stars spun through the air soundlessly, each striking one of the floodlights facing them. Each shattered and winked out as miniature lightning seemed to play about it, and in a moment the clearing before them was bathed in darkness.

Chiron immediately rolled forward, leaving the foliage behind and advancing upon the camp. With the dark armor held in front of him, he was barely visible.

Vandal and Roddi fell in line behind him, keeping Marinda between them. Vandal took the position on the right, where most of the guards would attack once they were inside the perimeter. Muse, the twinbots, and HiLo followed next, with Torb at the rear. All stayed in a line with Chiron's upraised shields.

They drew closer and closer to the fence, their approach momentarily unnoticed because of the darkness and the confusion on the far side of the camp. Suddenly, one of the guards stationed on the near side detected their movement and turned his spotlight toward them.

Chiron's twin armor panels shone in the spotlight's stark glow, but only for a moment, for Vandal lunged around the edge of the shield and fired a proton beam directly into the light.

"Go!" he commanded sharply.

Chiron lurched forward as his large wheels dug powerfully into the ground. In a moment he was speeding directly for the fence, closing the gap with grim urgency.

On his back, Cleera raised herself so that her head and shoulders stuck up above the shield. Gauging the area she expected them to enter, she extended her arms and fired laser beams from both, cutting through the fencing in two places ten feet apart.

That portion of the fence wire collapsed to the ground mere moments before Chiron reached it, to be flattened into the dirt beneath his wheels. They had breached the perimeter!

A battle rob near that section of the gate as they

entered fired at the shields in front of Chiron, but the densepak absorbed the energy, protecting those behind it. Vandal leaped out away from Chiron and leveled his protoblaster at the battle rob, firing repeatedly. Each shot hit a weapon in the mech's multiple hands, until at last it had nothing left to fire.

Vandal's next target was the high guard tower between the main building and the bunkers. Thrusting his missile gauntlet that way, he triggered a launch. The missile flew straight to the base of the tower, blowing up the supports on the far side. With a groan of twisting metal, the tower lurched sideways and toppled away from the group, crashing down upon a vehicle parked beside a bunker. Guards tumbled out, scrambling for safety.

"Nice shot, Vandal!" exclaimed Roddi. "I'd like to see the range score for that."

"We're not done yet," reminded Marinda, pushing him forward as more guards began to approach.

They had penetrated the area far enough now that they were no longer protected behind Chiron's armor shields. The angle no longer favored them. In fact, Chiron himself was not fully protected and had to do a quick turnabout so that he could back toward the cave entrance, shielding Cleera and Dr. Arcanus. Roddi hurried Marinda into position behind them, moving with Chiron's steady rolling progress.

The rest of the group were momentarily on their own. As dozens more of the CorSec troops advanced from the side to which they had been lured, and as more men and robots emerged from the main building, Vandal and the psybot team had to keep up the pressure just to avoid being overwhelmed.

As rayfire came their way, Jayray and Jom ran for cover behind two large boulders, firing back as they moved. Some distance behind them, Muse selected a group of advancing guards who posed the nearest threat and hurled a series of discharge stars their way. The first few struck mechs armed with simple laser weapons. Blue lightning crackled out across their bodies, disabling their circuitry and dropping them in their tracks. More of the stars hit human guards and stunned them with equal, if different, effectiveness.

The last star struck a CorSec cyborg, wreaking havoc on his artificial mechanisms, sending him into a twitching fit of jerking motions, causing him to discharge his weapon into a battle rob near him. The damaged battle rob sank to his knees, but swiveled around to grapple with the unexpected source of attack.

Jayray popped up from behind his boulder and unleashed three quick shots at approaching guards. Fire flashed over his head as he ducked back down to a safe position. But Jom now popped up from his hiding place several yards away and instantly fired at the same targets, their positions already in his mind from Jayray's view a moment before.

As Jom ducked back down, shots struck the boulder in front of him. Jayray once more fired off a salvo, dispersing those guards who had not been struck. Then both twinbots jumped up and darted toward Chiron and the cave beyond.

Vandal ducked as a shot flashed toward him. It burned a hole through his cybernetic arm, but the beam missed any servos or circuitry. He fired a missile into the ground directly before the guard who had shot him, watching as the resultant explosion of dirt and debris lifted the man off his feet and hurled him backward. Vandal glanced back and motioned for Muse and the others behind him to run for cover, then laid down a withering barrage of deadly beams with his protoblaster.

A ray blast suddenly scorched HiLo's arm, and the green psybot dove for cover behind one of the large boulders recently vacated by the twinbots. He started to peer up over the top to take aim, then saw that his attacker, a large Model 47 battle rob was practically upon him. He ducked back down hastily as a beam singed the air near him.

Advancing steadily on HiLo's position, the big battle rob walked on six segmented legs, its torso raised high in the air and a number of large weapons affixed to its arms. It moved toward the boulder behind which the psybot hid, angling cautiously around to get a better shot.

Its vision receptors fixed upon the area behind the boulder, but HiLo had not come into view yet. The battle rob took two more steps around the rock, its weapons weaving, aiming, searching for prey.

Then with an abrupt flash of movement, HiLo darted out into view. The battle rob quickly fired at the psybot's torso, or rather, it fired at the spot where it thought HiLo's torso was. The extendable psybot had fully retracted his arms and legs to their inmost limit, and now he scurried out barely three feet high. The deadly beam passed straight over his head.

HiLo ran in his odd, waddling stride directly beneath the tall battle rob's legs, moving as fast as he could, slapping a magnetically-timed charge on the mech's underbelly as he scooted underneath.

The battle rob stretched up as the blur of motion went between its legs, then it bent from the waist to peer down and under its own body, visually tracking HiLo and also curious about the device attached beneath it. It was about to draw a bead on the retreating psybot from this awkward position when the charge detonated, blasting the battle rob upward, scattering metal legs and debris in all directions.

The rest of the group were heading toward Chiron and the cave, with Vandal and Torb coming last. Vandal ran with a loping sideways stride, keeping his attention on the CorSec troops.

During the last barrage, many of the guards had taken shelter behind what cover they could find, firing only when they thought they safely could. But now they saw the intruders on the run, and emerged and attacked once more.

They had almost reached the cave. Chiron had not fully entered yet, and was holding his shields near the cave mouth to protect the others, but the twinbots, Muse, and HiLo had joined the others behind the long, wheeled psybot.

Vandal fired another series of shots from his proto-blaster, one of them hitting a battle rob in the lead. The beam did not fully disable it, but ruptured the mech's right pneumatic chamber. As the air pressure rushed out, the battle rob spun in an awkward pirouette, its flailing arms smashing into others around it.

With his next shot, Vandal's weapon clicked and whined, but did not fire. He yanked the power cell off and clipped on another. Throwing a glance to the big blue robot, who had been maintaining his own covering fire, Vandal asked, "Think we can buy some time to get into that cave?"

"Sure," Torb replied. "I've been saving a little something for a moment like this."

Still moving at his brisk, lumbering gait, the immensely strong psybot turned more fully to face the attacking CorSec troops as ray beams and projectiles passed perilously close to him. As he walked backward he activated circuits within his boxy torso. Panels in his sides snapped open, revealing stacked arrays of small missiles. With another click of circuits they were armed and ready.

Vandal fired proton beams near the first ranks of human guards to make them dive for cover, then launched two of his own missiles at the lead battle robs. The explosions were minor compared to the barrage next unleashed.

As they backed almost to the mouth of the cave, Torb began firing his missiles. Most were aimed at the ground immediately before advancing troops, but some were aimed at battle robs. Three or four shot out each second from his built-in launchers.

A wall of flame and smoke arose all across in front of the CorSec Guards as explosion after explosion blossomed. All of the humans that had not already sought cover ran at top speed for whatever bunker or building offered some hope of safety. Those battle robs not destroyed outright or disabled flailed about amid the confusion, uncertain what to do.

As the explosions continued, Torb and Vandal turned and ducked back within the cave. Chiron pulled back after them, leaving the long densepak panels propped across the opening.

Marinda rushed up to Vandal as he entered, throwing her arms around him in a fierce embrace. But as Vandal put his real arm around her in a reassuring squeeze, his eyes fixed on the interior of the cave with a look of alarm. The cave went back only a short distance, and he saw no sign of the tunnel he had expected.

"Damn! If this is the wrong cave—!"

"No," Marinda told him, turning to look behind her. "At least, she says it's the right one."

By the glow of Roddi's chest light, Cleera was using her wrist lasers to cut a square shape into the stone at the rear of the cave. When she had completed the square, she stepped forward and began to rap against the hard gray surface.

"It's here somewhere," Cleera said, half to herself, half to the others. "It's got to be! My programming can't be wrong."

Vandal tore loose from Marinda's embrace and strode quickly to the rear cave wall. "What is it? We haven't much time."

Cleera rotated her head quickly toward him. "The entrance had to be well hidden. I was told that much, and where to find the special controls." She looked back to the square she had cut into the stone and hit it again. Nothing happened.

Vandal detached his metallic hand and slipped off his missile gauntlet, stowing it in his pack. Snapping his hand back in place, he stepped closer to the cave wall and drew back his arm. With a sharp slam of his fist against the center of the square, fracture lines radiated out from the point of impact, then the stone crumbled and fell.

Set back several inches behind that spot was a metal panel slightly smaller than the square Cleera had cut. Vandal opened it with a wrenching jerk that tore the panel off its hinges.

"Thanks, Vandal!" said Cleera, immediately twisting control switches to turn on the power. She then pressed the buttons beside them in the sequence she had learned from the T-Beam message.

They were rewarded by a faint sound of powerful servos beginning to move. And then with surprising abruptness a large section of the cave floor began to tilt down, sloping toward the back and revealing an opening in the rear wall. It stopped when a sizable entrance had been cleared.

Vandal ran back to the mouth of the cave and peered out past the armor panels. The CorSec troops were already starting to move about, gathering themselves for an assault against the cave and those presumably trapped there.

"They're heading this way," Vandal said, then jerked his worried gaze back to Cleera. "You're sure there's a way out at the other end of that tunnel?"

"Yes. As sure as I can be."

"Don't have much choice anyway," Vandal muttered. "Everyone—get into the tunnel and on your way!"

Vandal watched as they started down the incline, checking to be sure even Torb and Chiron were able to fit through the opening. And as he watched he pulled bulky wrapped parcels from his pack and wedged them into niches within the stone near the cave entrance. Satisfied with their placement, he glanced back outside once more. The CorSec troops were approaching quickly, following behind their most heavily armored battle robs.

Vandal fired directly at the mechs in the lead, then turned, ran back to the rear wall, and pressed the buttons there in the reverse order to that which he had seen. He smiled grimly to himself as he heard the floor servos begin to whine.

He started down the incline, ducking under the top of the entrance as it narrowed. He advanced far enough to clear the end of the floor panel and reach solid tunnel flooring, then stopped a moment, looking back.

The heavy floor panel was nearly closed now. Just the barest of gaps remained, steadily growing smaller. Taking aim through that gap, Vandal sighted on one of the wrapped parcels he had placed near the cave mouth. He fired.

Flashing out even as the CorSec troops neared the cave, the proton beam ignited the plastic explosives instantly. A huge explosion resulted, setting off the other parcels as well.

As the floor panel locked in the up position, tons of rock and rubble collapsed within the cave entrance, sealing it completely, blocking the access of the CorSec troops, and locking Vandal and the others within the dark, uncertain tunnel.

27:
PROMETHEUS BOUND

THE DARKNESS OF THE tunnel threatened to swallow them up. Reverberations from the explosions still rang in their ears as they ran, and their footsteps echoed eerily from the stone walls around them.

Cleera was in the lead, knowing the way from her programming. She used a hand-held light to brighten the path before them. HiLo was beside her, back to his normal height once more and running with an easy, full stride.

The tunnel appeared natural, although the wavering glow of light revealed that the floor had been smoothed by cutting beams. Tire tracks and other marks indicated the passage of much equipment, and it was clear that the University had spent some time constructing the secret installation.

Jayray and Jom followed close behind Cleera and HiLo, one twinbot on either side of Dr. Arcanus, steadying the old magician and helping him as they hurried along. A short distance behind them were Roddi and Marinda.

"How are you doing?" the psybot asked the breathless young Earth woman.

"Okay, I guess," Marinda replied as she ran. "But it's a good thing I wear joggers."

Vandal caught up with the group, passing Torb and Chiron. He came up alongside Cleera, a light from his pack adding to the illumination.

"The CorSec Guards won't be following us down here," he told Cleera. "At least not right away." Glancing around the tunnel as they ran, he added, "I'm surprised the University didn't install lights along this thing."

"There may be lights," Cleera told him, her tone a bit sheepish. "I just didn't take time to look for a switch back there."

Covering another sixty feet or so, they followed a gentle curve in the tunnel until their lights failed to reveal anything in the darkness ahead. Only a metal railing loomed before them.

Slowing, the group drew together as those trailing behind caught up with those in the lead. Vandal raised his hand, motioning for the others to stop.

"Wait here a second," he told them, fanning his light across the floor of the tunnel until it reached the edge, where the railing ran to left and right.

Vandal stepped forward cautiously, playing the light around both ways, then turned and shined it against the stone walls on either side of the end of the tunnel. Seeing something on the left, he stepped toward it and reached out with his metallic hand. He grabbed something hidden from the sight of the others and pulled it sharply down with a rasping clunk. Lights suddenly blazed to life beyond the end of the tunnel. He had thrown the main power switch. Vandal turned to stand at the railing, and Cleera and the others in the tunnel came over to join him. Dr. Arcanus and Marinda squinted in the bright glow, shielding their eyes with their hands until their vision adjusted.

"Oh my," said Marinda, an incredulous look on her pretty features as she took in the sights around her.

"So this," remarked Vandal, "is the University's ace in the hole."

The end of the tunnel opened onto a cavern, stretching above and below them and out to each side. Beyond the railing where they stood there was a sheer drop of thirty feet to the cavern floor.

Running to the right of the ledge, a wide metal catwalk extended most of the way around the cavern wall. Iron stairs led down to the floor a short distance from where they stood. On their left side an open cargo elevator stood waiting, its gate open. The metal, all painted the same flat orange, was an odd intrusion of color against the cool gray of stone.

On the far side of the huge chamber were banks of electronic equipment, with cables leading into conduits, running all over the wall, and even reaching toward the roof of the cavern. Air passages had been cut straight through the mountain, their narrow shafts leading to unknown spots on the surface.

There was another shaft, not man-made, that dominated the cavern. It began at the northeastern end of the cavern and ran up at an angle, remarkably straight for a natural formation. From the cavern floor up into the shaft ran a set of large tubular rails, raised upon strong supports.

Sitting on the cavern floor was a small spacecraft, silver with red-and-yellow markings. It was larger than Vandal's downed vessel, but still small in terms of most interplanetary craft.

"It's just as the Uni told me," Cleera said appreciatively. "And it's beautiful."

"But will it fly?" remarked Vandal. Turning, he gestured toward the large cargo elevator. "Torb, Chiron, you'd better use that to get down there. The rest of you, let's go."

As the two bulky psybots headed for the elevator, Vandal led the rest of the group down the stairs to the cavern floor. Reaching the ship, they checked it over, examining the equipment.

Vandal glanced at the consoles near the cavern wall. "So this is where the University personnel ran their surveillance operation on Coreworld before they finally packed it in. I wonder why they didn't take this ship with them?"

"Something interfered with their plans," Cleera explained. "They made other arrangements for leaving the planet. Frankly, I'm glad they did."

"Let's get this thing ready." Vandal released the locks and pulled the hatch open. Looking inside, he said, "They must have assembled this here in the cavern. We're lucky they made it big enough to carry both personnel and equipment. There'll be plenty of room for all of us."

Marinda stood behind him, peering at the spacecraft's interior. It looked the same to her as Vandal's ship, but it seemed a bit less spartan.

"How long will it take to fuel this up?" she asked him.

"Fuel?" Vandal said oddly. "Spaceships have changed since your day, Marinda. Like most large vessels now, this one uses a fusion drive system. All we have to do is install those power cells and bring the electrical and control systems to full operating levels, assuming they still work."

"They'll work," Marinda said vacantly, fatigue showing on her face. "They've got to."

Vandal stepped back from the hatch opening and went to Cleera. "We'd better get the power cells put in first."

"Yes, you're right." Cleera glanced toward her psybot team. "Torb, Chiron, HiLo, can you give Vandal a hand with those power cells?"

"With pleasure," replied HiLo. "We're all eager to get out of here."

A sound came from the tunnel, the distant hiss and chatter of particle beams and weapons from outside.

Vandal glanced in that direction, listening intently. "They're trying to cut their way through the rubble. I guess I didn't buy us too much time."

"It's more than we would have had otherwise," Cleera told him. "But they must have figured that we wouldn't fight our way into an armed camp just to trap ourselves in a cave."

Vandal moved quickly to the rear access panels of the spacecraft to supervise installation of the bulky power cells. Chiron carried them with his long lifting arms while Torb and HiLo installed them. Vandal leaned over with a power wrench to bolt the heavy units in position.

While they worked, Roddi went to the rear of the spacecraft. A large plastic cover extended over the exhaust opening of the main engine. Tugging on the cables hanging from the edge, Roddi pulled the cover free and discarded it, staring for a moment into the mirrored surface of the powerful fusion engine. The feeder tubes and housings for the proton igniters glistened with the same stress-hardened, ultradense finish.

Vandal finished connecting the power cables and bolted the access panels back in place. Approaching Cleera, he said, "I want to check the readouts before everyone boards, just to be sure there are no problems. You can take a look too, if you want. What's at the end of the launch tunnel? It looks sealed to me."

"There's a barrier there," Cleera told him. "It's camouflaged on the outside to look like part of the mountain. There are explosive charges planted near the top to hurl it out of the way when we're ready. They're triggered from the ship."

Vandal gave a grunting nod of understanding and headed toward the spacecraft. With Cleera following, he strode up the ramp and through the hatch, going forward to the flight deck.

The controls were similar to those of other craft he had flown, and Vandal quickly found the test circuits. He switched them on, his eyes scanning the readouts and displays.

"So far, so good," he said. Next he flipped the main power switches one by one, feeding electrical current to all systems. Again he watched the readouts and displays, checking for any signs of trouble. "What do you think?"

Cleera studied the array of information before her. "Everything seems to be in working order. If there's a problem, it's not indicated here."

"All right, then. Let's get everyone on board. If the CorSec Guards outside suspect anything, we may have more to worry about than the troops trying to get into the tunnel."

They moved back to the hatch and called the others inside. After a quick last-minute check of the area, the psybot team and humans ran up the ramp and into the spacecraft.

Vandal directed Chiron and Torb to places on either side of the ship where cargo straps could be fastened. Chiron rolled into place and locked his wheels, and Jayray and Jom extended the straps around the centaurlike psybot, tying him down securely to the deck. On the opposite side, Torb was secured in place in the same fashion, distributing the two largest psybots' weight evenly.

Vandal pulled the hatch closed and pressed the small lighted panel beside it. Servos whirred and clicked, latching the door in place.

"Everybody strap in," he ordered. He guided Marinda and Dr. Arcanus to seats near the front of the ship, then checked to be sure HiLo, Muse, and the twinbots were all finding a place.

Returning to the flight deck, Vandal went directly to the pilot's seat. He saw Cleera taking the engineer's seat at the panel behind him. "You don't mind if Roddi is my copilot on this one, do you?"

Cleera fastened her flight harness. "Not at all. The only important thing is getting where we want to go."

Vandal took his seat and strapped in. Roddi slipped into the seat beside him and did a quick scan of the instruments. Working together, they began activating circuits, powering up the system for takeoff.

"All seals secure and pressurized," Cleera reported. "Proton igniters are operational."

Vandal took one last glance behind him, checking the interior of the spacecraft. As his eyes met Marinda's steady gaze they held there. She winked and gave him a thumb's-up sign, making him smile despite his seriousness.

Turning back to the controls, Vandal announced, "Stand by for ignition."

Flipping open the cover above the firing switches, Vandal held his breath a moment, then jammed his thumb down on the first button, then the second, starting the two-stage ignition procedure.

A shudder ran through the ship as the fusion engine

flared to life. An intense white glow came from the exhaust funnel, bathing the cavern in brilliant light.

Checking his readouts, Vandal said, "Seems normal enough."

Scanning the displays at the engineering panel, Cleera replied, "There's a minor electrical power drain I can't account for, but otherwise everything is at optimum level."

There was a sudden noise outside the ship. Sitting next to a viewport on the starboard side, Muse stared down the tunnel. A haze of smoke emerged from the tunnel mouth, and hand-held lights bounced through the darkness.

"They've broken through!" Muse called out sharply. "The CorSec troops are almost to the cavern!"

Settling back in his seat, Vandal said, "I guess that's about as much of a test as we have time for. Cleera, you know more about the barrier than I do."

"Got it," Cleera replied, checking the panel and finding what she needed. She pressed a series of buttons and listened intently. Seconds later, the sound of muted explosions came down the launch shaft. Cleera stared at the displays. "Remote sensors say the barrier is clear."

"Then hang on." Vandal pushed the throttle forward with a smooth, even pressure. Behind them the fusion engine roared into life, glowing like a small star.

Roddi studied his own screens nervously, watching the figures rapidly click upward. "Okay, Vandal, take-off thrust achieved."

Vandal's right hand shot out to the control panel and hit the button releasing the lock on the ship's rail rollers. He glanced out the viewport beyond Roddi and saw the first troops appear on the ledge, shielding their eyes against the intense glare. "So long, boys."

Lurching forward as the brakes released, the University spacecraft shot up the incline, following the rails that guided it up through the launch shaft. It gathered more and more speed as it thundered its way up through the mountain. The sides of the shaft were illuminated by the engine glow behind them, but it was all a blur, moving past too quickly to be seen.

Then with chilling abruptness the walls disappeared. The ship soared into the open sky, the dark gray bulk of mountain falling away behind them. They were off, heading toward space and leaving the accursed planet known as Coreworld behind.

28:
RESCUE IN SPACE

"MAINTAINING RATE OF ASCENT," Roddi announced from the copilot's seat, continuing to check the readouts on the panel before him. "We should reach escape velocity in another twenty minutes."

Already the atmospheric haze of Coreworld had been left behind, replaced by the inky blackness of space. Here the stars shone with unwinking clarity. Here the mountainous surface they had left minutes before sank back into a flat and muddled pattern of drab colors on the planet's night side. The thunder, the weapon sounds, the rush of air past their ship all faded away, with only the muted roar of the engine continuing.

From her seat at the engineering panel, Cleera frowned at data on her sensor display. "We may not *have* twenty minutes. I'm picking up ships from the main CorSec base near CityPrime. They're heading on an intercept course with us now."

"How long?" asked Vandal.

"They could reach us in twenty minutes—maybe sooner."

Vandal checked the control panel, but already knew the answer to his question. "This thing doesn't have much in the way of firepower."

"I know," Cleera agreed. "It was intended for escape, not combat."

"Sometimes it's hard to separate the two," Vandal replied grimly. "The CorSec patrol ships are faster than we are. Even if we outmaneuver them for the moment, they'll overtake us before we get a tenth of the way to Avalon. You'd better send a message to the University, Cleera, and let them know what's happening."

"Yes, Vandal," the lavender-and-white psybot replied. Vandal's words had a somber implication, but she knew he was right. Activating her T-beam transceiver, Cleera quickly framed a message containing all the important details and beamed it into hyperspace.

"Roddi," Vandal addressed his companion, "what do your displays show? Can we get any more speed out of this thing?"

The silver-blue psybot scanned the console before him. "I'm afraid we're already operating at our absolute peak. We have some electromagnetic shielding we can employ, but I doubt it will stand up against ion cannon fire."

"Not more than a microsecond," Vandal grunted. "I think maybe we'd better change course and try to gain us at least a little more time. Cleera, can you give me the coordinates on those CorSec craft?"

"Yes . . . wait! I'm getting a reply to my message."

Looking out the viewport beside him, Roddi exclaimed, "Oh, my . . . I don't think we really need the coordinates. I can see the exhaust glow of at least four ships heading toward us from the east-southeast."

Vandal waited a moment, growing impatient. "What's the message, Cleera?"

The pretty psybot's head swiveled toward him, puzzlement in her tone as she replied, "They only said, 'Stand by.' Nothing else."

"Stand by?" Roddi said incredulously. "What sort of a message is that? Are they too busy to answer?"

"I'll transmit another message," said Cleera hastily. "I'll tell them it's urgent."

"I rather imagine they should know that," muttered Roddi. He looked once more out his viewport. The glowing dots of light from the CorSec base were growing larger, steadily drawing nearer. "Oh, glitch!"

"We're going to have to do something soon," Vandal said seriously. "We're an easy target."

Cleera reported, still mystified. "The second reply is the same as the first—'Stand by'!"

Vandal glanced back at his passengers, his expression stone-hard. His eyes moved to Marinda's lovely face, and he felt his gut tighten as he saw her fear-blanched features.

At that moment, there was a sudden sensation, an almost electrical crackle, that caught everyone's attention. They all jumped, their heads turning in alarm. A rushing sound suddenly grew into a steady roar that reverberated through the ship.

"My sensors are going crazy!" Cleera exclaimed.

A crackling blue line shot past them with startling speed and bathed their ship in its glow. The line coruscated and pulsed along its serpentine path, and as it faded it spread laterally into thousands of tiny branches. Then it was gone, as if a great rip in the fabric of space had opened and closed.

Suddenly something else zoomed overhead and into view. Its glow faded as it slowed, revealing the lean and angular lines of a massive spacecraft—a spacecraft that had not been there seconds before.

Cleera stared out at it, recognizing its odd configuration. "It's the *Prometheus*!"

A voice now came through their conventional radio, blaring through the cabin speakers. "Sorry to keep you waiting, Cleera. Stand by for docking. We are matching our speed to yours and will guide you in."

"That's Dean McAndrews," Cleera announced. "They've come to pick us up!"

As cheers went up among the group, Vandal brought their ship alongside the hyperspace ship, slowly closing the gap. His display screen showed a diagram created by the *Prometheus*'s guidance signals, indicating the left docking bay was being opened. Vandal steered toward it. He cut all forward thrust, relying on their momentum alone to keep pace. Carefully, Vandal used the ship's lateral thrusters to nudge them toward the open bay.

Docking lights illuminated the bay, revealing the docking port near the center. Vandal guided the ship in, visually as much as by instrumentation. There was a soft nudge, then a more solid bump as they connected with the side of the *Prometheus*.

"The latches are secure, Vandal," Roddi said. "The port should be pressurized in a few moments."

"Good," replied the cyborg agent, glancing back at Cleera's console. Although the starboard viewports were now blocked by the larger ship, the instruments still showed the relative positions of the approaching CorSec vessels.

Cleera noticed the direction of his gaze. "We're down to about fifteen minutes before intercept," she told him. "We'd better transfer quickly."

"Suits me fine," Vandal said, unbuckling his straps and getting carefully out of his seat, well prepared for weightlessness. He turned off the console's power switches, leaving only the lights and life-support systems on.

Cleera released herself from her seat and worked her way back into the passenger area. "All right, let's get Torb and Chiron unbuckled, quickly! We've all got to board the *Prometheus*."

Jayray and Jom went to work on Chiron's straps. HiLo and Muse set about releasing Torb. In a matter of moments, both the large psybots were free and as weightless as their smaller companions.

Marinda and Dr. Arcanus gathered their belongings and moved as well as they could to where Vandal was standing near the hatch. As they all gathered there, Vandal checked the safety indicators by the hatch. "Okay, the port is fully pressurized. Let's get this thing open."

He pressed the control switches on the bulkhead and waited as servos released the locks around the edge of the hatch. Grasping the handle, he pushed the door open. There was a slight hiss of air as the pressure seals released. Vandal directed Marinda, Dr. Arcanus, and the psybot team into the docking port. The airlock chamber was small and could not accommodate them all at once. Vandal waited with Torb and Chiron as the others entered. Then, as he saw the hatch leading into the *Prometheus* open, he followed the two large psybots out and sealed the hatch on their small ship.

Within moments, they were all in the entry corridor of the large hyperspace ship. Facing them was a beaming Dean McAndrews with Jenna beside him.

"Thank God you all made it," said McAndrews. "We were heading here through hyperspace on a straight course from Avalon, so we intercepted your messages, Cleera. Sorry for the cryptic response."

"That's quite all right, sir," Cleera told him. "We're grateful you came for us. But the CorSec interceptors are getting closer."

"Yes, we wouldn't want to linger here too long, would we?" McAndrews gestured to one of the crew techs, who reached for the controls to activate the servos for closing the docking-bay doors. "We're increasing our cruising speed now, which will give us some distance on them, and by the time we reach the forward section of the ship we'll be ready to pop back into hyperspace."

Using the handrails that ran along the corridor's walls and ceilings, Jenna maneuvered closer to Cleera. "It's good to see you again. Wait until I tell you what's been happening on Avalon."

Before anyone could say anything further, there came an abrupt flicker of lights within the corridor. They came back to full brightness in a few seconds, but as they did the engines immediately shut down. As the great ship fell silent, the faint sound of the forward thrusters firing could be heard, then nothing.

McAndrews clambered frantically to the intercom panel on the wall nearest him. Pressing the button there, he called into the unit's microphone.

"This is McAndrews. What's happening up there?"

There was a long pause before an answer came, suggesting problems on the flight deck. Then finally Captain Isaacs's voice came through the intercom. "I wish I could tell you, Dean," Isaacs reported. "We've got a major systems failure on our hands. We lost power for a moment, and then all the computer-controlled systems, which is about everything on the ship, locked up on us. The engines are off and our braking jets fired. We're adrift in space."

"You've tried the backup systems?"

"Yes, of course," Isaacs snapped. "Everything's locked up and refuses to respond to our controls."

Vandal spoke up. "I'll bet they're responding to someone else's controls!" He threw a glance back toward the airlock and the docking port beyond.

"Oh, no," Cleera exclaimed. "The ship—that's what's causing the electrical power drain. There's some device hidden on the ship we brought that's doing this— something that's jamming the control systems."

Marinda was aghast. "The spaceship that brought us here? You mean it was rigged by someone, and we're deliberately being held here? How could anyone know . . .?"

Vandal seethed with self-directed anger. "They knew because they planned it this way all along, and I was too much of a fool to see it. This is exactly what they wanted from the start!"

"The *Prometheus*?" said McAndrews. "Then I've played right into their hands, myself! I've delivered the prize they've been seeking, right to their doorstep."

"But," said Jenna, "the Corporation sent agents to try to steal the plans—"

"A diversion—the Quintad never expected those men to succeed. They just wanted us to think we had thwarted their plan, so we would overlook their real intentions." McAndrews spoke into the intercom again. "Isaacs! Any luck yet?"

There was a pause, then, "No, sir. All systems are still locked up tight, no matter what we try. And it won't be long before those CorSec ships catch up with us."

McAndrews sighed and swore under his breath. His frowning gaze shifted to Vandal. The cyborg agent had moved back to the airlock door and was trying to open it. "What are you doing? If the systems are all locked up, that won't be operative."

"You're right," Vandal said after one more try. "We don't have much time. There are manual releases for these, aren't there?"

"Yes, but—"

"How long can you maintain atmosphere in here if your life-support systems are off?"

"An hour, maybe longer."

"Then," said Vandal, "get me a spacesuit. Have your men cut the ship's master and auxiliary power feeds. With no electrical systems working, I'll be able to open the hatch manually and get outside. I'm going to cut the small ship away from us."

Marinda pulled herself closer to him. "No, Vandal— it's too dangerous."

"Compared to what? None of us stands a chance in the Corporation's hands."

"Wait!" said Cleera. "Vandal's idea is a good one, but it will take time to suit him up—time we don't have. Let me take HiLo and Torb out there. Vandal can get us out the hatch once the power's off."

McAndrews considered it. What his psybot prodigy had said was true enough. That didn't make the decision any easier.

"All right," he told them. "Do it. The intercoms work on battery power, too, with no connection to the main control circuits, so I'll be able to tell Isaacs when to restore full power. I'll tell him right now to pull the main and auxiliary circuit breakers."

McAndrews did so, and within a minute the main lights went out, plunging the corridor into darkness. Red emergency lights, battery-powered, winked on a moment later, bathing the group in their fiery glow.

"All right, get ready," Vandal told them. Using his artificial arm, he flipped open the access panel on the hatch and extended the crank built into it. Turning it with powerful strokes, he continued until the latches released. He threw the hatch open and stepped aside.

As Cleera started through, Vandal handed her his protoblaster. "Here—this will cut through a lot faster than your built-in lasers."

"Thanks, Vandal."

HiLo followed her through the hatch, and Torb carefully worked his way through last. Once they were all well within the docking port's airlock chamber, Vandal closed the hatch and began cranking the latches back in place. As he reached the fifteenth revolution he could feel the hatch sealing tightly.

"We're ready," he told those inside the corridor. Looking through the small viewport built into the hatch, he gave a signaling wave to Cleera. "Let's hope they can handle this."

Inside the docking port, Cleera saw Vandal's signal and moved to the end of the chamber. "Lucky we don't need air," she said softly, locating the panel for the manual depressurization lever. "Ready, guys?"

Torb and HiLo nodded. Both knew the urgency of what they were about to try. Both knew the danger.

Cleera hoped they would survive it. There were still things she wanted to say to both these special friends. Flinging open the panel, Cleera grasped the broad lever, using both hands. Her eyes stopped on the large sign above the lever that stated in bold letters— "WARNING: COMPLETE DEPRESSURIZATION OF CHAMBER WILL RESULT WHEN LEVER IS PULLED."

Sighing inwardly, she jerked the lever back and

clung to it. Instantly there was a loud rush of air
escaping through the seals. The sudden flow drew
them even closer to the front of the chamber. Air
within the hollow cavities of their bodies whistled out
through their seams, adding a high-pitched chorus of
notes to the droning hiss around them.

Then all sound faded as there was no longer a
medium to convey it. There was only the awkwardness
of their movements in weightlessness, and the red
glow of the emergency lights.

Cleera pried loose the thick, multilayered seal that
had pressure-formed against the hull of the smaller
spacecraft by working up and down from the right side
of the chamber. HiLo did the same on the left side,
and once the bulk of it had been released they were
able to retract the entire fitting into the double walls
of the chamber.

Peering through the gap they had created, Cleera
could see the docking latches on her side of the port,
several feet away. Taking Vandal's protoblaster from
the holdfast at her waist, Cleera aimed at the latch.
She held the weapon as steady as she could and fired.
Half the heavy-duty arm disintegrated as the proton
beam hit it. She took aim again and fired a second
time.

The latch broke free and Cleera headed for the
other side.

HiLo was already working on that latch, firing at it
with a laser pistol. He had burned only a third of the
way through it when Cleera reached him.

The pretty lavender-and-white psybot motioned him
out of the way and strained to see her target in the
poor light. Aiming carefully, she fired at the center of
the remaining section.

The arm parted in a spray of glowing fragments, and

the smaller ship lurched slightly as it broke free from the *Prometheus*. As the docking port jarred in reaction, Cleera nearly stepped through the gap. HiLo grabbed her arm and steadied her, holding on to one of the handrails within the chamber to secure his own position.

They had cut the other ship free, but that was only half the job. The sabotaged vessel still floated alongside the hyperdrive ship, close enough to interfere with the large vessel's control systems.

Cleera motioned to Torb and HiLo. They had discussed her plan in the chamber while Vandal cranked the seals tight on the hatch, and understood what they must do next.

Torb took his position at the outer edge of the chamber, directly in front of the smaller ship. HiLo moved behind the big psybot, floating horizontally and extending his arms and legs until he was able to place his hands against Torb's back and his feet behind the handrails on either side of the hatch. Floating above Torb, Cleera stood on his massive shoulders, bracing herself against the top of the airlock chamber. She looked down and saw that HiLo was gripping the ridges on Torb's back to keep him from slipping away and knew they were ready.

There was no way to give a verbal order without air, so Cleera tapped Torb on the side of his head with her foot, then braced herself once more.

Braced in three directions, Torb placed his broad hands against the side of the small spacecraft and began to push it away. He knew only too well that HiLo was bearing the greatest amount of stress, so he kept his movements slow and smooth. Although HiLo was built for cargo work and was sturdy, Torb did not want to damage his friend.

As Torb's mighty servos and thrust pistons strained forward, the spacecraft that had carried them from Coreworld began to move away. Reaching the limit of his arm length, Torb lost contact and stopped pushing.

The smaller ship kept moving, drifting farther and father away from the *Prometheus* and toward the planet below. Within a minute it was three hundred feet away and still falling back.

Cleera climbed carefully down and worked her way to the rear of the chamber. HiLo pulled Torb back from the edge as he retracted his limb sections and reoriented himself. They peered through the viewport, gesturing at what they had accomplished.

Within the entry corridor, Vandal turned to McAndrews. "They've done it! The ship should be out of jamming range now. Restore the power! And get everyone down the corridor, past the second airlock hatch!"

McAndrews pushed the button on the intercom and told Captain Isaacs to close the circuit breakers. He waited, holding his breath, to see what happened next.

Tense seconds crept by, then the main lights flickered on within the corridor and throughout the ship. They brightened to full power and held.

"Get those docking-bay doors closed," McAndrews ordered the crew tech, "now that they'll work." Into the intercom he asked, "Isaacs—are your controls responding?"

After a brief pause, the captain's voice came back. "Yes, sir! There was still a trace of interference for a moment, but all systems are now operational."

"Get us moving again, and prepare for hyperspace jump."

"Yes, sir."

McAndrews motioned for everyone to move back as Vandal gave a thumbs-up to Cleera through the viewport. Once they were all on the other side of the second airlock hatch and had sealed it, they started depressurization of the section they had just vacated.

Moving to another intercom unit here, McAndrews called the flight deck again. "What's the position on those CorSec ships?"

"Interception in ten minutes, sir," Isaacs's voice came back. "And they'll be within weapons range in five."

McAndrews turned to Vandal. "The airlock is so slow. We're going to have to be ready to go as soon as they've gotten in from the docking port and the entry is pressurized."

Vandal nodded soberly. "Even then it will be close."

Two minutes dragged by. Then the lights lit up on the airlock control panel. It was safe to open the outer hatch.

Cleera pressed the controls that freed the hatch and swung the door open. They pulled themselves through, then gave Torb a hand as he entered the corridor. Moving as quickly as they could, they closed the hatch and resealed it.

They started toward the second airlock door and saw Vandal gesturing toward the aft wall of the lateral corridor. Cleera could read Vandal's lips well enough to understand what he was telling her about the pressurization.

Cleera motioned for HiLo and Torb to join her against the wall and to hold the handrails. They braced themselves as well as they could, locking their joints into place and tilting their heads back flat against the wall's padded surface.

The other psybots and humans were running forward to the passenger section immediately behind the flight deck. As they strapped into whatever seat they found first, Captain Isaacs's voice announced over the loudspeakers, "Two minutes to weapons range."

Marinda was sitting next to Jenna and Dean McAndrews. As she nervously buckled herself securely in place, she saw McAndrews looking at her.

"Miss Donelson, I presume?" said the Dean.

"Yes! At least, I used to be, a very long time ago."

"You have a real treat in store for you," Jenna told her with a reassuring pat. "We're about to enter hyperspace."

Marinda swallowed hard. "Why not? I've been through just about everything else in the last few days."

On the flight deck of the *Prometheus*, Captain Isaacs studied the readouts and displays on his flight console. The CorSec ships were drawing ever nearer.

He checked the indicators for the hyperspace systems. They were just entering the ready margin. Flexing his fingers somewhat hesitantly, Isaacs reached out and pressed the switches activating the special engines at the center of the large spacecraft.

Approaching from behind and slightly to one side, the CorSec pilots had the ship in their sights and were readying their targeting grids for a disabling shot. They saw the strange blue glow emerge across the domed surfaces amidships and spread along the tubes of the power grid. They saw the enormous ship brighten to an intense blue, and a tiny point of coruscating light near the nose of the craft intensify and spread, erupting into lightninglike discharges bending back along the sides of the ship.

Then in a flash, the *Prometheus* shot forward into that point of light, sucking the residual glow along behind it. It vanished in an instant, leaving the CorSec pilots with nothing in their sights but dazzling spots before their eyes, and the clear impression that the ghostly ship had never been there in the first place.

29:
THE PLAN REVEALED

IT WAS MORNING IN CityPrime; murky sunlight streamed down, glinting dully off the corroded splendor of a once glorious colony. In the massive building that was Corporation headquarters, Roman sat behind the desk in his private office, frowning an irritable and dangerous frown. He tossed an empty vial of rejuvenation fluid into the waste chute and straightened his clothing once more over the invisible seam in his chest. He again read through a report printout sitting on his desk, then crushed it angrily in his hand. For a moment he almost threw it into the waste chute as well, then thought better of it and fed it into the document destroyer.

Roman gave a slight jerk of surprise as the door to his office was thrown open. An unannounced visitor stormed in, petulant and bristling with anger.

Rising to his feet, Roman put on his mask of cordiality. "Razer, my darling, you're back. I've been waiting for a message from you."

"Have you?" said Razer with barely controlled emotion. Her beauty was savage, her eyes flashing with near-murderous intensity. "Have you indeed?"

"When did you return?"

"Minutes ago." Razer slapped a bit of dust from the sleeve of her jumpsuit, her unblinking gaze never leaving Roman's face. "I was halfway to Trasker's Island when I heard the report of the spacecraft taking off. I knew there was nothing more I could do, so I turned my helijet toward CityPrime and came straight here."

Roman moved toward her, exhibiting a certain caution. "I don't blame you for being angry. Vandal and those psybots have apparently eluded us this time, though not without considerable help from our adversaries on Avalon."

"Yes," Razer replied hotly. "And not without considerable help from someone much closer to home."

"What do you mean?" Roman studied her, a muscle in his face twitching a bit as he saw her draw her weapon from its holster. He half expected her to use it on him.

"What do I mean? I mean this! This, this thing you had me draw from the armory, made it impossible for me to kill Vandal or that blasted psybot of his. Look at this!" Razer clawed at the housing of the small protoblaster and the weapon came apart in her hands. It was clear from the missing fasteners that she had previously dismantled it. "I was beginning to think I was losing my touch," Razer told him. "But the more I thought about it, the more certain I was that I simply could not have missed that many times. I thought the weapons I was issued might be defective, so I took them apart. And this is what I found."

The beautiful eliminator thrust the opened weapon toward Roman, pointing an accusing finger at components within it. "What I found was not defective parts, but a surplus of parts. And quite a fascinating surplus at that. In what should be a conventional weapon I've discovered miniature optical circuits, and a complex computer chip, and a deflection yoke built around the beam emitter."

Roman looked at the gun's interior, his face expressionless.

"Strange parts for a weapon," Razer continued "But not as strange as how they make it work. To confirm my suspicions, I tried firing at a close target. Perfect bull's-eye. Then I tried again, with a 'Wanted' photo of Vandal stuck over the target. Same distance, same point of aim. Do you know what happened? Do you? The beam deflected a good three degrees and missed the photo by nearly four inches."

She stepped closer to Roman, clutching the pistol in a trembling fist. "This damned thing, and the other weapons you gave me, were deliberately programmed to miss anyone visually resembling Vandal or his psybot. And perhaps the girl as well. I can't be sure in her case, as I had nothing to test it on. I want to know why, Roman. Why?"

Roman studied her for a moment, his eyes shifting from her steady, demanding gaze. At last, with a heavy sigh, he said, "All right, my dear. It's only right you know the truth. The weapons were indeed rigged. And I, though I am ashamed to admit it, was indirectly involved in this deception. Unwillingly involved, I might add."

For the first time, a trace of hurt as well as anger showed in Razer's exquisite face. "How could you do this to me? You, of all people, must know how important this was to me."

Roman put his hand on her arm in a consoling gesture, his look pleading, his deep, resonant voice solicitous and apologetic. "It pained me deeply to put you through this. Alpha deemed it necessary, and I had no choice but to follow his wishes."

"Alpha?" Razer stared oddly at him. "This was Alpha's doing?"

"Yes, but what I am about to tell you I am technically not supposed to reveal to anyone. You see, everything, from the very beginning, was staged—all guided with one purpose, one goal, in mind. Alpha is obsessed with obtaining the University's hyperdrive ship, the *Prometheus*. He devised a means of getting it here, and tried to seize control."

"Then the girl—this Marinda Donelson—she's not an original Earth colonist?"

"Oh, yes, she's genuine enough," Roman replied. He turned and walked back to lean against the edge of his desk. "She was indeed left behind, unknowingly, by the landing parties so very long ago. She would be there in *Glory* yet if the hidden compartment had not been stumbled across by a vile man who recently docked with the ancient ship. A salvager and black-marketeer. Most likely a grave robber, when the need moved him. He thought he could turn a tidy profit by bringing news of the secret suspension chamber to Alpha." Roman smiled grimly. "Of course, his payment turned out to be very permanent and not terribly tidy."

"But," said Razer, "I don't see how, if she was genuine . . ."

"It was simplicity itself. After all, that suspended-animation cabinet was nearly out of power anyway. And there was existing circuitry for sending out a distress signal once the power reached a certain point. We merely provided a means for the equipment to transmit that signal far enough to reach Avalon. Put yourself in their place. You know how intellectually curious they are about mysteries, especially one as tantalizing as a repeating transmission coming from a starship abandoned centuries ago."

Razer lost a small trace of her angry look. "Yes, I can well imagine. They could not rest until they knew the answer."

"Which is exactly why they sent Vandal and that psybot of his to investigate. But what they could not know is that everything was arranged to make it appear that we were trying to stop them, when in truth we really wanted to use them all as bait."

"Then it was no accident that the CorSec ship that fired upon them only disabled their craft instead of destroying it?"

"Of course it was no accident," Roman replied with a bit of a chuckle. "The officer who fired that weapon was our top marksman. His precise aim and timing were crucial to bringing Vandal's ship down roughly where we wanted it."

Razer tossed the disassembled weapon on the desk top and frowned at the map. It showed most of Coreworld's western hemisphere, with marks on it to indicate Vandal's progress and a large X on Trasker's Island. She said, "Then you knew all along about the University ship hidden on the island?"

"My dear, I learned about that ship within a month after they evacuated that base. One of my agents found a way into the cavern through an air shaft. I've been saving the knowledge of that vessel a long time, waiting for an opportunity to make use of it. At the same time we were modifying the beacon circuitry on *Glory*, we installed a special jamming device on the island ship."

"But how could you be so sure Vandal would try to reach it?"

Roman made an expansive gesture with his hands. "What other choice did he have? The University gave him the information, counting on what they thought was a safe plan. Besides, to be absolutely sure, Alpha had me place similar jamming devices on a number of vessels at the CorSec base—vessels made reasonably accessible, in case he tried to steal one of them to escape. Either way, we were assured that whatever ship Vandal used would carry means for disabling the *Prometheus* so we could capture it."

Razer's eyes flashed. "And you used me to make sure the *Prometheus* would come for them, didn't you?"

"Certainly you were part of it. Don't you understand? We had to keep the pressure on them. We had to make it seem as if we were really trying to stop them. Who could be a more convincing threat than you? And we had to make certain that the University would feel compelled to send the hyperdrive ship as a last resort. It was all set up very carefully."

"So I see. What a pity it was not successful."

Roman's features clouded. He picked up a small metal paperweight from his desk and began toying with it. "Yes, a great disappointment. Someone's timing was off for the patrol ship launch. Somehow, the crew of the *Prometheus* were able to break the small ship free and reestablish control before we could reach it. What should have been a monumental success instead became a disastrous failure!"

Roman gripped the paperweight tightly in his fist, an angry and uncontrolled force briefly manifesting itself. Then as he calmed he realized what he had done—saw the small dents in the hard metal surface. That would not do. That would not do at all. Distracting attention from it, Roman shielded the dented areas with his cybernetic hand and quickly put the paperweight away in the top drawer of his desk.

Razer's attention was elsewhere anyway, her eyes clouded with thought. "Incredible. Some of our own men were killed in the fighting. Machines were destroyed. All for the sake of Alpha's plan."

"Only a handful. And if it had been successful, it would have been a small price to pay for the secret of hyperspace. A secret we still intend to acquire."

"How utterly ruthless Alpha is," said Razer dreamily. "And how utterly brilliant!" She put her arms around Roman's neck, her look, her voice, as seductive as they were angry. "You could have confided in me. I do not like being deceived and used."

"Alpha would not permit it. He doubted you would go along with such a charade, and anyway, he wanted your responses to be as genuine as possible. I argued against involving you but with Alpha it does not pay to argue too loudly."

"Yes. I can understand that. And I suppose I cannot truly blame you for protecting yourself and your position." She leaned closer and kissed him, slowly, teasingly. Her dark and wicked beauty was never more tantalizing, Roman thought, than when she balanced precariously between murderous rage and physical desire. "We both have such great disappointments to endure. Such very . . . great . . . disappointments."

Roman returned her kisses, and found his own pulse quickening. "Yes. Perhaps we can console each other, my darling. We both certainly deserve a bit of rest and recreation. You have been through such a great deal, and I have been standing by here for far too many hours. I should be going back to my quarters in a moment, just as soon as I make my report to Alpha. Tell you what—why don't you go on ahead of me and make yourself comfortable. I shall be along shortly."

"An excellent suggestion. But see that you don't keep me waiting too long this time."

*   *   *

Gary Alan Ruse

It was evening on the part of Avalon where the massive University complex sat within its atmosphere domes. The hyperspace vessel, *Prometheus*, had returned four hours earlier and was once again sheltered within the crater which served as its hanger.

Dean McAndrews walked into the large meeting room on the same level as his office. Jenna greeted him with a warm smile, which he quickly returned, and his smile continued as his look took in those gathered before him.

Marinda sat between Vandal and Roddi, freshened up and looking a bit more rested. Dr. Arcanus sat near them, looking quite dapper. Cleera and her psybot team were all present as well.

"Miss Donelson," McAndrews began, "I want to welcome you officially to Avalon. I'm sure you'll be pleased to know that your blood test shows you have no trace of plague virus. In fact, your blood chemistry shows a remarkable resistance to all types of diseases, perhaps because of the unorthodox suspended-animation process you went through. You're uncommonly healthy."

Marinda sighed happily and settled more comfortably in her seat. "That's a relief. But I hope I'm not going to be just some sort of museum piece around here."

"Oh no, not at all. After you've had a chance to look around I'm sure you'll find any number of interesting projects to work on. Rest assured, you will be a most welcome addition to our group."

Vandal fidgeted, never quite comfortable around any of the University officials. "When do you want a full debriefing?"

"Considering what you've all been through," replied McAndrews, "I think tomorrow will be quite

394

soon enough. After that, we can start thinking about future assignments, for all of you."

Cleera looked down with pride at her repaired leg. The scorched and patched panel of her thigh had been replaced, as well as the damaged internal support. She felt whole again, new again. She knew she had changed, though, for within her psychogenetic brain she had learned important new data about herself and her friends—about her very existence. It was an existence she was truly eager to explore.

"Dean," she said to her boss and mentor, "do you think you can do anything for Dr. Arcanus? He gave up virtually everything he had to help us. Any chance we can return the favor?"

"Oh posh!" said Arcanus.

"Count on it," McAndrews told him. "I'll have to speak with the University Board first, but I'm certain we can replace your show equipment with brand-new gear. If, that is, you still wish to continue performing, and if you furnish us with the specifications."

"If?" Arcanus drawled dramatically. "If? My dear young man, performing is my life. If you insist on helping, I would not think of refusing your generosity. I am, in fact, already envisioning the greatest, most monumentally stupendous magic show ever conceived! An interplanetary extravaganza!" He smiled wryly. "Free tickets to you and your friends, of course."

"Well, then," replied McAndrews, "if everything is resolved for the moment, I think we should call it a day and just enjoy this evening. Maybe even go out and celebrate."

Jenna's mouth twisted up in a knowing grin, her pretty eyes rolling. "I love it when he gets reckless."

Marinda turned toward Vandal. "What about it? Want to go out and celebrate?"

The cyborg agent's sober look remained. "I'm not much for big parties."

"Well," said Marinda, playing with the collar of his cloak, "how about an intimate dinner for two at some nice restaurant? I'm dying to wear that pretty red dress again. And I haven't had anything decent to eat in ages."

Vandal eyed her with a hesitant look, finding it difficult to resist either her enthusiastic gaze or her undeniable warmth and charm. His expression thawed a bit, relaxing into a trace of a smile.

"Maybe," he replied.

"For two?" Roddi exclaimed, with an exaggerated shrug of dismay. "Oh . . . glitch!"

Then the silvery-blue psybot joined in the warm laughter that filled the room.

About the Author

Gary Alan Ruse served as an official correspondent with the U.S. Army Corps of Engineers in Vietnam and was Information Specialist of a Group Level P.I.O. office, editing a newspaper and writing for various military publications. While in Vietnam, he became interested in military research involving animals and in experiments in behavioral control through radio implants—an interest which gave birth to his first novel, HOUNDSTOOTH. He was born in Miami, Florida, in 1946 and attended the University of Miami, where he graduated with a B.A. in commercial art. While there, he also studied film, stage, television, and photojournalism.

His first sale was to *Analog Science Fiction Magazine* in 1972, and *Analog* has published a number of his other short stories. His novels include, A GAME OF TITANS, THE GODS OF CERUS MAJOR, and MORLAC: *The Quest of the Green Magician*.

In the vast intergalactic world of the future
the soldiers battle

NOT FOR GLORY

JOEL ROSENBERG

author of the bestselling
Guardian of the Flame series

Only once in the history of the Metzadan merce-
nary corps has a man been branded traitor. That
man is Bar-El, the most cunning military mind in
the universe. Now his nephew, Inspector-General
Hanavi, must turn to him for help. What begins as
one final mission is transformed into a series of
campaigns that takes the Metzadans from world to
world, into intrigues, dangers, and treacherous dip-
lomatic games, where a strategist's highly irregu-
lar maneuvers and a master assassin's swift blade
may prove the salvation of the planet—or its ulti-
mate ruin . . .